EXTENDED STAY

JUAN MARTINEZ

EXTENDED STAY

THE UNIVERSITY OF
ARIZONA PRESS

TUCSON

The University of Arizona Press
www.uapress.arizona.edu

We respectfully acknowledge the University of Arizona is on the land and territories of Indigenous peoples. Today, Arizona is home to twenty-two federally recognized tribes, with Tucson being home to the O'odham and the Yaqui. Committed to diversity and inclusion, the University strives to build sustainable relationships with sovereign Native Nations and Indigenous communities through education offerings, partnerships, and community service.

ISBN-13: 978-0-8165-4797-5 (paperback)
ISBN-13: 978-0-8165-4798-2 (ebook)

Cover design by Leigh McDonald
Designed and typeset by Leigh McDonald in Adobe Jenson Pro 10.25/15 and Hardwick WF (display)

Publication of this book is made possible in part by the proceeds of a permanent endowment created with the assistance of a Challenge Grant from the National Endowment for the Humanities, a federal agency.

Library of Congress Cataloging-in-Publication Data
Names: Martinez, Juan, 1974– author.
Title: Extended stay / Juan Martinez.
Other titles: Camino del sol.
Description: Tucson : University of Arizona Press, 2023. | Series: Camino del sol: a Latinx literary series
Identifiers: LCCN 2022016012 (print) | LCCN 2022016013 (ebook) | ISBN 9780816547975 (paperback) | ISBN 9780816547982 (ebook)
Subjects: LCSH: Noncitizens—Nevada—Las Vegas—Fiction. | Illegal immigration—United States—Fiction. | Immigrant youth—Nevada—Las Vegas—Fiction. | Haunted hotels—Nevada—Las Vegas—Fiction. | LCGFT: Horror fiction.
Classification: LCC PS3613.A78645 E98 2023 (print) | LCC PS3613.A78645 (ebook) | DDC 813/.6—dc23/eng/20220516
LC record available at https://lccn.loc.gov/2022016012
LC ebook record available at https://lccn.loc.gov/2022016013

Printed in the United States of America
♾ This paper meets the requirements of ANSI/NISO Z39.48-1992 (Permanence of Paper).

For my parents, Alvaro and Susana

FOREWORD

A HORROR STORY BECOMES EVEN MORE unsettling when its protagonists are at their most vulnerable—as youth, as migrants, as working-class people. Such is the journey for Alvaro and Carmen, a Colombian brother and sister duo who escape their troubled homeland, seeking safety and a fresh start in America. But like many others who arrive with big dreams and small pockets, that transition from their former life to the new one is fraught with obstacles and setbacks. Instead of pursuing the dream, they find themselves persecuted by a nightmare.

For Martinez, that nightmare is not figurative—not exactly. And that's how *Extended Stay* distinguishes itself from the many other narratives about migrants who receive an unkind welcome from a capitalist society that further disenfranchises the poor. Alvaro and Carmen's limbo is the Alicia, a Las Vegas hotel that will not let them leave.

Why the Alicia becomes such a prison for the siblings is a mystery. Though the hotel is unquestionably otherworldly, readers will wonder about the dark energy that Alvaro—who witnessed the massacre of most of his immediate family—brought with him. He is tormented by the event, racked by survivor's guilt, and in exile. All that emotional baggage was bound to manifest itself somehow, so why not in the Alicia, "the sort of place where you could forget yourself"?

If the Alicia is the ideal building for a haunting, then Alvaro makes a most appealing ghost, embodying the way society makes phantoms of the unwanted and the undesirable. In the American context, this includes low-wage and undocumented workers. When Alvaro and the other employees of the hotel become distressed, they have little recourse, and no path to rescue, intensifying their senses of loneliness and dislocation. So when Alvaro is struck by a moment of clarity and muses, "Where you are, what this place is, there is something here that is hungry and wrong. This is not home," his statement applies not only to his immediate surroundings but to the city, the country, and even the memories that plague him.

Until recently, the discourse behind immigration was romanticized with the iconic Statue of Liberty on Ellis Island and the Emma Lazarus poem, "The New Colossus," whose final lines read,

> Give me your tired, your poor,
> Your huddled masses yearning to breathe free,
> The wretched refuse of your teeming shore.
> Send these, the homeless, tempest-tost to me,
> I lift my lamp beside the golden door!

Those sentiments have changed in tone since the late nineteenth century, particularly with the recent anti-immigrant rhetoric and policies coming from the highest offices in the United States. *Extended Stay* is a stark warning of where such a climate will lead: to the corruption of "liberty and the pursuit of happiness," a dystopia whose maxim is best reflected by the inscription at the entrance to hell in Dante's *Inferno*: "Abandon all hope, ye who enter here."

—*Rigoberto González*

EXTENDED STAY

PART ONE

Courier (Colombia)

CHAPTER 1

ALVARO'S FAMILY WAS SINGING. HIS baby sister, Alba, included, but they stopped when the Fiat stopped. Carmen would have said something. She'd have gotten them in trouble, but she wasn't there. She had schoolwork and insisted on being old enough to be left at home unattended. Plus, Alba's swim meets bored her and she didn't feel like she should go. Alvaro agreed—he didn't want to go either but he had just dropped out of college again, for the third time this year, and he didn't feel like he had much in the way of an argument. He had been lolling about the house, putting empanadas on his parents' tab at the country club, having vague thoughts of taking up architecture (Dad could talk him through the math). They'd all figure out what was wrong with him, why he couldn't make himself go to classes, why he cried when there was no reason to cry.

The day had just made it to noon, the trip from Barranquilla to Ibagué barely clear of the dead-fish smell of the coast, the sun in full force when the girl tapped on the glass with her enormous gun. *A gun*, he'd tell you later. Not a rifle.

The girl with the gun asked them to please step out of the car. She was calm. She was polite. She wore a bandanna over the lower half of her face.

The girl with the gun had hazel eyes, like Carmen. It was just Alvaro and his baby sister, Alba, and his mom and dad and scores of other families, strangers all, everyone dazed and stepping out of their cars like it was normal, no big deal.

It did look normal. It looked for all the world like a routine roadblock, an ordinary traffic stop. The military set them up to look for guerillas, but the guerillas set them up just as often to look for kidnapping targets, and now that the guerillas were on the run, now that their world had crumbled, you didn't know who it was. Maybe common criminals, or paramilitary, or who knows, and that's what he'd try to tell you later, what he'd say to you, what he could only whisper. That he did not know, had no idea. One roadblock was indistinguishable from the other. Everyone used the same prefabricated pieces to build the structure, the same smoothly swinging steel-and-rope arm blocking the road, the same procedure for pulling people out of the car.

The family joined the crowd gathering by the shoulder of the road on a lazy curve overlooking a trampled field, a valley just beyond: a low, flattened cup of green and mist. Time refused to settle nicely into the story when he told it to you, and now you're having the same problem. It all happened all at once, he told it in the wrong order, he got the names wrong. He asked you to remember that he was not named after his own father, that Alvaro wasn't actually his name, but that he had done his best to think of himself as Alvaro, to call himself Alvaro, that he'd explain it to you later, and then forgot to tell you why.

He knew that they had left early in the morning, that they had been stopped around noon, but when they stood on the curving road, it was already late in the afternoon, the sun was already giving up.

His sister's swim meet wouldn't be until tomorrow. They had time, they could still make it, even if this lasted however long it was supposed to last. His mother stood in front of him and held his sister's shoulders. Alba was ten, old enough to know what was going on. She cried, but when they decided to move closer to the edge of the road, she did so calmly. His father, too, was calm. He whispered, "It's going to be all right. They do these all the time."

He wanted to ask if they'd be interested in Dad and the family because Dad worked for the oil company, but he knew better. Dad worked in research and development and had done graduate work in the States, but the family had no money, none whatsoever.

The girl who waved them toward the crowd with her gun was not much older than Carmen. Sixteen. Maybe seventeen. She could hold the gun, she could point with it, she could presumably shoot it, but she was so tiny.

His parents had spent the bulk of their lives traveling. After the kids were born, the family had lived in Curaçao and spoke some Dutch, some Papiamento. They had lived in Venezuela in the middle of a jungle. A worker's camp, Dad an engineer for a hydroelectric dam. They had spent some time in Ohio when Dad was finishing up his PhD, returning to Colombia only at the insistence of Mom's extended family, and of Mom herself: They missed her, they wanted them here, grandchildren included, they'd been gypsies too long. *Come home*, said the family. *We don't belong here*, he wanted to tell the girl with the gun. *We never have.* They hadn't spent enough time in this country to be kidnapped.

A guerilla rode on the back of a Kawasaki motorcycle and, through a megaphone, told the crowd to face the field. Another Kawasaki followed, lime green, where another guerilla, an open laptop dangling, checked the license plates of the idle cars.

They have a database, Alvaro thought.

There was some relief in knowing that much. Because his family really did not have any money. They could barely afford to get him to college, which they could not have done at all without Ecopetrol's sizable subsidy. They could afford to get him to a doctor—they'd made the appointment, they'd figure out what was wrong with him—but his parents constantly fretted about affording anything, and now they fretted about him dropping out of school again. About what troubled him. They told him, *You can tell us anything*, and he kept quiet. Cried. He couldn't get himself to classes, didn't know what was wrong with him, it was his first time alone, away from home. And now he was home again, a big disappointment. They went out for dinner, his parents fretted. He or his sister signed for an empanada at the country club, they fretted. They fretted and traveled, never staying wholly fixed to one place, so they had nothing in the way of savings. He'd hear his parents talk about money, argue about it. Say that they should have stayed put. That they should have saved.

His dad whispered, "If they start shooting, roll down the hill and act dead."

He nodded and whispered the same thing to Alba, grateful that Carmen wasn't here. She wouldn't whisper, wouldn't comply. She'd fight. She'd yell. Alba nodded and whispered the same words to their mom, and she cried the whole time but she did so quietly.

They faced the field. A foot away from him, a trucker left the crowd and sat on the edge of the highway, and the guerilla zipped past with his megaphone and told him to get back, which the trucker did, but lazily, slowly, a man having a hard time taking the people with guns seriously.

All the truckers laughed and huddled and moved about and had no problem engaging in conversation. They must have seen the fear on Alvaro's face and on the faces of his whole family, because they tried to reassure them. The truckers told them that drivers on this route were stopped all the time, that the guerillas hardly took anyone in these fishing expeditions and that half the time it was what they loved to call "information campaigns," one of the chiefs talking at them for three hours about land redistribution and Marxist ideology. That the men on the Kawasakis handed out booklets on their history and encouraged you to read and take notes and ask questions. That the captive audience was thanked for their time and then released unharmed.

One of the Kawasakis roared past again and the megaphone told the trucker to shut it. The trucker waved him off. Laughed.

The day waned, the air cool and gentle. Alvaro shivered. He'd been shivering earlier too, when it was hot and humid. Mom shivered also. So did his sister, his dad. If they shoot, burrow under bodies, act dead. He thought, *My whole family will do the same. We'll be fine. The trucker told us we'd be fine.*

The trucker would know, he'd been here before.

The moon crawled out, too bright, the field overlooking the valley clear in the horizon, as was a sky choking with stars. The world turned dark blue and silver blue and placid. Even the quick rip of gunfire sounded unrushed, brief, distant. Laughter burst here and there among the throng of civilians, so the gunfire didn't feel serious. Not to him, not to them. Hundreds of their own kind gathered by the side of the road, the kind of people who carried no guns, who did what people with guns told them to do. Nothing to worry about. The trucker told them the only thing to worry about was the military. Because when the military intervened, things got bloody. But then the trucker drew their attention to the heart-beat and the murmur of distant helicopters.

The trucker said, "They're far. They know what they're doing. They're not going to endanger us."

The landscape above the valley stretched flat. There was nothing to worry about. Alvaro could not stop shivering.

That was when they called his father's name through the megaphone.

Alba said, "No, no, no."

Mom sobbed.

Dad asked him to take care of his sister and mother until he returned. Dad was being asked for his ID, the young man and the boy on the Kawasaki already there, and Dad pulled it out of his wallet, the ID a dirty cream color and poorly laminated and smudged, he'd never gotten it updated, and there was comfort in being witness to the process, it was so sane and orderly, as planned as the whorls of the Colombian seal stamped in a dead and faded green.

Alvaro could not stop shivering. He wanted to intervene but he could not bring himself to say or do anything. What was he? He was just a kid, he had never held a gun or gotten drunk or anything. The family barely had enough to keep going, to pay the maid, to travel, to pay for the country club. It would only be later that he would think, *That's not poor, that's not poor at all.* What did he know? What was he thinking?

"Dad's got nothing," he said. "We don't have any money."

The boy on the back of the motorcycle checked his laptop. He stared at the antediluvian photo of the father, with its muttonchops and big hair and wide lapels. He rechecked the laptop. The boy leaned into the driver and whispered, and the driver whispered to another guerilla by Dad's side. Another person roughly Alvaro's age. Everyone in charge was too young. They all should have been in school, himself included, they should have been somewhere else.

The boy said, "Take the whole family."

━ııııı

They walked for hours by clear moonlight, the underbrush and trees etched in the dead, pale-blue light. His sister fell twice and scraped her knees, their mother grew quiet, Dad turned and told him again to take care of the family. Then said it again. Then again. Alvaro nodded and said yes every time, but Dad forgot or he wanted to make sure or else he was so nervous he could only repeat himself. He said it and he rubbed his son's back. "Take care of the family." The smell of spearmint brightened the cool, wet air, their shoes brushed the grass, the sound carried far into the night. An army helicopter whirred in the distance, but it did not follow them deeper into the mountainside. Either it never found their trail or did not care or knew better, decided that to follow would endanger civilians, like the trucker said, the trucker who also said that everything would be all right.

They were not alone. In front of them and behind them were other families, a few lone men, a few shivering teenagers, the line of civilians flanked by guerillas, some older and clearly in charge. The younger ones were younger than he was, men and women both, all wearing rubber boots and armbands, their bandannas no longer obscuring their faces but bunched around their necks, their faces flat as the moon, bored, blank, unperturbed, unalarmed.

━ııııı

They stopped in the middle of the trail, the rut deep with the footsteps of strangers, and one of the men whistled, and someone else laughed, and one of the hostages ran in the blue light and was shot. Alvaro heard the shot before the man had fallen, and so didn't know if the man fell by accident, if he tripped just before the shot was fired, but someone leaned in and shot him again two times in the back of his head. The body twitched and lay still. He remembered his sister saying, "Poor thing." She looked at the body, she did not turn away, the body twitching still, and she said it softly, holding their mother's hand.

The guerillas told them to stay, to not move, to not run away. The men with the guns left the family and the other hostages in the middle of nowhere, where they waited, one of their own already dead, the poor thing. Dead and nameless.

There was no talk of leaving, no talk at all.

The other men arrived within the hour. They came at the exact time that Alvaro thought, *Let's leave.* Alvaro could have run, the whole family could have, they had time, but what if they were watched? They had been warned. The body lay still not too far from where they stood. The men and women and boys and girls gathered close, huddled in a cloud of their own breath, not talking. They shivered. They cried, but they made an effort to keep quiet. When the other men arrived, the whole group turned in unison. *We are a herd*, Alvaro thought. *We are cattle.*

Four of the men wore black bandannas and military uniforms and gum boots, and the fifth a bright-yellow soccer shirt, his right arm missing, his face visible and streaked with scars, one of which bit into his left eye. The other scars were still raw, the skin held together with thick, black thread, but the thread wormed in and out of the puckered skin as though it had fused into the body, as though it should have been removed a long time ago and no one ever got around to it. The other men held guns but the scarred man carried a machete in his left hand. Most of the right forearm had been chopped off and the tissue at the stump was puckered and seamed. The men wore no armbands, were much older, in their forties, and when the one-armed man spoke, the others laughed. Their teeth had been removed. Their mouths were blacker than the night. Their faces were moonlit, distinct, but the countryside swallowed their laughter and their words.

The one-armed man called his father by name. The one-armed man said, "I'm Ernesto. Remember me? Remember Ernesto? Remember what you did to my family?" Alvaro thought of Bert and Ernie, of a broken Muppet, of this heavily injured, heavily scarred man sharing the same name as a *Sesame Street* character. *This is all a joke*, he thought. *This is not happening.*

Ernesto swung the machete deep into his father's thigh and his father fell to the ground, the blade still lodged deep inside him. His father did not make a sound. Neither did he or Mom or Alba. What was there to say or do that wouldn't make it worse?

They are going to chop all of us, he thought.

He was remembering it wrong. He had been crying, whimpering, yelling. His mother and sister too. His dad too. His dad moaned and said, *Please* and *No*, and when he held his arms in supplication, Ernesto's machete sliced off half of his father's fingers, the fingers still intertwined.

The men pointed their guns at the screaming family and did not tell them to be quiet, and the eyes of the men were dead, their faces plain and visible in the dead, blue moonlight, in the night that was like no night you could imagine, and the family would not make it, they would not leave this place alive, not his dad and not him and not his sister or his mother, and he could not hear himself scream, but he screamed like his dad screamed.

Ernesto screamed too, mocking his dad, and when he chopped off Dad's arms at the elbows and his feet above the ankles and cauterized them with flame and tourniquetted them with twine, the forest lit up with the animal sound of his father, and the birds answered back.

His father had no feet, no arms.

The men propped him against a tree so he could watch while they raped his wife, Alvaro's mother. No one turned away. Alvaro could not turn away because they pressed a gun against the side of his head. It went on for no time at all, it went on for hours, it did not happen, he did not see it happen.

He did not see the little girl either, pale and blond and out of place, as she peeked from behind a tree and smiled. She wore a dress or she was naked. She was as old as his sister but he had no way of telling, could not tell you how he knew or why she put a finger to her lips.

Quiet.

The men were drunk, the men had no teeth, the men were naked from the waist down, their feet still encased in gum boots, their parts caked in the blood of his mother, the boots and their thighs and their scars and the stump of Ernesto's elbow all caked in blood too.

His mother made a low and awful sound from her bloodied face. She was bloody everywhere.

There was a gun pressed to the side of Alvaro's head and he watched it all, and no one but him saw the little girl, who watched it all too, no one saw her walk to him, her feet blue in the moonlight. No one saw her, no one heard her. How could they? She wasn't there.

She did not say, *Give them to me and you live.*

Give them, they're dead anyway, you'll die too. Give them to me.

Sometimes there is no sound, and she is not there, sometimes it turns out that he did not watch, that he shut his eyes, but he can't lean in on the memory. Sometimes he wants to tell himself that it happened at a great distance, but the men clustered the family in a small patch of land. So what distance? None. He was close enough to smell what he did not want to smell.

Will you give them to me?

They sliced his mother's stomach open and all her dark, wet secrets spilled. She moaned like an animal abandoned by the side of the road. She tried to bring the coils and cords back into herself, but her fingers had been broken, a nail had been pulled off, and she could not do it.

They gave his sister a gun. They told his sister to shoot Mom, to put the gun against Mom's mouth and pull the trigger. They said, *Right here,* and tapped her mother's cheek, and laughed, and the little girl who wasn't there asked once more if he'd give them all to her, if he'd give her the broken pieces of his family, and then she said, *Look*, and she pulled back the bark from the tree to reveal a black, ropy, wet mass, something alive and throbbing behind the fabric of the world, some other awful pain that waited behind the awful pain of his mother, and the little girl laughed when the men laughed. She laughed with them. His sister cried and held on to the gun with both hands and could not lift it, not until they slapped her and told her they'd rape her if she didn't do it, that they'd let her go if she did. (*Will you?*) His sister crawled to their mother, the men alongside her, and she dragged the gun to their mother's temple, and she shot her. They told her to shoot again, that her mother was not dead yet, that if she loved her mother she would put her out of her misery, and the men meant it. They were no longer laughing. Whatever pleasure they had taken in what came before was gone, they were all business, and his sister did what she was told, and the body of their mother stopped convulsing.

You shoot your brother, they said.

Will you? said the girl who wasn't there.

He heard them say it, he did not hear them say it. He did not hear his sister say yes or no, and he'd like to tell you that he didn't say yes, that he didn't say, *Yes, take them, I give them to you, let me live*, but that much he remembers. That much he can confirm. He said yes. His father slumped on the tree, his face swollen and blotched, his eyes red and black. If Dad was crying, there was no way to know, no way to tell. If he said anything, if he wanted to say anything, there was no way to tell. Dad's mouth was a mess and the eyes half blinked, half opened.

Alba put the gun to her brother's mouth, to his mouth. The barrel tapped his teeth, and her hands shook, and the metal chipped his front tooth, the crack small and unimportant and still unfixed, and she could barely lift the thing, but she did not pull the trigger, her hazel eyes enormous in the moonlight. His sister. He made fun of her. He dressed her up. He told her these awful stories just to make her cry. (Like, she was a fan of the Care Bears, and he told her that they would help her just like they helped the kids in the episode, but the bears were popular, they were busy, so there was a waiting list, and they wouldn't be able to help until she turned eighty, they couldn't see her until then.)

Alba shot the man holding the gun to her face. She aimed for the chest but hit his leg instead. The man did not shoot back, was presumably in too much pain, too much disbelief.

Ernesto laughed. The other men laughed. Ernesto brought the machete down on Alba's hand and the hand fell off, still clutching the gun. The other men kept laughing, one of them pried the gun off the fingers, one of which cracked.

When Alvaro was ten, when he was Alba's age, he read every issue of *Condorito* the day it came out. Half the gags involved an amputation, with the bone and muscle as round and as neat as concentric tree rings. His sister's stump looked like that, like a cross section, like a cartoon, before it gushed and bloomed and before his sister cried and before they put the bloodied gun in his hands and told him to shoot.

They shoved him close against her, shoved the gun up against her temple and said, *Shoot.* Then they sliced off her left foot, still in its sneaker. Then Ernesto jabbed the machete deep into her thigh, jabbed it so deep that he had to prop a gum boot against Alba's side to pull it out.

Alvaro shot his own sister.

They pulled him away, pulled the gun from him, left him on the ground. He could have gotten up, he supposed, but he did not try, could not try, and the men around him knew and did not bother. Ernesto crawled by the wet mess of his father and behind the tree against which his father slumped, moved right past the girl who was not there and found something and dropped it in a dirty envelope lodged between his armpit and stump, then dropped something else before he licked the seal shut. They had the same ancient envelopes at home in some forgotten drawer— flimsy, pale blue, edged with blue and red. Aerograms. You used them when writing to friends abroad.

Dad had already died, though Alvaro did not know when it happened, or how much his father had seen. Ernesto gave him the envelope. It had a name and an address on it, both from Bogotá, and he was told to deliver it in person.

"Your sister was supposed to do it," Ernesto said, stump pointing at the crumbled mass of limbs on the ground.

CHAPTER 2

CARMEN WOULDN'T LOOK AT ALVARO, wouldn't ask.

She huddled and drew on her sketchbook, and kept herself low. The family had long limbs, and they were all unusually long and lanky, Carmen in particular.

He'd been told she cried when she heard the news, but in the days between Bogotá and Barranquilla, the tears had stopped and she seethed, she raged, she kept to herself. He had told her he was sorry and she said he had nothing to be sorry for.

But she didn't know, didn't want to know.

He said, "We'll be fine," not believing it, his sister not believing it either, realizing only then that their dad must have felt the same.

Dad said they had nothing to worry about because that is what you said.

You said it, you hoped it was true.

▬▪▪▪▪▪

Two months later, he received a letter from the other Alvaro, the one his father had been mistaken for, and a letter from Ernesto, both men apologetic, both saying that if they could take back what happened, they would. That neither was knowingly a "bad person" (both used the same phrase). The other Alvaro had moved his family to Santiago de Chile that year.

Ernesto was still at large, still in the jungle, but the letter came postmarked from Bogotá.

Alvaro learned that neither he nor Carmen knew their extended family too well. That their grandfather was too old to care for them. Brother and sister spent the bulk of their days together, him still shivering, in their grandfather's squalid row home, in a part of Barranquilla he had not known, the room hot, and his sister still not asking.

What everyone knew about Carmen was that she was brilliant. She could draw anything you asked. She had their dad's appetite for numbers, for structures.

She went to school and returned, and he realized how relieved he felt at not having anyone giving him a hard time about dropping out. Carmen didn't care. His grandfather didn't quite know. In the fog of their grief, it was hard to tell how anyone else felt.

She had not asked what happened, and the worry was that she already knew. She knew so much. The worry was that she would ask.

What everyone knew about Carmen was that she was sullen, that she did not smile, that she had Dad's capacity to keep herself closed off. That she did not cry easily, unlike Alvaro. That she barely cried at all after they lost Mom and Dad and Alba.

What he knew was that she was afraid. She had night terrors.

She cried in her sleep.

They had to share a room and a fan, and the fan whirred and kept the stuffy room bearable, and the noise partly obscured Carmen's nighttime mourning. Did she know she cried? Alvaro didn't think so. They ate whatever the maid fixed for them, and on the third night of the awful soft spaghetti with the too-sweet sauce and the shredded chicken, he tried to bring it up, but she shut him down.

"I've got schoolwork," she said. "Some of us still do."

She held a red forkful and he wanted to tell her what he'd learned, that you included the index finger as well as the ID of whoever you killed to verify identity. That was what he carried back to the highway in the aerogram envelope: Dad's index finger and ID.

The phone rang. The calls came at dinner, and he answered because his grandfather couldn't hear the ringing, and because Carmen never got up. It was his job now, he supposed, to see who was on the other end.

We're coming. We're coming for you.

It sounded like Ernesto, the broken Muppet, the man who had written to apologize. The one who said he was not knowingly a bad person.

Carmen asked, "Who is it?"

"No one we know," he said, and the lie sounded like the truth because he couldn't be sure.

We know you talked.

They're coming for us so we know you talked. They're coming for us so we're coming for you.

There were other voices.

Others called, told him to keep silent, told him that they knew he had talked, that it was no use.

We're coming for you and your sister.

He tried telling them the truth: He had told no one, he whispered that never in a million years would he think of telling anyone, that he hadn't even told his own sister, who was here in the same room. That even if he tried to talk he couldn't, the words wouldn't come out. He couldn't say anything. They said, *We know you talked* and he kept mute, the terror a dark ribbon squeezing the air from his lungs, squeezing whatever was left of him, whatever was not stripped away on the road to Ibagué.

Once, the voice at the other end of the line sounded like Alba. A little girl told him that they were all waiting for him, that the house waited for him and his sister both, and that night it was hot and sour in the room, and he woke from a dream where his parents ate at a long table that pulsed. The faces of his mother and father were fine, the same long faces he remembered from childhood, but when he sat by their side the faces were bloodied and mangled, skin shredded, a long flap of his mother's cheek succumbing to gravity and falling in a wet heap on her plate. She ate it. Alvaro thought, *I should be frightened*, but he wasn't. He wasn't scared until he realized that Alba was missing, and until he saw her holding hands with the pale girl from the forest. The girl who wasn't there, had never been there. He woke up with a shock, a sudden squeeze of the heart. The phone was ringing and there was no one in the house and he had no idea how long he had been asleep.

It was no use telling the voice otherwise, no use explaining that it was a mistake, that they'd made a mistake again, that he hadn't even told his sister what happened.

Here's what he most wanted to tell the voice, because now he thought of it as a confidant, as the only entity that would understand: He had no desire to go back, no real need to talk about what happened. The only way to make it through was to keep going forward. To forget. To never talk of it again.

That the police had asked, that Ecopetrol had asked, that his sister had asked—he could say nothing.

He had no words.

In the last two weeks, the callers learned when he was alone. Carmen had school, but his grandfather's schedule was erratic, and even so, the phone rang only when he was alone in the hot house. He didn't know how they knew. He supposed they didn't. He was mostly alone. He was mostly in the house.

He knew they could not stay. That was all.

"Let's go," he said one night. "Dad wanted us to go back, so why don't we?"

Carmen said, "Why don't we wait and think about it?"

They had a tourist visa that was good for another three years. They could fly in, lie about where they were going to stay, and they'd make their way to a safe place, away from the voice and reach of the people Carmen didn't know about—the people they were on the run from.

The phone rang. Their grandfather coughed and turned up the sound on the television.

He said, "What's there to think about?"

The Ecopetrol check had just arrived, and the money felt bigger than any single sum they'd seen, and it was written out to the both of them. Later they'd learn that it wasn't much at all. He'd tell himself they didn't know, that he wasn't to blame, but here's the truth, here's what he'd tell you even if he couldn't say it at the time: He lied. He didn't tell her about the calls. He didn't tell her that he was afraid. He wasn't honest.

Instead he said, "If we do it now, we won't be missed. We'll be gone before anyone has time to stop us."

Carmen tore a sheet from her sketchbook and handed it to him. "That's what I drew this morning," she said.

He unfolded the sheet. She had put the head of Mickey Mouse on the body of an enormous octopus, the tentacles digging deep into desert ground. A lone saguaro cringed from the cracked ground.

She said, "Maybe it's a sign?"

"To go or to stay?" he asked, then corrected himself. "To go. Let's say it's to go. We'll fly to Orlando and see what happens."

There was no one who said no because they told no one, not even their grandfather. Not the social worker whose visits were haphazard and useless. Not the Ecopetrol folks whose check they cashed.

You had to buy round-trip tickets because one-way trips raised questions upon arrival.

They flew, and on the Avianca flight, an ad from the Colombian board of tourism claimed that the only danger about the country was "wanting to stay." It was the decade following the triumphs of Álvaro Uribe, and Colombia was supposedly better. There were no kidnappings, nothing bad could happen to you anymore—not on the roads, not in your home, and so the story felt particularly fraught, particularly *off*. Because what happened to them was no longer supposed to happen.

That's it, he'd say to you, though you'll forget.

You'll forget him, you'll forget the story, you'll forget why he told the story, or who you were then, who you are now, all of it gone.

That's all of it, he'd say, looking at his hands, and you still dreaming, still looking at his hands, counting his fingers.

PART TWO

Foundlings (Las Vegas)

CHAPTER 3

THAT AFTERNOON AT SUNSET PARK was the first time they had all been together—Alvaro, Carmen, and Alvaro's coworker Ellie. Alvaro didn't have a car. Carmen wanted to go back to Colombia, and Alvaro had been desperate to show his sister that Vegas was OK, that it was a good place to regroup, and so he talked to Ellie. Did Ellie know of anywhere in Vegas that was nice? Green? Less . . . ?

He couldn't find the word for how the city felt.

Less dead? Less harsh?

Ellie was Irish, born in Belfast, but she had lived in Nevada forever, and loved it, and she wanted to prove that there was life here, something other than streets and dirt and desert, that you could find fields and water and something like wilderness, so she drove them to the park. She pointed at trees, at volleyball courts, at picnicking families. Smoke from barbecues rose, fragrant. A Mexican radio station played at full volume.

He drank in the bright sun, the black water of the artificial pond, the auburn ridge of mountains in the distance, the flat, pale blue of the Vegas sky, the panicked geese.

Most of all, he relished the stone face at the heart of the pond: an Easter Island head as tall as him. Pigeons rested on the head and took off when radio-controlled boats buzzed too close. Carmen propped her sketchbook on her knees and drew the pigeons, the boats, and the stone face. She drew the old man in the pale-yellow trousers and the albino goose that followed the old man from bench to bench.

He thought, *Why did the old man move? Why did the goose follow?*

"I bet they know each other," Carmen said. "I bet they've known each other for years."

She drew the man, but she had him riding the goose in midflight, borne to who knows where.

It was always a shock to see her draw. A shock that his sister could be so good, so talented, that she could conjure a likeness out of nothing.

When he drew, he could barely manage stick figures, and no one else in the family was any better. They were a family of engineers, good at structures, bad at art, but Carmen was the anomaly. She was good at everything.

She moved away from him, closer to the edge of the pond, and kept drawing. Her hair hung low over her face. His little sister had dressed all in black since they came to Vegas, each of her nails sporting the same Sharpie-drawn pre-Columbian figure. Carmen the Goth.

He thought, *If Mom could see her, what would she say?*

Ellie stood in her long skirt and held a Budweiser, her hair bright red in the dying light. She was pale for Vegas, she claimed, and too fat. But she moved with grace.

She hunched close to Carmen and talked. Carmen shrank from Ellie like she shrunk from Alvaro and everyone. He wanted to go to them, but Ellie was already getting up, she had given his sister something—money? A note? A gift?

He couldn't tell, he didn't know if he could ask.

He had not seen his sister talk to anyone, not like this, and it felt like it wasn't his business. He wasn't Dad, after all. Carmen nodded, laughed, put whatever Ellie had given her away, went back to her sketchbook.

He blinked and Carmen and Ellie were covered in blood, every limb wet and slick. A roach fell from Ellie's hair.

He shivered in the heat and blinked and found everything had returned to normal. The sun and the breeze threw trembling shadows on his sister and his coworker. You could mistake the shadows for blood. He had been seeing things that were not there, but he knew it was nothing to worry about. No need for panic. They were safe now. The blood came back, the vision of the forest, the dream of the little girl—it all loomed, but it was all in his head, he knew that much. He still cried. He was no longer sad.

Ellie sat close to him and said, "You're getting better."

A shadow fell on her, then passed. It did look like blood, it moved like blood, but it was just moving light and lack of sleep, and so he nodded, he let her know that he agreed even though he didn't know what she was talking about.

For a moment, he thought she was talking about their trauma, but Ellie didn't know, he had told no one, but then he understood. She meant his skills as a line cook. She had spent the better part of the decade in Nevada. First Reno, now Vegas. She had worked as an office assistant for years but had to give it up because of carpal tunnel. Now she was a waitress at the Alicia. She still had to wear braces on her wrists. In her late forties, Ellie was old enough to be his mother, too old to be a friend, but she was the only friend he had.

He nodded. "I'm still slow," he said, "but I feel like this week's better than the week before. Better prep."

"It's the grill you're getting the hang of, hon. At least."

"That's all you," he said.

It was. Ellie had saved him.

He would have been fired had it not been for her. He could still get fired, for all he knew. Ellie had told him there had been a time when it didn't matter. You could pretty much walk into any kitchen and get a gig. Not now. Not even after the economy had picked up and investors came back. Vegas had busted, like it always did, and now it was waking up again.

Even Fremont, the old heart of Vegas.

It was where the city built the first cluster of hotels and gambling halls, not far from where the first band of settlers found water. Ellie had promised to drive them to the site, Desert Springs, where people had stopped because they found an oasis.

Everything he knew about Vegas he learned from Ellie, even if Ellie herself knew nothing about him or his sister. Ellie was the one who told him of the investors who arrived from elsewhere, tore down whatever they wanted to tear down, and replaced it with something new. The money sprung like the Desert Springs water, like a miracle or a mirage. Like a force that couldn't possibly be there or, once there, run out.

"I have to go soon." She sat on the grass. "I can give you guys a ride back if you want."

"We'll take the bus," he said. Carmen wasn't done drawing, and he wasn't ready to go back either. "Thank you."

"Happy I could show you the nice part." She stared at Carmen. They could barely make out what she drew, but the strokes came down hard on the page. She said, "I have a sister too. She's in Ireland. We never talk. She never calls unless she wants money. Never calls unless there's trouble at home. We were never as close as the two of you. Never so sweet." Ellie was nearly done with her beer. "Your sister's at a tricky age, hon. Fifteen's *awful*. It gets better. You and your sister, you'll do just fine."

He felt lightheaded and lighthearted. Carmen's Nevada ID insisted that she was fifteen, but she was actually two years younger. He was seventeen, but his papers said he was twenty-two. There was a weird joy in knowing how little his friend knew about them.

He didn't know what to say, and he didn't know why he blushed, but she smiled and patted his back, and her hand felt good and warm, and again he remembered the troubling shade—how her fingers looked like they were coated in blood, how it was all in his head. It was so good to have nothing to say—to be understood. *Yes*, he thought. *We'll be fine.*

Ellie said she'd see him tomorrow and walked away.

For the first time in months, Alvaro and Carmen had nothing pressing to do and nothing to worry about, a Sunday without homework or a breakfast shift.

Carmen said, "This is the first time I've seen the city."

"We've been here," he said. "We've seen it."

"Not since the Greyhound, and we drove in at night," she said. "We hadn't seen the Strip until now. Like, when I get on Paradise for the bus, you hardly see it at all. And back from the room it's just Ogden and Fremont and all those other dinky streets, and there's nothing there. Like, *nothing*. You see Charleston and it's wide and full of those weirdos, that's it. And all those bars. That giant screen. It's like they keep building and they don't see you, like they don't see *anything*. I wish it could all go away. Like, imagine this place with nobody, nothing."

The old man moved benches and the goose followed, and it was so friendly, so sweet, and so unlike the goose he saw when the family first traveled abroad, to Canada, before they moved back to Colombia. He forgot whether it had chased Carmen or Alba. He'd heard a cry and found one of his sisters wailing, chased by a giant bird going after the bit of bread in her tiny fist.

He said, "Why do you think he's moving benches?"

She pointed at the cluster of geese behind the old man. "If they stay too long, the other geese get wind of it. This way, his special goose gets the bread."

"Oh," he said.

The old man and the goose found a way to keep themselves apart.

A toy yacht the length of his arm ripped along the edge of the pond and scattered ducks and grackles in its wake.

"This city's so *stupid*," she said. "Everything's so *loud*. No one thinks there's other people around."

She was right, but he didn't think it was so terrible. The boats were annoying, but music wafted in from the volleyball courts and from the picnics and from all around, all of it faint and welcoming. And the air smelled good, cooled by the water and rich with the green of the grass and the faint sharp tang of trees and scrub. Even the water from the pond had a good smell to it. In Fremont, it was all hot asphalt and drunks and bright lights, or it was dark and just as hot, just as redolent of burnt rubber.

Carmen said, "I hate it here."

"You don't," he said, though he knew she meant it, and though he hated it here as well.

She wiped her nose. The sun buzzed low and orange in the sky. The light summoned clouds into its core, and the mountains felt like they'd been cut out and dropped in the distance. Like they weren't quite real. Like they stood in a set.

"You don't hate it," he said again. "It's not bad. I mean, it's not *so* bad." He pointed at the old man, the pale goose. "*This* you don't hate."

She smiled from beneath her bangs and it was like they were kids again. Real kids. Back in Colombia.

They had to go soon. Driving took fifteen minutes, but the bus to Fremont took well over an hour, a long, slow jaunt along Eastern on a route that didn't run that often or that late on Sundays.

Ellie had left over an hour ago, though it felt like she had just said goodbye.

"No," Carmen said. "You're right. This I don't hate. This I kind of like."

He said, "Why don't we go back?"

"We've got time."

"I mean *back*," he said. "Back to Colombia." Whoever called, whoever said they were coming, had lost them. They were in a new country, and they had new numbers. Maybe it'd be fine. And why was he so afraid? The worst had happened. "This was stupid," he said. "This was such a stupid idea."

"That was all you," she said. "That was your stupid idea."

He pulled at a strand of grass. *We know you talked*, the voice had said, but he had kept it all inside. One time Carmen caught him hanging up, asked him what was up with his face, who had called. What had he told her? Maybe she knew. Maybe, deep down, she understood.

She had thought about going to the States too, she had talked about it, but he had been the one to plant the idea in her head. And before him, Dad. Because Dad loved to talk about how they'd all end up over here, how it was such a better country—how the place made so much more sense than the chaos and corruption of Colombia. So maybe he was innocent, or at least a little innocent. It was hard to tell now.

"I know," he said. "I know it was my stupid idea. But let's go back. Let's call it quits or even or whatever, and let's go back."

We're coming. We know you talked.

He hadn't. And they didn't belong here. They knew no one.

She closed her notebook and stood up. "You're right," she said. "This I like."

"We'll do it," he said. "I'll get us back."

"You promise?"

The gaggle of geese waddled too close to the albino, and the old man spread his hands and yelled and they all scattered, their wings awkward and half-spread, most of the flock earthbound. There was nothing sinister about it, nothing remarkable. The ground was dry, the sun almost set, the sky pink and red. Later—much later—he would know why he remembered the park. Why the wings and the honks had stayed with him when so much else had vanished. Later he'd take the geese for a warning, convinced he had missed something.

"Alba would have liked the park," Carmen said. "She would have *loved* the geese."

Alba had been dead for four months, and so had their mother and father.

Four months to the day.

He had done his best to forget. He had no intention of marking the day, of making a big deal out of it, he told himself that he thought of it every day, so why make any one random moment of pain and grief more special than the other? But the anniversary snuck in, as nimble and fleeting as a shadow.

Alba would have loved this day, it was true, but he couldn't bring himself to agree. They had mostly avoided talking about their family. They had to. He had to, at any rate. He couldn't do it just yet.

———

They made their long way back home. It took a transfer, and it took forever, and Carmen drew and stared out the bus window.

Fremont waited, alight and full of noise on a Sunday night, but they walked into the part of it that kept itself dark, the part they now called home.

CHAPTER 4

ALVARO DREAMED OF HIS DEAD sister. In the dreams, he wore the same cheap chef's pants he wore to work. He chopped and prepped—chopped badly, prepped slowly—while orders piled up and Alba watched and shook her head. *Tell her*, Alba said. *Tell our sister what you did.* The kitchen bloomed, the tiles the wrong shade of green. The grill hissed. In the dream, morning was soured by disapproval, as though the hotel itself knew he had no right to be here.

Not after what he had done to his family.

Will you give them to me?

The voice came from the tiles, and in the dream he said yes once more, though he knew he shouldn't, though the part of him not in the dream said no.

Carmen woke him up at three in the morning, an hour before she was supposed to, her face damp, and he asked her what was wrong, confused because he thought he was still dreaming and Carmen looked like Alba, though they were three years apart. The whole family looked too much alike. Long limbed, with big noses. All oddly attractive. "Your mother's so beautiful," he heard. "Your sisters too." He didn't know what to say. Didn't know what to say when he was told his father was so handsome, or that he looked so much like him. All of them too long.

She had not let go of his shoulder. He had asked her again what troubled her.

"Nothing," Carmen said.

She shuffled to her corner of the room and fell asleep again. Her inflatable mattress was small and thin, red on the top, navy on the bottom—a pool toy bought at the 99-cent store. She wanted him to have the bed because he was the one who had to get up early, who had to work. They had not slept well, neither one, not for months.

They barely had enough to make it from week to week. They had meant to go to California, and had no real idea how they made it only as far as Las Vegas. And she didn't care for the magnet school, didn't like the long bus ride, or the kids, or the math courses. And when he fell asleep again, it was Alba who waited for him.

Maybe it's just our earplugs, he thought. *Maybe we need better ones.* Because they could hear the other tenants. A child called out for her mother. Others too. More than one child called out for more than one mother.

━━ɪɪɪɪɪ

They lived on a block of Fremont that was still unbought and undeveloped— their extended-stay motel hunched next to the fading sign for the Chevalier and the bright-green Peter Pan that pointed west. They could pay by the week, and they could pay in cash. Signs stickered to every floor told residents the same thing over and over: "If you hear the alarm, call 911." They'd had to call 911 five times. The windows were barred, and so was the whole place, all of it gated and spiked and wired shut, and the floor of the laundry room crunched with broken glass, and the people they ran into were red eyed and broken and always asked them if they had any change, if they could help them out, anything helped, a quarter, a dollar, enough for a loose cigarette. Their own room reeked of cigarettes, though he did not smoke and was afraid of drinking—the one therapist in Barranquilla told him not to, not until they figured out what was going on. He suspected the room had always smelled like cigarettes, but it did have an ancient television set, and the set did offer a pretty impressive selection of channels.

He and Carmen watched whatever played on Turner Classic Movies, unless Carmen had dibs and then it was just animal documentaries.

They walked the five minutes from their nightmare efficiency to the bus stop, and they waited for the city bus that would take her to the actual school bus. The bus came only once every hour, so they arrived well before because otherwise she'd miss school entirely, and he'd have to leave her in the apartment by herself. They'd done that once before and didn't want to do it again. They were too old to hold hands, though part of him wanted to. Their father had had a nervous habit of stroking his children's back when they walked together. It was good when he was little and then insufferable as he got older—Alvaro couldn't explain it, didn't know why he repelled at the touch—and then on the night of the roadblock his father did it again, he did it for the last time, both to Alvaro and to Alba, and that moment was part of the problem, part of his unease. The gesture was so loving, and it was also irritating, and it didn't matter that it was the last time, didn't matter that Dad was about to die. Alvaro shrank away. His dad reached out to comfort him and he shrank away. And now Alvaro wanted to do exactly what his dad had done, his hand hovering by his sister's shoulder blades, but he restrained himself.

Instead he said, "I mean it. We could go back."

Carmen fidgeted with the straps of her backpack.

"We could," he said.

Carmen said, "Let's." She pressed the back of her hand against her mouth and stifled a yawn. "I'm sorry I said it was your stupid idea. Like, it was and it wasn't." In the dark, it was impossible to see her eyes. "I thought maybe it'd be better here. But it's not. It's not better *anywhere*."

The bus arrived and his sister left for a part of Las Vegas he did not know.

▬▪▪▪▪▪

He walked to the Hotel Alicia, still thinking of the nightmare. Still apologizing. Still not fully awake.

Fremont was still dozing at five o'clock, all of Ogden quiet, the neon off. Two Metro cops chatted with a homeless man about his lost dog. The Metro cops wore reflective vests over round stomachs. The homeless man wore stained red sweatpants and an olive T-shirt. He gripped a leash. He said he had paid good money for it at PetSmart. Honest money.

The homeless man said, "Please help me find her."

—•▮▮▮▮

The Alicia lurked behind El Cortez, on a street Alvaro liked because it kept itself out of view. You could not see the parking lot or the empty pool or the wrought-iron cages. You could not see much of the Alicia until you were already in it. He had seen the boss himself only once before in real life, during orientation, a short man with a bushy handlebar moustache, a Texas accent, a Yosemite Sam tie.

The boss had stood on the rickety ballroom stage and said, first, that hopefully they'd be able to renovate the convention space, but that for now they'd be focusing on the casino area. That Cara Holdings were so proud of what they'd done so far. That they'd hear of the awesome and hard-working crew the boss had assembled, that he'd tell the investment group himself—that he couldn't wait until the Cara folks flew in from Seattle. That the Alicia might be down, but not out—that she had a great history but an even greater future—that she was tiny compared to all those other joints in Fremont, and maybe not as hipsterish, not as bopping, but so what? That things were picking up all around, you could feel it, couldn't you? The boss stood in the weak light of the Alicia's sad chandelier. Any problems, anything wrong with the hotel, anything needing attention, the boss wanted to hear about it.

The chandelier rustled, blinked, gave up. A pale redheaded woman in a tight plum blazer clicked her way over to a generator.

The room buzzed with work lights. They revealed peeling wallpaper and flinching furniture, everything cracked and dirty and wounded. Even the room didn't want to be in the room.

"Call me B.," the boss said. "Or call me crazy. But call me."

No one laughed.

The staff was mostly Mexican, so B. added, "Loco. Call me Loco."

Alvaro had called B. the week before because a third-floor suite poured roaches from the nozzles of a cracked Jacuzzi. He liked to walk the empty, narrow corridors on breaks and before and after shifts. The rest of Fremont did not appeal—too many lights, too many drunk people stumbling and shouting—but the Alicia stood dark and small, forgotten, the sort of place where you could forget yourself. Management shuttered three of the hotel's five floors and used the crumbling sixth-floor penthouse for its offices.

You could walk for hours and run into no one. You could, if you wanted to, step into an empty room and cry. You could avoid your own room a block away with the fading photo of your mother, father, and sisters. You could avoid your own living sister. He turned the nozzle because there was talk in the kitchen that the pipes were not working right, that the guts of the Alicia badly needed fixing. His call went straight to voice mail. B. never called back. It had been a week since B.'s speech.

It had now been a month since the Alicia reopened. Things did not look good.

▬ııı

The casino proper had not been truly renovated. The room had been repainted, the booths and banquettes and stools freshly upholstered, but B. spent the bulk of the Cara money on a lighting design inspired by the Golden Nugget. One of the croupiers said that it was like walking into a yellow Crayola.

The light did not hide the main floor's problems: The scratched slot machines, screens milky with age, backs and sides clumped with dirt. The long row of windows facing Ogden—the one decent and somewhat well-trafficked side of the hotel—overlooked the planned site of a religious protest in the coming days. Three weird, angry men already walked the block and held massive photographs of aborted fetuses. The men walked only alongside the Alicia's windows. They kept their signs occluded from the Big Eastern, the dying Western, the back of the Chevalier, the lights of Fitzgerald's and the Golden Nugget. They could have marched along the length of Fremont Street, right down the middle of the covered street if they wanted to, Las Vegas didn't care, but the Alicia drew their attention and anger. The place was a magnet for malfunctions.

The slot machines refused to cooperate. Four rows of electronic poker and keno units went dark.

The felt on the gaming tables pilled. Maintenance patched two rips on the anchor craps station with duct tape—unheard of, as far as Alvaro knew.

He didn't know much, granted. He knew that few chose the Alicia willingly, that bussers and servers avoided this hotel—it had a murky reputation, it closed down as frequently as the ghostly shells on Paradise and Flamingo. There was talk of frequent thieving, late paychecks, unresponsive bosses. All of it seemed to be true, and none of it mattered much. Alvaro had worked a previous casino gig, at Fitzgerald's just down the street, but he lasted less than a week before the kitchen caught on to his severe lack of cooking skills. The Alicia took him in. And Ellie was right, he'd improved somewhat since he'd been here. It helped that they didn't get much traffic—he had time to practice, time to screw up and get better. He thought of what happened on the road between Barranquilla and Ibagué, still struggling to explain to his coworkers why his English sounded wrong, mostly trying not to talk at all, to keep to himself, also worried that his chipped front tooth would finally give way at the next meal.

He told himself what he told Carmen: They didn't have to stay. They could go back.

Never mind that he was getting better, that the distance was helping. Never mind that he spent all their money on a fake work visa.

He still did not know if his forged papers would fly, but they were surprisingly better than what most of his coworkers came in with. Some brought wrinkled photocopies of a Social Security card. That was fine, apparently. The money he had spent on the forgery could have kept them going for six months. They could have left Las Vegas and ended up elsewhere.

That was something else he hadn't told Carmen: that he had misspent their money, and that she was right, they had no business being here.

The main floor of the Alicia, the casino and café and lobby, looked fine if you did not look closely. It looked about as respectable as any other establishment in Fremont. Same with the papers, he told himself. The papers were fine because no one was looking closely.

And now it was time to leave.

He would go in, he would work his shift, and he would tell them he was leaving. They would go back to Colombia, or they would go to California, but they would leave. He had led them to the wrong place, but he could fix it.

—·····

In the morning, from five fifteen until seven thirty, he spent the bulk of his time prepping. The kitchen followed the same decrepit logic as the rest of the hotel, so the room stretched long and narrow, the ceilings low, one door leading to the dining room and the other to a walk-in freezer, and through the freezer to a door into a narrow service alley.

If he needed to pee, and he if had the time, he walked the length of the dining room and into the bathrooms just off the pit. Washed his hands. Sang "Mambrú se fué a la guerra," as per ServSafe regulations—the video suggested "Happy Birthday" or "Row, Row, Row Your Boat," but he stuck with "Mambrú," thought of his family, looped through the bit that went "Que dolor, que dolor, que pena." What pain, what pain, what sorrow.

He cleaned the kitchen himself, though of course the janitors, too, made their circuit and scrubbed, and he wiped the boards, wiped the knives, segregated surfaces. Before he handled one bit of food he had to take a daylong certification course. He had not known this, had not known anything of work. He had not known you dreamed of work. He watched a video. He watched and took notes and a computer quizzed him, and later at work, when he messed up, someone helped. Someone offered corrections. The entire kitchen surface bandaged itself in green tiles, the walls almost humming a pale, dead olive, the floor and the ceiling included. He could get most of the dirt off the grout but not all of it.

The room echoed.

Whatever he said, it came back thick with someone else's words and rustle and breath. They had no one in charge of prep, so he and the other two line cooks chopped a host of onions and green peppers. The mushrooms arrived presliced, each bag as heavy as an infant. You picked the bag up and propped it next to the cutting board and defrosted it, timer on, at room temp.

The servers arrived surly. The graveyard shift did all right with tips, but the morning breakfast crowd was notoriously stingy.

Ellie, big and brassy in her uniform, peered over his shoulder. "Hope you get them tiny," she said, holding her pinkie in front of him. "Like so. Smaller. Don't want another return." The room swallowed her words, mixed them up with the thud and chop of his fellow line cooks' knives on onions and peppers.

Last time, three of his omelets had come back. It was, as Ellie herself had noted, an improvement. "You'll get there," she said.

Alvaro nodded. Ellie thought he was from Mexico, because pretty much everyone else here was from Mexico. It was easier if people didn't think he knew too much English, easier still if they did not know where he came from.

"Oh boy," she said. "Oh honey."

The pack had not been sliced open yet but Alvaro could smell what Ellie saw. The mushrooms were gone, spoiled. The stink crept through the milky plastic, which was moist and slippery enough to require two hands. He nearly dropped the bag anyway.

Something jagged poked through the plastic, a pale-pink needle. He had almost slapped it away. It looked like a tooth, but it was too long. He pulled it out of the bag. He should toss it, but the trash was too far away, and so he put it in a pocket, though it smelled awful, evil.

The mushrooms practically glowed through the plastic. "We're not serving those," he said.

"No, hon. *No es bueno.*"

"It's fucking *bueno* enough. For fuck's sake." Alvaro and Ellie turned. The room always made it difficult to place voices, but mornings were particularly hard. And the voice was new. At first, Alvaro thought it was the boss, but all they shared was a Texas accent.

The man was in his early twenties, wiry, blond. He stepped between them and tore open the bag. The stench reminded Alvaro of family drives to the coast of Barranquilla. The mushrooms smelled like rotting fish.

"What you do is you pick out the good ones," the stranger said. He wore a suit, but the suit was navy, not black, and it was expensive and fit well, so Alvaro knew he couldn't be a cage boss or a dealer. The stranger picked through a couple of the mushrooms. "The good ones. You fucking *comprende?*" He held a mushroom that was half gone, the edges a sick pink. There were no good ones. The stranger's cuffs darkened and stained from the mushroom sluice, but he kept going.

"We don't serve rot," Alvaro said. "Why would you think we'd serve those? That's a ServSafe violation." It was. It was in the video. If something had gone bad, you tossed the whole thing.

"Dude, fuck ServSafe," the stranger said. "We're broke. Seattle wants us saving every fucking penny. So fuck ServSafe, and fuck you, señor high and mighty. You know that? Know we're broke? Think we can afford to throw food away? Pick the good ones and rinse them and serve them. *Comprende?*"

"We're not serving those," Alvaro said again.

Ellie said, "Some of them look OK."

Alvaro grabbed the bag and tossed it in the trash. "We can't afford a violation," he said. "A new bag of mushrooms maybe we can afford."

"Dude, I could so have your job," the stranger said. "I'm so having your job."

People could do that, Alvaro supposed. They could just fire you. Let them. He was done here, done cooking, he couldn't even do it right anyway. He and Carmen could go elsewhere. Maybe Los Angeles. He washed the slime off his hands. Said nothing. Moved to the freezer to pick out another bag of mushrooms.

Please, he thought. *I'm doing what I'm supposed to be doing. Leave me alone.*

He thought of Alba in the dream, his sister shaking her head in disapproval.

"You know what?" the stranger said. "Fuck you. You're fired. *Comprende* fired?"

"We've got morning coming on," Alvaro said. His station waited. "Fire me after breakfast."

Let him fire me, he thought. *I'm done here. I don't know why I ended up here.* He remembered his father and mother singing along to *Don Giovanni*, the Fiat chugging along the coast, Alba wordlessly humming "Madamina, il catalogo è questo," Carmen busy drawing and deep in her own world, all of them alive and certain that everything would be OK and that Colombia's troubles were not their own. He thought, *Just let me be.*

He sliced open the new bag. Rotten also. It smelled worse than the first, the mushrooms soft and half-eaten by black and pink growth. Fungus on fungus.

"*Comprende?* Fired." The stranger turned to Ellie. "How do you say *fired* in Spanish?"

The voice that answered was not Ellie's. "It's *despedido*, and you're not firing anyone." Alvaro first saw the Yosemite Sam tie, the same one from three weeks ago, then the rest of him: B., shorter than Alvaro by a head. "Come on. *Git.*"

The stranger did not move.

"I said, *git*." B. peered at the bag while the stranger left. Ellie busied herself with side work: the folding of napkins, the filling of pepper shakers, the clacking of mugs.

"We can't use this bag either," Alvaro said. "Sorry."

"Not your fault, compadre," B. said. "Thank you. Don't have too many folks standing their ground like that."

Alvaro's arms crossed and his elbows locked. *Take a picture and it'd be Dad, not me, standing here.* He unfurled his arms. *I'm not him,* he thought. *Don't stand like him.*

"Look, we need people like you," B. said. "If the Alicia's to make a turnaround, we need people looking out for quality. Find a good bag, get to prepping, all right? Anything wrong, anyone gives you any trouble, you call me."

Alvaro nodded and walked back to the freezer and then turned. Better not to say anything. "I did," he said. "I did call you. We got roaches on the third floor. I called your cell. Left a message."

"That was you?" B. said. "Couldn't understand a thing. Sorry. Not used to your accent."

He stayed quiet. What could you say? Sorry?

B. took up the slack. "We'll get that fixed, I promise. Soon. Soon as we can." B. made it to the door before turning and addressing Alvaro one more time. "Where you living? You living close?"

"Close," he said.

"Why don't you live here? Rent free. You can help out with quality-control reports." B. typed in the air. "Easy peasy." He fiddled with his tie. "Talk to my assistant. Soon as you can—tomorrow?" He didn't wait for Alvaro to say yes, to say no. To say, *I have a sister.* "I'll tell him you're coming by tomorrow."

The clangor of the shift was finally coming on—he could hear the breakfast crowd assembling just outside. Ellie returned, clicking together two empty mugs. The BUNN coffeemaker, reliable and steady as a mule, poured out the coffee. There was no time, no helping it. *I'll talk to the assistant*, he thought. As soon as he had a break tomorrow, he'd talk. He'd talk first thing. It'd be a great thing, not having to pay rent.

"I will," he said. "Thank you. Who's your assistant?"

"Surly jackass you just had a pissing contest with is who." B. walked off, smiling.

When Ellie swung open the kitchen door, Alvaro caught a glimpse of the breakfast crowd. Not a happy bunch.

Ellie pinned the first five tickets. "No one wants mushrooms," she said. "Thank God."

"If they do, we'll find a good bag," he said.

She swung back into the café and balanced a tray of coffee mugs. He thought of her carpal tunnel. Life is hard. Life is hard all over. Remember that. Remember and don't complain.

She returned. He was already behind, he was so slow. And the grill not nearly hot enough. One egg wasted already. "That took courage, hon," she said. "B.'s right. It's not every day you see someone stand up for himself like that."

"The assistant was wrong," he said.

"He's B.'s son," she said. "He can be wrong all he wants."

The next eight hours proved long and hard, and enough went wrong to spare him from having to deal with thinking much at all. *I didn't know*, he thought. Had he known, he may have acted differently. Maybe. He could not tell. Fortunately, the job blurred into a mess of dropped skillets and misunderstood orders, and it kept him too occupied to really think or dread the meeting. Unfortunately, the hours exhausted themselves before he had time to really prepare, to really think about what he was getting himself into, and then he found himself outside the hotel, knowing he'd have to talk to the hotel owner's son tomorrow, whom he had pissed off in a fit of self-righteousness. He was right, though. He was doing the right thing.

I'll have to tell Carmen too. Tonight.

Why did he dread telling her? Why did he want to keep it all to himself?

He found himself regretting everything, ashamed of his work clothes, of the stains and the smell of sweat and grease and food. Very much wanting out. He thought of Ellie again, and reminded himself that life was hard, and that things could be worse. He thought of the homeless man who missed his dog. *I'm here. I did good.* He imagined Alba next to him, shaking her head. Disappointed. Disapproving. *It's a promotion,* he thought, *or it's free rent.* A way out, at least, for him and Carmen. He thought, *What's the worst that could happen?*

CHAPTER 5

ALVARO HAD PICKED UP THE Asian noodles trick from Ellie. You reserved some of the hot water and stirred peanut butter and vinegar and hot sauce in the pot, and you had a pretty solid go-to dish for weekdays, when neither he nor his sister had time to shop and cook.

He cooked at work and he cooked after work.

In Colombia, a maid always cooked, so the surprise was how long it took, how it could consume so much of his time, how far less mysterious it was. How boring too. And how grateful he was for that boredom. Cooking ate up so much of his time that he found himself crying less, too busy to be sad, all the more so because cooking took so long at home.

They had bought the two-range hot plate a month before. He had not wanted to. He felt they could do just as well with the cheaper version, but his sister insisted and he relented, though the extra expense set them back.

You were supposed to put in cilantro and shredded cabbage and carrots, but they didn't have those. Last time they walked to the 99-cent store, the vegetables all looked as suspicious as the bag of mushrooms at the Alicia.

He could have stolen the supplies from the kitchen. They wouldn't be missed. He thought of his mother and Alba—how the both of them would not approve.

Carmen did not need to know that he had been nearly fired, but he couldn't help himself. He told her.

She laughed. She said she had been very nearly put in detention.

"What did you do?" he asked.

She showed him. She'd been drawing. She drew panel after panel of the same story, the same big-eyed girl battling the same immense monster. The monster was all tentacles, the girl all courage. They ate and fought over the remote. The cook won. He switched from a documentary on the mass migration of wildebeests to a black-and-white movie. She had homework to finish, but she said it could wait. On the screen, a wealthy family found a man they mistook for a bum. He had been living in a landfill, and the family took him in, made him a butler. They didn't know he was like them—educated, wealthy. Wealthier, in fact. He was all for being their butler, for helping them out, though he could leave anytime he wanted, could pretty much raise money at the drop of a hat, the whole living-in-a-dump thing being more of a choice than a necessity.

During his worst days at the Alicia, he tried to think of it the same way. He was only working the job as a lark. They didn't really belong here. They had come to the States just to try it out, just to see what would happen. They had not come because they lost their immediate family, or because they no longer felt safe, or because they had no other option, had no one on whom they could rely.

A child wailed next door.

He said, "They're offering us a room at the Alicia."

"You said we were leaving," Carmen said. "You didn't tell them we were leaving?"

"I did," he said. It felt close enough to the truth to be true. "They offered us a room. So we would stay. Just for a while longer. We'd save money. I might even get a raise. We could get back sooner. It'd be easier if we saved some money." It was possible, he supposed. It was absolutely possible he was telling the truth. "We could fly back if we had more money. If we had *any*."

Carmen's noodles clumped at the bottom of the bowl, and she cut them with a fork.

He asked, "What do you think?"

She was still chewing when she answered. She pointed at their barred windows, at the wheezing AC unit, and said, "And leave this palace?"

"Funny."

On the screen, the man had returned to the dump, though he still wore his tuxedo. Alvaro had not changed out of his chef's pants. He owned a pair of jeans but wore them as little as possible. They hated the laundry room in the extended stay, and the other laundromat required a four-block walk in the worst of the heat, through two streets that had looked dodgy when they first arrived but seemed to be getting better. That was Fremont's perpetual promise: things were getting better, things were turning around.

"You said 'us,'" Carmen said. She pulled out her sketchbook, the book of algorithms propped on her lap for support.

"We can put Discovery back on if you want," he said.

She sketched his face: the long nose, the big eyes, the lashes his mom said belonged to some large creature. A wildebeest. A deer.

"I don't mind," he said. "We can watch some animals."

She said, "So they know I'd be coming along? They know about me?"

She drew him and all he could see was how much like his father he was. How many features they shared.

"Do they need to?" he said.

Carmen drew wings on him. She drew a pair of thick goggles over his forehead. She turned him into a steampunk version of himself, because she was a nerd.

She shared that much with their dad. She hated math but it came easily to her. They didn't own a computer so she wrote down her programming assignments in longhand and transcribed them at school. *She'll be fine*, he thought. They didn't need to worry about colleges yet, or about what they would do to pay for them. The plan was that they'd start saving, but that idea had been shelved along with California, and so they were making do, barely. But the money problem loomed and worried him: Carmen wouldn't be eligible for most scholarships, and he wasn't sure where she'd qualify for in-state tuition. He assumed, he didn't know. And he didn't know how he could tell her they were going to go back and be so certain that they wouldn't. That their life was here. In the States. Where no voices reached him through the telephone. Where no one, not even Carmen, knew of what he had done. He didn't even know if they could risk using her forged papers for school. He supposed they'd have to. He had paid so Carmen could keep her real name, but he'd have to keep calling himself Alvaro. And the money they spent on rent could be saved.

Carmen had finally opened her book of algorithms. They fought over homework occasionally, less so these days.

Less so after she reminded him that he'd dropped out of college twice, that Mom and Dad had had to pick him up midsemester from the Javeriana, that he had squandered God knows how much money on his wasted schooling, so who did he think he was to be telling her to do her homework. Didn't he know she was pulling all As?

She said, "You got to tell them. It's not like I can sneak in and out." She drew an octopus, a door on one of its tentacles. "They'd find me."

He said, "You had a bad dream last night."

"I know," she said. She opened her homework and worked at a string of commands that he had no way of understanding. She nested a parenthesis within another one and each felt like it buried itself deeper into a world he had no access to. A locked door. She explained code to him once, how all programs operated on a series of conditional clauses, how it all boiled down to a few basic operating procedures. *If, then. If this, then that.* The rest he could not follow, but there was a real joy in learning it, in knowing that most algorithm errors hinged on faulty closures—on parentheses missing their partners—and an even greater joy in realizing that his younger sister knew so much more than he did. He only wished he could help more. Dad would have been able to.

"I've been having them too," he said. Better not to mention Alba. Better not to say, *But at least we didn't dream of what happened on the road. At least you didn't dream of what I saw there. At least you didn't see what I saw.*

You didn't do what I had to do.

Carmen could have been in the car. It was a miracle she had stayed behind. It was a miracle he had survived.

If, he thought.

If she'd been there, then what?

"I know," she said. "I know you've been having them too. You talk. In your sleep, you're always talking, always mumbling."

He grew cold, said nothing.

She said, "I never know what you're saying." She dotted a string of commands he had no way of reading and waited for her to say something else. He was hoping she'd share her dreams, that they could talk about them.

But he could not start. He could not say, *I dreamed that Alba showed up at the kitchen,* because it would have meant talking about the one thing neither could bring up.

She said, "I dreamed I was in the hotel already."

"You've never been," he said. "You don't know what it's like inside."

"It's a dream, dummy." She doodled on the margin of her program: door after door after door. "You dream whatever you like. The hotel was bright pink, all of it. Fuzzy."

It wasn't. The inside was too bright, but it was yellow, not pink. But she was right: you dreamed what you wanted to dream.

"And I dreamed you were lost in there," she said. "I couldn't find you, couldn't see you. You kept calling me. You called me on your cell phone and you called me on these old landlines. You kept saying you'd be right back."

She was back to her homework. He turned off the TV. If he made it to bed right now, he'd have about five hours of sleep. It was enough, usually.

"That's when I woke up," she said. "I think that's why I was trying to wake you up." She closed her notebook, capped her pen. Done. "Just making sure you were still there."

He felt too young, wrong for the job. The panic traveled from his lungs to his heart. He had no business taking care of his sister. He had no business telling her that everything was going to work out, though he said it. He said it and he did not believe it and he could tell Carmen didn't believe it either.

CHAPTER 6

ALVARO TOSSED THE BURNT MEAT and hoped nobody saw him. The panic did not arrive, though he waited for it, the familiar squeeze in his chest. He had just imagined Carmen hiding in the kitchen, a blur of white against the green tiles, Carmen lurking because if she missed the bus, that is what he would have asked her to do, to hang out where he could see her, but nothing went wrong this morning. She made the bus. He had not messed up, had not dawdled, and the panic of the night did not blossom into paralysis. He had taken the longest showers when they lived in Colombia and now he was in and out, because they had no time in the morning, could not afford the time, and when he cried, he cried for a reason. Maybe it'd be better at the Alicia.

By all accounts, he should have been fired.

Everyone in the kitchen knew it because everyone else had worked in a kitchen before and didn't have to ask Ellie for help, though Ellie didn't have time, and though her experience prepping and on the line had occurred years ago in Reno.

He ruined another patty. It was hopeless, he couldn't get the meat right.

"It gets easier," someone in the kitchen said.

Someone else echoed it. The kitchen filled itself with voices, all of them rich and cheerful and Mexican, and in the echoes and chaos he heard his nickname, Galán, which they'd taken from a Vicente Fernández song about a good-looking charro who couldn't ride a horse.

He said, "Sorry." He was holding up two orders, everything on the plate but the meat. "It's almost ready," he said.

The kitchen laughed. Other patties waited, one close to done, others less so. You waited until the meat sweated. He sweated himself, the heat soaking through, the fear of messing up keeping him alert. You could use the back of your sleeve to wipe off sweat, but that was not ideal. You used a towel, a clean one, draped over your shoulder, but he had forgotten to do so. Four patties looked ready. He moved those to the side of the grill, where they would stay warm but not burn. Unless he did it wrong.

The kitchen said, "You'll get it, Galán. Just remember us when you're up there. Tell him we want a raise. Tell the boss we need to find the thief. Tell the boss everything is falling apart."

But they said it laughing. Most of them lived near Nellis and drove in. A few of the dishwashers lived like he did, nearby in a motel where you paid by the week or the month.

What thief? What were they talking about?

He set the meat where it was supposed to go. He fixed the plates. Ellie swung in and picked them up and swung out.

The doors closed.

Whatever Ellie balanced on her tray—the food he'd just made, the mugs of coffee—must have fallen immediately after, because the sounds carried clearly: a thump, broken plates, a body on the floor, screams. The rest of the kitchen craned toward the café, reluctant to leave their stations.

He ran to help, his face still hot and wet, surprised by his anger. He was angry at Carmen because he thought she was in the hotel, and he was angry at Ellie for being fat. For falling. He had an appointment, he was supposed to see the boss. A free room. Free rent. The people in his life weren't helping. Thinking, too, that he almost had the hang of the grill, that he would have gotten it down if he could have worked a couple more orders. People got in the way of work. The thought came twinned with an image of Ellie and her elegant waitressing—so cheerful, so sweet, so efficient. She had been at it for years. *So could I*, he thought. He could do it for as long as he needed to. Indefinitely. Maybe forever. You worked until you grew old and could no longer do it.

The café crowd parted around the mess of Ellie's tray. A busboy was already working at it with a cloth, the broken plates already gathered. It was a marvel—the gliding efficiency, the orchestrated competency. No one saw it. He had barely missed it himself. No one paid attention, and Ellie herself had already picked herself up.

He said, "Ellie? You OK?"

She ignored him and ran the length of café, her apron flying.

You could hardly see her, she darted between tables so quickly. He ran after her. His station lay abandoned. Had he left meat on the grill? It'd be on fire now. It would smoke and spoil.

Ellie said, "Easy, easy," and ran after a shadow on the wall.

A woman in a neon tank top screamed. A waitress dropped a tray of drinks.

Ellie darted past the tables and followed the noise, and Alvaro followed.

"It touched me!" someone screamed, then screamed it again. "It touched me!" Louder now. Impossible to tell if it was a man or a woman.

He ran after Ellie, and it was only when he got closer that the shadow grew into a chocolate Labrador. Big. About the height of a four-year-old. Goofy smile. The dog held herself still and then when they ran after her, she ran too. Barked. Panted.

The dog lumbered and wagged her tail and knocked over a glass. Three diners pulled out their cell phones. He thought, *I'm someone's story now.* A woman in Colorado will pull out her tablet and show her friends a photo: *These two café workers chased a dog through the casino. Craziest thing.* He tried circling around the dog, Ellie on one side and him on the other, but she squeezed past them, into the pit, and Ellie ran after her.

The pit was just as thinly peopled as the café, so the dog lumbered between rows of slot machines, a happy beast in a narrow yellow labyrinth. She barked. She was happy, he could tell. She was enjoying the chase.

His family had had dogs while he and his sisters were growing up. Poodles, mostly. Their neighborhood in Barranquilla was the first to bring them in, these fancy dogs imported from Miami. The dogs were later bred in the country, and many of them were set free later still. Or they ran away. Their owners had not spayed or neutered. You knew, because feral dogs roamed the better Barranquilla neighborhoods for years afterward. They lingered by the edge of the Cervantes school. They moved in large packs, barking at anyone who drew too close. How they survived he had no idea. The dogs had never been meant for the Colombian coast, and they quickly joined up with the rangier street dogs that lived in the shanties and the fishermen huts and the refineries.

Carmen and Alba had tried bringing one of them home from school. He remembered now, chasing the Lab, because neither sister struggled with getting the dog to come with them. They didn't have to chase the dog, whose white coat had been stained with the mud and the dirt of the roads. They just walked and the dog followed. Hungry, maybe. Waiting for a treat.

"Wait," he said to Ellie.

She stopped, and the dog stopped as well, the dog's tags jangling against its collar. She must belong to a guest of the Alicia. Dogs weren't allowed, but that wouldn't stop anyone. People smoked in the nonsmoking rooms. They brought in their own liquor. The Alicia was just glad to have their business.

He crouched and cupped his hand.

The dog drew in, sniffed, and sat and stared.

Ellie petted the dog's glossy fur and inspected the tag.

"The girl's name is Clarabelle," Ellie said. "And she's far from home."

"Out of Vegas?" he asked.

"Not quite, hon," she said. "Says Summerlin. The suburbs."

Clarabelle had to be taken care of, her owner found, though Ellie had just called the number on the tags and had gotten nothing. No voice on the other line. No voice mail. He remembered Carmen telling him about her dream, about him calling and promising he'd be right back but never returning, lost on some floor of the Alicia. He remembered the homeless man from the day before. The man who had lost his dog. It was hard to imagine Clarabelle on the street. Hard to imagine that she had it rough, she was so healthy, so sweet. Alvaro thought, *It's not him, he's not the owner, it can't be, but if it is, we'll find him.*

Ellie shook her head, rubbed the place on her elbows and back of her wrists where she said the pain snuck in. And Clarabelle stared at them both.

Carmen and Alba had tried talking him into sneaking the poodle into the house, but their mom didn't want the street poodle in the house. He told on them. He forgot what their punishment was, but it couldn't have been too much, he hoped. He was doing what his sisters had done. Him and Ellie. They walked the dog back to the kitchen, where they would keep her until they found her owner, or until their shift was over. They would keep the dog here without B. or anyone higher up knowing, which did not bode well for Alvaro, now with him figuring out if he could bring Carmen into the hotel. If he couldn't, screw them. They didn't have to live here, didn't have to lift the weight of the rent money. Something would work out.

Clearly the dog meant something special to Ellie. He didn't even know why the two of them had agreed to keep it quiet. They had not even said anything. Did not need to. Ellie had worked these jobs longer than he had, and he trusted her, and so they walked Clarabelle into the kitchen, where everyone stopped and clapped and petted her and settled her in a corner. *No one had to know* is what it came down to. Everyone he worked with could know, but the people upstairs could not.

Or he could tell, like he did on his sisters. He could use the dog as leverage—one more thing he had to offer B. and his assistant, one more bit of currency he could trade in for the good of his sister. The secret of the dog.

He'd tell, he'd never tell.

He didn't know.

He worked until he got the call to head upstairs, and when he did, Clarabelle sat still in her corner, working at a patty he'd overcooked. There were less of those as the hours progressed. His feet ached. He felt old, sore from standing and moving all day, and he thought, *But I'm young, I'm young and I'm not fat like Ellie and I have no reason to feel this tired, this sick of my body.* He rubbed his calves, wiped his hands on his apron before he remembered ServSafe. You washed your hands at the handwashing sink. You did not cross-contaminate.

He was certain now that the dog belonged to the person he'd seen on the street talking to the cops. The poor homeless man in his dirty green shirt and dirty red sweatpants. He must be so worried for his dog. *Please help me find her,* he had said. Alvaro wanted to find him, to tell him Clarabelle was all right.

"We'll find him," he said to the dog. "We'll get you home."

Ellie called the number twice between orders and her side work.

Nothing.

It was time for him to go upstairs and face B.'s assistant, and he thought again about the street poodle and its dirty white fur. How Alba and Carmen cried when he said he'd tell their mom.

I'll never forgive you, Alba had said. *I'll never forgive you if you tell.*

Alba fed the dog for weeks, on the sly. And then he did too. The siblings took turns. They tried keeping the dog in the yard, but the poodle couldn't be tamed: it ran away and rejoined the pack.

He had no time to think about what he would say, how he would say it. That was the worst part, the most awful thing about his rough English. Everything came out wrong. Too blunt. Shorn of half of what he wanted to say. He wanted to talk like the people he saw in the movies he loved, and instead he sounded like a dope. Like a joke. He pressed the button on the elevator and left a greasy print on the light. He had not washed his hands before he left. You were supposed to. Before and after and during. He thought of his living sister, the one he had been charged with keeping safe, and hoped it would work out. *I should apologize*, he thought, wiping his hands on the apron again, which he should have taken off, which he should have left behind.

CHAPTER 7

THE ELEVATOR OPENED ON THE wrong floor: three. Alvaro waited for a fellow worker to step in, but no one did. Someone must have called it and given up, a wandering guest maybe, but he recognized this floor, he had walked it before. B. had shuttered it, so it was almost always unvisited. Not today.

Two figures huddled in the corridor.

Their shadows moved, and their bodies followed. They didn't see him step out of the elevator. They didn't see him walk toward them. Their gaze fixed on the carpet, their hands buried in the flowers-and-thorns pattern of the carpet, searching. He had no time, B.'s son waited for him upstairs, and the whole business with the dog already delayed him, but what if they were intruders? He imagined the son upstairs, angrily checking the time on his phone.

Alvaro was late, he was so late, and now the son was angry.

"It was here." In Spanish. A woman's voice.

He recognized them both then. Marisol had just been moved from cleaning to serving, thanks to Ellie, who had taken her under her wing. By her side huddled her boyfriend, Umberto, in chef's pants much cleaner than Alvaro's.

They must have pressed the button before they realized they'd lost something.

"Can I help?" Alvaro said, not wanting to, angry at them but angrier at himself for even asking. He had to go. He had to get everything settled so he and Carmen could move in. Everything about the hotel was *sticky*, he realized. You tried doing one thing and ended up stuck doing another.

"It's nothing," Marisol said. "It's such a little thing. I'm so stupid."

"She lost a photo of her grandmother." Umberto pointed at the intersecting corridor. "We were over there, but we looked already. So now we're looking here."

Alvaro said, "I can help." He hoped they could see his impatience. He had no time to help, but he remembered his little sister Alba, how she *always* helped, how she fretted over losing anything. Family mementoes were extra special—how she howled when she lost a photo, a keepsake. And now Alba was lost too. He'd never find her, whatever was left of her. "I'd be happy to do it," he said, and did not bother to pretend to smile.

"Yes," Marisol said, "yes please. Thank you."

"I'll look again over there," he said, eyes fixed on the flat black planes of the intersecting corridor. No light there, and precious little here. Would they have noticed him had he kept quiet? If he had stepped out and said nothing and hovered by their side, unseen, unheard. It was what he wanted, why they had left Colombia.

To vanish. To be left alone.

B. hadn't even bothered to connect this corridor to the house grid, the only light the muted red of the EXIT signs. Alvaro shivered. Afraid now, not sure why or of whom. Not of Marisol and Umberto, and not of whatever could happen upstairs. He was supposed to talk to the hotel owner's son, but that was forever ago, he was so late. He had expected to be fired. He wanted to be fired. He could not bring himself to quit, he saw no other way to bring in money. Now he worried about missing a meeting he never wanted in the first place.

It's sticky. This place is so sticky.

He imagined Carmen looking for him like Marisol and Umberto looked for what they'd lost. Huddled, talking low. Shadows, mostly.

He had been here before, down this same corridor, thinking of his dead sister, his father, his mother. This was one of the floors he could spend time on and no one bothered him, no one thought of visiting.

Which is why he'd wanted to stop himself from saying hello, why he'd wanted to make himself invisible to Marisol and Umberto. Because you'd only meet here if you didn't want to be bothered, didn't want to run into people. He wanted to be elsewhere, but the corridor had pulled him in, even before he recognized his coworkers. The elevator had opened. The Alicia invited him into herself.

He could still hear Umberto and Marisol, their voices clear though they crouched on the floor, Marisol insisting that she brought the photo with her but that she kept it in her purse. That she never took it out of her purse. Umberto said that they'd find it. Alvaro imagined the couple combing the carpet forever, people off their shifts but trapped in the hotel.

They could have been anywhere. They should be anywhere but here.

Umberto must have roommates. Marisol too. Umberto lived in North Vegas, Marisol near the base, but they met up in the Alicia. The hotel accommodated them, which was fine. Good for them. There were so many empty rooms. He supposed he should feel happy for them, or at least envious.

The fear came at him in quick, cold stabs, light as a knife.

Marisol's disappointment echoed down the corridor. She said, "Forget it. I have other photos. I'm so stupid. I don't know why I brought it."

That was his cue: if she was giving up, that meant he could give it up too. She hadn't lost anything important, after all. Photographs didn't matter.

She sounded on the verge of tears, and the frustration that he felt came twinned with a curdled sliver of anger he held on to. It was stupid, he thought. It was stupid of Marisol to be so upset about a photo, and it was stupid of him to be helping. Umberto insisted that they keep looking, that hope wasn't lost. That he was sure they'd find it. In Spanish, he sounded nothing like the cartoon the kitchen made him out to be. He remembered

Ellie, otherwise kind, saying, "Is Umberto! Is . . . *fuego!*" Though in all fairness, Umberto had just set one of her carpal tunnel braces on fire.

Alvaro leaned against a suite door, still close enough to hear their conversation, knowing he should be heading upstairs. He could just walk down the corridor, pretend he looked already, wish them luck. Or he could wait for them to give up. They were never going to find it. The hotel must have swallowed the photograph like all large buildings swallow things: without thought, without malice.

The door yielded, the click so loud he imagined Umberto and Marisol hushed and annoyed by his presence. Alvaro the interloper. He stepped inside and half-closed the door, and he could hear them still, their search uninterrupted. He wanted to hide in the room, but he shrugged off the thought. They knew he was here, and they knew he was helping.

He meant to close the door completely, but the index card taped above the door stopped him. The card read, "This door is LOCKED."

It wasn't.

It couldn't even keep him out when he leaned in. He did not close it, all the same, because the note sounded so strident, so sure of itself. The room was gutted, the lazy Susan shorn of its TV, the two twin beds stripped of their floral comforters. On the wall, in place of a painting, the same writer had taped another card: "A SOOTHING landscape." Where the lamp used to be: "Environmentally friendly LED lamp." On the wardrobe: "Esther's SPECIAL things." The index cards pointed to all that was missing, and there was so much, much of it sad. Meager. On the nightstand, next to a card that read "Esther's favorite BOOKS," was a card on which "iPad" was scratched out in favor of "Hymnal." It sat next to a card that read, "FAMILY BIBLE."

A stain spread over the carpet, a faint pink in the poor light. Next to the bed, he found a pair of children's boots, small and black, out of place and out of time. That is where he found Marisol's lost photograph. Next to the boot.

That is where he found a card that read, "Esther, WAITING."

He imagined a child staring at him from beneath the bed, her eyes too bright in the darkness. He imagined the child crawling toward him. Her dress rustled against the carpet. In the bad light, it'd be impossible to tell if she smiled, but he was sure she'd smile, like she was happy to see him, her face pale, her hair light—a healthy child, abandoned in an abandoned room.

He shook it off.

He imagined them all in on it. Umberto and Marisol pretended they lost the photo, left the index cards behind, Carmen letting them know that her brother was afraid, telling them everything she knew and suspected. This dark room was her revenge for what he did. And everyone in on this *joke*, all of it orchestrated so he'd be afraid.

The thought made no sense but it stuck around anyway.

Fright did that, he realized. It made you think the unthinkable, the impossible.

The AC kicked on and another wet card fluttered to a corner. He did not know if it was "SPECIAL things" or "Hymnal" or "Teddy Bear," not even when he stood close, Marisol's photo still in his hand. You stopped thinking and assigned blame.

But I was afraid before, he thought. *I was afraid because I thought the hotel wanted to keep me here.*

Esther's SPECIAL things.

That was her name.

Esther.

Umberto and Marisol talked, oblivious.

He reached for the card but couldn't bring himself to pick it up. Another card waited just out of reach, half-buried in the same soft growth that bloomed in the carpet. The cards were breadcrumbs. Bait. Or nothing at all, nothing out of the ordinary. Just a child livening up her room with cards. Kids did weird things, after all.

He could almost make out a set of letters, but they snaked into themselves. Maybe the card said "Father." Maybe it said "Mother." The word blurred even as he thought of his own dead parents.

"Where is her mother?" he asked no one. "Her father?"

"Below." A man's voice. It came from the corridor, from the other side of the half-opened door. "Her mother's in the pit." The voice belonged to an old man who wore the plum blazer of the Alicia.

"Esther," Alvaro said.

"Esther's mother is in the pit," the old man said. He pulled out a cigarette. "And you're supposed to be upstairs. They're waiting for you."

"You're not supposed to smoke."

"You're not supposed to be here." The old man jabbed the unlit cigarette at the ceiling. "They're waiting. We're all waiting. Don't you think we know already? Don't you think we know who you are?"

"Who are you? Who's Esther?"

"Esther's mother is the one you should be worried about." He pulled out a lighter, a greasy Zippo, and in the poor light the old man's eyes shone a dead white. "There's a debt." Smoke, a smile, two missing front teeth. "You owe. You made a promise. Don't you think we know? Don't you know that's why you're here?"

"We don't," he said, and wondered why the old man said "we." "I don't owe anyone."

"Go upstairs."

Maybe Esther was here. Hiding. Ignoring him. He remembered his own sister ignoring him when she was deep into her homework, and when he himself was bored, and wanted company, wanted someone to listen to him.

"Esther," he said again.

The old man said, "You should go. They're waiting for you upstairs. Avoid the child and avoid the mother."

Alvaro nodded, the photograph secure in the pocket of his pants, the jagged tooth safe in another. He had been struck by how roomy the pockets were, how much space they had, when he was first asked to buy his uniform. They were bigger and baggier than any pants he'd worn. Pants you would not wear in real life, checkered in black and white. He thought,

It's part of being here. Part of the penance. How the pants will keep their stains until you wash them. How your skin will smell of the kitchen even after you shower. That's work. That's what work means—that and people telling you what to do.

This man, this very old man, had been doing this work for years. He had been at the Alicia forever. Alvaro wanted to ask the man how he stayed—if he had decided or if it just happened, but he was not sure the answer would help.

"Charleen's going to come up any time now," the old man said. "You don't want to be here when she does."

"Charleen?"

"The mother."

⸻

Marisol took the photograph and hugged him before he had a chance to tell her that he had not taken a shower, that he smelled like the kitchen. How Umberto could look so clean was a mystery. They had worked the same shift. Umberto's hair was neatly parted, and his pants had no stains, though the cuffs were singed. Even his shirt was unwrinkled. Alvaro wanted to shrink into himself. To be far away. To go back into his little room and turn on a movie and be elsewhere. He hugged Marisol back, wanting to cry.

They were all here away from their families.

In the photograph, the grandmother stood by a much younger Marisol, both women using their hands to shade their faces from the Guanajuato sun. Which he had never seen. Before coming here, he had hardly left Colombia.

I think I've come from so far away, he thought, and here's this girl, here's this man, and they've traveled too. They may have seen worse. They may have lost more, for all he knew. He had not asked and did not want to ask right now. Would they even tell him? He didn't think they would. They weren't the kind of people who sat around and cataloged their misfortunes. They had work and families and more work. Marisol slipped the photograph in her purse and snapped it shut.

Alvaro said, "A little girl had it."

He led them to Esther's room (*Avoid the child and avoid the mother*), so they could talk to the old man, possibly confront the little girl. But the room stood empty and unlocked. He expected the index cards to be gone as well, for the room to stand as bare as a stage, but they waited where he left them, Umberto commenting on their weirdness, Marisol mute.

On the bed, at the very center, he expected to find a final card. He *wanted* to find a card, and he wanted the card to read, "Esther, napping," but what he found instead was a chunk of short, spiky hair.

■IIIII

Umberto pushed the down button. Alvaro pushed up.

Up dinged first, so Alvaro left his friends in the corridor. He imagined the old man and the little girl leaving their hiding place—they'd been in there hiding the whole time, he imagined, watching them, all three of them, Esther and Esther's mother and the old man in the plum blazer, and now the three headed elsewhere, the girl still looking at an index card whose words he could have sworn said a name, maybe even a familiar name, or maybe "Father," which at any rate he'd never get to read but would come into focus anytime now, just as soon as he stopped thinking about it, he was sure.

CHAPTER 8

THE PENTHOUSE OFFICES BROODED DARK, hollow, and green. Green carpet, green walls, dim light. The offices stretched across the entire sixth floor, joined together by a single, uninterrupted hall decorated with flamingo murals over crumbling marble. The marble had not been cleaned in years. The walls looked like they were rotting. The flamingos fared no better.

Nobody manned the behemoth mahogany desk. Alvaro despaired. He had lolled about, he had missed his chance. No more free rent. They'd given up on him.

A beige telephone ran and would not stop ringing, nobody answered or walked over or typed, the cavernous room as empty as the interior of a shipping container. A ship. Nobody at the helm.

He very much wanted to pick up the phone, to make it stop ringing. He was tired, the day had been long and hard, so he couldn't help thinking of the phone as a disconsolate baby. Late in the night at their extended stay, the walls gave up and let in the wailing of children. The wailing sounded as though it came from all the rooms, and it would not stop, so they usually put on old movies and fell asleep to that. Even if he knew who these children were, which he did not, he knew it was a bad idea to comfort them. They were somebody else's business. He did his best not to think about them or engage with them on his way to and from work. He had his own worries, and he had Carmen's worries, and he had Carmen to worry about.

Rooms like these, rooms at the top, came with panoramic windows, but the Alicia covered them with plywood. The plywood had been half-heartedly spray-painted green to match the marble. Through the gaps, he could see some neon and some evening sky.

He walked to the desk, the desk ornate and also rotting, and picked up the wailing phone. "Hotel Alicia," he said. "Can I help?"

"You're not my son."

Thank God I'm not, he thought. He recognized the voice. "I just got here, B. Your son must have stepped out for a moment. I was running late."

"Tell him to call back," B. said. "Tell him we got to talk about the two passages. Tell him Cara's worried."

A notepad waited by the phone. "Will do," he said. He found a ball-point with the hotel's name misprinted on the barrel ("Hotel Acilia") and was about to write down the message when he realized that B. must have called before, and that someone else must have written down the same words. "Two passages. Call B." Alvaro underlined "Call" and wished B. a good day.

"Make sure my son gives you a good room," B. said. "Nothing on the third floor."

Alvaro thanked him and hung up. The only place to sit other than the office lobby chair was a broad whale of a couch—broken, filthy, green-blue corduroy—so he walked to the boarded windows and shifted back and forth against the plywood panels.

Down below stretched Fremont like an enormous beast, the spare roofs punctuated by vents and antennae, all of it a single structure, the body of the creature snaking up and down, east and west. The sun was nearly setting, the light a darkening blue, the neon bright and clean. Beyond: the lone exclamation mark of the Stratosphere and the remote mute land of the Las Vegas Strip. He and Carmen had not walked farther than Charleston, with its abandoned theater and its 99-cent store.

The two of them had no bank account, no savings. *We are never getting out*, he thought. He spent half his paycheck on rent. It would take him at least six months to put the Alicia and all of Fremont and the rest of Vegas behind him. He thought, *Just head back east. You started in Florida. Consider returning. Where you are, what this place is, there is something here that is hungry and wrong. This is not home.*

This is no place for you or Carmen.

"We're so glad you're going to stay here," a woman said. Alvaro did not see her come in. He had not even seen where she came in from, but he knew it couldn't be the elevator. He would have heard its clunk, its protest.

She stood a full head shorter than he did, a riot of red hair and freckles and a slim black dress. A plum blazer, rumpled. "Sorry," she said. "We had to get your papers from downstairs. Hope you weren't waiting long." She put a manila folder on the desk. Copies of his forged documents. She extended her hand. "Winifred," she said. "I do people around here."

He shook her hand and introduced himself, all the while thinking, *Where is B.'s son?* He had fretted over seeing him again and now fretted over his absence.

She fanned his sham life in front of him: copies of his forged passport, his forged work authorization, his forged driver's license, and his forged Social Security card. "Everything looks in order," she said.

It wasn't. They had to know. The creeps at Lost and Found—surely they knew. They knew everything. The brothers—fat, doughy identical twins in matching overalls—had names, but the Alicia took to calling them by their roles. They'd call in ICE. They would get him deported. Carmen would be left on her own. He felt light—afraid and resigned and ready to confess. They knew, they had to know, how could they *not* know?

Winifred slid two smudged papers his way. "We need you to sign these forms," she said. "Sign and we'll be all set to go."

He read them, slowly. He read them again.

"I'm not clear on what this says," Alvaro said. "What does B. want me to do?"

Winifred laughed. "Who the hell knows?" she said. "Keep an eye on things? Quality control, he said. He trusts you. He wants you here."

"My sister lives with me," he said. "I take care of her."

"The room's got two beds."

"B. would not mind?"

Winifred shrugged, and the shrug told him all he needed to know about where he worked.

Alvaro signed.

"Free rent, right? Why the fuck ask why?" B.'s son said. He stood behind Alvaro, holding two key cards, still wearing the same suit and shirt from the day before. His French cuffs still showed the juice of the rotten mushrooms.

"Alvaro, this is Dan Melmot," Winifred said.

"We met," Alvaro said.

Dan extended his hand and Alvaro had no choice but to shake it. "Come," Dan said. "Let's see your new digs." Dan moved to the edge of the room and adjusted the plywood, shutting Las Vegas out of the Hotel Alicia, and he shot Winifred a look, a warm dart of the eyes, and Winifred responded in kind. Sweet. Surprisingly sweet, given Dan.

So.

The penthouse offices had more room than was apparent at first glance. And Dan liked Winifred. You learned these things without meaning to. They crept up on Alvaro before he realized how he had put them together, how easy it was to put them together.

The Alicia herself was not that easy. The building refused to settle into coherence. Every time he passed the courtyard, the three ornate wrought-iron cages turned almost human—three bodies wrapped in wire, hunched and sad. They once kept tropical birds there, the kitchen staff told him, way back in the Alicia's heyday, when the hotel was known as the Splendor. Now the cages stood open, unlocked, and every time he passed them, they looked like medieval torture devices. B. wanted the pool ready for summer, but all that meant was that the grounds crew had swept the leaves from the dry base, that they had removed the two orange cones from the edge closest to the casino entrance. Someone could fall. Someone would, inevitably. A dumb kid would jump headfirst and break his neck. They'd get sued. But it had not happened and B. had not worried. *That's the kind of thing I'm supposed to be looking out for*, Alvaro realized. *That's why I'm here*. He could feel it, in this room, in the corridors, the need to look out for the interests of the people wandering the hotel, and for the Alicia too, her profusion of cramped corridors. B. was right. The Alicia was so much smaller than most of the other buildings around her, and so much more interesting. She was special.

━ ┉

The three descended in the noisy elevator to the fifth floor, the oldest unrenovated wing of the hotel where once, Winifred told them, a flamingo escaped from the cage by the pool and loped the narrow halls.

CHAPTER 9

"THANK YOU," ALVARO SAID. "WE'LL bring our stuff in tonight."

They had already given him the key cards, but not before checking and rechecking them. The cards tended not to work at the Alicia. The locks liked to freeze. But these doors worked. These locks worked. All was in order.

Room 54 was brightly lit and airy, though the fifth-floor hall had stretched dark and narrow, the lighting limited to one high-efficiency bulb and the red glow of the EXIT signs. You wouldn't know it now, inside. He could have been in any room on any open floor. Two twin beds, freshly made, took up most of the space, arranged much like Esther's beds two floors below. The window overlooked the soon-to-be-working pool and the empty flamingo cages. Winifred moved near the beds and sniffed, Dan trailing. Alvaro appreciated the concern. Some of the shuttered rooms stank of cigarettes, and no amount of aerosol disinfectant could fix it. The space they'd given him was clean, free of dust, better in every way than his old room, his and Carmen's. A real bed waited for her at the Alicia.

"So you like it?" Winifred said. "Because we have a couple of others if you don't."

"This is perfect," Alvaro said. "Thank you."

"How about you tell my dad?" Dan said. "How about you tell him what a great fucking job Winifred is doing? Got that, compadre?"

Alvaro could have ignored him, but the day had been too long. "How about you stop with the barking, compadre?"

"I could so have your job," Dan said.

"You say that," Alvaro said. "Call your dad. Call him and tell him you want me fired." Dan did not move. Alvaro remembered the message on the penthouse notepad. He continued, "Call your dad and tell him what you want to tell him, I don't care, but let him talk too. He wants to chew your head off about the two passages."

Dan fiddled with the dirty cuffs of shirt, Winifred inspected a smear on the door. They'd leave him alone now. He wasn't sure what B. meant, but likely it was some of the service corridors connecting one part of the Alicia to another, the halls narrow, stuffed with secret arteries shooting every which way. The corridors ran everywhere and crossed each other at odd, unnecessary places. If Dan ignored the message, if Dan was avoiding whatever needed doing, it mattered only in that it would get him out of the room.

"We should let you get settled in," Winifred said. "Dan, Cara emailed asking again about the locks. We're on that, yes?"

Dan Melmot—son of B., ignorer of his father's messages, all-around asshole—moved to leave, did not answer, did not want to answer. He touched the long, flat door handle.

The walls shook.

The world went dark.

Winifred screamed.

"It's just us," Alvaro said. "Outage." Outside, through the window, the lights of Fremont blinked and sputtered and resumed their glow, but the Alicia kept herself dark: the room dead, the whole floor, down to the lights in the pool five floors below, the half-filled water black, the parking lot an empty cavity.

But then Fremont went dead too, all the neon and the screens out, and then all of Vegas, the waning afternoon light over the city the color of a bruise.

"What's that?" Dan said.

Alvaro could hear it, a great humming that drowned out all other noise, as though they stood near a river. He thought of the Magdalena, he thought of the Caquetá. He heard the same muddy rush of water.

▬▬∎∎∎∎

The three walked the narrow corridor close together, their faces a faint red, their features blurred and scattered in the long shadows. *Night will fall before long*, he thought. In Fremont proper, night never really came, not fully, not until you had an outage. Just a few blocks away, however, all you'd get is a shoddy row of hotels and few streetlights. He thought, *That's where my sister is. I should be heading to my old haunts before full dark.*

"We should let your dad know what's going on," Alvaro said.

"Like he doesn't know already," Dan said. "Like he doesn't always already know already."

Dan stopped short, and Alvaro ran into him. Alvaro was going to ask Dan what he saw, what was going on, when he realized that Dan had been stopped short by his own sentence.

Winifred took out her phone and dialed. "He's turned it off," she said, "or I'm not getting a signal." She dialed another number. They walked while the phone signal negotiated the hotel's odd walls. Someone answered. They walked while she listened, plugging her right ear with her index finger to block out the sound of rushing water. "Utilities is on it," she said. "So is the shift manager. It's totally an outage."

"So all we're doing is tracking a fucking water pipe," Dan said. "Because why?"

Alvaro wanted to say, *Because it's your job*, but he resisted.

Alvaro wanted to know. He had been running away for so long from what he had seen, had been keeping it inside for so long, had told no one, had not even told anyone they had left Colombia. No one knew. They'd been away for months. They must think something horrible happened, they must be worried—there were still people left who cared enough to worry, he supposed. Hoped. About Carmen if not him. When you run away from one thing, you run headlong into another. When you keep one secret, you want to know what secrets others keep. What secrets a building keeps.

They turned a corner and stepped into absolute darkness. The sound of rushing water surrounded them, it deafened, it came from everywhere, the air itself turned wet and cold. They neared the source. That much was clear. Alvaro could feel Winifred pull something out of her purse. Her phone again. The screen shone with a weak glow and he could make out the shuffling outlines of their bodies against the walls.

Dan pulled out his phone, tapping the screen until it grew bright. "Wait," he said, tapping the screen again. His phone now sported the animated image of a torch.

They moved farther into darkness. Winifred's phone blacked out every few minutes, so their light waned while she thumbed the screen out of sleep mode. The walls breathed with the light.

The walls were, in fact, moving. They shook violently, they grew still, they grew angry again.

Alvaro felt one with his hand, the surface wet, sweaty, and cold. And thrumming. He ran his hand down the shudder of the wall and crouched and felt the floor, and the floor yielded with a wet shudder, it yielded with a sigh, his hand pushing into the rot of the wood. The floor sank and sagged and shook and refused to stop shaking. Alvaro thought, *The floor's giving birth.* Behind him, Winifred stopped.

Dan, ahead, did not.

"Stop," Alvaro said. "Dan, stop. Dan. *Dan.*"

Dan did not, Dan kept going, but the sound of the hotel erased all other sounds. When Alvaro screamed Dan's name, even Alvaro could not hear it. The world cracked and crumbled.

He jumped to drag Dan to safety. Missed.

The floor's contractions yielded. A rush of water burst and flipped Dan's limp body to the ceiling, shot him up legs first like he weighed nothing at all, his legs making an awful cracking sound, then the water dragged him into the hole in the floor, sucking him down into blackness.

Alvaro reached into the blind hole, managed to get a hold of Dan's shirt collar, the floor sinking below them. He dragged Dan back, sticking close to the mess of gummy wood and ruined carpet. The water subsided, the awful noise abated, and his ears now hummed with the ghost of the sound. He could hear things he did not think he should be hearing: the noise of the casino, the insistent winning melodies of the slot machines on their perpetual loops.

Dan moaned. The pipes disgorged their contents. The hotel whistled: the emergency generator, warming up long after the emergency began.

The one solitary bulb in the hall returned to life. Too bright. Winifred said, "Oh God," because blood coated Dan, blood coated all of Dan, as though he had been dipped in a bucket. As though it was not his own. A tear on the shoulder of his suit revealed a gash. His pants were in shreds, his legs exposed, wet and red. Alvaro could make out what he was pretty sure was bone.

Dan's bloody legs still dangled in the hole, so Alvaro clung to the floor and dragged himself and Dan out. The hole spat out a cluster of broken tubes.

"I just called 911," Winifred said. "Called the lobby too. Someone's coming."

She grabbed his shoulders and pulled. "Come on come on come on," she said.

If this were a movie, he thought, *she'd find the strength*. But all she could do was budge them, and it was useless, a useless waste of energy. "Get out of the way," he said. "Move back."

She held on. She pulled at him when her small hands, and it was useless but also painful, he hurt all over, and the pipes burst again, all the walls cracked open, as did the floor and the ceiling, and a black, skittering rush descended upon them.

At first he thought it was just gray water. The mass hitting them moved like liquid. The tubes disgorged themselves in black heaves, the smell peanut, rich. Almost pleasant. He had never been close enough to a cockroach to smell one.

The roaches poured over them and he resisted the urge to scream but Winifred did not resist. Winifred indulged. At full volume. The roaches continued their transit, the press of their carapaces light and constant, their shells, their chittering, their spindly, feathery antennae, the awfulness of having all these light little appendages dotting your whole body. Coating your whole body. Your body. It is you I'm talking to—the you he is telling his story to, the you who counted his fingers. The roaches bore under clothes and ran blind circles on his legs. He smacked a hand against his thigh and a spot as big as a fist turned wet. Turned warm. Ran down to his ankle. He closed his eyes and felt their transit over his eyelids, his nostrils, his lips.

———

"They're gone," Winifred said.

Winifred stood by him, her red hair a fiery contrast to the dank and the dark of their surroundings. He didn't want to say it, and he didn't want to see it, but he had no choice. He pointed to the bugs dangling from her hair. "You still got two," he said.

She brushed them off and shuddered.

"Dan," he said.

"Oh God," she said. "Oh fuck. Dan, say something."

"Sure you want to live here?" Dan said, his eyes still closed.

The three slumped in the corridor and waited for help. Below them, through the hole, they could make out a dark, shuttered guest room, the noise of the casino carrying through unknown channels.

He could not reach his phone. Normally he'd be home by now. Carmen needed to know that he was OK, that nothing had gone wrong, that the blood on him was not his. He wanted to wash himself off. He wondered, briefly, if maybe he could sneak into an empty room and use a shower, so his sister wouldn't have to see him like this (*like Mom, like Mom in the forest*). But he could not even move, not without disturbing Dan, whose breathing was shallow. The blackout. He had seen how far it spread, how it erased most of Fremont, their little room at the pay-by-the-week included. She must have arrived there around the same time that it happened, so his little sister would have been in the room by herself when the lights went out, and she must have tried calling, and he must have missed the call. He had not taken out his cell when Winifred and Dan had. Carmen left jaunty messages, particularly when she was worried. He remembered the one she'd left when she hadn't heard back from anyone on the road to Ibagué. She'd said, *You must have forgotten me.* She'd said, *I guess you've all found a new sister.* She waited for him now, he imagined, alone in their small room, and all of those children waited in rooms just as small, just as crowded and stuffy. His sister, in the dark room thick with old cigarette smoke—his sister, doodling in her notebook by whatever light leaked through their window.

He thought, *Wait till she hears what just happened. Wait till she hears about the room with the index cards. Wait till she hears about Ellie and Clarabelle: we chased a dog, and she's here with us, here in this hotel. In hiding.*

Just wait.

The slot machines chirped their short song, then chirped it again. Someone yelled, and it was the kind of short, happy yell that anyone working in a casino grew accustomed to. A big win. Followed by a big loss. A crowd echoed the yell. Applauded. The world below, the world of gamblers and croupiers, continued with its business and in doing so insisted on its perpetual lie: Nothing of consequence had happened and nothing of consequence would happen, could happen.

Everything was fine.

CHAPTER 10

BECAUSE THE EXTENDED STAY AFFORDED them no privacy, Alvaro and Carmen had gotten into the habit of knocking before opening the front door. Power had not returned to their neighborhood.

It was just past two in the morning, the air hot, stifling. Odd silhouettes lurked on the street corners, barely visible through the bars that kept the world from the building. Alvaro could make out the lone glow of a cigarette, the intermittent red light of a motorized scooter, the glare of a wheelchair.

"You're a mess," Carmen said, but Alvaro didn't feel like a mess.

He felt deeply alive, buzzing with life, inexplicably elated and angry. *Why aren't you worried?* he thought.

She drew by the light of a candle. Her hands projected shadows onto the paper, so the ink and the pencil shook themselves to life when she dropped the notebook and hugged him.

He didn't feel any pain then either. Just relief. He thought he would hurt, but he was fine. And she was fine. She had not slept and she had school tomorrow, but that was fine too.

She made a face—she grimaced, like he had told a bad joke—and touched a spot just above his left eyebrow, and pain burst through him, a bright jolt.

"Sorry!" she said.

He hadn't realized he had been hurt until she touched that bruise.

He hadn't felt a thing on the walk home, the key cards to a new room on the fourth floor still in his hand, the chaos of the Alicia safe behind him. B. had called to thank him, to let him know that he was on his way to the hospital to see his son. That he wanted Alvaro to go too. To get checked up. That's what workers' comp was for, B. had said.

Carmen asked, "What happened?"

He told her about the pipes, the great burst of water, his brush with death, the person who almost died. The boss's son. Whom he had saved.

"That was stupid," she said. "You hear a big noise and you *walk* there? 'Yes, let's just see what's down that way *where we can't see a thing*, why don't we.'" She wiped her forehead, but it grew sweaty again.

Maybe she didn't understand. He had almost *died*. He had almost died and now he was back. "It wasn't like that," he said. "We had to do our jobs."

The room bristled with candle shadows, and he grew uneasy and hot, the AC still dead.

She was back to her drawing, but her hands threw shadows over the lines. She must have finished her homework hours ago.

"We can move in tomorrow," he said. "After school. After my shift."

"We're not moving," she said. She put her notebook in her book bag, dropped the book bag by her half-deflated bed.

They had to inflate the bed every night, and he sometimes wished he had listened to her and bought the more expensive one, the bed that came with an electric pump that just plugged in, but they had no money.

"We're not moving," she said again. "Not to a place that blows up just because. Not to a place we don't know. Not again."

"It's safe." He held up the key cards. "It's a different floor."

She pulled out another sheet, and for a moment he thought she was going to tell him something. Maybe she needed a guardian's signature. No, she just needed another surface. She drew, she kept drawing, she wouldn't stop. She didn't understand.

He said, "The floor did *not* blow up. The pipes burst. That's different."

She drew, but she was also listening, he could tell.

He said, "I've worked at the Alicia long enough. It's fine. It's safe." He waited for her to tell him he was lying, that he didn't know anything, but he was telling her the truth. The Alicia was a half block away from Fremont Street, so the hotel avoided the worst traffic: the drunks, the fights, the angry tourists. They'd be fine.

She yawned.

He grew quiet, and in doing so recognized something of his father. How he could never admit he was angry. How he would always talk in the same measured beats when he was sure he was right and the rest of the family was wrong. Alvaro moved to the window, where hot air puffed through the bars and the mesh screen. "We are moving," he said.

"Whatever," she said. "We just do what you want, all the time."

"We don't always do what I want."

She yawned again, tired. Unyielding. Arms crossed. No, they were not moving.

He said, "And it's not like I want us to go," though he did, and he knew he did, and he knew he was lying. He wanted it more than he could say. He didn't want to say he wanted it at all, but he also didn't know why he didn't even want to make that admission. Like it was dirty. Like he wanted to drag his sister into something ugly. He felt flustered, ashamed, the heat in the room intensifying.

The key card lodged against something in his pocket and pressed against his leg.

He said, "If we go, we save enough to leave." He touched the throbbing knot on his forehead. It woke him up. "We could go. We could move back to Colombia, or back to Florida. Or we could go to California. We're so close. We would only need to stay for a few more months."

"Whatever," she said, hands against her ears, her words loud and harsh enough to tear into the dead neighborhood. She woke up the night.

A child wailed in the next room, and that woke another one. The toddler cried. Wailed. "Ma! Ma! Ma!" An older kid wailed for their mom and dad to come over. The voice was high and piercing and could have belonged to a boy or a girl, there was no way of telling. From above, from below, their neighbors thumped on the wall. Alvaro and Carmen had done that too, when it was late and someone was too drunk or angry or happy, and the noise of other lives tumbled into theirs.

Carmen said, "What*ever*" and thumped on the wall, her palms black from her drawing. "Whatever!" She hardly ever yelled, but she found a register that drowned out the children, drowned out the thumps. "This is our place too," she said. "We live here."

She grabbed her backpack. He thought she was going to throw it at him, but she threw it at the wall where the children asked for their mom and dad. "Shut up!" she yelled. "Just shut up and go back to sleep."

"It's for three months, maximum," he said. "Maybe less." The backpack leaned against the wall, undamaged. They had bought the cheapest one possible. Carmen insisted on beige so she could draw on it. She had drawn a complex set of whorls with a Sharpie and was at work on a pre-Columbian figure—eyes and head peeking from the whorls. "Probably less."

He did not say, *It's like a family over there. B. said that we were a family.* He did not say it because Carmen would mock him.

She would say, *Some family.* Or, *Don't kid yourself.* Or, *Let's not talk about family.*

Because they could not, not until more time had passed.

Not until the dreams stopped, or at least until they stopped for one of them.

He could say what his dad had said when they moved back to Colombia from the States. He could say, *We are doing this for you. We are doing this because of you. So you can be happy.*

Carmen had drawn a figure from the San Agustín baths. He had not recognized it until now. It peeked through the whorls and held its small arms to its chest, it's mouth open, full of teeth, its eyes small and frightened. Half-animal. You wouldn't think it was pre-Columbian. It looked more like a character lifted from the Cartoon Network.

They'd seen the site together, on a family road trip the previous summer. Even then, there were roads that people weren't supposed to take, but the country was changing and everyone was eager to travel. Nothing bad had happened.

"It's fine," he said. "You'll see."

"Then let's go," she said, arms still crossed. No longer yawning. "Let's go right now."

"Tomorrow after school," he said. "After work."

"It's five minutes away." She jabbed her arm at their door. "Why not go now? We check it out and if it's fine, we move in. But I want to see it before I take my stuff. I want to see what we're getting into."

The figure hid in the whorls of the backpack. The first sculpture they'd seen was like that, hiding in plain sight until it emerged. The baths too. The smooth, dark slabs with their grooves for water to course through. The sculpted pool that you could mistake for a natural formation. Carmen had liked it, but Alba had complained, cranky from the drive. They'd driven all this way, for this? If you removed the signs, the posts guarding it, you could have walked on it and not known, not unless you looked down.

Carmen had been the good one, Alba the bratty one. That's what Mom said when the sisters were out of earshot.

Carmen had been the favorite.

"What's there to see?" he said. "It's a hotel. It *looks* like a hotel."

She squeezed the air out of the mattress.

"The room has two beds," he said. "We'd each have one."

"Whatever," she said. But she sat down next to her backpack, slumped against the wall, not minding the wailing children. No one had come to comfort them. Each night, he heard the rustle of the vinyl, her sad attempts to get comfortable. The bed leaked air.

Carmen flipped the mattress and pressed and squeezed and blew on the mattress again.

He said, "You were OK with this plan yesterday. You *wanted* this. What happened?"

"You show up bloody and bruised," she said. "And you're like, 'It's all fine.' Like it was OK you got hurt."

She was on the ground, the candle so faint he could not tell if she was crying or not. She sounded like she was.

She said, "People can just—"

She didn't finish.

She didn't say, *You're all I have.* She didn't say, *You could have died.* She didn't even finish her thought, but he finished it for her, because they had both learned that lesson.

She was going to say, *People can just die.*

"Let's just go tomorrow," she said. "It's fine."

They turned off all the lights. *Wait,* he thought. *Just wait till you're inside this place.* He could not sleep, and his sister shuffled and turned in her corner, also awake and uneasy.

"It *is* fine," he said. "You'll see."

The room burst into light and noise, his eyes closing against the glare. The power had returned.

Carmen had turned everything on in his absence: the fluorescent light by the kitchenette, every overhead bulb, their one lamp, plus the television, the bathroom fan, the radio.

They both flinched, and then went about turning everything off, quieting everything down. The AC wheezed to life, the air weak but mercifully cold. *It will be fine,* he thought, remembering Dan touching the door in the Alicia and the world going dark. *This is different. This is a different odd thing. Nothing to worry about, nothing worth mentioning.* He had not told Carmen about the little girl's room and her index cards. Or about the dog. Or about the roaches. *I told her about the pipe bursting,* he thought, *I didn't tell her what was inside. Better not to. Better to focus on the good.* That wasn't a lie, not really. She did not need to know. Besides, there were enough things they didn't talk about. These were small omissions. Oddities. Not worth troubling over, not worth the energy or the bother.

PART THREE

House That Believes It Is Not a House

CHAPTER 11

ALVARO WASN'T THE ONLY ONE who felt off. The whole crew of the Alicia drifted, uneasy without the presence of her owner. The kitchen had seen no one in plum blazers since the night of the accident. A whole week and no B., no Winifred, no one to tell them what to do. It was a relief, at first. The kitchen didn't need management to function, but you felt their absence all the same. Management usually lurked in the pit and kept an eye on the kitchen in other ways. The crew was well aware. The cameras rested in the ceilings—fat, glossy spiders. But there was no one looking right now, no one to worry about, no one to answer the phone. No one at the helm.

"Winifred's in the café," Ellie said. "Your friend."

Alvaro nodded and tried to keep an omelet together but it fell apart on the grill. He moved too fast or not fast enough. *So at least one of them is back*, he thought. Good.

Ellie petted Clarabelle and the dog looked at the Irish woman with adoration.

Alvaro yawned and a thought came to him from nowhere, from deep inside the walls of the hotel: *There was never a good time to be good, to do good*. You could try to help, as long as you realized you would mostly fail. Tell her now: Tell her it's a bad idea to keep the dog. Get the dog out of where no dogs belong. Winifred's coming, she'll see Clarabelle, she'll call animal control. But Ellie didn't want to leave Clarabelle alone at her house. The dog whined, she told him. The dog howled and keened if she lost sight of her.

Ellie said, "Your friend's out there and she looks pissy, hon."

━▪▪▪▪▪

The hair moved even though the rest of her sat composed, a burst of red in the green of the café. The other diners clumped together, but Winifred sat alone.

She jabbed at her laptop and he thought, *Why aren't you upstairs? Where have you been?* The pipes had damaged a small part of the fifth floor but spared the penthouse offices above. She had taken off her plum blazer and draped it over another chair, and she'd set a pile of folders on still another chair. She had colonized the table. When had she come over? He had imagined she slept in the hotel, like he and Carmen had been doing for a full week, like he supposed B. did until he was told that B.'s house was in Boulder City, a long drive from here, and that he commuted every day.

She jabbed at her keyboard again and said, "Fuck." She cleared the folders from the chair when she saw him and said "Fuck" again at the screen and waved him over.

He wiped his hands on his apron.

"This fucking thing," she said. "Cara wants these numbers today and B.'s fucking gone and it's not fucking working."

She poured too much sugar into her coffee and stirred. The rim of the mug was too perfect, devoid of cracks—nearly all of the Alicia's china was damaged. Ellie must have selected the mug fresh from the dishwasher's shabby offerings. Poor Ellie. Afraid of the plum blazers. Winifred pointed with her spoon and dripped coffee on her keyboard.

He recognized the spreadsheet from Carmen's homework, and he saw the error because it was the kind that drove his sister crazy. *People are careless*, Carmen said. They're sloppy and they blame the machines.

Alvaro said, "You're missing a parenthesis."

Winifred pecked at the cell and closed the nested equation and the numbers almost settled into comprehension.

"Two more." He pointed. "Here." He had to lean into her shoulder to point at the other open formula. "There." Her skin was pale and freckled and she couldn't be much older than he was, and here she was—an adult with an adult life, a citizen, a real person, a real job. He felt like a kindly ghost.

The numbers resolved into a graph, a bright-red wave that shot upward and refused to turn level.

Winifred smiled. "Still off."

She pulled out a pack of cigarettes from her purse, no lighter, and waited for him to proffer one. The best he could do were the complimentary matches by the bus tray. *She and Dan have that in common at least,* Alvaro thought. *They're both smokers.* But they're also salaried. They own cars. They had not dropped out of college.

The hotel brought all of them together, though. It created a kind of democracy. It wasn't just B. welcoming him here. If you could be of use, you were drawn in and asked to stay.

"Let me see," he said.

She tilted the screen. "You're cute," she said. "You know you're cute, right? Bruises and all?"

He couldn't look at her, the blood hot in his face, so he kept his eyes on the screen and hoped he wasn't blushing. He found the error before she exhaled her first cloudlet of smoke, the errant graph turned into an elegant sine wave, each crest slightly bigger than the one it preceded, until it hit the last pulse, where the line shot up, turned jagged and violent—an angry snake.

He had not bothered to look at the footers. He'd been looking at the numbers and the equations so intently, he had not realized that he was looking at the ebb and flow of the Alicia itself.

That's us, he thought. *That angry upward jag—that's where we are right now.*

He could feel it too, how the hotel had more guests this week than the week before. The café could barely keep up with orders.

"That's Cara." Winifred pointed at the spike. "Cara and us," she said. "The hotel has these little swells and then it calms down and then it goes out of business. Gets sold off." Her index finger had a spray of freckles, and her nail was painted silver, and he followed the nail as it went through each cycle. "Since 1905. A couple of months of full occupancy and then it's a snoozefest."

He nodded. Every five years, the hotel shut itself off, turned off its lights, and slumbered for seven years. Every twelve years, the same pattern. Every year but this year. "Cara's trying to go big," he said. "Cara and B."

"That's the thing," she said. "They could have bought it outright, but they got B. involved. And soon after B. hired me, Cara started asking me to keep tabs on him."

"Did you?"

She shrugged. "So much fucking trouble for such a dinky property." She was nearly done with her cigarette. "I bet I'm not the only one keeping tabs. You too, right? They talk to you? I bet they do. They will, at any rate. And for such a dinky property." She'd looked into the hotel's past, she told him. The hotel had been around under one name or another for over a hundred years. The Splendor, the Alicia, the Enchanted Hunters, the Bright and Risen, then back to the Splendor, back to the Alicia. It did not look old, just shabby. There was nothing about it that suggested a history, or a previous name, or a sense of who stayed here, who worked here. Who left and why.

He thought of the cages on the patio. Birds lived here once.

"Cara's going big, bigger than this place is used to," Winifred said. "Go big or go home, right? Or, I don't know, go dinky and you can go fuck yourself." She snapped her laptop shut. "I'm sending these before they throw another fit," Winifred said. "Can you help me with the rest, cutie-pie? Later?"

The door swung and Ellie came out with two trays. Clarabelle barked.

"Did I just hear a dog?" Winifred said.

"You heard the kitchen," Alvaro said, unsure if he meant it as a lie. He didn't want Ellie in trouble, and he wanted Winifred to stay put. And for the dog to shut up. *How easy would it be*, he imagined, *to keep her muzzled. You could get something for her mouth (bought at PetSmart with honest money).* He said, "Sometimes we bark in there. When people are cooking and you want someone out of the way, you bark."

"Really?" she said. She stubbed out her cigarette, which was mostly gone, the smell of tobacco more fresh than stale.

He shrugged.

"So it's like a zoo in there, you're saying," she said. "Like this whole other world."

That much was true. She squeezed his shoulder, gathered her materials, and told him she'd stop by again tomorrow. Again he wondered why she kept herself away from her own office, but he had a good guess.

She wanted out of the building.

She was as close to the outer boundary of the Alicia as you could be without setting foot outside. You could take the service corridor to the back of Ogden from here, the part of Ogden no one bothered with. Now that B. and Dan were gone, now that they were otherwise occupied, she had no reason to be in the penthouse, but he remembered the landline marooned on the enormous desk, convinced that it was ringing now. That it rang for Winifred. It rang and kept on ringing and no machine would pick up the call. *No one at the helm*, he thought again. There is no one at the helm because the Alicia steers herself.

The pit glowed its awful yellow, the machines all occupied and furiously chirping, and he wanted to go back to the kitchen before he saw anything. A voice he could not place asked him to turn away from the pit, but he did not. Winifred had already gathered her things. They were done. He would not have seen it had he not been looking at Winifred—her neck, her lips, her dark lashes, her pale skin, the electricity of her hands and hair. He looked at the pit because he did not want to get caught leering.

That's when he saw his sister.

Carmen lurked by a *Star Wars* slot machine, the Death Star spinning, Carmen's backpack yellow and lurid from the light. She moved her hands up in the air like the whole family did when they talked. Wild gesticulators all. Carmen dipped out of sight, an old man close to her in the crowd. Plum blazer, red eyes. Red even from this distance.

The man from the room with the index cards. The man who told him to stay away.

Carmen was supposed to be in school. They had walked to the bus together this morning. She was not allowed in the pit. No one under eighteen was. Alvaro did not know if he was angry or if he was afraid, but the old man followed his sister too closely, and he had no business with her, and Carmen had no business here, in the gambling part of the Alicia.

He returned to the chaos of the kitchen, but only to tell Ellie that he needed to go, that he needed to find Carmen. That she was running around in the hotel. Again he thought of Clarabelle. *Muzzle her. Tie her to a post.* But it was his sister he was thinking of, not the dog. His face no longer hurt, but his reflection on the stainless door of the walk-in freezer reminded him that it was still swollen and bruised. That he was still not quite himself.

CHAPTER 12

CARMEN COULD HAVE GONE ANYWHERE. Four corridors connected the pit to the rest of the Alicia, and she could have chosen any of them.

Alvaro knew this much about the hotel: It had been expanded with no real thought or plan, the original structure stretched thin and grown tall, the passages narrow and all intersecting so that one always ended up where the machines waited with their birdsong and promises of easy money.

He could not think in here, nobody could.

He stepped into the courtyard, the pool half-filled with gray water. Soon the pool would be full of children, but for now a few just played around the edges, swimsuits on but dry. No one had jumped, yet. The Vegas sun flattened the bricks and tile of the yard. Too much light. No clouds. All heat. The hotel snaked around the tiny courtyard, brick and stucco turned to smooth cement that was cracked and painted over, the sun baking all color into off-white or gray or pale yellow. The children's skin was off too. Leeched of color.

The three cages were still empty.

B. didn't plan to keep live birds, but Alvaro would not have been surprised to find plastic flamingos pinned to the ground on aluminum legs.

The children didn't seem to mind the heat, the sun, the lack of color. Must be more pleasant by the water.

He sweated in his chef's pants and his T-shirt that had not been washed for at least four shifts. He must stink, even if he couldn't smell it. The sweat evaporated almost as soon as he grew aware of it. He didn't belong here with the guests. He had to go, but he needed a direction, he needed a clue, and there was nothing. The children played. He remembered the room strewn with index cards, and thought of Esther *here*, among the children, the old man telling him that he didn't want to be there when the mother arrived. The room where you found things you didn't know were lost.

He ran and the children squealed.

One of them said, "Marco!"

Carmen never said "Polo!" when they played. Alba would. Carmen cheated by keeping silent, but when she was little, she giggled, and that would give her away. He had been afraid that he'd never find her, when she was younger and he had his hands over his eyes. That he would miss her. Or that she'd run off and he'd get into so much trouble. Or that—eyes dutifully shut—he would run headlong into the diving board and bonk his head. He grew afraid and then he'd peek, he'd cheat, but the sisters cheated also. They giggled and moved and tried to throw their voices.

She doesn't belong here, he thought. She should be in school.

Maybe she is. Maybe he imagined her in the pit. Neither of them had slept long, and lack of sleep made you see people who were not there, next to people they did not know and could not know.

He had almost convinced himself by the time he made it to Esther's room on the third floor.

━||||

Carmen stood by the closed door, the old man walking away as soon as the elevator doors groaned open.

"Hey!" Alvaro said, but the old man shuffled into the dark of the corridor.

Carmen stared at the floor.

Had she seen him at the pit? Did she know she was in trouble?

He tried to remember what his dad had said when the family first found out that Alvaro had dropped out of college. They didn't know about the crying yet. They didn't know about how he could not get out of bed, and he never had the chance to tell his parents about the worst—about how easy it would be to kill himself. How you could slip out of this life and no one would care, why would they, no one would so much as register his absence. He could barely register his own presence. Alvaro had come in from the capital, suitcases piled in the living room. The news was a week old already. He had hoped the anger had abated. It hadn't, nor had his dad's disappointment. Alvaro could tell, even though his dad talked softly. *Because* he talked so softly. He marked his words. Dad said that he was not angry, just disappointed, but oh, he was angry—angry *and* disappointed—there was no hiding it. Dad had sent the rest of the family away, Carmen and Alba off with Mom at the country club. What did his dad say? He could not remember, but he did remember his own face growing hot and flushed, all of him shaking and afraid and angry too. All of him wanting to say, *This is not me. I did not mean to do this. I don't know what came over me.*

Esther's door was closed. No index card to tell the world that the door was locked.

Carmen tried to turn the knob before he could stop her, but surely the old man had already told her not to. Surely he had said, *You do not want to meet the mother. You do not want to be here.*

"What did he say to you?" he asked.

His sister kept her hand on the knob. She tried to turn it.

"Carmen?"

His sister shook.

No, he thought. *Don't let her distract you. She's acting up to distract you.* "You're supposed to be in school," he said. "Carmen? What happened? What did the old man say to you?"

He did not ask, *Do you know who is on the other side of this door? Did he tell you?*

He said, "You don't walk around with strangers. You don't let them take you places. What happened? What did he do?"

"He's not a stranger," she said. "He's Jacob. He works here. Like you. He *knows* this place. He knows *things*."

"No," he said. "You don't trust people just because they tell you to. What did he do?"

"He didn't *do* anything," she said. "He just wanted help. He said he needs us." She chewed her nail, the Agustín drawing on the nail looking alarmed, the top of his head gone. "And he wanted to help me. *Us*."

"We don't need help," he said. "We're fine." It felt good to say it. He almost believed it. "We're totally fine."

Her backpack sat by the door unzipped, papers spilling out. Carmen's drawings. He could not make them out and he did not want to, not right now. He wanted Carmen far from the door. Again he thought of Ellie's dog, picturing her muzzle wet with blood. Something waited in the room, you could hear a rustle of anticipation. Whatever lurked and brooded wanted them to stay. *You don't want to be here*, the old man had said.

He stuffed papers into the mouth of the backpack and waited for his sister to explain herself, but she stayed in place, her hand on the knob.

One of the doodles was of a dress he'd never seen his sister in: floral, old fashioned. She had drawn it on the back of an official-looking document. He turned it over.

A suspension letter.

She hadn't been to school in days.

Carmen—the smart sister, the one who never got in trouble, the one who could write code. The one who was going to college.

Alvaro thought about how he had dropped out, how he had failed his family, how he could not fail what remained of his family. His father must have wanted to hit him—the thought came out of nowhere, but it felt unarguably true. Not that his dad would. Alvaro could. Right now, he could. Smack Carmen's mouth. Teach her to pay attention, to be serious. Nothing too hard. He wouldn't break her jaw. He wouldn't hit hard enough to draw blood. (*Her muzzle wet. Her muzzle wet with blood.*) No. No he wouldn't hit hard or at all. No. Never in a million years. Dad wouldn't, he wouldn't. All the same, the thought must have crept to a part of his father's brain, because it had crept into his just now.

The same anger. The same fear. The same love.

The thought bubbled and burst. *Never*, he thought. He'd never hit her. Never harm her.

He held the letter. The drawing was so good, so familiar. Imagine someone you knew in that dress. Your mom. Alba. Carmen wouldn't look at him. It was his fault she had been suspended. It wasn't, but she'd blame him anyway, he could tell. He had dragged them to Vegas even if he didn't mean to. He had pulled them here even though he had meant to leave. He wanted to say, *I'm sorry*, but mostly he wanted her to realize that he had been trying. He had been trying so hard.

He said her name like you would say something foreign. She wrapped herself in silence. She wouldn't respond, wouldn't look at him. He zipped up her backpack and tried to ignore the index cards jammed into the edges and slipping out of books. Study aids. Flash cards. Nothing to do with Esther.

They had to get out of here before the door opened. Before the mother came back.

"You can't—" he started. "You can't just get suspended."

"Jacob said you shot her," she said. "He said you shot Alba. He said that's why we're here."

He felt himself go cold. His hands trembled, and he thought of the children by the pool, the children without color who played as though nothing could happen to them. They lived in a place where you could count on being safe. Even if unattended.

She asked, "Did you?"

Her eyes had the same ring of hazel as Alba's. Their whole family looked disturbingly alike. She was crying. She said it again, as though saying it would make it go away. "Did you?"

"No," he said.

Meaning, *I had no choice. They had a gun to my head. They said they were going to rape her. They said they were going to chop off her hands.*

Meaning, *Yes, because I loved her. Loved Mom, loved Dad.*

"No," she said. "No, you wouldn't do that."

If there was a time to tell her the truth, it was now. Maybe she wouldn't speak to him. Maybe she'd scream, or yell at him. But she could forgive him, she'd have to.

They were all they had, and they had to forgive each other. Because they had to talk about what they were going to do next, and because they were all the family they had, and because they had to keep going. They could not stay here, not for long.

"Why did you get suspended?" he asked. All of him wanting to tell her about the night in the forest—the family's last hours together, the girl he dreamed up in the midst of the blood and the carnage. *Will you give them to me?* You could, you could give them up, that was the worst of it. What you would say and do to keep yourself alive. She didn't know. *Tell her,* he thought, and the Alicia told him not to. He could almost hear the hotel. A real voice. Soft. The voice of a woman. The glint of teeth in the dark of the corridor. He asked, "Why did they kick you out?"

"I screamed," she said. "I ran out, I guess. Last thing I remember was the teacher doing a lesson I could have sworn he did *last* week, I swear. Towers of Hanoi. Recursive algorithms. These combinatorics anyone with half a brain could do in their sleep. All this stuff anyone who's actually paying attention would know. I caused a scene, I guess." She looked at her hand, which held the knob that would not turn. "I was thinking of Alba. I could have sworn I saw her in the school, by herself. She stood by the board, by where the teacher sits when he's not boring us with stuff he already told us. But I could have sworn I saw her here too. In the hotel. I keep seeing her *everywhere.* Jacob says she's here. That her ghost is here. He knows things. About me, about *us.* Stuff he shouldn't know. Like, stuff he has no business knowing. He says he knows us, and he says Alba's here

waiting for us. He told me he'd show me." She shook. She tore the edge of
the frayed nail. "He said you shot her."

Tell her.

Tell her.

"It's not her," Carmen said. "It's not Alba either way. It's not, because
she's dead and the dead don't come back."

But they did, he thought. You could not keep them safely tucked away.
They troubled the edges of your waking life and infected your dreams.

Tell her.

━ ⅠⅠⅠⅠⅠ

Alvaro walked Carmen back to their room and by the time he made it
back to the kitchen, it was chaos: orders piled up, prep trays in disorder,
Umberto putting out a fire he had apparently started in a cereal bowl.

Ellie had left a piece of paper by his station: "W. stopped in again. Says
to call her."

He checked his cell phone: Winifred had called five times, and she'd
texted, but the phone had lost to the Alicia. The messages all said the same
thing. Cara wanted them to open the two passages, they wanted more
traffic, they had little time. They had only a couple of days. Could he help?

He called and got her, and she told him she'd come for him tomorrow.

His eyes burned. He'd gotten no sleep. His poor sister—alone in their
room and also not sleeping. He wanted to say, *Yes, yes, come get me, please.*
He didn't say, *My sister's suspended, and I don't know what to do with her,
and I don't think we're staying here. Not for long anyway. We don't like it here.
We don't like what it's doing to us.*

He said, "Fine," and when he hung up and Umberto told him that
Marisol's photo had gone missing again, that she didn't know what to do,
and could he help? he said, "Of course."

━ ⅠⅠⅠⅠⅠ

He knocked on the door to their room and hoped to find his sister in better spirits. He also hoped she wasn't there at all, so he wouldn't have to look at her face or answer her questions or lie to her again. She was there. He didn't know if he was relieved—he was so sure he wouldn't find her.

Carmen put away whatever she was sketching. He didn't ask her about homework. He didn't ask her about the rest of her day, but he hoped it was fine. He wanted to tell her that it wasn't just her. The hotel could trick them. They saw what wasn't there. Heard things that were not true. There was nothing to see, not really. Nothing to learn from old men. Nothing to fear.

"What?" Carmen said.

"Nothing," he said. He was about to say that Jacob wasn't lying. How the old man knew was anyone's guess, how he knew who they were, what they ran from. He could have explained, or tried to. "Nothing," he said again, and saw the blank, wet void that had once been his father's face. The limb that had been hacked off. The severed thumb. How they shot his father, how they pressed the gun against his mouth, the mouth of the son, immediately after, the barrel still warm. The tooth that cracked when the barrel of the gun jabbed his mouth. How the trigger followed its own oily logic. How it felt like he had nearly no control over it. How he had no control over anything.

"It's OK," Carmen said. She was crying again. "It's OK, it's not like you—"

Again she meant to say something and stopped herself. Again she had said enough. Betrayed what she meant to say.

It's not like you.

They each sat on their respective beds, the flowers and thorns of the carpet an impassable gulf. Alvaro thought again of how his dad used to nervously stroke the backs of his children, and of how that had annoyed him. How it had made his skin crawl. How he could not stand to be touched. And how he very much wanted to do what his dad had done to his own sister. Stroke her back. Bring her some sort of comfort.

She would not go near him.

It's OK, he thought. She said it was OK. It must be. They had not slept, and so he fell into the folds of his clean, new bed convinced that things were getting better, that his sister understood, that he had meant well. That he had brought them here with the best of intentions.

⸻

They had not slept and so he had no idea how long he had been asleep, how badly frayed they both were, when his sister woke him up in the middle of the night, screaming.

Another nightmare, he thought.

Their room was cold and dark, their beds soft, but Carmen could not settle. He followed her screams, half-asleep still, his heart beating so fast it hurt his chest. She sounded like he was on the verge of killing her. She sounded like she was being murdered.

She had leapt out of bed and was now shrieking in a corner of their little room, and he staggered to her side, thinking all the while, *Nothing's all right. Nothing's OK.*

She was such a small, long thing, her figure mostly kept out of sight by shadows. An oversized T-shirt swallowed her form, and it must have been how she huddled, how she cried, that triggered the confusion.

She looked just like Alba.

She knows, he thought. *She knows even if she doesn't know. Even if she refuses to believe it, even if I won't tell her.*

He would, though. He told himself he would. He shivered and gently put his hand on his sister's back and said nothing, because he was not ready to give himself away. Because it was too late in the night for the conversation, and because he had carried his guilt for so long that it felt familiar, a welcome sourness lodged in his clenched mouth.

He thought of the old man with the red eyes, and his own eyes burned. He'd never sleep again, nor would his sister, not until he told her what happened.

He stood by her side, thinking, *Please wake up, please fall asleep. Please.*

She didn't.

He left her in her corner and settled into bed and thought, *Please please please.*

—·····

In the morning, Carmen screamed again.

She huddled in the early-light shadows of the room, blue light leaking into the corner where her hands scrambled, all of her blurred, her mouth a gash of black, a torrent of sound.

My sister looks like a dog that lost a bone, Alvaro thought, not fully awake.

Neither was Carmen. Her eyes fluttered closed.

A muzzle. A muzzle wet with blood.

A week before, when they still lived at the extended stay, she had grabbed his shoulder and shaken him into consciousness. He tried the same thing. She stayed put when he shook her.

Her shoulder felt too bony. She wasn't eating enough. *Don't ask her what's wrong,* he thought. *You don't want to know. You don't want to know what she was up to with Jacob either. With the old man with the red eyes.* She wouldn't wake up, and her hands shone blue in the bad light of the Fremont dawn, and whatever she looked for she did not find.

Her shirt hung on the shower rack, already dry. Before she'd gone to bed, she had wrung it in the sink and scrubbed soap on it and wrung it again. She had put on one of his T-shirts to sleep in because they had done no laundry, and now the T-shirt was covered in dark smudges. She must have been drawing. That must be charcoal. And now she crouched and would not respond when he shook her, though she had little time. They had to catch the bus in an hour, and she had not yet taken a shower—no, no, she didn't have to go to school. She'd been suspended. How could he forget?

He said, "Wake up."

She screamed and the sound tore at his ears and filled the room. She pulled at this shirt with her nails, each still showing the little faces she'd drawn. She tore another nail, the raw edge snagging and catching on his sleeve. *They're going to call security*, he thought. *They're going to think I'm killing her.*

He asked her again to wake up, and she screamed and scrambled for whatever she wanted to dig up from the corner of the room. His poor sister.

Dawn light pooled into the room and revealed what she'd done.

She had scrawled on the walls, first with a broken Sharpie and then with her own bloody fingers. She had drawn row after row of cockroaches, and you could mistake them for the real thing in the bad light. She drew with ink and she drew with blood, and now she crawled away.

She had not seen what happened to Alba, but she replicated their dead sister's crawl. After the machete. After Dad died. After they put the gun in Alvaro's hands and laughed and told him to shoot.

He put his hand on Carmen's mouth to quiet her, but he pressed lightly, afraid of hurting her and afraid of her teeth, and so did little to muffle the sound. She screamed louder.

He slapped her, the slap hard, louder even than her scream, all of Alvaro shaking.

All of Alvaro glorying in the violence—how wrong it was, how good it felt.

His mouth was locked in an awful open smile, he couldn't help it. It didn't matter. Carmen didn't know. Carmen was still screaming. He was still smiling.

He slapped her again.

Carmen's eyes sprang open.

She ran out of the room.

The soles of her feet shone in the yellow light. He followed her, hoping she was OK, hoping she wouldn't run into anything because he had no idea what she saw with her eyes half-closed. (*Your smile. She sees your smile. The smile of the person hitting her, that's what she sees.*) What did she see? Not the corridor, not the Alicia. Something else. *She's still dreaming,* he thought. *Maybe she'll think it was a dream, my slapping her.* His hand still stung. He was afraid, he wanted her to get better.

He ran, knowing he also did not want to get in trouble with the Alicia. They had just arrived. They had just been given their room. He didn't want them to lose it, to go back to their sad old room filled with the sad noise of Fremont, all of it seeping in with their sad AC: The wailing of children they did not know, the fights of strangers, the crunching of glass, the cough of smokers and the sour tang of old cigarettes, the drunk laughter of kids his age walking to bars he could not afford, had no time to go to. He slapped his sister because he loved her, but he also slapped her because he was afraid. He did not want to lose what little they had.

You did what you had to.

I could have done better, he thought, telling himself again that it was not his job, that he was not her father, that he had no idea what he was doing.

He needed to lock their door behind them, he needed to put on shoes, thinking all the same, *Fine, I'll leave you out there,* and knowing all the while that he wouldn't—that he would spend the whole day, his whole life, looking for her if he had to.

Someone had closed the blinds in the lone corridor window.

He opened them to the shadows of the Alicia's courtyard, with its empty pool and the wrought-iron cages, the interior of the hotel so obscured he only recognized the outlines because they were already familiar. He walked through the courtyard every dawn when he came to work.

The middle cage stirred. An animal lurked. It wasn't a bird, because the shape huddled, and you could almost imagine paws in the shadows. Clarabelle, maybe.

Keening.

He stared until he realized that it was Carmen down there, the white of her T-shirt catching the growing light, and he ran down, still barefoot, the carpet cold and rough, and then the ground—also rough, still hot from the day. His poor sister, troubled by dreams and sleepwalking. And by what he had meant to tell her, and by what he had held back.

━ ·····

He stood close enough to smell her sweat, both of them crouched inside the narrow cage.

Her eyes bulged, her face close to the ground, hands buried in the dead leaves and tossing the stray wrappers and newspapers lining the cage. She clawed the mess with both hands. She grunted. They'd seen a caveman movie together, a bad one, phony and flat, and that is what she reminded him of—an actor playing the part of a cavewoman, badly. She would have found it funny, had she seen herself, but he could not, it wasn't funny. His sister Carmen cried, she couldn't find what she was looking for, she couldn't find it because it wasn't there. She dreamed it up, this missing thing. She could have been looking for their family, long buried, or the parts of their family they could never find, what they could not recover from the road to Ibagué: their mother's earlobe, the back of their sister's head, most of the left side of their father. First, when he waited in Bogotá, he had assumed that the missing remains waited belowground, that the remains had been buried, that one of the men suffered a burst of kindness and decided to give the family a grave, and he only later learned that he was wrong. That animals likely took off with what they could.

You won't find them here, not in Vegas, he thought, but his sister dug anyway.

You won't find anything.

He was wrong.

His sister pulled a photograph from the mass of leaves, and he recognized it immediately.

They had taped it to the wall of their old room, and he had assumed they'd unpacked it in their new room, but they had not, apparently, because here it was, outside. His sister must have grabbed it from the wall. Grabbed it and buried it here, in her sleep, when he himself had not noticed.

Who had taken the photograph? He did not know. It must have been the maid, because the whole family appeared. It was Alba's fifth birthday, a Hello Kitty balloon floating taut, all of them gathered around their Barranquilla table, all of them singing to the little sister. They all stared at the birthday girl, and the birthday girl stared at the Hello Kitty cake. No one suspected their world would change in any way.

The week of Alba's birthday, they were almost swept away by what looked like a trickle of water running down the middle of a street. It was Barranquilla's rainy season. You weren't supposed to cross if you saw water, but everyone did it. They themselves had just done it. The car stalled, the water rose, the car moved along on its side, threatening to tip. Muddy water seeped in through the bottom of the windows, and it was Carmen who suggested they just roll down the windows and climb to the roof of their car, which they did—the whole family huddled up there until someone saw them, a maid from one of the houses on the dry side of the street. The maid tossed them a rope and each of them walked through the pull of the flooded street, everyone but Alba, who piggybacked to safety on her dad's shoulders. They stayed calm, and Alvaro remembered thinking, *That is us, that is our family.* Unflappable. Resourceful. Nothing bad could happen to them. Whatever came, they could handle it.

He inched closer to Carmen. His parents looked so young in the photo, Alba so sweet. All of them unchanged, unchangeable. Carmen focused on the field just beyond the photograph, and it was then that he remembered Marisol and her own lost family photograph. *Carmen didn't hide it,* he thought. *The Alicia did.* It's the Alicia hiding these. Secreting them. Drawing them into herself.

Why?

Someone could close this cage right now. They'd be trapped, they could both scream and no one would hear them.

The hotel could swallow them whole.

He took the photo from Carmen and turned it over. A flattened square of Scotch tape hung to one corner, dirty from the burial in the cage. He put the photograph in his pocket, but he wanted to rebury it. There was nothing in the photo but pain, nothing but people who were dead and unrecoverable, even the two who lived. He and Carmen unrecognizable in the photo. Too happy. Their sleep untroubled.

Carmen woke up and nearly fell into the wrought-iron bars, but he held on to her.

"Oh," she said.

The air blew cold from the desert and rose hot from the ground.

"It's OK," he said.

"Look," she said, and pointed.

On the third floor, a little girl in a dress stared at them through a window. He recognized the dress: it was the one Carmen had drawn. The girl could have been Alba's age. The girl waved, and the light caught something feral and off about her smile.

"It's not her," he said. "It's not who we think it is."

And it's not the other girl, the one in the forest, the one who asked—

Will you give them to me?

Will you?

She was never there. I dreamed her up.

Carmen shivered. The girl in the window shivered too, the light blurring her into the contours of her room. Carmen's wrist was too bony, all of her too small in his T-shirt, her skin hot and feverish.

He thought, *This is getting worse. Carmen's getting worse.*

They had to leave.

He could feel the way the hotel wrapped itself around them, the cracked walls curving, the corridors narrowing. Every EXIT sign a lie. (*This door is LOCKED.*) They'd end up in the pit no matter what.

Leave.

They had the safety of their room at least. The twin beds. The AC.

They had another week and a half until their next payday.

Hang on, he thought. *Hang on for a little longer and then we get out. We move on.*

Maybe back to Barranquilla. Maybe California. Anywhere they could find that was not here, not this awful place that remembered everything he had been trying so hard to forget.

He had forgotten that birthday week, it had slipped by like so many other memories of Colombia, and what he felt now was a wish that the photograph never existed. You could bury it and forget—forget what? Everything. Everyone. Everyone you loved. Everyone you hurt. Every lie you told. Every secret sorrow. You could forget yourself.

Someone would remember it for you.

How did Jacob know about Alba? About what happened on the road to Ibagué?

Alvaro had told no one. He had not betrayed himself. He had kept quiet.

I should toss the photo, he thought. He kept it close to him.

Their room waited, the AC a marvel to behold. Cold air, a steady, pleas-ant hum, no danger of it shutting off for no reason in the middle of the night, no water dripping off the unit and onto the carpet. He thought of taping the photo to their wall, sure that the dirty square of Scotch tape would be enough. It would hold. No. No, he did not want to find it gone again. The walls shone a dead blue. No, worse still: he did not want to wake up and go through the day and fail to notice the absence of the photo, the void of the people pictured.

Their father, their mother, their sister.

He said their names, thinking, *We're safe.*

We're safe for now.

A shadow moved across the wall. He was falling asleep, startled when he realized that the shadow was actually a cockroach. It scuttled across his sister's drawing, the live thing blending for a moment with the things she'd drawn, as though she conjured the insect into life, then it sank out of sight into a corner.

Better not to move. He didn't want to wake up Carmen. He didn't want her to know about the roach. It wasn't the same floor as the one with the pipes. She doesn't know, couldn't know. Who knows why she drew cockroaches? She was fine here, even if he kept waiting for the walls to shake, for the shadows to stir like they did in the corridor—for the walls to sweat and shiver and break.

The room stayed put. The cockroach kept itself out of sight.

Carmen said something to him. He could not make it out, but he remembered what she had said before, that she'd seen Alba walking in the hotel, and he had seen her too, had seen someone that could have been Alba, the blurred girl in the window, and then he saw her in his dreams, Alba wandering the pit and the corridors, her mouth open and toothless and wet and very red, Alba wandering into Esther's room and into the safety of the green kitchen, Alba about to form a word with what was left of her tongue, and then he woke up.

CHAPTER 13

THE KITCHEN COULD BARELY KEEP up with all the food the café asked for, though it was too early for anyone to be there. But every table was full. Every table was hungry. On most mornings, Alvaro had a moment to settle into the rhythm.

Today it was chaos.

He felt heavy and dumb. The bad night lingered—he could not shake off the dream of Alba and her red mouth. He cooked and grew certain that his sister waited for him and for Carmen in some corner of the hotel, stirring in the shadows (*that's not her, that looks nothing like her*). The light in the kitchen was too dark, the air sour, thick with steam. The noise all wrong.

He kept hearing his name and turning around. Nobody called. Nobody had time to call, the orders thick on the pins, Clarabelle barking with joy at every server coming into the kitchen, all of them learning to walk around the Lab without so much as giving her a glance. He wouldn't kick the dog. He could, it'd be easy, but he wouldn't do it. Maybe Carmen had gone back to sleep. Maybe she at least felt better.

We'll sleep tonight, he thought. *She'll feel so much better. We both will.*

He had promised to call at first break, which wouldn't be for three more hours. He told her to call if she was afraid (*if you see her, call if you see our sister with her red mouth, her wet muzzle*), or if she needed anything. "You'll be fine," he said. Carmen had half-smiled, she'd held up her hand and waved her fingers. He made her promise she wouldn't leave the room. And she wouldn't talk to Jacob, she wouldn't talk to anyone. If you don't leave the room, nothing bad could happen to you. You were safe where you slept.

The kitchen doors swung open and he caught a flash of a plum blazer and red hair: Winifred, trying to make her way in. She nearly collided with two servers carrying full trays out of the kitchen. The trays fell, the clatter harsh and ringing.

Winifred turned to help, then ducked when Marisol ran past her, Marisol's full clattering tray held aloft. Marisol apologized. Winifred got up, waved an unlit cigarette, sidestepped the mess on the floor, and tried once again to walk into the kitchen.

Clarabelle panted and stood next to Alvaro, ready to greet the newcomer.

"No," Alvaro hissed. "Down." He tapped Umberto on the shoulder. "Hide Clarabelle."

Umberto threw his dishtowel at the dog, which covered roughly half her face and left the bulk of her body visible. They had no time.

Ellie, he thought, *why is the dog still here? And where are you?*

It was as though he had conjured his friend out of thin air. Ellie stood right by Winifred and motioned wildly at them through the bustle, her arms still in their carpal tunnel braces, and then swung into the gap between the café and the kitchen and blocked Winifred's line of sight with her apron. They moved like characters in a terrible sitcom. A comedy of errors. He was too tired to find it funny.

He moved, hoping that he looked convincingly busy. That he did not look as though he was blocking what was going on behind him, which was what half the staff was doing. *That dog*, he thought. *All for that stupid dog. Jesus Christ, Ellie.*

Umberto whisked the Lab into the walk-in freezer and closed the door behind him. Alvaro guessed he was keeping the dog company so she'd stay quiet.

Ellie pulled Winifred aside and asked her to look at the comp line that snaked around the hostess station—too long, by far, and could B. see about adding more shifts, hon?

Winifred's red hair bristled, but she smiled at Ellie and made a note of it on her phone, and kept trying to catch Alvaro's eyes all while Alvaro tried to keep up with his skillets and look like someone who was not partly responsible for hiding a dog.

Marisol came back, her tray empty. She moved close to Alvaro.

"Can you talk to Winifred?" she said. "Can you get Winifred to talk to B.?"

He didn't even need to ask.

He knew, even through the fog of no sleep, even though he felt as old and red eyed as Jacob.

He said, "The photo's missing again."

Marisol nodded.

"We lost one too," he said, "but my sister found it."

"Everyone's losing things," she said, "and they're not big. They're little. Keepsakes. Drawings. All family things."

No one in the kitchen wanted to take it up with Lost and Found. They handled property loss and inventory control, they fixed the network of cameras in the pits, they called in Metro when Metro needed to be called in. They had also called ICE on occasion, when they felt like it. When they found themselves disliking someone on staff. No one knew it for sure. No one doubted it. There were no raids, nothing happened in the Alicia proper, but they had all seen friends snatched. And not just fresh arrivals. Marisol and Umberto's friend Andrés had lived in Vegas for twenty years and just last week, right as the pipes burst, he was detained and now he was being bused back to Mexico.

Alvaro thought he heard his name again, and when he did not turn around, he heard it again, much louder. Winifred. She stood next to Ellie, out in the packed café, and Ellie held her tray in the most innocent way possible. Winifred motioned for him to come over.

"I'll ask her," Alvaro said, and left the chaos behind: the dog and the man hiding the dog in the freezer, the pile of orders, the worried waitress, the echoes, and the green tiles.

"Everything OK?" Winifred asked.

He said, "Yes," but thought, *Everything's wrong.* "Marisol lost a photo," he said. "A waitress. Others too. Everyone's losing things. Have you heard from Lost and Found? Anything about keepsakes going missing?"

"You mind, cutie?" she said. "The passages?"

Right. Right, right. He remembered they'd talked about opening the passages, the men from Cara wanting them open soon. He had said he'd help. The kitchen was falling apart, however, and he couldn't possibly leave, not right now—

"Come," she said.

He followed her, his gaze fixed on her swaying back, the back of her neck, the semaphore red of her hair. The two made their way through a door he had never noticed before, older than anything he'd seen in Vegas: cracked wood, scratched and stained, painted and repainted, on which a crumbling newspaper had been used to cover a broken window: a faded glossy employment ad for the Hotel Alicia, formerly the Hotel Splendor. *Workers wanted. No experience necessary. 1958.* Another grand reopening. Alvaro followed Winifred down a set of dark stairs and thought, *This place just won't die. It keeps waking up. It refuses to be put to sleep.*

<hr />

"Dan's much better," Winifred said. "Hospital's letting him out tomorrow."

Alvaro said that he was glad, and remembered Dan's broken leg, how he was covered in blood. He could have died. Alvaro could have let him fall into the broken pipes. It would have been easy. Your hands slip, the body falls. You wouldn't hear him. You'd just see his open mouth, his face fade into darkness. He wouldn't suffer. Why wouldn't Dan stay in the hospital longer? Why come back? Alvaro found himself irritated and surprised at being irritated. His cracked tooth ached. His tongue played with the tooth, despite his own best advice. Leave it alone. He kept silent. Dan getting better was nothing to be angry at. But why would she bring it up now?

They walked beneath the Alicia, just the two of them, under a gaudy yellow light, down a passage whose cement floor was painted and texturized to look like sand. The walls were freshly painted too, the smell bright and chemical. Murals. Beaches and long stretches of ocean and parasols and scattered flamingos, their feet jabbed into the sand. He thought, *Those birds don't belong there, they don't make sense.* But nothing belonged down here. Not even them.

He did not say, *I was hoping we'd get dinner.* Thinking too: *Where is this urge coming from?* He barely knew her. He had not realized he wanted her until now, as though this desire belonged to someone other than himself. It felt like a fever, like a flu, like he'd been infected. He could not afford to buy her dinner, not on what he made. He wanted to kiss her, but instead he said "Yes" to whatever it was she'd just said, and he blushed, he felt so young. *I'm not ready*, he thought. *I'm not ready for anything.*

The corridors disagreed.

He walked and could not let go of that thought—that the corridors themselves were waiting, and that whatever preparations B. had made, whatever the people of Cara wanted, it was the corridors that were now ready. And impatient. What was missing was Winifred and him, the two of them.

The passages sloped into wide double doors whose handles were padlocked and wrapped in heavy chains. Nearly every other door in the hotel used key cards. These doors had not been repainted. They had not even been refinished. They reeked of old casino. Trapped air, old cigarette smoke, spilled drinks, heavy, unmoving bodies.

"So Cara wants this open by noon," she said, holding a ring with keys. "We got a day before the protest. They want everything open."

"What's behind it?" he asked.

When Winifred moved, her hair moved in opposition, on all sides, her hair and her mind at odds with each other. Even in the light of the mural, she looked formidable. Beautiful and freckled and pale. "Not sure," she said. "Not Ogden, for sure. And not Fourth Street." Her hair was dark and thick and lovely, a mess of wires in a ponytail.

What's behind you? Who?

The corridors knew. Cara knew. If the corridors could talk, they would volunteer the answer. They would say, *Open us up. We've been waiting.* He said, "I bet B. doesn't know."

He felt eyes on him. Told himself, *There's someone behind you. Turn around.*

"B. doesn't exactly care," she said. "This was supposed to be open weeks ago. When the Alicia opened. He held it all back for the paint job. The lights. We were waiting on flamingos on the fucking walls."

He asked, "How did you meet B.?" He resisted to urge to turn around. If someone lurked, she'd tell him. She'd see whoever it was.

She was too transfixed to hear him. "I bet you they link us to another casino, like on the Strip." She put one finger on the lock and traced the curve and the whorl of the metal. "Like the Excalibur to the Luxor. Or the Palazzo to the Wynn and the Encore."

He didn't tell her that he'd never been to any of those places, had never really left the orbit of Fremont. He asked again, "How did you meet B.?"

Winifred traced the pattern on the metal. Absorbed. Enthralled. She wore the usual tight plum blazer and a white shirt that was mostly buttoned. Her hair was dense, wiry, impossible to control. He had tried and failed to ignore Winifred's proximity. When she leaned in on the door, key in hand, the wreck of the ponytail pressed against him, and her perfume had a sting and a spice to it. Limes and cinnamon and money.

She said, "B.'s doing his best. He's never run a casino before." The corridors seemed to say, *We know. We need him not knowing.* She traced a loop on her own neck with her finger, she traced what looked like calligraphy on herself, traced it over and over on the freckled skin of her neck, her expression distracted. Absent. "He's never dealt with people like Cara before."

The corridors waited, impatient. He could almost hear the hotel. What the hotel, what her corridors would say, if they could talk. *Come on. Come on come on come on.* Already he knew: It was a bad idea, their being here, opening this door, leaning into each other. She wasn't answering, did not want to answer, would not talk. Why persist? He persisted.

He asked, "Who is B.?"

"Who are you?" she said. "You're not in charge, OK? And you're no line cook. I've seen you chop. You haven't been doing this long."

He did not know what to say. For his first few months in the States, he'd come up with plausible backstories in case anyone asked, but no one did, and now all his stories slipped out of reach. "The staff is losing things," he said. "Keepsakes. Photos. Mostly photos. I think we have a thief."

"Photos?" she said. "Who do you think you are? Who are you?"

She waited for his answer, but all he could register were her eyes, her hair, the skin of her neck. She asked again, "Who are you?"

The corridors whispered their secrets, but he could not make out the words. The words submerged. The gist too. He knew better—he should have known better—he could have told himself the truth, that it was all in your head, that what you heard was coming from deep inside your own skull, your own imaginings. The hotel didn't speak. The hotel didn't dream. You did, and assigned the words and the dreams to the building and its corridors.

Still.

What he said was a faulty transcription. "You did something terrible," he said. "You did something terrible to someone you loved."

She flinched. She pulled a sheet from her purse. He looked. His own face stared back at him. His own poorly reproduced features on the HR photocopy of his passport.

She knew. She had caught him.

His skin grew cold and clammy, and his hands shook, but a part of him insisted on the lie. *There I am,* he wanted to say. *Everything you need to know about my life comes from forged documents. Anything of consequence. Fill in anything you need that you don't already have.*

She said, "Is this even your name?"

He could have said yes and it would have been the truth, almost, but pointed to the padlock instead, his skin cold, his hands still shaking. "We shouldn't open this door," he said. "I don't care what B. says."

She wouldn't look at him. She looked just behind him.

Someone's there, there's—

Stop making so much noise.

The corridors echoed.

He turned.

Lost and Found lurked by the painted flamingos. The twins lumbered in the shadows, silent, in identical overalls, wearing yellow rubber gloves. *They see everything, they—*

"They'll tell," she said, and turned him away from the corridor and the twins.

They were the only things moving under the eyes of the animals in the murals, the still painted ocean, the glare of the fake yellow sun. The twins kept quiet. Watched. Judged. He didn't know, didn't know why he didn't care, why he and Winifred had to do this. They cast long, busy shadows on the receding corridor and on the padlocked door.

He touched the padlock, thinking, *This is a bad idea. This is a pretty terrible idea.*

They're watching.

Because something was wrong with the Hotel Alicia, with the twins, something was wrong with all these corridors, though he didn't know what exactly, and Winifred knew more than she let on. And she had something on him now. She knew he wasn't who he said he was. He felt feverish.

Worse has happened, he told himself as he unlocked the passage. The worst had already happened, had happened months ago, in a country where the worst happened as a matter of routine to everyone.

—||||

They opened the doors to glare and noise and a host of men and women tapping on slot machine screens, tapping cigarette ash. Another casino. The banner read, "Welcome to the Big Eastern." The gamblers resembled birds. The same crane of the neck. The same eyes. Winifred asked him if he'd seen an earring, that she'd lost her earring. He almost said, *Maybe Lost and Found took it.* He crouched and helped her look. The twins had gone already. Alvaro had so little time. He remembered Marisol and Umberto on some other floor, the lost thing moved to some other corridor, both crouched low to the ground like Carmen in the flamingo cage. They could not find the earring. He did not see the photocopy either, the one of his forged passport, though they had dropped it, they must have dropped it somewhere. A token, a sacrifice. They'd each given something up. They gave up. Already the gamblers moved from their banquettes and loped, cards and cigarettes and drinks in hand. They moved toward him and Winifred. They moved past and around them, a great migration, Alicia-bound.

It was only then that he remembered to check his phone. He had not heard it, and he had assumed it had not rung, but you could never tell.

Ellie had called. She had called, and she had texted.

"Marisol's missing," Ellie wrote. "Poor Umberto's going out of his mind."

"Help?"

The phone weighed nothing in his palm, but it was all he could do not to drop it. If he dropped it, he didn't know if he'd ever find it, if the corridor would let him find it. He was shaking again, afraid. There were other texts.

"We can't find her anywhere," Ellie wrote.

"Alvaro, where are you?"

"R U OK?"

"Umberto says you know where she is, where she is, where she could be."

"Hon pls help I hope yr OK r u OK?"
"Pls help."
"HELP."
"We need u."

The messages had been sent hours ago.

CHAPTER 14

MARISOL GOING MISSING WAS ALVARO'S fault. Never mind how or why.

That's what he'd tell Umberto, what he'd try to explain to Winifred, but they weren't in the kitchen, and he gave up on texting them and tried calling, but the calls didn't even go to voice mail. They sank into silence.

Surely they'd know. They'd smell the guilt on you as easily as they'd smell Winifred. They knew what you did, who you neglected. Lost and Found had seen (*they see everything*) but it was so easy to give yourself away, you gave yourself away all the time, and every attempt to right yourself veered by these rooms.

The hotel swallowed their efforts to reach each other.

But they'd know. They'd see his face and they'd know he was to blame, and Umberto could do whatever he needed to do. Take his revenge. Ask him what'd he'd done, and Alvaro could tell him the truth—that he didn't know, had no idea, but he'd done *something*, he was sure. He felt like he committed a terrible crime but he didn't know what the crime was, and he walked through the welter of the kitchen preparing an apology. A confession.

There was no one here he knew.

Everyone was newly hired. The hotel burst with activity and the kitchen was stocked so full he could not move, and so he asked the throng of hairnets bent over the steaming dishes and the hissing grills. No one turned and faced him, they were too busy. Surely they knew Umberto. And everyone knew Ellie. Loved Ellie. The two of them worked so many shifts. Someone here must have seen them and witnessed Umberto's panic.

He grabbed a shoulder and tried to pull a man from his station. The man resisted. Alvaro couldn't blame him. Move away and you could ruin the order. Alvaro had ruined enough.

"Please," Alvaro said. "I need your help."

The man finally faced him. It was Umberto.

"You found her?" Alvaro said in Spanish. "She's OK?"

Umberto didn't say anything. His face registered no recognition, no worry, nothing but a desire to get back to the grill, where a brown lump was quickly catching fire.

"Umberto?"

The man shook his head. Alvaro couldn't let him go.

The man smiled, said that he had to get back to the grill, that Alvaro had the wrong man.

"That's not my name," the man said. "I'm not who you think I am."

Alvaro apologized, but the words that followed were the ones he had been saving for Umberto, Everything's fine, there's nothing to worry about, and he left the kitchen with its host of strangers and stared at his phone, hoping for a call or a clue.

▬ ▪▪▪▪

The pit glowed yellow. He had no room to move here either. The whole world had decided to gamble at the Alicia. Soiled bodies pressed into his own soiled body, and he made his way in the sweat and heat of strangers.

He tried to remember how empty the place had first felt, how he could wander into a corridor and see no one.

How the place kept him safe from too many faces and too many questions.

One day the floors and the pit were empty and now they thrummed, and he thought of the pipes, how they brimmed and burst, how the roaches poured out, and how the guests were very much like that: a burst of activity, a rush, a skittering. An infestation.

You were a ghost before.

You could wander onto any floor and see no one, be seen by no one.

That was how he had found Marisol and Umberto in the corridor. The third floor—where Marisol's photograph first went missing.

—————

He found himself in the elevator, but the elevator refused to take him where he wanted to go. He pressed the button and pressed it again. Nothing happened. Someone had fixed it so that the shuttered floors wouldn't light up. Soon none of the floors would be shuttered. They'd open all the rooms. All the corridors. He pressed 4, which did light up, but the elevator still didn't move. He stepped out and into the service stairs, the light still poor and flickering, no one thinking of the parts of the hotel rarely seen by guests—not yet.

Maybe you should tell B.

It was time to fix the lights and get the hotel ready for everyone.

—————

Ellie waited in the third-floor corridor and worried at the braces on her wrists. Clarabelle sat and panted and leaned close to her human. They didn't belong here. You could keep a dog if you needed one, of course— that's allowed. But Clarabelle wasn't a service dog, she didn't even belong to Ellie, and the hotel wanted her gone. The hotel wanted her thrown out a window. Let the children in the pool deal with the mess: the splayed body, the burst of red, the muzzle, the broken bones, and the ruined meat. She'd come to harm if she stayed here any longer. Didn't the dog know? Didn't Ellie? Ellie was on her phone and said, "Hello? Hello?" and for a moment he worried that she wouldn't recognize him. She'd act like the man who looked just like Umberto but wasn't.

"Oh hon," she said. "I've been trying to call. I called you a million times."

"What happened?" he asked. "Is Marisol OK? Where's Umberto?"

He petted Clarabelle. The poor dog whined and rested her muzzle on his hand, as uneasy as her owner.

Ellie pointed at a closed door. "He's in there," she said.

"And Marisol?"

She shook her head and worried at her braces. The dog barked and behind the door a sound came, a low whine that didn't sound like Umberto. He remembered the road to Ibagué: when you were in distress, you didn't sound like yourself, you didn't sound human.

Ellie pounded on the door and said, "Sweetie, come out. We're here. It's OK. Come out."

"Umberto?" he said, thinking, *Is it really you?*

He knocked, tried the knob, imagined himself kicking the door down. The door glistened. The knob felt warm, alive and fleshy.

"What happened?" he asked again.

Ellie told him.

━ ▪ ▪▪▪▪

The café had picked up almost immediately after he and Winifred had gone. Ellie didn't ask him where they went, why Winifred needed him, which was just as well, and she didn't blame him—didn't say he had been needed at the kitchen. (And he hadn't been. Not really. So many new people had come in.) They worked their shift, Umberto only occasionally setting things on fire, and it was only hours later that they both noticed that Marisol had gone missing.

She would have said goodbye, Umberto was convinced.

It wasn't like her to go. She'd never do that. The worst thing, Umberto told Ellie, was that he had not noticed. He had been so busy with the orders that he had not registered Marisol's absence, though they were working the same shift. He *should* have noticed.

Umberto told Ellie that it was the hotel, that there was something wrong with the hotel, and he wandered into the café shouting Marisol's name. Ellie asked him to quiet down.

She didn't want him to get in trouble, didn't want him to get fired.

He was too worked up to do any good. He shouted Marisol's name but wasn't thinking straight.

Ellie spotted Marisol's pad and apron by a table, and the people who sat and waited for their burgers said they hadn't seen anything, that they'd been waiting for their food for so long now that they deserved it for free. But Marisol was not their waitress, they couldn't remember who their waitress was, but it wasn't her. Not a Mexican, for sure. Ellie picked up the pad and it was sopping wet, stained a pale pink.

Not blood. Something else. It smelled like food gone bad, like rot.

Like bad fish.

Umberto didn't want to go to Lost and Found. He didn't want to call the police. They didn't have papers. He didn't want Marisol to get into more trouble. Maybe she was fine. Maybe he was wrong—she'd gone home was all, and hadn't told anyone.

That was when Umberto said he saw her. He ran and Ellie ran after him, followed him down the service corridor and up the stairs and now here they were.

▬▪▪▪▪

"So you found her?" Alvaro said. "She's in there?"

Ellie shook her head. "He wasn't thinking, hon." Clarabelle whined and both he and Ellie did their best to reassure the dog. The dog was the only one making sense right now. They needed to get out of here. Anyone could see that. You, for example. *You'd leave in a heartbeat*, he'd tell you, his hand pressed under his leg, aware of how closely you tracked the movement of his fingers. How you tried to count them. Maybe they knew and no longer cared. They needed to go before—what?

We're coming for you.

You talked and now we're coming for you.

He shook off the thought. It was so easy to scare yourself. So easy to abandon people. But they couldn't leave Umberto here. You didn't do that. And you really didn't do it if—

We're here.

Alvaro said, "So he was chasing no one?"

"I saw a little girl," Ellie said. "She ran and she giggled, she must have thought it was a game, but she was too tiny. And she looked *nothing* like Marisol."

"That's who he chased?" he said. "And she's in there? With him? The little girl?"

Ellie took off one of her braces and folded herself and cried. She said she didn't know, that she was sure he was alone. She squeezed her arm until her hand turned pale. "It hurts so much," she said. "I don't know why. It's been hurting since I got here. It's never been this bad."

He knocked again. He kicked the door and his shoe sank into the wet wood. *It's going to burst again*, he thought. *The wood's going to burst and the roaches are going to pour out and this time there'll be no saving us. We'll sink, all of us will sink.*

The door might as well have been a hunk of rotting meat. The wood sank into the room. Some stuck to his pants. He imagined himself stitched inside a dead animal and pulling himself out by ripping through the flesh— the wood was hot and soft and bloomed with mold, most of it black or pink and threading in thin strands, giving off a sweet smell. He gagged. He could hear Ellie doing the same.

The room was all rot.

The walls glowed from the Vegas sun, their wetness and their sweet, thick stink so heavy that he nearly missed Umberto in the corner.

Umberto tore at the wall with his hands, his fingernails cracked, his fingers bloody and stained with the black and pink life of the room, all of it soft and yielding. That was what Alvaro saw, what he'd tell you he refused to believe he saw. Because Umberto dug into the walls with his bloody hands, and the walls yielded, and what they revealed was more life. More mold, all of it slick and wet and defiantly alive. In the dry heat of the city, the room was like nothing he'd ever seen—a sopping sponge, a beating heart, black and pink and marbled.

He thought of flesh again, he thought of meat, and he resisted the urge to sink his hands into the walls, to pull the rot off and stuff it in his mouth.

Umberto clawed, wouldn't stop clawing. "She's in there," he said. "I saw her. She's in here."

Umberto pulled at the soft mess of the wall and what he revealed was more of the same—fistfuls of wet rot, broken pipes, the only trace of anything human Umberto's own blood, which the mold took in.

"Hon, stop." Ellie put her injured hand on Umberto's wet shoulder.

Alvaro said, "We'll find her, I promise." He grabbed Umberto's bloody hand, but it slipped away and kept digging. "She's not here, but we'll find her." He remembered his time in the corridor. How Winifred stared at the twins. How neither said anything. "I'll talk to Lost and Found, I'll talk to B.," he'd said. "B. likes me. They won't call the cops." Marisol was fine. Probably. She had ended up somewhere, she had gotten lost, the hotel needed her. Maybe she had listened to the voice in the corridors.

Ellie said, "You see? It'll be fine. Marisol is here, or if she's not here, she's fine. But she's not in this room."

"She's dead," Umberto said. "She's gone." He grabbed a fistful of soft wall and threw it on the sopping carpet. "She's in here."

Ellie told him that there was no way of knowing, that it made no sense to think that way, that he didn't have proof, didn't know. "Don't despair, hon," she said. She'd been there herself, she reassured him. She imagined the worst because of course you did. But eventually everything worked itself out, everything would be fine.

Light shifted and moved about the walls. The room pulsed. Ellie took Umberto by his hands, said he needed tending, told him she'd take care of him, that they'd drive over to Marisol's apartment.

Ellie said that maybe Marisol felt poorly and had to go, didn't have time to tell him. Or tried to tell him and the call wouldn't go through. "It's happening to all of us," she said. "We're all losing calls." He had nothing to worry about, at any rate. They'd find her, and she'd be fine, she'd be fit. Umberto would see.

EXTENDED STAY | 127

Alvaro followed as they walked down the hall, and Clarabelle kept close.

"And look," she said, "we're all helping. Alvaro's going to ask the boss. He's going to see if anyone here saw anything. It'll be OK."

Alvaro said, "I'll find help." He patted Umberto like he had patted Clarabelle, like you would a dumb beast. "You don't need to worry about Lost and Found. They work for B., they'll do what he tells them."

He resisted the urge to apologize. Why blame himself? Why did he think he was guilty? He walked out of the damp room and thought, *I should let B. know. Winifred too.* They needed to get this floor fixed, they needed to know that it wasn't just the fifth floor. They had to get the Alicia ready for new visitors.

They needed to make the walls solid again.

It wasn't until then that he thought about the dog. Clarabelle had not gone into the room when he kicked down the rotting door. He had walked in and Ellie had followed. The dog had stayed put and keened, and it was only when they walked out that she padded after them.

She's smart, he thought. *Smarter than us. Smart enough to keep away.*

So why did he want to kill the dog?

Why did he want to break her legs and gouge her eyes?

━▪▪▪▪▪

He needed a shower.

You couldn't wipe off the mess, you couldn't get rid of the stink—it coated his fingers and his pants. He didn't find the smell offensive, but he knew that he should. He smelled like an animal trapped and dead and long forgotten.

CHAPTER 15

HE KNOCKED, SLID HIS KEY card, and walked into the order and cleanliness of their room, the good, clean smell of bleached linen, the drawn curtains letting in the fury of the Vegas light. The AC hummed and kept the room icy.

The good news was that Carmen had stayed in.

She sketched at the little desk by the window, her bare feet propped on the sill. Her bag was open, the textbooks inside. Less of an issue now, he supposed, now that she'd been suspended. *Whatever*, he thought, *I'm not Dad*.

The bad news was that she wanted to talk—he could tell from the ugly way she contorted her face, from the way she edged her stupid sketchbook away and inspected him. Her eyes were rimmed with red. Tired. Didn't she know he was tired too? That all he wanted was sleep? Was she that obtuse? It'd be so easy to shut her down—you could do it, you'd be doing her a favor. Just tell her to shut up before she even says a word. Just smack her mouth. Once. Once would be all it takes. He had already slapped her when she was sleeping, when the bad dreams had turned her into an unthinking creature. And now she wasn't thinking either. Of what was best for them. She looked like she was going to scold him, like she knew he'd done wrong. Thought wrong. And it wasn't fair, was it? Because usually it was him who wanted to reach out, who wanted them to talk, and it was her who froze him out.

He walked into the bathroom before she said anything, turned on the shower, ignored the knock on the door. The water fell and washed off the day—the stink of the kitchen, his time with Winifred, the rot of the room on the third floor. He tried to forget about Umberto, about poor Marisol, but you couldn't very well do that, could you? The poor girl was missing. He'd talk to B., he'd get B. to help. He'd make sure Lost and Found didn't interfere. He could make it right.

Marisol's fine, she's at home. She just didn't tell anyone.

He could imagine himself doing the same thing. You could leave your sister here, go deep into the bowels of the hotel, find another room, leave the chaos and the hurt and just forget it all. Forget even yourself.

▬ꞁꞁꞁꞁ

Carmen waited. She had fixed them peanut butter sandwiches, their meal of last resort but also one of their favorites since they had come to the States. They had no supplies. She must have gone shopping, must have made her way to the 99-cent store while he worked and opened the basement corridor with Winifred and talked to Ellie and Umberto. She was supposed to stay in the room. Besides, they didn't have much money. Not until payday. They needed it to last the rest of the week.

"I hope that's all you bought," he said, and bit into the bread and the peanut butter.

"What happened?" Carmen said. "Ellie called the room phone. She wanted to know where you were. She sounded so worried."

He chewed. He forced himself to swallow, to drink warm water from the tap. "It's bad enough—" He couldn't finish. She was his sister. She meant well, they had to eat. So she didn't understand that they had nothing—that even a necessary expenditure threw him into a panic. So what? Why would she care? Why would she care about *anything?* "Nothing happened," he said. "I was just busy, that's all. I had to leave the kitchen. Ellie needed help."

That much was true. It was his job now, helping.

Helping the Alicia.

He expected her to tease him, to say, *Some help you are, dummy,* but she kept quiet.

He could slap an answer out of her.

She threw her hands in the air and sighed, rolled her eyes, and it was too theatrical. It looked like she was playing a part. Bratty Sister. Angry Teen. He didn't know what to think—maybe she was being sincere. Maybe she knew better.

Maybe she knew what angry worm turned in his heart.

What—

Stay inside, he wanted to say. *Stay away. Keep away from me. There's something—*

But again he couldn't finish the thought. The hotel protected them—they'd been given free rent. By the next paycheck, they'd have actual savings. They each had their own bed. He'd been promoted. Good things were coming their way—finally.

The problem was all her. The suspension. The attitude. The questions.

"So nothing happened?" she said.

He shook his head. *Not a lie,* he thought. They didn't know what happened to Marisol, but that didn't mean anything, not yet. All they knew was that she had left her shift early, which people did sometimes, and if her boyfriend worried—well, who could fault him? Boyfriends worried. You worried for those you loved. You wanted them safe, you wanted them close. You wanted the best for them.

Carmen opened her sketchbook. "I've been drawing," she said. "Ever since we got here, I can't stop." She ripped out a page and showed it to him: an open mouth full of teeth revealing another mouth, another set of teeth. She waited for him to respond, to take the drawing from her, and when he didn't, she let it fall on the carpet. She said, "There's something wrong with this place. You have to talk to Jacob. You have to get us out of here. I can't stop drawing. There's something wrong with my dreams. We shouldn't be here. You know it. I know you. I know you love me. I know you care. I know you wouldn't—"

The phone rang. It was good that they had a landline. They'd save money on their cell phones. Carmen picked it up and said hello and put the receiver on the desk. "It's Ellie," she said.

Alvaro hoped for good news. There was none. Marisol had not gone back to her apartment, the roommates hadn't seen her, Umberto didn't know what to do. "I'll talk to B.," Alvaro said. "I'm sure it's all fine."

"What happened?" Carmen said.

"Nothing." He finished his sandwich. "Everything's OK. It's just a work thing. When are you back in school?"

She didn't answer. She pulled another sheet from her sketchbook and showed it to him: a hotel room at night, a broken flashlight in one corner, an indistinct pile in the other. She pointed to the pile. "I don't know what that is," she said. "I don't know why I keep drawing it. It's like my head's cracked open and all these things are pouring in. These *images*. Like someone's talking to me." She pulled at a hangnail, and the little San Agustín face she had drawn stared back at him. "Like we've landed in the middle of a conversation. I don't like that we're here. I don't like that we had to come here. I don't like that you won't talk to me."

"I talk to you."

She shook her head. "You don't. You think you're talking to me but you're not. Dad was bad, but you're worse. You think you know all these things, but you don't."

"I never said I knew *anything*," he said. "I'm just trying." He could open the door, he could go anywhere, he could leave her here. Didn't she know? He wasn't Dad, he wasn't supposed to do this. He wasn't supposed to be in charge. "It's—I'm trying, OK? I'm trying to get us out of here. I'm trying to find a way for us to do OK. For you to—"

"Whatever."

"Don't say that. Don't just say 'whatever.' Don't."

She shrugged and he wanted to smash his plate on the wall, to make her flinch, to make her see how unfair it was. It'd be so easy to hit her. Didn't she know, wasn't she grateful knowing that he *could*, that he had chosen not to? It wasn't any of his business what she did, what she felt. He wasn't much older than she was.

He put his hand out. Palm down. Conciliatory, calm. The hand of a person in charge.

He said, "You're not happy here. You want to go back."

"I don't," she said. "I know we can't."

"I know you don't want to be here."

She faced the window. The sun smeared the edges of the Fremont buildings. There were other buildings, there was life outside the Alicia, life and daylight, but they had to stay in the room and talk it out. She would realize he was right. He was keeping them safe.

He said, "We can go back. All we need to do is save a little money. We've got a chance if we stay for a little bit. You've got school, I've got a job." He put one hand on the wall. "We've got this room."

He didn't know if she understood how rare that was, how wonderful and weird. To get a free room? Just like that, without even asking? Some kind stranger just going, *Please, here, it's yours.* All he had to do was help out, take care of whatever needed taking care of.

Like the rot in the third-floor walls.

Or like the walls his sister had scrawled on. She had drawn even more roaches. She had covered the bottom half of every wall in the room with her drawings.

He hadn't noticed, not until now.

He'd been so caught up—first the shower, and then trying to avoid talking with Carmen, and then the talk, long and exhausting and pointless, because she couldn't see, she didn't understand. He thought she had stopped when he had woken her up the night before. She must have continued drawing this morning.

She drew cockroach after cockroach, a long and steady stream pouring out of the corner where he'd seen the single actual roach. Back in the extended stay, he had stumbled on a commercial for an exterminator where a bug crawled across the screen, and he'd been startled at his own disgust. He knew the bug wasn't real. His body responded anyway. Disgust jolted him—the urge to itch, to brush insects from his arms, to leave the room. His sister drew extraordinary likenesses. She had worked long and hard on the shells, on the shading, on the antennae. The bugs felt *off*, though, but he didn't know enough about the anatomy of bugs to know what was wrong. Too many legs? Something about the long pincers? He bent down to examine them in detail and expected the drawing to come to life.

"I'm sorry," Carmen said. "I don't know what happened. I got carried away. I don't know why bugs."

Maybe she'd heard. Maybe the old man (Jacob, the traitor) had told her.

Whatever.

He shook his head and let out a heavy sigh, like you would in the same situation. Nobody would blame you for being too theatrical. You'd worry, of course. Maybe your sister wouldn't believe you. You'd tone it down. Try to sound not so much angry as hurt. Disappointed.

"I'm disappointed," he said.

"I'm sorry."

"They'll take it out of my check," he said. They wouldn't. B. wouldn't care, wouldn't find out.

Her shoulders slumped. She wasn't crying, but she was quiet, and he knew that she was sad and ashamed, and he'd tell you that he felt no shame, no sorrow, no sympathy for Carmen. He felt nothing but pure, heartfelt elation.

"*Our* check," he said. "That's what we use to eat. What we'll need if we want to get away."

"I'm so sorry," she said. "I'll fix it. I'll paint it over."

He wanted to tell her that she'd done nothing wrong. There was nothing to fix. None of this was her fault, but the words wouldn't come out, and he wanted to apologize. For bringing her here. For making her feel guilty. For not dying along with their rest of the family. He wanted to tell her what Ernesto had told him, in that letter. That he wasn't knowingly a bad man. That was good. That he was trying his best. But the words wouldn't come out and what did come out was a long, choking sob—it startled him.

It scared her, he could tell. She flinched, shrank away.

She'd seen him cry before. He had cried plenty before and since their life in Colombia ended, but he hadn't done so for days.

Scared, still shaking, she was now close to him—Carmen, his sister, the only family he had. Now she hugged him. And it was awful. Awful to hug her and to cry and to not know if he was manipulating her or not, if he was truly sad or if it was all still part of the same ploy. To make her feel bad. To gain her sympathy. He didn't know, and he didn't know why she was so scared, why his crying disturbed her now when it hadn't before. All he knew, all he could tell you, was that he had not expected to sob, had not encouraged it. Besides, he was right. They had no money, nowhere else to go, and everything was mostly fine, everything would work out. Her dreams would subside. The walls would get painted over. Marisol would be found. All would be resolved. That's what happened in all the movies they loved. Fortunes were restored, the good rewarded, their virtue and lives untarnished. If they were changed, they were changed for the better. That's what would happen. Carmen would see. All would be set right because he loved her, and because he wanted what was best for her, what was safest. He said nothing and watched his thoughts, tried to follow the stream of words that wouldn't come out, the ones that rose and festered and broke through, bloody and violent, remembered the voice in the corridors, the voice speaking to you right now. *Someone else is talking,* he thought. *Someone else is thinking these awful thoughts.*

But who, if not him?

There was no one else to keep silent or to talk. There was no one else to blame.

CHAPTER 16

ALVARO WENT UPSTAIRS AS SOON as he woke up. He needed to find B. and couldn't reach him on the phone, so there was no way of knowing if he had heard about Marisol.

The penthouse office space was still dark, plywood still covered the windows, but the room buzzed with life this morning. Management moved about, the tails of their plum blazers struggling to follow, B.'s people stepping in and out of rooms and answering their phones. No Winifred in sight. She could help. He'd see her, he was sure—he'd spot her hair in the bustle, call out to her, it'd happen any moment. But she wasn't here. He didn't know anyone in this room, which was supposed to be mostly empty. The hotel didn't want anyone here: just the eyes of the flamingos on the murals, the plywood and the marble and the pink growth peeking through. People belonged elsewhere.

He heard a loud Texan laugh, the Yosemite Sam tie a flash of red between two heavy, half-open doors. He walked into B.'s office before the door closed.

"Dan's back at home, son," B. said. "He wants to thank you. He'd be here in person to do it, but we're all a little busy with the Cara group coming in. Did you see how we fixed it all? Go to the third floor, *poof.*" He swept his hands. "Like nothing happened."

Alvaro tried to smile. "I need your help," he said. "Marisol is missing."

B. fiddled with his tie and looked concerned. Tried, at any rate. B.'s heart wasn't really in it. The phone rang and B. made a show of ignoring it. *You,* the gesture implied, *are far more important than this clearly very important call.* The man ran his fingers along the blade of his tie.

The phone kept ringing.

"Marisol's a waitress," Alvaro said. "She was in housekeeping, but she's a waitress now. She's been missing since yesterday. Her boyfriend's concerned. He's worried about her. But he's also worried about the police. About Lost and Found and ICE."

"He's got nothing to worry about. Lost and Found are good people." He smiled and pointed at Alvaro. "I only hire good people. The *best* people."

"He doesn't want to get her in trouble," Alvaro said.

"I'll talk to them. They can look at the cameras, see if they can spot her. You've got nothing to worry about, son. Lost and Found, they're good people. They wouldn't call the authorities on your friend."

"They've done it before."

"Not under my watch, son." B. pointed at the still-ringing phone. "I should take this. Can you hang on?" He didn't wait for an answer. He picked up the receiver and didn't even so much as say hello. He knew whoever waited on the line. He listened, then reassured the voice that he was taking care of it, that they had nothing to worry about, that everything would work out fine. "I promise," B. said. "Not under my watch, no sir." He hung up, smiled, and ran his fingers over the cartoons on his tie.

The man in charge.

Alvaro said, "You asked me to keep an eye out."

B. smiled and winked. "You bet."

"There are problems," Alvaro said. "Mold eating at the walls. A door came apart. I don't know what it is but it can't be good, can it? You shouldn't be able to peel a wall with your hands."

"We'll get that fixed," B. said. "I promise you. We won't have none of that under my watch, no sir."

Every time B. said that, Alvaro believed it less and less. B. missed too many things, was too quick to reassure, didn't seem to register that there were serious problems. And it wouldn't do any good to insist. Insist and he'd just smile again, wink again, promise you that he was on it, that he'd take care of it, that you had nothing to worry about. That was B.'s job. The job of management. To lie. To pretend everything was fine even when it wasn't. The truth was that B. didn't know the hotel, didn't know what went on here, didn't know who went missing, who passed through. B. didn't know, didn't need to know, didn't care.

"How's your sister?" B. asked. "She better?"

Alvaro stared at the whorls of marble, his fingers numb. His whole body had gone cold.

Winifred must have told him, or the twins in their overalls who saw everything. B. must have found out about the sleepwalking. And the suspension. And her wandering the casino in the company of an old man. Things got around. Everyone here belonged to a family, after all. You kept an eye on each other.

"I hope she's better," B. said. "We really are glad you're here, son. We can use all the help we can get."

The phone rang again. It was time for Alvaro to go. He didn't know why he wanted to stay. He still didn't know why B. had kept him here, and he didn't know to ask, *Why me?* He wasn't sure he'd like the answer. Living rent free at the Alicia was a stroke of good luck. You didn't question that.

B. pulled out a pen, the same one Alvaro had seen before, the one misspelling the hotel's name. "Mold, fifth floor," B. said. "Got it."

"Third floor. Not fifth. Third."

B. nodded, wrote nothing down.

Alvaro said, "What's going on?"

"With the mold?" B. picked up the phone and pressed the hold button. "We'll find out. We'll take care of it."

What's going on with the hotel?

That was the question Alvaro had meant to ask. He could try asking again, but it wouldn't do any good. B. wouldn't answer. B. would talk, he'd keep talking, and they'd get lost, and whatever Alvaro would get would be not quite a lie, but nothing useful at any rate.

Ask anyway.

"I'm glad Dan's OK," Alvaro said. "I'm glad he's better."

B. clicked his ballpoint and waited for Alvaro to leave. The phone rang again.

"Your son was injured, one of your workers is missing," Alvaro said, thinking, *You said we were like a family.* "What's going on with the hotel? B., what's going on?"

"Nothing," B. said. "Nothing bad." He clicked and clicked again and ignored the ringing phone. "Why don't I show you? You'll see. Nothing bad." B. pointed at a spot on the great marble slab of wall and Alvaro missed what B. said next—*Follow me* or *Let's go*—but the intent was clear, because B. got up and Alvaro followed, and what looked for all the world like an ordinary section of an enormous marbled room was actually an opening.

You couldn't see it unless you knew it was there. Until it was shown to you. *A secret passage*, he thought, and remembered the ones he'd seen in movies. You turned a lever or jiggled a candelabra and a door glided open. Or you leaned against the wrong spot and the wall rotated, and you were suddenly elsewhere. You found the treasure, the catacombs, the secret laboratory, the torture chamber. You found the lost girl—or her skeleton.

You didn't need a lever in the Alicia. You didn't need anything. You just needed to know that the entrance was there, and that it waited for you.

B. smiled in the dark of the passage and winked. "You got nothing to worry about, son." He faced the darkness, the bulk of his back enormous. The sides of his belly pressed against the narrow passage. "The elevator won't go where we're going. The stairs are steep, and we can't get a light in here, not yet, but you'll be fine. Just watch your step."

They descended. The air grew moist and sour. Alvaro did his best not to touch the walls. He could not see, and while he had no way of truly knowing, he suspected that the same mold he'd seen elsewhere grew here. He imagined the mold ripening, breaking off into long strands, reaching for whoever made the mistake of coming this way. He could almost see the spores in the darkness and held his breath—he didn't want to inhale whatever the Alicia sloughed, her dead skin or her living essence.

B. told him to follow his voice. The passage grew byzantine—a left here, a right there, a set of suddenly steeper descents. Vinegar in the air.

Alvaro grew hot and sweaty and did his best to follow, to stay close to his guide. B. smelled like he had not showered in days. His body gave off a ripe, awful stench.

B. said, "Seattle wants an elevator built."

To where? Alvaro thought. *Where are we going? Why are you showing me this?*

If they fell, if they fainted—if anything went wrong at all—no one would find them. B. could turn around and kill him. B. could leave him in this labyrinth and he'd never know how to find his way back.

Maybe he wants to get rid of me, he thought. *Maybe I asked too many questions.*

He followed nonetheless, like he'd done on the road to Ibagué. Like people tended to do. Cattle. Sacrificial lambs.

Easy prey.

"Son? You all right?"

Alvaro remembered when he'd first set foot in the penthouse. The phone had rung. B. on the other line. The same ballpoint pen. He'd been asked to take a message. *Cara's worried.*

"Is this the passage Seattle was talking about?" Alvaro said.

"They got nothing to worry about is what I told them." B.'s breathing grew heavy. The poor man didn't get much exercise. "'No sir,' I said."

"Passage to where?"

"Almost there. You'll see."

━━⅏

They stepped into one of the Alicia's corridors. Alvaro's relief came mixed with disappointment. He didn't know what to expect, but he certainly didn't expect *this*.

More of the same. More hotel.

He'd tell you later that his problem came from not paying enough attention, from not listening hard enough to whoever whispered the same insistent warning. From not knowing you were there, we all were, our mouths open, our throats raw.

The hallway stretched longer than the ones on the floors he knew. He had never walked down this particular hallway, he was sure of that much at least. But it was just an unusually long passage, narrow and thick with the same bad, vinegary air of the passage he had helped Winifred open, but there was nothing he needed to see. B. was just wasting his time, leading him nowhere.

B. flapped his arms, both arms fully extended, and it was only then that Alvaro saw what B. had wanted to show him all along.

The floor didn't hew straight. It curved and rippled. The floor below them warped, the floral carpet dipped and rose as though following a hiking trail in a field. None of the doors were quite straight either. The doors curved and sank, the room numbers unreadable. They looked like numbers only if you didn't stare at them for too long. Corridors spiraled from the hallway and curved as he followed B. The floor branched off. Alvaro thought of ants and worms, of the paths they left behind, the homes they made with their mouths.

They had gone deep underground.

B. said, "We found these yesterday." He pointed at a fork where the corridor split into four cavernous openings. "They keep growing. The hotel's just making us more rooms. Isn't that a hoot?" He jerked his head up. "Plus, Seattle's doing this funny thing. See?"

Alvaro didn't, not at first, and then he did: strings stretched from the ceiling into the darkness. Someone had nailed the strings along, nearly all of them red—a single string was green. Green was the one that mattered. Red meant stop. Green likely meant a way out, back to the passage and the solid geometry of the world above. Light poured from what looked like the same fluorescent lights as the ones upstairs, but even the light felt counterfeit. And the strings—why strings? From B.'s description, it didn't even sound like B. knew. All B. knew, all B. seemed to care about, was that the hotel was growing, that it kept growing, and that they'd soon have room for as many people as they wanted. Infinite rooms. Maybe the pit would grow too. Wander long enough and you'd find a roulette table that felt soft and moist. Alive. Nothing would be straight or tooled. Nothing here would feel like what you'd find upstairs. They were inside something else. Something *wonderful*. Something alive and magical.

"You see?" B. asked. "You feel it?"

Alvaro could. The voice he heard inside his head was much louder, much clearer here, much more persuasive.

He couldn't wait to show Carmen.

She'd love it. Who wouldn't?

Wouldn't you?

But better to wait, better to keep this revelation from her until she was ready. She was so angry right now, and so afraid. Better to let her settle down.

━━━

They followed the green string back to the mouth of the original passage, and it was only then that he sensed how truly gigantic the Alicia was—how fast and how enormously it had grown in a single day. *I'm part of this growth*, he thought. It was why he was there. He had been chosen. B. had asked, *How's your sister?* She walked the same floors, breathed the same thick air. She was here too. With them. With all of us. She was part of it. He'd tell her soon. And she'd see—the promise of this place, its great and strange beauty. She had nothing to worry about. They could come down here, she could draw these wavering corridors and patches of live light. She could get it all down on paper. It'd be better than their time in the park, better than Colombia, better than anything. And they'd follow the green string home—back to their rooms, back to safety. You couldn't get lost. B. and the people of Cara had seen to that. All you had to do was follow your path. Such an easy thing. You did the same thing in large airports. You picked the right color on the carpet, on the tile, on the arrows—there were signs everywhere, you just had to know where to look. They were safe here. Taken care of. All was in order.

He heard a scream. Distant. A woman's voice.

I didn't, he thought. *I imagined a voice. Or I'm confused. I confused one thing for another.*

No one moved through this floor. No one knew they were here. The doors were still wet from their birth. No one living belonged this far below.

You *could* get lost. You could, if you didn't belong.

Alvaro said, "The waitress could have gotten lost in here." He coughed.

They had already taken a few steps up the original passage, the air just as moist and thick but nothing you couldn't live with. Not as bad as he remembered. Why had it bothered him so much? B. grunted, busy navigating their way up, his breath heavy with exertion. It was possible for Marisol to be down here. Maybe she'd wandered in by mistake. Maybe she'd heard a voice in the darkness and followed it down to the corridors, and now she was lost. Because no one told her to look up. No one said, *Follow the green string.* Maybe that's what happened, or maybe she had decided to leave her job and boyfriend and tell no one. People did that. You didn't necessarily have to assume the worst. People came, people left.

A part of him doubted the other. A part of him became convinced that he could hear Marisol asking him to come back, to find her. She had turned the wrong corner or opened the wrong door, and now she had no string to guide her, no room number to read, nothing to go on. She opened door after door and they all led downward. She stumbled down the roots of the Alicia and the lights that were not really lights flickered, and her screams grew more distant, harder to hear.

He stopped.

He didn't know if he had imagined those screams.

"You hear that?" Alvaro said.

"No," B. said. "Hear what? There's nothing down here. No one. Not yet."

"I'm going back," he said.

B. grunted, and the grunt felt like enough of an answer. *Suit yourself.* "Phones don't work down there," B. said. "They go off. You can't even turn them on."

"I'll be fine," Alvaro said. "I'll follow the strings. I'll find my way back."

But B. was no longer there, and Alvaro was not sure if he was talking to his boss anyway. Maybe he was talking to himself, or to Marisol, or to you. He was sure of one thing at least—the hotel wouldn't lead him astray. He was home. You couldn't get lost if you had already found your way home.

CHAPTER 17

ALVARO MISSED CARMEN. HE WANTED her next to him under the bad light of the soft corridor. She would see what he failed to see. She could draw the impossible geometry of the Alicia. She would guess why the place had changed, and she'd do so as easily as she had guessed why the albino goose followed the old man at the park. She was so quick.

He felt slow.

The sour air had shifted and thinned. It was difficult to breathe, difficult to move, but he moved all the same, keeping his eye on the red strings nailed to the ceiling. *I'm bound to find a work crew*, he thought. *Maybe they've seen Marisol. Maybe they've heard her.* Marisol had screamed. That must have been her voice. He was sure he'd heard a voice, faint and afraid, even if he couldn't quite bring himself to believe it. He was also sure that he had a job to do—that's why B. had brought him here, why he'd showed him the corridor (*Nothing bad*), and this was his fault after all. Marisol wouldn't have come here if—

We found these yesterday, B. had said.

Alvaro had not put it together until now. The Alicia had opened up her secrets right around the same time he had helped Winifred unlock the corridor above. *It would have been* directly *above*, he'd tell you—he'd insist—and when you asked him how he knew, he'd smile and promise you he'd explain, but that he had to keep going, because we were running out of time. How long did Marisol have? The unlocking of the upstairs padlock, the birth of these passages, Marisol's absence. He didn't have to tell anybody that he played a part. When he found Marisol, when he brought her back, she didn't need to know that it was his fault—that he played a part in her absence. Umberto didn't need to know either. Alvaro didn't need to confess. He just had to fix what needed fixing.

Did Winifred know? They had opened the passages above and had triggered *this*, whatever this was, below. This *growth*. This life.

The corridor splintered into four malformed fingers, each with its set of melting doors fading into darkness. He wouldn't follow any of those.

No strings on the ceiling, no way to get back. He shuddered.

She keeps growing, he thought.

He hadn't seen those corridors when B. had led him down this way. He must have missed them, and again he wished he had Carmen along—his sister, who missed nothing, who wanted out of the hotel. Even if the hotel had their best interests at heart. *Nothing bad*. Nothing to fear. He steadied himself. Carmen wanted out but she kept a cool head. She'd make fun of him for being such a worrywart.

She must be in their room, cleaning up her mess. How did you erase the insects? An eraser would smudge, and she didn't have paint. He didn't know how she would fix it. She said she would. She kept her promises.

You have to talk to Jacob, she had said, and he would.

Oh, he would. He'd tell the old man to leave his sister alone. She was young and troubled, and she could not sleep, and Jacob had no business telling her lies. Even if the lies were the truth. Carmen didn't need to know about the forest and their family. Jacob needed to understand that they had no one left, no one living, and the calls had followed him to Barranquilla, the voices had promised a reckoning, and so they couldn't go back. Colombia wasn't home. What he'd say to Jacob was what he said to himself—yes, he knew he had promised her they'd go back, but he needed to calm her down, he needed to buy some time, to make things right. And if Jacob didn't listen, he could choke the life out of the old man. It'd be easy. Jacob was frail. You could break his bones. You could pulp his face until it revealed its true face, the true face of us all—raw, red, wet, and soft. Better to punish Jacob than to admit failure. He wouldn't keep his promise to Carmen, they wouldn't go back, but Alvaro was in charge, and that's what you did when you were in charge.

Don't touch the wall, he thought.

He touched the wall.

He sank a finger into what looked like wood and paint and plaster. The corridor yielded, the stuff inside wet and spongy. He had torn a hangnail earlier in the week, he must have cut himself when he was prepping— nothing major, a tiny cut, it hadn't really registered—and he knew only because the stuff of the Alicia burned on the cut and the hangnail.

She's disinfecting me, he thought. His finger stung. The wall hissed as it took him in.

He popped the finger out when the wall sucked at his body. The wall had tried to pull him in. He hoped Marisol hadn't made the same mistake. The wall *wanted* him. It was hard to resist—he felt the same vertigo he'd felt anytime he walked along the edge of a cliff, when he was very high up and a perverse part of him told him to jump. He could imagine himself jumping, he could see himself doing it, and what frightened him most was how easy, how reasonable the suggestion sounded. *Why not jump?* And he *could*. He could dive into the soft walls, and where he'd go, how far he'd fall—he wouldn't know until he tried. He stared at the green string and thought, *You've been here long enough. They need you upstairs. You need to make sure Carmen's OK, and you need to help Ellie, and you need to talk to Umberto.*

He had only taken a few steps when he heard her again. He hadn't imagined it.

The sound was faint and distant, but unmistakable.

A woman screamed.

He followed the scream to a knot of corridors, each leading into darkness. The strings ended right before the black began, the strings dangled and brushed the carpet. B.'s associates had only made it so far, or the corridors were new, or the strings had been cut.

Cut with teeth.

With pincers.

He imagined the bugs his sister drew, the fat bugs with the wrong antennae, the bodies that moved like no bugs he'd ever seen. The woman screamed again. It didn't sound like Marisol, but he wasn't sure he could tell, if he could recognize anyone's screams—no one sounded quite human when they screamed. He imagined the bugs running over Marisol, Marisol trying to brush them off and screaming and one jumping into her mouth.

"I'm here!" he said. "It's going to be OK. I'm coming."

He stayed put and faced the darkness and didn't dare enter it.

The scream refused to die down.

No, he thought. *I won't. I'll die. I don't know what I'm walking toward.*

A light flickered to life, as if on cue, the corridor closest to him now visible. He thought he could see handprints in the murk of the light and the bulbs flickered, the darkness ate the edges of the doors and carpet, and the light waned, greenish and alive.

A light that wasn't a light.

A sign hummed, promised an exit, but the letters faded and a dark growth spread over the Plexiglas.

The scream was his mother's scream, his sister's scream.

He recognized their voices. He had never left the jungle, he was still there, and this corridor was a bad dream—a bad dream inside another bad dream.

He knew he shouldn't walk into the newly lit corridor, that it was a trap, that nothing good would come of it (*Nothing bad*, B. had said—B. had *promised*) but he found himself walking in the counterfeit light, and so it was no surprise, no surprise at all, when darkness returned.

The light died. He was too deep into the Alicia to double back.

He was already lost.

The scream grew louder. He followed the sound because he had nothing else to follow, and because he had to help.

If.

If he could help, he would. Even if it wasn't Marisol, he'd help. Even if he didn't know what to do. He walked and expected to stumble, to hit a wall, to brush an insect from his hand, or for the wall to peel off and stick to him.

The strands brushed against him, he didn't imagine the sensation this time, he could feel the mold on his arms and on the back of his neck, but he ignored it and moved toward Marisol, or toward what sounded like Marisol and also like his dead sister and his dead mother.

He wanted to let her know that he was close, that he was almost there, but he was afraid of what would happen if he opened his mouth. What would crawl in? He held his breath, he followed the swell of the scream, and stopped only because he was sure he was close, he was almost there. The woman screamed behind a wall or a door, she screamed behind the partitions grown by the Alicia, and the scream filled the dark with its urgency. Other sounds too. Rushing water. Skittering. He had to open his mouth. He had to reassure her. Calm her. He didn't want to, because he was afraid, because the bugs would stream into his mouth, because he could hear the bugs, not imagined now.

The bugs crawled over the bare sliver of skin between his pants and his socks. One crawled up under his pant leg, and when he brushed it off, it plopped wet and heavy on the ground.

The same bugs from above.

The pipes will burst, he thought. *They're going to burst again.*

The rustle and murmur rose. *She's in there*, he thought. *Alone.*

Not alone: the rustle of the insects drowned all other noises. They must have to crawl over each other. The room must be thick with life.

"Marisol?" he said. He found the door and felt for the knob—hot, sticky, soft—and tried turning it. He was about to try again when the screams stopped.

"Don't open the door." The voice belonged to a little girl, to a bad recording of a little girl—low and rough and wet. A girl with a bad cough or a fever. No one he recognized. He tried the knob again and his fingers dented the soft, warm metal. An overripe fruit. It wouldn't turn.

"Please don't," the little girl said. "Please don't open the door. You don't want to come in here. You can't. You don't want to see what's here." The little girl laughed. "There's *so much* here. And Mom's coming." The bugs skittered in agreement. "You don't want to be here when she comes."

He remembered the old man's warning. *Charleen. The mother.*

Charleen's going to come up anytime now.

He said, "Esther?"

What he heard in response was an awful sound, a great, ripe fruit hitting the ground. Another scream. You wouldn't know it was a little girl in there. He tried the door again and said, "Are you Esther?"

"That won't work," the little girl said. "You're just making them angry."

Esther's SPECIAL things.

He said, "Where are we? What is this?"

"You're in the dream," she said.

"I'm awake," he said, unsure.

"The dream of the Alicia. She dreams and we all dream with her."

"I'm not dreaming."

"We all are. We dream what she dreams, all of us who serve her, me and my mom and Jacob and your sister and you."

"I don't. I'm not."

"Mom's coming."

"Charleen?"

"She's been looking for you," the little girl said. "She has a knife and a smile *just for you*. She *loves you*. She says she loves your whole family. We're all a big family down here and we *love you so much*, we've got a song for you in the Nightmare Room. A song for you. A song for your sister. A song for Alba too. She's been looking for you for *so long* and now you're here, and Mom will be here soon. Don't open the door. Don't move. Stay here and we'll sing, we'll all sing together."

The insects grew louder.

He could feel them crawl by the door. All you had to do was follow the river of sound. There were more of them. If you ran, you'd step on them. You'd burst so many of their fat, little bodies. Try not stepping on them. Try being considerate.

She had not said she was Esther.

Who was she?

"Don't open the door," she said again. "You don't want to be here. She's coming, she'll be coming down the mountain, Charleen comes round the mountain with a song and a knife."

"I'm looking for Marisol."

"I know who you're looking for." The voice was low, rough, wet. "You're in the wrong place."

"She's a friend. I think she might have gotten lost. Is she in there with you?"

"No one's in here."

He tried the knob and remembered Umberto, remembered sinking into the rot of the doors aboveground. He could do the same. He could sink into the Alicia and never come out. He could disappear, and would that be so bad? Would it be awful? Would anyone care?

Carmen would.

Your sister. The sister who lived.

Charleen's got a song for her. A song and a knife.

"Let me in," he said and pressed on the soft wall. The wall stuck to his fingers. "Let me out."

The little girl laughed. "That's not how it works. That's not what we want. That's not what the Nightmare Room is for."

Don't ask, he thought.

"Tell me a story," she said. "Tell me a story and we let you go back, back to your sister and your friends. We come for you later. We let you live a little longer. We'll come for you and your sister. Tell me a story about your sister. We come to you with our song and our knife and our friends. Tell me a story, big brother. Tell me a story and put me to sleep."

He should run long and hard and fast. He should put as much distance between himself and the room, the little girl in the room, the little girl and her mother (*You don't want to be here when she comes*), the mother and her knife. Run long enough and you'd find light, maybe, you'd find a way out, find the green string again, make it upstairs—

And leave, he thought. *We go as far as we can. We get away.*

But he leaned into the door instead, and he pressed his body once again into the soft, quivering tissue of the hotel, and it stung this time—it hurt—and he screamed his way through the pain, and the moldy fabric stuck to his lips and licked his throat and nostrils, and it didn't matter, because he had to break through, because the little girl could be lying. Marisol could be in there. He needed to help. That's why he was here.

He had made a promise.

The wall yielded.

The room glared, sullen and empty. Twin beds. The wallpaper half-torn. A TV that once sat on the lazy Susan had been thrown to the floor.

It could have been his own room, for all he knew. The rooms all looked the same. The windows were open, and he could smell the Fremont air— the burnt rubber and the exhaust and the hot breath of wind blowing in—and it took him a moment to realize that he was no longer underground, that he had burst into the daylit world, and that he was alone.

No little girl here.

The note on the bed read, "Esther's SPECIAL things."

Esther's room. The third floor.

He looked under the bed, but Marisol's photo was no longer there, and neither was Marisol. He expected the old man to come back—to tell him he better go, that Charleen was coming and he didn't want to be here when she made her way to the room, did he? He'd say what he had said before. Stuck in a loop. He felt a void in his stomach. But there was nothing to fear, nothing be afraid of. He was alone, and the air was the air of the city, sour but nothing like the belly of the Alicia. He just needed to get back to work, back to the café, he needed to finish his day and to figure out what he and his sister would do next, how long to stay in the relative safety of their lodging, his work, before fleeing.

They couldn't stay, not for much longer, not here. *Nothing bad*, B. had said, but B. didn't know. Worse, B. didn't want to know.

Alvaro found himself arguing with the room, talking at the walls. "We're fine," he said. "We're safe." He held himself like his father did—his right arm crossed over his chest—and he shivered, and didn't know why he talked, didn't know why he needed to hear himself talk, and he realized that he'd found Umberto, mad with grief and despair, in the exact same place the day before—

The little girl stood in the corner closest to him, her dress long and floral and nothing a little girl would wear. Not in this century. Not in Vegas.

A bonnet obscured her eyes. Her smile gleamed in the daylight. She had so many teeth.

"You're not looking," the little girl said. "You don't know. I told you not to come in. You made us a promise. In the forest, you promised. Will you give us what you promised?" The girl pointed at nothing. "You won't. You will. Why pretend you won't? You're not ready yet, and *she's here*, Mom's here, can't you see she's here?"

She pointed at the carpet.

A bug crawled and turned its bulk from him, each leg rising and falling to its own otherworldly rhythm.

When he turned back, the little girl was gone.

She was never here, he thought.

She couldn't have been. The voice was the same, but he had imagined her—of that much he was sure—and he wanted to shake off the sight of her as badly as he wanted to clean his hands and legs, which still stung with the remnants of the mold. He wiped his arm and tried to get it clean and nothing worked. He walked and realized he had failed—he had not found Marisol, he had learned nothing of her whereabouts, and he despaired when he imagined what he'd tell Umberto and Ellie, what'd he'd have to hide from Carmen so she wouldn't worry. He was so consumed with guilt that he failed to register the change in the light until he was already in the elevator—it felt thicker, gauzier, as though the weather had changed and threatened rain. It never rained in the city. You never saw a cloud.

The thick light followed him into the café. No windows had been built this deep into the Alicia. In the kitchen, Clarabelle sat in her usual spot, barking joyously, welcoming him back.

His sister was there too. Carmen sat on the floor and petted the sweet brown dog, and Ellie stood by her side, both of them now running to him in the heat and bustle of the kitchen, their faces so relieved and so full of happiness he could only smile, he could only hide his dread.

Why was his sister here? What was wrong? Why was she so *happy*?

They closed in on him, they were already by his side, they had already made their way and he had somehow missed their transit. He blinked and they were there.

Something's wrong, he thought. *Something's wrong with me.*

His sister clung to him and cried with relief.

He was afraid they were going to ask where he'd been. He didn't know what he could say. He didn't know what lie he was going to tell them.

CHAPTER 18

UMBERTO TURNED AND WAVED, HIS station aglow with flames bursting from two unidentifiable pieces of meat. Alvaro tried to wave back, even though Carmen hadn't let go, didn't seem ready to let go.

He felt lighter than he had in days, like his brief time underground had removed a part of him that was bothersome and unnecessary.

He blinked again and the kitchen staff had changed places. Everyone had shifted. His sister had stayed put. She sobbed and clung to his shirtsleeve.

Marisol must be back, Alvaro thought. *That's why Umberto's here, why he's so happy.* And that was why his sister had made her way to the kitchen. Marisol's return would explain his sister's expression, her joy and tears and relief. But Carmen didn't know that Marisol was missing. He'd kept that from her. Carmen hadn't even met Marisol.

His sister felt too thin—she had the bones of a bird.

"Where have you been?" she said. "We called." She sobbed. "We called and we called and we called. We were so worried."

"Everything's fine," he said.

Ellie stared, her eyes wide and tired. "We couldn't sleep, your sister and me." Ellie's forearms, he noticed for the first time, were considerably darker than her hands and wrists. The Vegas sun had tanned her skin, but the carpal tunnel braces safeguarded part of her.

He had been lost in his thoughts, only now aware of how tightly wound he'd been, and only because he felt relief.

Finally, something good had happened. Marisol was back. Marisol was fine, he was sure, and not below, not screaming, nowhere near the little girl in her Nightmare Room. About whom he'd need to tell B., he supposed, if he ever found B. Management needed to take care of her, or B.'s Seattle partners and their labyrinth of strings. They could get the little girl out. He himself had emerged unscathed from the bowels of the hotel. The Alicia had kept him safe. He had nothing to fear and so—

We couldn't sleep, Ellie had said.

Carmen smiled, her breath rank from a morning of worry.

A morning and a night, he thought. *A full night's worth of worry.*

She was red eyed, her lids heavy and smeared with eyeliner.

He had been gone a day. He opened his phone to confirm. It was Tuesday now. Yes. He had gone downstairs with B. and emerged twenty-four hours later. *It felt like nothing*, he thought. *I blinked and I was back.*

But the new light—the light in Esther's room—was wrong. And the trail of corridors were just as wrong.

The kitchen and the people in it, mostly strangers, insisted on everything being fine, so maybe he could work on forgetting, on letting go, on remembering he had his own set of troubles to focus on. His own family.

"Everything's fine," he said again, and he believed it. "I got a little lost, but I'm fine now. Everything's going to be fine."

Carmen wiped her mouth. "Don't just leave," she said.

Now you know how it feels, he thought.

He said, "Umberto's here."

Ellie patted her apron and smiled. "He says Marisol called. She's sick with the flu and she'd gone to CVS. That's why we couldn't find her, hon. She'll be back soon, he promises. Soon as she's fit."

The kitchen bubbled with new orders, new people, and new life. He remembered the man he had mistaken for Umberto, who looked exactly like his friend. *Maybe that's not really him*, he thought. *Maybe it's the other one.*

Umberto thanked him again. The order he had put on the grill turned black and burst into flames. *Must be him.* You work next to someone, you get to know them. He'd worked next to the tall, cheerful, clumsy man for weeks. You got used to a person's tics. How they sat and held themselves when they told you their story, for example, or how he knew you stared at his hands, counted his fingers, when you thought he wasn't looking. You'd know that person anywhere. The real Umberto stood before him.

"She's fine," Umberto said, "but she had me so worried. I kept thinking that the hotel swallowed her up, ate her up, but she is fine and she wants to thank everyone for their concern. She says to tell Lost and Found, no worries. Tell the boss too. No worries."

Those are my words, Alvaro thought. "*Swallowed.*" "*Ate her up.*" Or the Alicia's words if not his own. The voice in his head that was not his voice—the voice of the hotel. The Alicia shared her dreams, her thoughts—the voices in the corridor, the voice of the little girl behind the closed door. The voice intruded, oily and gleeful. Bloody as the muzzle of the dog when he'd be done with her. Bloody as the face of his sister when he'd be done with *her.* Unrecognizable. The voice speaks to Umberto. The same words. The same violent message. *Will you give them to me? All of them? Will you?*

"Get to work, Galán," said the kitchen. "We got orders."

"Don't leave," he told his sister.

Umberto wouldn't look at him. They each faced a mountain of tickets and prepped their share of meat and onions, they cracked eggs and scrambled them on the grill, all while Alvaro tried to keep an eye on Carmen. She could leave at any moment. Lose sight of her and she could vanish. She didn't. She stayed close to Clarabelle. She wouldn't leave his side, not now. She wouldn't dare. She wouldn't wander, wouldn't go away, because now she was afraid, it was all over her blotchy face—and what a relief to see that fear. *I could leave you*, he thought. *It'd be so easy to leave you.* Just walk below where we all waited, all of us ready and willing to receive you. Carmen tracked his every move. She wanted to make sure he didn't wander, didn't go away, and he wouldn't, of course he wouldn't, even if it'd be easy to do so. Easier than all other alternatives. Ellie had loaded a tray with food and darted into the café. Alvaro was already behind. Catch up. He squeezed water on a sausage patty and the bottle nearly slipped. The morning shift was going to prove heavier today than ever before. So many people came in, all of them hungry and impatient, and it was his job to keep them full, to feed them, to get their order right. It was so easy to get the orders wrong. As easy as lying to your own sister. Again he thought of Ellie and how she had helped him, how she had helped Marisol.

Alvaro said, "What's Marisol's number?"

Umberto busied himself with pancakes.

Alvaro asked again. He kept his eye on the burning meat and on his anxious sister. "I should call her. I'm so happy she's OK."

"You don't need to do that," Umberto said. "She'll be back tomorrow. You can tell her in person."

They had managed to get their orders out, but six tickets waited, they were so behind, and so it was best to say nothing.

Carmen leaned against the sickly green tiles. The dog panted by her side. Umberto could set her on fire, he was so close. What Alvaro felt he could not put into words, not his own anyway, because even the shimmering voice drowning the part he recognized as himself—the real him—shivered.

But nothing's wrong, he thought. *Why be afraid if everything's fine?*

He said to Carmen, "Go to the room."

Carmen wouldn't budge. She was stubborn, like the rest of their family. Like him. Like everyone except little Alba, who always got along, always wanted to get along, never gave anyone any trouble. Alba, who proved stubborn only at the end.

Ellie said, "Go, hon. I'll keep an eye on your brother."

Don't just leave, Carmen had said.

People left all the time. They came and went, lived and died. The biggest thing that could happen happened all the time, *would* happen to all of them sooner or later. *Don't just leave.* His sister understood. Lose sight of your family for an instant and you wouldn't see them again—they'd be changed or gone. Carmen didn't want to go, but he wanted her back where it was safe, where he wouldn't have to think of hitting her, of slapping all the worry and love out of her until she was as clean as a sacrificial lamb. A pleasing offering. Better that she be out of sight. Out of the way.

Ellie said, "You can sneak Clarabelle into the room too, if you don't mind." She handed the Lab a treat. "She's not supposed to be here." Carmen hugged the dog and the dog chomped away at her food with joy. The kitchen was always full of smells, and now the smell of wet dog was part of the mix. Ellie put on her braces. "You'd be doing me a favor," she said. "Please?"

Carmen snapped the leash on the dog. Alvaro thought of the homeless man again. (*Bought the leash with honest money. Bought it at PetSmart.*) Carmen didn't hug him again. She kept a wary eye on the kitchen as she took Clarabelle's leash and followed Ellie. Alvaro took his eyes off the grill so he could track their progress. Ellie and Carmen and the dog hunched and darted. They crossed the café, Ellie blocking their transit from public view with a tray—a heavyset, middle-aged woman and a teenage girl and a big dog doing their best to be invisible, to not get in trouble, and everything in him ached to follow. To make sure the elevator took them to the right floor. To make sure Carmen kept herself safe from harm. That was all. It wasn't much, was it? That was all he wanted from the Alicia—to keep him and Carmen and his friends safe.

Ellie came back, her tray empty.

The café bustled. They had so little time, he should cook as much as he could before Winifred came back—before she and B. wrangled him into something else. Before the hotel reclaimed him. He'd lost a day. The protest was happening, but he couldn't remember if it was tomorrow or the day after. Maybe it had already happened. He needed to help. Poor Ellie. It didn't look as though she'd slept. *I haven't even apologized*, he realized. He knew the weight of worry, and he hadn't even thought of that weight on Ellie until Carmen was gone, and now Ellie was too busy, and he couldn't pry the half-formed thought that had lodged in the back of his head—it had been kept out by the bustle, by the insistent but wordless presence of what he guessed was the Alicia, though you couldn't tell, you couldn't know for sure, and by his sister, and by his own fatigue, which only registered now. He couldn't stop yawning.

Keep to the order. Turn the meat before it blackens and smolders.

But the thought had arrived, fully formed.

Umberto's lying and Marisol's here, she's lost in the Alicia and—

Better just to cook and leave things be. Marisol would be fine, and he didn't want to confront Umberto, didn't even want to turn and face this man, *really* didn't want to know why he would lie. Worse still, he didn't want to go against the hotel's wishes. The building wanted silence. Another want intruded, a force that belonged to something else, and it coated his every thought. He didn't know what it was, this dream that the Alicia dreamed. Didn't have to. A place changed you—a city, a neighborhood, a hotel. A story. You arrived to each with your own fear, your own hunger, and you found yourself taking on the cast and the appetite of where you were. You couldn't help it. *Better to let the Alicia have what she wants*, he thought.

Say nothing.

"Why are you lying?" he asked.

Umberto pretended not to hear him.

"Where's Marisol?"

"Why are *you* lying?" Umberto replied, spatula a blur. He played with the burning meat. "Why don't you tell them where you were? What you found? Why do you lie to your sister?"

"That's different." It was. Alvaro was trying to protect Carmen. He didn't know what Umberto had done, but Umberto wasn't protecting anyone, certainly not Marisol.

How we must have looked, he'd tell you: The men worked side by side, each busy with his station and neither able to get any distance. Was

Umberto as repulsed? Alvaro itched. He wanted to brush an insect from his arm, but there was no insect. There was just this repugnance that settled on his limbs. How awful, to work next to someone who kept a secret from you, someone who knew what secrets you kept from those closest to you. Umberto smirked. *Fuck him.* "I'm going to management," he said. "I'll tell them. I'll tell Lost and Found. Tell me where to find Marisol or I'll tell them you're involved. They'll call the police. They'll call ICE."

Umberto's expression did not change.

He's a good man, Alvaro thought. *He loves Marisol. He's sweet, bumbling, he wouldn't harm her. I know him.*

You don't.

"You won't," Umberto said. "You won't call anyone. *I'll* talk. I'll tell your sister."

"Tell whoever the fuck you want." Alvaro dropped his towel on the pile of rags and said, "Tell them everything." He thought of Dan and the rotten mushrooms.

Fuck this place.

He walked to the pit. He'd find B. or Winifred. Get them to fix what needed fixing, find Marisol. Call in the proper authorities. He didn't have to walk far.

A cluster of plum blazers gathered and talked on their phones and pointed at the corridor that he and Marisol had reopened. Clumps of new people streamed in, but they bottlenecked where the overhead lights blared yellow, so their faces pulsed with a sick, sallow glow. The crowd gave off a sweet, heavy smell, and the AC couldn't quite keep up with the trapped heat of so many bodies.

He knew he should have stayed in the kitchen, because more orders came in and the staff needed all the help they could get, but he had to talk to B., he had to let them know that Marisol was still missing, and that Umberto was involved. Umberto was lying. They needed to find her before—

Before what?

Something was coming. Something *awful* was coming. He could feel it in the walls, in the air, in his bones, in the chaos of his own thoughts, which he didn't quite recognize as his own anymore.

He could even feel it in Winifred's face. There she was, in the cluster of blazers, pretending all was fine. Her face saying otherwise. The rictus of panic. *There's no one at the helm because the Alicia steers herself.* He waved at the red hair, at the unlit cigarette dangling from her lips (she'd help, he was sure, she'd get him to Lost and Found, she'd help him find Marisol), and he kept his mouth shut when he saw why management was panicked.

Eight pale men hovered by the roulette wheel. They wore fleece and tapped on their smartphones. Alvaro had never seen them, but he knew who they were. They presided over the staff of the Alicia as though they owned them.

Because they did.

The people from Seattle had finally arrived, and they did not look happy, and Winifred looked genuinely afraid, and so he swallowed his own fear and moved toward them, and walking helped a little. It made him realize that he had ignored the worst part of what Umberto had said.

Why don't you tell them where you were? What you found?

Umberto knew about the Alicia's undergrowth, that much was clear, but he also knew that Alvaro had made his way below, which meant that she—the hotel, the thing that spoke through the hotel—talked to Umberto. Talked to everyone. *We're hearing the same voice.* He found himself listening once again, but he couldn't make out the words, he could hear nothing in the noise of the casino, and that was the problem. That was what he and Umberto and everyone here kept forgetting: the hotel had things to say, and they kept listening, even if they didn't quite know what she said, what she wanted from them, though she very much did *want*. You couldn't escape her hunger, and you couldn't stop listening even if you didn't realize that you were listening, and that you had been listening all along, and that you had been nodding, had been agreeing.

That's what Winifred was saying, what he heard as he walked toward her.

"I hear you," she said to the pale men from Seattle. "I hear what you're saying. I hear you."

CHAPTER 19

"BUT YOU DON'T." SAID A pale man in a black turtleneck. "If you did, we wouldn't be here."

The man had shaved recently, his neck red and raw. Angry bumps dotted the skin, and when the man scratched, Alvaro caught a glimpse of his neck tattoo, words in an old-fashioned script that looped and curled around the flesh. The man could not stop scratching. Alvaro followed the whorls as they dipped in and out of view and then resolved into a readable phrase: "Serve all, save none."

The man was too pale for Vegas, his skin clammy, freckled, and doughy. Press your finger against it and the indentation would stay in place.

The other men in the group were also built for the Pacific Northwest, strangers to the heat and sun of Nevada, uncomfortable in the recycled air of the yellow pit. They wore too much fleece. They checked their smartphones. They frowned. They scratched at their skin.

They all had the same neck tattoo.

Winifred cocked her head and smiled. "Steven," she said. "Steven? You've got nothing to worry about. The passages are all open, everything's fine."

"I don't think you're hearing me." Steven looked like he wanted to cry.

Winifred's posture was fixed. Her smile too. She dropped her cigarette and didn't pick it up. A band of sweat shone high on her freckled forehead. A terrified woman, doing her best to look not at all terrified.

"I promise you," Winifred said. "We've got everything under control."

She extended her arm. Alvaro recognized the intent of the gesture. She meant to pat Steven, to reassure him. *Touch him and he'll scream,* he thought. Her hand remained just out of reach. "Isn't that right?" she said, nodding. "Don't we?"

She won't touch him, he thought. *She can't. Touch him and the indentation will stay. He's uncooked dough. There's something wrong with his skin.*

With him.

Something wrong with all of them.

"Alvaro?"

The pale men were all looking at Alvaro, as was Winifred, and it was only because he had the foresight to nod when Winifred had been nodding that he had a moment to catch up, to realize that she was addressing *him* now, and that he was expected to offer reassurance.

"We're on it," Alvaro said, sure that he was lying, and that Winifred was lying too, also sure that the hotel had just swallowed more of his life. Whatever troubled him below troubled him still. He missed cues, time skipped, he daydreamed blood and hurt, he wasn't quite himself.

People spoke and he did not listen.

Steven tapped on his smartphone. "Because they're saying the locks aren't in. And no one's finding passages where the oracle promised us passages. The passages spring elsewhere. The tributes can't find their way. Our sacrifices are nowhere near on target. We follow the oracle and chart the growth and we protect the new passages, but nothing's on target. Nothing. And you can't speak for the person we need to speak to. We need to hear from Melmot. Where is he?"

Winifred's smile stayed in place—wide and dazzling in its beauty, and wholly unconvincing.

Better not to say anything, Alvaro thought.

"B.'s here," Alvaro said. "On his way for sure. I saw him just now."

I saw him a day ago.

Alvaro had no business lying, he had no business here at all, but he needed to help Winifred, and he saw an opportunity. He could help Marisol. He pointed at the lurid yellow blare of the ceiling. "He's up there."

Steven craned his head, his neck stretched taut—the skin all rash, the words unreadable and bloody.

"He's up there," Alvaro said again, growing more assured. "He had to deal with some missing waitstaff."

"Not a sacrifice?" Steven said.

Alvaro shook his head and thought, *Oh no. No. None of us are. All of us have sacrificed enough.*

Winifred said, "B. made that clear. No one on staff, none of us. The contract made that clear."

Save none, read the tattoo.

"It's the locks," Steven said, his eyes brimming with tears. "The locks and the path. Stray from the path and you'll get lost. You'll run into the retribution. Melmot kept his people from the path and so they have nothing to fear. They will be rewarded. Spared. They need not run into the children nor the mother. They need not worry." Steven cried now, his face transfixed with joy. "They need not worry," he said again. "They need only rejoice. They are here to witness her awakening, to see her through and tend to her needs. To see that she is kept in check. Which she is not." He glared at Winifred. "She is *not*. She grows. She stirs when she is supposed to slumber. She dreams. Why does she stir? Why won't you hear me? Where is Melmot? Why is she so engorged? Why has he let her go unchecked?"

"Melmot's coming," Alvaro said. "We've all been busy looking for someone. Marisol Ramirez. She's lost."

"She's not," Steven said. "No one's *lost*. Not yet. You are not listening, none of you. Your friend is here." He pointed at the ground. "We know the paths, we have set the guides. We know who strayed from the path. Your friend strayed. Where is Melmot? We have looked and we have called and nothing. What is he hiding?"

Winifred could no longer hide her dread, her face damp, her mouth pinched.

Alvaro grew less afraid, more sure that he was in control, though he'd tell you now he wasn't sure at all that it really was him. Maybe *her*. The Alicia. Who else could be so confident?

"I can take you to Melmot," he said, "if you can help us find Marisol."

Steven nodded—a man sold on his power. A man whose every wish was granted, whose assistants gathered and tended and said yes, all the time yes.

No one says no here, Alvaro thought. *Not to him. He'll believe anything.*

Alvaro motioned for them to follow, and the group walked away from the pit. *I'll get caught.* He led, his heart steady, sure that he could string them along, that Steven would believe what he told him.

They moved along the service corridor that ran parallel to the pit. Everyone missed it but the staff, who used it when the elevators jammed and you needed to make your way around, and Alvaro hoped that if he traced a circuitous-enough route, he'd stumble into Melmot or he'd figure out how to get what he needed from Steven. Maybe B. really was in his office. They'd get there, eventually. If he wasn't in his office, surely he was in the secret arteries of his own hotel. *He's hiding. You won't find him. Melmot's gone. The captain's left the ship and no one's at the helm because the ship steers herself.* They'd find him in the green recesses of the penthouse between the rotting marble and the stained plywood.

If Alvaro could deliver his boss, the men from Seattle would help him find Marisol. *That much was true*, the voice inside him whispered. That much he could count on.

There was hope. He'd find his friend, he'd be redeemed.

Maybe that was why when he heard footsteps, he found himself smiling at Steven, whose cheeks shone bright with tears. Steven had not bothered wiping himself dry. The group followed Alvaro, and he followed the sound.

The corridor was wet, slick with mold, the smell sour enough to make Winifred gag. Alvaro stared at the floor. Pink and black strands coated the carpet. The men from Seattle wore hiking sandals and the kind of gear you'd wear if you were out in the mountains, in wilderness. *They don't belong here*, he thought. *They don't know how to dress, don't know how to move, how to breathe in the heat.* That was why they scratched and tore at their own skin. They didn't belong. The Alicia didn't want them.

Their steps grew louder, their rhythm odd and clumsy. Strange. Strange, too, that he was so sure of what he was doing, that he had somehow roped a group of people, Winifred included, into following him to a dark corner of the hotel, and stranger still that his plan had yielded a result.

Melmot was close. Alvaro knew that much even if he could not explain how or why. You could believe in the truth of your own lie. He believed in nothing right now. No one. He couldn't even trust his own eyes. He blinked and people shifted. His thoughts too. He didn't know B.'s but had found him anyway, had lied but turned out to be telling the truth, he had guessed right, he'd gotten lucky.

No, not lucky.

He'd been told. The Alicia had taken care of him, had poured her secret voice into his ear. *I'm hearing her*, he realized. *Even when I don't know what I'm hearing, when I'm pretending I don't know, when I'm sure I don't understand her. I'm hearing her all the time. I'm listening. I'm doing her bidding.*

"Here he is," Alvaro said.

A form emerged from the void of the corridor.

"Thank you," Steven said. "Oh, thank you."

The form lumbered and leaned against the wall, and the men from Seattle frowned when the figure finally came into view.

"Wrong Melmot," said Steven.

Dan was finally back. He leaned on crutches, and he'd put on a dress shirt and a tie, but he wore sweatpants, with his shirt untucked, and fresh stains spread over his attempt at a work outfit. Dan spit on the floor. He balanced a can of Skoal and a Diet Dr Pepper bottle between his crutches, the bottle sloshing full of spit. The rubber tip of the crutch missed the edge of a stair and the boss's son nearly fell. Dan grew pale.

"Dad's not here?" Dan said. "He said to meet him here."

Steven turned to Winifred and whispered. She shook her head. She put another unlit cigarette to her lips. Alvaro couldn't believe that these people were in any way responsible—that they were in charge, that he depended on them for his checks and his livelihood and any chance of he and his sister doing well. But here they were.

Alvaro said, "B. said you'd speak for him."

Dan nodded, and so did Steven, and Alvaro wondered if he had gone too far, if there would come a time when he'd get caught. They'd figure out he knew nothing, had nothing to give them. All he had were words. Lies. All he had was what he could not say.

Tell me a story.

Will you give them to me? All of them?

Here is what Alvaro saw before he realized what was going on: Winifred's cigarette in midair, Winifred's mouth open and aghast, the squeak and scuttle of sandals, the stain on the steps, the peculiar smell of the hotel, the ring of his cell phone at the worst possible moment, and he hoping it wasn't Carmen, not now, wondering how the Alicia had even allowed a call, Steven's chin dotted with blood, Steven turning and thanking Alvaro once more (*Thank you! Oh, thank you!*) and Alvaro hoping Carmen would hang up, because it *had* to be her, hoping, too, she wouldn't call again, because he didn't want her connected to the men from Seattle, to Steven.

Here is what he knew: a key cord had been severed.

Time had skipped once more, he'd tell you. He lost those crucial seconds as easily as you'd lose your keys or the thread of the story or the reason for why you were hearing it in the first place.

He had lost a minute. He had blinked and everyone had shifted again. It hadn't been a problem before. He could fake his way through the gaps, people could talk and he could pretend he understood, but no one was talking.

He didn't know why Dan was sprawled on the floor, why the crutches lay useless against the wall, why Winifred looked like she was screaming though she made no sound, why she put her hands against her mouth and forced herself to keep silent. He didn't know why the men scuffled uneasily in their sandals. A raw, keening howl filled the corridor. *That's Dan*, he thought. *Dan's screaming.*

Dan coughed blood onto the floor and the sound continued unabated, so it wasn't him.

The sound came from Steven.

Alvaro couldn't tell you why Steven keened, why he howled, why he wouldn't stop making that awful, inhuman sound, but he could tell you what he learned: the man from Seattle screamed when he beat the living shit out of another human being.

Steven was not done. No questions now, no tears, no speeches. Dan's blood coated Steven's sandals and sockless feet. Dan's leg had given out again, a dark stain where Alvaro remembered bone and tissue laid bare, and Dan crawled—tried to crawl—but he had nowhere to go. Steven jammed his foot on Dan's neck and Dan's head cracked against the floor. *So much bone*, he'd tell you, tapping his own head with fingers you could not stop counting. We have so much bone up here. Not enough padding. Something else had broken. Something else had given way.

He'll die, Alvaro thought. *Let him.* He owed nothing to Dan, nothing to the Melmots.

We'll come for you and your sister, Esther had said.

Will you give them to me? she had said.

The same girl in a different continent.

The hotel pulled at his insides. You could not put it into words, though words bubbled to the surface of the blood, the viscera, the hunger for what you kept safe inside, the thirst for blood—Dan's, his family's, everyone's. All of us a potential sacrifice, yourself included.

Steven served the hotel, and the hotel served Steven.

No one said no. No one told the tattooed man to stop. Steven pulled out a small knife from his fanny pack, Alvaro close enough to read the brand etched on the handle. X-Acto. *Charleen's got a song for her*, he remembered. *A song and a knife.* Steven held the knife to Dan's ear and cried, and Alvaro thought of all the awful secrets he kept deep inside himself—what he could not say to Carmen, what he could not admit to himself. That he was a coward. That when he was afraid, he did nothing, and that he did nothing to save his family. That he gave Alba up so he could live. And so now Dan would die. The part of him that wasn't him shrugged off Dan's death. As would you, because whose fault was it, really? You didn't know him, he wasn't family. Let him die.

Let him.

"You've got B. already," Alvaro said.

They'll believe anything, he reminded himself. They were too sure of themselves.

Steven stopped, knife still in hand, fanny pack unzipped. The men from Seattle could kill them all. No one would know. Carmen would never know what happened to him. Steven stood much shorter than he'd initially appeared, his rash much worse—it looked almost infected. It glowed. The smile he'd come with was still intact, teeth bared, a dot of blood on his chin. Dan's blood. Poor Dan. What was important now, Alvaro realized, was that he not lose more time, that he not let himself be pulled into the dream of the Alicia. He willed himself present. He took in the entirety of the man in front of him: Steven's cruelty and insanity, Steven's certainty. *Tell that man anything and he'll believe it.* The knife drooped in his hand.

"That B.'s not here, that he's elsewhere," Alvaro said, "is not important. You know that. You've got him. He serves you." Alvaro pointed below, as Steven had done, and it was a wonder to see Steven's reaction—to see how easily he fell into kinship, to realize he didn't know that Alvaro was just parroting the man's own gestures, the man's own words. Even the words of the tattoo. "Serve all," Alvaro said. "Save none."

"None," Steven said, crying still and nodding. "*None.*" He returned the knife to the fanny pack and zipped it shut.

Dan gurgled.

It was awful to be that close to someone in pain. Dan needed to go back to the hospital. He needed an ambulance.

More awful still was the necessary task of ignoring Dan. Alvaro had to focus on Steven, had to let Steven know that Alvaro could deliver what they wanted.

Dan tried to stand up but slipped on his own blood. It was disturbingly easy, Alvaro would tell you, to leave a fellow human being on the floor. You could ignore their pain. You could let them bleed. Alvaro had done so before. Ignoring the pain of others opened a window into your own body, and you felt a vertigo, an automatic empathetic rush, all while your heart squeezed into itself—it wasn't unpleasant. Dan wasn't family. He was just a crumpled body, a body in pain, and Alvaro was trying to help, and the only way he could help was by pretending he did not care, even if a part of him truly did not care.

"I can take you to B.," Alvaro said. "I told you that. I gave you one Melmot already. I can give you the other."

Steven's face glowed wet and pale and red. "She speaks to you," he said, placing a blotchy hand on Alvaro's shoulder and squeezing hard.

Winifred shivered. She picked up her cigarette from the ground and took out a lighter, and one of the men from Seattle stopped her, his hand a mess of welts.

"I have asthma," the man said, his neck a bright red.

"She speaks to me," Alvaro said. That at least wasn't a lie. "Esther too."

"The Daughter speaks to you," Steven said. "That is marvelous. Marvelous news. The Daughter speaks to few. She speaks to none of us. We sacrifice but she speaks to none of us. Only the Mother. The Face Beneath the Face slumbers. But the Mother speaks. The Mother and Daughter reward us." The tears were tears of joy this time around, and no less frightening. "The Daughter keeps silent."

"Take me to Marisol, help me find her, and I'll give you B."

Steven turned to the asthmatic, and the man tapped on his smartphone. "We have forty minutes, tops." He looked at the angry welts on his wrist.

"That'll be enough," Steven said.

"We'll need Dan," Alvaro said. "You won't get B. without Dan."

Steven scratched, wouldn't stop scratching, a gesture that felt like begrudging assent. *Dan gets to live, fine, whatever.* The men from Seattle were pressed for time. Winifred too. Winifred who kept herself from her penthouse desk. Winifred in the café, with her graphs. Winifred who did her best to stand as far from the orbit of the Alicia while still being inside. *Winifred doesn't want to be here, and Steven and his people can't stay, not for long. The hotel won't have them. They're an alien substance. A bad graft.*

Winifred said, "We need to call a doctor."

Steven pulled at a chunk of the wall. It yielded, pale and pink and translucent, and he jammed the stuff into the moaning, crumpled heap that was Dan. Steven forced Dan to swallow a handful. The stuff quivered and shivered as it wormed into Dan's mouth. Steven jammed heaps of the sour living jelly into Dan's other wounds. Alvaro began to understand why these people worshipped the Alicia. The hotel—the stuff that composed the hotel—spread and insinuated itself into all of them. *Me too,* he realized. *It's inside me.* They were all infected. The jelly flowered into hundreds of strands, bristling and alive, and slipped into Dan through his wounds. Alvaro thought of spaghetti, he thought of fungi, but mostly he thought of underwater creatures, the kind that never saw the light of day.

That's the Alicia, he realized. *That's what we're in. We're in her and now she's in Dan.*

She's in all of us.

Dan no longer bled. The jelly hissed as it fingered its way in. Dan screamed and grew calm. The jelly had burned Steven's hands—they were a bright red now, as though they'd been scalded—but it did the opposite for Dan. It *healed.* It saved. It was a balm, even as it hurt Steven and the other men.

Alvaro helped Dan get up. Dan, hoarse, said what sounded like *thank you.* That he could talk at all was a miracle. Alvaro found the crutches and wiped the rubber tips with his kitchen apron so Dan wouldn't slip on his own blood. *Remember to clean the apron*, he thought. *Get a fresh one. Don't go into the kitchen with blood. Don't infect anyone.* The jelly bristled in Dan's quickly closing wounds. The jelly stuck to Dan's lips in thin strands that wormed their way around split skin. *The Alicia healed*, he'd explain to you. *She helped her own.*

But Seattle worships her, he thought. *Why does she hurt them? Them and not us?*

Why does she love us?

Winifred said, "I can help Dan."

"I'm fine," Dan said, his voice weak. "I'll help Alvaro. I want to find Dad. We find Dad, you leave us alone, yes?" He turned to Steven.

Steven tapped a blotchy finger to his blotchy forehead and smiled.

Dan said, "I'll help."

Winifred lit her cigarette. "Fuck."

"Don't smoke," the asthmatic said. "Please don't smoke. It's *rude*."

"Fuck it," Winifred said. "I'll come too."

Steven's rash had crawled to his cheek. Alvaro didn't think they had forty minutes. The men from Seattle needed to step outside right now. They needed to breathe air that the Alicia had not touched.

Every corridor thick with spores. Every breath thick with the particulate matter of the hotel.

Dan limped along, Winifred steady in her heels.

"The protest's tomorrow," she said to Steven. "Let's find B. Let's get all ready for what you all want tomorrow."

"Marisol first," Alvaro said. "You tell us where she is. Then B."

"We flew here because it was time," Steven said. "Because Melmot lets her run wild, and so she grows engorged." The man practically glowed, an incandescent red, his skin so inflamed it pulsed, but his smile dazzled. When he patted Dan, there was a madness in the air like none Alvaro had ever witnessed. Dan winced, yes, but he also smiled, as though Steven had not tried to kill him earlier. Dan would pay. If they could not find the father, Steven would take it out on the son. The son smiled anyway.

"We'll find Dad," Dan said. "I promise."

A sacrifice.

Alvaro thought of Abraham.

What God wanted was what the Alicia wanted, what Steven wanted too: your own flesh and blood. The people you loved.

"Your friend's below," the asthmatic said, glaring at Winifred. "Follow me and we'll find her."

"How do you know?" Alvaro said. "We follow the strings?"

The man tapped on his smartphone. "We got cameras, motion sensors." He swiped with a swollen finger. "We know who's here and who isn't. When She lets us see. We can't see right now." He ran the red finger down and up. "But when She lets us ask, we ask. We asked. She answered, the Mother has. Your friend's below."

Winifred said, "Didn't you ask her where B. was?"

"She won't say."

"She doesn't know, or she won't tell you?"

The man walked, his breath laborious. "She won't say," he said again. "But you know. You'll say."

Alvaro followed the asthmatic man, and Dan followed Alvaro. Winifred trailed. Steven and the other pale men stayed behind.

Dan's breath was shallow. He sighed with every step.

As they made their way deep into the hotel, a fat fist plopped onto Dan's shoulder—a cockroach too fat and oddly shaped to be a cockroach. A bug like no bug they'd ever seen. Dan yelped. Alvaro brushed it off Dan's shoulder and it fell onto the steps with a wet thud and scrambled out of sight. The narrow corridor rustled. Insects scattered. A sandstorm. A rustle of twigs and leaves. The asthmatic pointed the light of his smartphone at the ceiling. But there was no ceiling. What they saw instead was an ocean of insects. Bugs crawled over each other and dangled inches from their heads. Dan yelped again. Winifred too. The asthmatic gasped and said that there were too many, that if you wanted any proof that Melmot was slacking, that he wasn't doing his job, the ceiling was proof positive.

He poked at a bug with the phone and the bug tried to crawl onto the glass. Alvaro thought of poor Marisol. She must be somewhere below, and they needed to find her, finding her was all that mattered. How else could Alvaro make things right? How else could he be forgiven? *No, really,* he tells you, and when he tries to grab your hands, you flinch. How else? Dan's angry sobs, the end result of the pain and grief and now disgust—Alvaro didn't know what to do, what to say, what comfort to give. Neither did Winifred, who kept quiet, who did her best not to breathe the thick sour air. Alvaro couldn't tell Dan that it would be all right. Dan was a mess, and Alvaro couldn't tell him the truth—that he'd seen worse, that Alvaro had actually felt better now than he had in months, that he'd stopped crying for no reason, that he no longer grieved, that he dreamed when awake, and his dreams shared the blood-soaked lust of the Alicia, that Dan had no idea, none whatsoever, of how bad things could really get. They walked beneath the crawling insects.

"Welcome back," Alvaro said.

CHAPTER 20

THEY FOLLOWED THE RED STRINGS past the insects and into darkness. The strings had multiplied, so before they lost their light, Alvaro saw a knotted, dangling red mass—a giant cut open, its circulatory system laid bare.

They were sure to find Marisol, the asthmatic explained, because the Alicia couldn't lie. The hotel—the thing beneath the hotel—took everything literally. "You'd think that was a problem," the man said, pointing to his phone. "You'd think language would be a problem, interface would be a problem, but code doesn't lie either." He wheezed and took in the damp, sticky air. "We can't talk to her, but the app can." Alvaro wanted to tell him that his sister was a gifted programmer, that she was in a magnet program, but he resisted. The less Seattle knew about him and his family, the better. The man had grown silent, as had Dan, even as Winifred continued to curse, to remind them what a terrible fucking idea this was. She wasn't wrong. Better not to think about Dan's injuries or the asthmatic's neck. The neck had turned a dark purple before the Alicia completed extinguished their lights. The app functioned, barely. A sickly glow. The man's skin too.

They walked and followed the man into a warm, sweaty chamber.

I'm inside a fever.

This is the inside of a sickness.

"She's here," the man said.

Dan said, "Are you OK?" Dan himself sounded awful, but his voice had grown stronger while the asthmatic's had weakened.

The man from Seattle had barely squeezed the words out, and everything about the voice was worrying: the words came out tight and constricted, failing. *We'll never find our way back if he stops breathing*, Alvaro thought. They didn't even know the man's name. If he died, who would they tell? He must have a family, someone who cared for him. Everyone did. Even these weird, pale creatures whose skin the hotel blotched— these men were loved, someone loved them.

"What's your name?" Alvaro asked.

"She's here," the man said again. "Stay put."

They couldn't see, couldn't tell if the man was telling the truth, because they stood in absolute darkness, the rustle of insects filling the room.

"My name doesn't matter," the man said. His voice had grown so faint it barely rose above the insects and what had just disturbed the insects. "Steven doesn't call us by our names. To spare us from the Mother. Stay put. Don't say anything."

Alvaro turned. He heard Dan and Winifred turn as well.

They faced the source of the sound—a bare limb brushing against a wall, he imagined, or a hand rubbing against another. Something wet too. A trickle of water. Some kind of liquid. Nothing like the bursting pipes.

Maybe it is, though, he thought. *Maybe something will burst.*

Maybe you.

A hand brushed his hand, brittle as a leaf. He gasped but kept quiet.

Don't say anything.

The asthmatic said, "Give these to your friends. Hold on to them. Don't move."

Alvaro did. He hoped Dan and Winifred would be able to hold on to whatever it was they were supposed to hold on to, but there were no guarantees—not with Dan's crutches and not with his recent injuries, and Winifred couldn't even hold on to her cigarette. Whatever they each held was no bigger than an index card, and it crumpled easily, and he could tell Dan was nervous because he rustled the little gift he'd been given. Winifred kept quiet and cool. Alvaro wanted to tell Dan to keep quiet, to remind him that they had been told to hold steady, but that's when a light bulb flicked on. You could hardly call it a light, it was so wan and erratic, this ghost of a light bulb.

The asthmatic stood by a pale-pink wall. His finger rested on the light switch. Insects crawled over the man's sandals and sockless feet, but he ignored them. He also ignored the insects that burrowed and transited inside the walls, which they could see because the walls had grown soft, translucent, and wet. *That must have been the sound*, he thought. But liquid barely dribbled from the pores of the walls, so the sound must be coming from elsewhere. The asthmatic placed his swollen finger over his lips. *Shush*. Alvaro nodded. Winifred sucked on her unlit cigarette. Dan hyperventilated. Alvaro wanted to tell him to calm down—to keep quiet—until he saw what had transfixed Dan.

The Alicia can't lie.

The hotel had not led them astray. They had found Marisol.

He knew they had found her because the skin from her face had not been removed, not yet, though the woman in the blue tracksuit closed in on Marisol's cheeks, her X-Acto pulling at a long strip that curled from the neck and ripped at the back of Marisol's ear. *That's Charleen*, Alvaro thought. *The mother, that's the mother who comes round the mountain with a song and a knife.* But Charleen wasn't singing: she had short blond hair, a pursed mouth—the room that was no room, the room that moved around the hotel. *The Nightmare Room.*

Marisol's clothing lay in a red heap by the strips of skin. Her apron, her pad for orders—they'd been set in a tidy spot. Neatly arranged.

Charleen didn't stop doing her work when the lights were turned on. She went about her business. Her tracksuit's sleeves grew darker and wetter even as they all stood in horror and watched the woman flay Marisol.

You don't want to be here when she comes.

That's what she wants to do to you, he thought.

That's what she wants to do to Carmen.

That's what we want, what all of us want. You too. That's what we want from you, this little red gift.

It's what we want from everyone.

The ribbons of skin piled knee high in the corner. The pile shifted. A ribbon slid from the others, the whole pile glistening from fat and tissue and blood. The ribbon dropped onto the floor. A bug crawled, its pincers tight around another lopped piece of Marisol. Nothing you could identify. Charleen had said nothing, had not turned around, and only then did it occur to Alvaro to look at what he held. An index card, the word "INVISIBLE" stamped on it. He remembered Esther's room.

FAMILY BIBLE. Hymnal. A SOOTHING landscape.

Esther's SPECIAL THINGS.

Charleen worked at the skin behind Marisol's ears. The body of his friend slumped, but her limbs had locked—arms and legs extended and stiff. Like she had no joints. Like she was a mannequin. Her eyes were closed, her mouth open. Most of her hair was lopped off. *Her hair's in the pile,* he realized. *The bugs took it already.* Her scalp shone bright with bone. Charleen broke her silence and starting humming as she went on with her work, and it was awful to recognize the melody, the theme song to an ancient sitcom—awful because he remembered that Alba and Carmen watched the show with him when Dad was in grad school and they all lived in Ohio, the winters never as bad as Mom insisted they were, all of them safe and warm in their tiny room in Akron and in thrall to the one TV station they could get, which played programs cancelled long ago.

Charleen knew nothing of this, of course. She knew nothing about him. But they shared the same taste in TV, because here she was humming the theme to *Three's Company*.

Come and knock on our door, the words went. *We've been waiting for you.*

But Charleen had no words.

Her humming was as mechanical and jerky as the swing of her arm when she cut into Marisol's neck. Most of Marisol's skin had been removed, everything but the face, but that was next.

Charleen's been waiting for you.

Waiting for you with a song and a knife.

This song was the wrong song, the knife the wrong knife.

He'd been dropped into a world that was close enough to pass for his own, but nothing in it behaved like he expected it to. What could he do for Marisol? He could watch. Keep still. Keep silent. He would have to tell Ellie. He would have to tell Umberto, who had lied and said that Marisol had spoken to him, who said she was fine. He had lied or he had been lied to. *The hotel called Umberto*, he thought. *The hotel took on Marisol's voice.* The hotel swallowed Marisol's memories, her photograph. The Alicia took all of it in. All of Marisol. How it must hurt—to die, to feel the bite of the knife, to know that you were far from home and loved ones. How no one would know.

Marisol opened her eyes.

She opened her eyes and stared at the room and her mouth contorted in fury. The wet muscles of her neck tensed. The bugs startled into motion, as surprised by Marisol as Alvaro and Dan and Winifred and the asthmatic were. Marisol's mouth opened and the long, brown feelers of an insect emerged, followed by the insect itself, a fat bug that stretched the lips thin with its bulk. Others followed, a steady stream of insects carrying forth pieces of the dead girl—nothing Alvaro could identify. All he knew was that the pieces, bloody and black, belonged inside the body, and that nothing could live, nothing could be allowed to live in that condition, with no skin and no viscera. Marisol's eyes were beautiful. Hazel, like Alba's. He had never truly noticed them before—how light they registered, how close to green. Even in the dead light of the Nightmare Room, her eyes were beautiful, and the eyes scanned the room and there was no terror in them, nothing but fury, and the sound she tried to make must have been a scream, it must have been something like a scream, but it was stopped short at the windpipe, and from her neck another insect pincered out. *It's giving her a tracheotomy*, he thought, *so she can breathe*. The dead thing that had been Marisol insisted that it was alive. It made a sound that passed for a scream and that's when one of them finally broke.

Dan screamed.

Marisol's teeth had been mostly removed. A few remained. She smiled at Dan.

So did Charleen, who turned and held her X-Acto high, the tip capped with a shred of skin. Charleen, the mother, scanned the room and tilted her head and looked for all the world like an insect herself—a creature of impulse and stimuli. *Knock on her door. She's been waiting for you.* But she couldn't see them.

Marisol could see them just fine, though, and she tried forming words, and the wet, taut muscles of her arm tried to point, but she had no strength, nothing but a rage that felt close to ecstasy. Because her mouth contorted into a scream, but she also smiled. At them. At him.

At Alvaro.

Charleen fixed her gaze on the source of the sound—on Dan, quiet and shivering now—and she took a few steps his way.

Marisol kept her hazel eyes on Alvaro.

I'm sorry, Alvaro wanted to say. *I'm so sorry.*

Marisol tilted her head.

We're coming.

We're coming for you.

We're coming for you and your sister.

He recognized Marisol's voice, though it had joined a chorus. It was the voice he heard in the corridor, when he was with Winifred, the voice of the hotel and the thing beneath the hotel.

The Face Beneath the Face.

Yes that's us me you yes.

Hello.

Hello we've been waiting.

Whatever stared at him through Marisol's eyes was no longer Marisol herself, though she was still there—a part of her was still the same, and it was that part that was angry. He had let her down. He had betrayed her somehow. He had let her die.

I am so sorry, he thought.

Waiting for you.

Open up.

The thing that had been Marisol hissed, the air coming out through her toothless mouth and the hole in her raw throat. There was no forgiveness to be had, nothing to be gained from talking. There was no one to save.

The asthmatic took a step back and motioned for them to follow. Winifred was the first, her index card bent tightly around her cigarette. Marisol tracked them, her skinned hand flapping, the bones and ligaments and muscle bright with blood. Bright and beautiful. How wonderful it was, to see it all laid bare. What was inside them all. Inside his sister. Inside Clarabelle. You could so easily uncover these truths. All it took was a knife. A knife and a song and a human body. How these bodies failed us all. The asthmatic's face was as red as Marisol's flayed body. Alvaro had been allergic to the dust of the Barranquilla tennis courts when he was a child, and the man's face reminded him of his own skin when it was inflamed—puffy and red, the eyes reduced to slits, the neck engorged and pushing into the face. The man scratched his ballooning cheek and it bled. That thing that had been Marisol rejoiced. An insect crawled over the man's red foot and over his hiking pants. *It's going for the blood*, Alvaro thought.

We all do.

The bug crept to the man's neck and sank its pincers into the red flesh. The man grimaced and kept silent. Other bugs joined the crawl in a long, slow line. A funeral procession. They climbed the man's pants. They moved so easily, so efficiently.

Marisol's eyes burned with joy.

The man twitched, his whole body convulsing, his hands jerking open. His card fluttered out of his hands, the stamp clear and legible as it made its gentle descent. An errant leaf.

"INVISIBLE."

Charleen saw the man, but she kept the tip of her knife on Marisol's chin, and leaned in for a kiss, and her lips collapsed into worms. Alvaro thought of shredded paper, of jellyfish, of spaghetti. Charleen's mouth split into a live flower. She breathed and shivered life into Marisol's open, ecstatic mouth. He kept his grasp on the index card and willed himself quiet.

Winifred too.

Dan clambered away, the crutches landing on the skittering rush of insects and making a sound equal parts wet and brittle. *He can't run away,* Alvaro thought. *Charleen will get him.* Charleen turned her head in Dan's direction but did not move, and the man with the swollen face, the man from Seattle, the man who was being eaten alive by bugs—he stayed as still as he could, even as Charleen became something other than Charleen. Even as Charleen melted into herself, as her eyes and mouth wormed into the air. Even as Charleen took her first step toward the man, and even as the bristling appendages that flowered toward him licked at the air, hungry, and even as Marisol herself convulsed into a mass of openings and filaments. The air hissed with the wicking and slashing of the two things that were not Marisol and not Charleen. The air flicked and chittered.

The man kept quiet. He fell to his knees and raised his arms, his red face rapturous, *grateful,* his lips so plump they could pop if you touched them. *Save none.* Insects covered his legs, a living carpet.

Alvaro brushed the insects off the man's pants. Winifred hissed, shook her head, jabbed her hand at the exit. "Leave him," she mouthed. "Let's go."

Alvaro pulled at the insect that sank into the man's neck, but the thing held fast, the other appendages wrapping around his own fingers. The pincers stuck to the skin of the neck, they wouldn't let go, so he cracked the feeler loose. *You could do that,* he'd tell you. You could absolutely kill these things. *Don't lose the card*, he thought. *Remember you're invisible. You've always been invisible.* And he doesn't laugh, doesn't sound like he's making a joke, when he tells you that it's never changed—that he's always been invisible, even to you. He was prepared for Charleen to lunge at him. He tensed and waited and thought, *We'll die anyway. I might as well help.* He had waited on the road to Ibagué and done what he was told and his family had died. It was a bad idea to listen, to do what you're told, to believe the people in charge, the ones who convinced themselves that they knew what they were doing. They didn't. Look at them. The man did not resist, did not pull away, did not help himself, and the worms of Charleen licked the air and came ever closer, and Alvaro thought, *Winifred's right. We should leave. We have no business here.*

Dan had already left. Winifred lingered by the door, horrified. Stay a moment longer and you'll be alone. They'll leave you here, because that's what people in charge did. That's how management moved about the world.

And so Alvaro helped. He pulled the man to his feet. Was he breathing? The man gasped, his hands clawing at the swollen neck, at the place where the insect had torn into the flesh. The neck bulged around the punctures, and that the man could walk at all was a miracle, that he could breathe, however poorly—that, too, had no explanation. Also without explanation: why the bugs narrowed in on the man.

Alvaro and the man walked into darkness, Winifred somewhere ahead, and Alvaro did know if the mass of worms followed—if Charleen and Marisol hovered close or if they stayed and finished their work. One wasn't done with the other. Human skin still remained on Marisol's face. Charleen and her knife could have returned to their work. Sometimes he felt them close, he imagined the brush of the wormy appendages on the back of his neck, and he felt the cold weight of their bodies fast on his back. They walked so slow, the man could barely walk, even as he guided them to safety, the sick glow of his phone offering a flickering map. Arrows. Warnings. Winifred pressed them on. Again he thought:

The insects wanted him. Not us. There was something odd in realizing that the hotel, the thing beneath the hotel, had preferences. Had likes and dislikes. It disliked Seattle. *Because they use her,* he realized. *They groom her, they worship her, but they use her all the same.* The bugs worked in concert with the Alicia. Parasites. He had walked into an ecosystem. He was part of it now, and so were the Melmots and Winifred and the men from Seattle.

The asthmatic guided them, but he could only squeeze Alvaro's hands or tap his shoulder, correct him when they headed the wrong way by pulling at his shirt, and Alvaro tried to imagine how Dan would find his way out. Tried to and failed. You couldn't. Not without help. They moved so slowly. Dan wandered deeper into the Alicia. Into the darkness. On crutches. *I keep leaving people here,* Alvaro realized. *I bring them down here. I gave them Marisol, gave them Dan.*

"Stop," the man whispered, finding his voice. His phone shone on the ceiling and revealed a mass of green strings, wet with mold.

"You need to leave," the man said. "Both of you. Leave me here. You need to leave and take your loved ones with you. Let Steven know that the Mother cannot be controlled, that She is waking up and cannot be put to sleep. Let him know that no sacrifice will do. I don't know what happened, why she swells." He tapped at his phone. "She no longer hears us."

"Why do you—" Alvaro wanted to ask why the men worshipped The Alicia, but stopped himself. "Why do you talk to her?"

"She calls us like she called you. We sacrificed like you sacrificed. She rewards those who make offerings."

Winifred said, "You profit?"

The man nodded. "Wealth. Long lives. We lose our names but gain a century."

"What does the Alicia want?" Alvaro said.

"Nothing. The Alicia slumbers. It's that thing beneath the Alicia that *wants*. Hungers. That's what you hear, what we all hear."

Winifred fiddled with her cigarette. "You give her people."

"Stories." The man coughed. "We give her stories. She wants our secrets. Our names, our memories."

Alvaro said, "What is this? Where are we?"

The man coughed again.

"Who gives a fuck?" Winifred said. "Seriously. Fuck this place."

"It's not a place," the man said. "We're not anywhere. We're not in a place. We're not in—" The man coughed up blood, mucus, a long, ropy strand of mold. Black and pink. "She's inside us. All of us are infected. You too." The mold bubbled in his lips. "Your dreams. The voice you hear. Your dreams of violence. Your guilt. What you won't tell her. That's what She wants. She *knows*. You hide the worst from her. She wants your secrets."

Winifred's mouth pinched. Her hair moved.

What terrible thing did you do?

What terrible thing are you hiding?

"Winifred?"

"Nothing," she said. "I've done nothing, OK? Let's go. You heard him. Leave him."

Alvaro ignored Winifred. He carried the man.

He expected the voice of the Alicia to thank him, but he heard nothing, and it was no surprise that he heard less and less from the man as they made their way into a corridor that looked familiar—a corridor that looked solid enough to pass for a real space, even though the light was bad and the ceiling was festooned with broken clumps of red string. It felt real enough.

The man had led him to safety and no longer moved, no longer breathed. His eyes were open. Alvaro closed them. *I should find someone*, he thought. *I should tell someone.* But he had no time, he no longer had time to be kind to people he did not know. Winifred took the man's phone, and Alvaro thought of grave robbers. But she was right. Now that they knew what they had to do, their priorities were simple.

"I'm finding my sister," he said. "We're leaving."

"What about B.?" Winifred said.

"We have to leave."

"Get your sister to safety, fine, but help me, OK?" she said. "How are you going to get out of town? Get B. to cut you your last check and you can leave. You think you're going to *walk* away from this thing? Do we even know how big it is?"

It's inside us.

You.

All of us.

You can't outrun it.

She said, "Help me."

"We're leaving," he said again.

They had to get on a bus and go. But Winifred was right. They had no money. Carmen could not know what he had seen. The less she knew, the better. The less he knew too. None of this was his business, and it troubled him, that he'd be so eager to stay, so *hungry* to stay, and all it took was Winifred's words, even as he doubted the words fully belonged to Winifred. *Inside all of us.* He had no choice, though. Not *his* choice, no one else's, even as the voice troubled the back of his mind—that he listened to the words that belonged to no human, that the Alicia whispered and suggested and he did her bidding, they all did, Winifred included, even when they resisted. Even when he was sure he was doing what was best. He had to think of Carmen. He had to keep her safe. He thought, *We still have the room at the extended stay. We paid till the end of the month.*

The light dimmed. Insects poured from unseen holes in the wall and were already hard at work on the body of the nameless man. Alvaro could barely make out the swollen foot in its sandal with its odd set of straps. "Keen," the logo read.

Insects covered the logo, they poured fast onto the body, and Alvaro wished the dead man well and left him to the corridor, grateful for the man's help. Troubled too. Because the man had served Steven and the others from Seattle, and whatever happened—what happened to Marisol, what could happen to Dan, who was now lost, what was happening to them all—the asthmatic man had been part of it, he and Alvaro and Winifred and everyone in the Alicia, all of them enmeshed, and all Alvaro knew was that he had to get Carmen to safety, that he had to do it before anything else happened, before he heard the voice again, before he felt the Face Beneath the Face deep inside him, and before the voice shifted inside him. They left the body behind, and he tried to shake off the thought of Dan on his crutches, alone and terrified.

"I'll be back," he said.

Winifred lit her cigarette.

"I will," he said. "I'm not lying. B. will cut me a check, yes?"

"If you find him," she said. "Big *if*. We can do it, though. We can do this if we work together. Get these morons off our backs. Then we run. We get the fuck out of Dodge."

"See you in the pit." He ran to his room, afraid he'd find it empty. Afraid he'd open the door and see no one there, his sister gone. Or changed. *All of us. All of us infected.* He remembered Marisol's wet, red body, her beautiful, inhuman eyes. How she hungered. How she screamed, though she had no voice and no teeth—no soul. How she resembled nothing he'd ever seen, live or dead.

Here is what he knew, what he learned: the more he tried to resist, the more he tried to leave, the more he hungered to stay, the greater the force that kept him in the Alicia. *Save none.* They had nothing keeping them here, nothing but the voice that told them to stay, the voice that assured that the hotel had been waiting. All this time, across great distances, it had been waiting.

CHAPTER 21

CLARABELLE BARKED WHEN ALVARO KNOCKED. They were still there, still safe. The relief didn't last long. The dog sat alone in the room, barking, and whining. No trace of Carmen.

The beds were neatly made, the shades drawn, the room bright. It was still day somehow. He didn't know if daylight meant he had not been below for long or if he had been there the whole night. He didn't know, didn't know why he wanted to check, didn't know why he yawned even as he panicked, didn't realize that a part of him was trying to remember the last time he slept. He had dreamed of Alba, Carmen had woken him up, and now Carmen was gone.

He expected their room to be ransacked. He expected a broken door and blood on the walls, but their space was untouched. And empty.

"Carmen!" he said.

Clarabelle barked.

He kept saying his sister's name while he checked the bathroom and snapped open the shower curtain. Nothing. He checked under the bed. Even her backpack with its hand-drawn whorls was gone. She was playing a trick on him. A practical joke. He'd show her. The moment he saw her, he'd slap her face, throw her to the ground. He'd leave her here. Abandon her. Let her bleed into the mold of the Alicia. His eyes burned. What a horrible joke. And what a horrible joke his whole life was. "Not funny," he said. Why did she want to mess with him? Why did it all feel so familiar?

He'd lived it before. This anger, this crouching under the bed—he'd lived through it already. Whoever doing it now wasn't him. An actor on a set. A movie on a loop. Why would she leave? How could she leave Ellie's dog behind? His sister wouldn't do that. She loved animals too much. She wouldn't do it.

He checked his phone. Nothing.

He texted, "Where are you?" and waited.

Charleen could have dragged his sister across the corridor. The shivering worms that flowered out of Marisol's red limbs could have pulled her apart. Jacob could have taken her. She could have been taken somewhere by a dirty old man and—

And so now he shook, now he found himself with his hands over his mouth.

She doesn't know. She doesn't know this place.

What it can do.

What it can make you do.

He couldn't breathe, as starved for air as the man he'd left behind. What the hotel didn't know was that Carmen had to be OK. Nothing bad could happen to her. Nothing could happen because she was lucky, preternaturally lucky, and she was fine, he was sure of it, she—

Dead.

She's dead, she's with us, she's fine.

Fine, he thought. *She has to be. I'll find her.*

Slow down. He couldn't help anyone if he panicked, if he forgot to breathe, if he was close to tears. If all he could do was pet a dog. Clarabelle whimpered in sympathy. *Good dog,* he thought.

"Carmen is fine," he said.

Clarabelle panted and whined.

The dog padded to the closet door. Which he had missed. He looked everywhere twice, he had called out her name, and he had missed the obvious. He did that. He did that when he stopped thinking. He didn't see what was in front him. *Maybe I'm dreaming.* He opened the door and imagined a world where Marisol was fine, where the asthmatic had never led him below, where the walls of the Alicia stood as solid and trustworthy as they pretended to be. Nothing lurked, nothing crawled. Everything was exactly what it looked like.

Carmen hid in the closet.

She had shrunk herself to nothing in a corner, draped in the deflated pool toy she had used as a bed at the extended stay. For one awful moment, he thought she was dead, that someone had killed her and covered her body, but then she moved her face when he called her name again. She flinched. Her arms locked. Just like their father. Like him. He'd never seen her do that. Usually she drew when she was upset, she held her sketch-book like it was a fucking shield, like it could protect her from the world, but now she gripped her arms tight around her, hand clenched over the locked elbow, and he thought of Dad—his kindness, his worry. How Dad lied when he told them it would all be fine. How Dad believed his own lie. Alvaro said her name again and he shivered. The vinyl's red underside colored her skin and for one awful instant he remembered Marisol's flayed red body.

"We can't stay here," he said. "We have to go."

Carmen shivered. He couldn't see her eyes. If he could make eye con-tact, if she would only look at him, everything would be OK. He could get her to move. They had no time.

The dog whimpered.

"She wouldn't come into the closet with me," Carmen said. "There's something *wrong* with me. She kept smelling me like there was something wrong with me."

"There's nothing wrong with you."

Carmen pulled the vinyl tight around her, and she was so small, so frail, just bones and a smudged, oversized T-shirt and dark lipstick, dark eyeliner. Her nose was wet and red. She'd been crying.

He said it again, "There's nothing wrong with you." Maybe he meant it. What else could he say?

Clarabelle joined them. The dog licked Carmen's tensed hand, and Alvaro could see the faint beginnings of a smile, of some kind of hope, but Carmen wouldn't move, and he couldn't bring himself to touch her. *She'll scream if I come close*, he thought.

He said, "We have to go."

"I was going to," she said. "You left me here with the dog and I wanted to. I *knew* we had to. You weren't here."

"I'm here now."

She wouldn't move. She wouldn't look at him. "How do I know?"

"It's fine," he said. "We're fine. It's going to be OK."

"Don't lie," she said. "Why do you lie? How do I even know it's really you? Why are you lying to me?"

"I'm not lying," he said, thinking, *I'm not. Not now.* "We just have to go." He didn't even try to insist on the other bit, on the thing his sister seemed most bothered by—that it wasn't him standing here, that it was someone else. Someone who looked like him. He remembered Umberto and the man who looked just like Umberto.

His sister petted Clarabelle but kept herself on the floor, wrapped in vinyl.

"What happened?" he asked. "What did you see?"

"Did you find Marisol?" she asked. "Ellie was worried, she said for you to call her. She called to check up but also to tell you she was worried." She bit at a nail. "About Marisol. About Marisol's boyfriend."

"I'll call Ellie," he said, dreading the call. What could he say? *Marisol's dead. Something happened to Marisol. She's dead and her eyes were open and she had a face that was no face at all.* He shook himself out of the reverie. Marisol was gone. They were still here. Still themselves. "We have to go. I'll call Ellie when we're out of the hotel."

Because Ellie had to go. Even the stupid dog had to go.

He gathered the clothes she'd folded in the hotel dresser. She was so tidy. He had tried to be organized too, but his stuff was in piles. At least they didn't have much. His sister had not moved but he had somehow managed to get everything ready. Now all they had to do was to walk away.

His sister needed to change, he didn't even know if she had put on pants. They'd need the inflatable bed again. Who knows where they'd end up? But they were ready. Nearly ready.

He said, "Why won't you get up?"

"How do I know it's you?" she said.

He remembered, dimly, that she'd asked the question before, but that felt like forever ago. He found himself too tired to argue, to say anything. *I'll drag her from the closet*, he thought. She was so small, so bony, so weak. He'd drag her all the way out of the Alicia if that's what it took.

"It's me," he said. "Who else could it be?"

"This place—" She wiped her nose and he saw, with a shock, that she'd bitten a nail to the quick. Beads of blood welled on the curve of her ring finger and streaked across her upper lip. She sniffed. "With this place, you never know. I don't know *anything*. There's something you're not telling me. Jacob—"

"I'm telling you we have to go. Everything's going to be fine, but remember how you didn't want to be here. You *don't* want to be here."

She said, "We're really leaving? We're really going back?"

To what?

To where?

We're home.

He said nothing, which he hoped she'd interpret as a yes.

"And it's really you?" she said.

She got up, her skinny legs poking out of the oversized shirt. His poor sister. "This place," she said again. "This *city*. There's something wrong with this place."

He nodded. About that much they agreed. Their clothes were packed, but he left out a pair of black jeans for her. She pulled them on. She finally looked at him. Her brother. Last living member of her family. Whom she loved. Whom she trusted, had no choice but to trust.

They left the AC on and the key cards on the bed and the door as open and vacant as Marisol's toothless mouth.

Carmen squeezed his hand, her skin hot and sweaty. Feverish.

"It's you," she said. "It's you."

He wanted to say yes but kept quiet, because she was talking to herself, giving herself a measure of reassurance that he could not offer. *Let her have some comfort,* he thought. She followed, his indomitable sister now afraid, feeble, sickly. Blessedly meek.

They walked down Ogden in the morning heat, past El Cortez, until they stopped at their old building. The extended stay. He'd been smart to keep the keys. She wouldn't step into the room, tired and weak as she was.

"Someone broke in," she said.

It was true.

The door leaned into the room, its top hinge dangling, a tooth on its way out. He thought about his own cracked front tooth. About which he could do nothing.

"If you hear an alarm," the sticker read, "call 911."

No one had called.

The light bulbs had been smashed. The AC was on but it could not compete with the hot air blowing in from the street.

Whoever had broken in had left burnt tinfoil behind. And cigarette butts, broken glass, cans of generic soda. Dr A+. They had cut up foil and pasted it on the window, but they had razored off small squares, each square no bigger than his thumb, row after row after row. The Alicia loomed through the little squares, and so did the impossibly clean Peter Pan sign, the Plexiglass foot delicately pointing west. You could make out the Chevalier, the Big Eastern. You could see so much of Fremont from where they had lived, and he had somehow missed it.

She said, "You said we were leaving."

"We are." He put their bags on the bed, but thought better of it. The floor felt cleaner. He found a clean spot behind the bed, safely out of sight of the open door. He patted the bags. "We're out of the hotel."

Clarabelle wouldn't go in. Neither would Carmen.

Carmen said, "You said we had to go." She stood by the broken door, arms locked, her face a blur in the sunlight.

He could not make out her features or her disappointment. What did she think? That they'd get on a bus right away? Fly off to Colombia?

They had zero money. Like, *zero*.

"We will," he said. "B.'s going to write me a check. We just have to find him. Winifred's helping." The bags were better off on the bed after all. Broken glass littered the carpet. He'd have to sweep it, pick up what he could with his hands. They didn't have access to a vacuum cleaner.

They'd have to be careful, but they wouldn't be here long. He would remind her to wear shoes. Socks at least.

He said, "It'll take an hour. A day at the most. That's not long." He knelt and picked up a piece of glass and cupped it in his palm. "And we're not in the hotel. We're not in the hotel, so it's OK." He pointed at the broken door. "I can fix that."

"You can't leave me here."

"I just need to go back and do my work and that's it. We get paid, we go."

She cried again and he desperately wished she had her sketchbook out. He wished she'd go back to being who she'd always been: sullen and whip smart. A smartass. Instead she kept herself hunched, small, and sad. She stepped into the room and the dog reluctantly followed.

"Why can't your friend write you the check?" she said. "Winifred?"

"I'll ask her, OK?" he said. "Maybe she can. I'm sure she can." Not a lie. She could. She could have offered. She didn't because she needed him. "I'll go right now and get her to give us what we're owed. And then we'll leave."

She wiped her nose and in the darkness it almost looked like was nodding, giving in.

"Watch your feet," he said. "There's glass everywhere." He had picked up so much glass but had hardly made a dent, and he knew he was right. His sister was so wrong. You couldn't go anywhere without money. "I'll get it all taken care of," he said. "We can get the check and get on a bus. We'll go to California."

His sister talked low, something about Jacob, the old man again, but he didn't hear it, and he didn't want her to repeat it. What mattered was that

196 | JUAN MARTINEZ

she had calmed down. She had agreed. She'd stay here, where she was safe, and he'd go, and he'd try to get paid early, and then he'd leave.

The dog nuzzled against Carmen.

"Can we keep her?" Carmen said. "Can she stay here?"

Ellie.

Ellie had to leave too, of course. She couldn't stay. Winifred too. They all had to go. Everyone had to go before—

Before what?

Before the Alicia woke up. Her dreams were bad enough. What had already happened was bad enough, but it was about to get worse. He could feel it in the hotel's damp, dead air, which followed him down to their shabby room. He hadn't left the hotel at all. The hotel followed. He could feel it all around him. The voices of the corridors and the murmurs of the bugs that coursed through its walls. He could feel it deep inside himself. Charleen was bad, Esther too, but something else was coming— wrapped in the hotel, sheltered, it waited. The Face Beneath the Face. The thing that the men from Seattle loved and serviced.

Serve all, save none.

He'd do his best to help his friends, but what mattered most was keeping Carmen safe. He'd do his best to get Ellie out, he owed her so much. But he had very little time.

He said, "Of course we keep Clarabelle. She stays with you. Watch her paws, though. There's glass everywhere."

It was clear, so clear now that they had left the Alicia. They couldn't stay here, no one could. They had to go, the Face Beneath the Face was coming, and he didn't know what it was and—

Carmen had pulled her sketchbook out of the bag, and the pre-Columbian creature she'd drawn stared at him with startled eyes. She leafed through her drawings, she pulled out a Sharpie, and he caught a glimpse of the sketch she'd done right before the move to the Alicia: a little girl facing off an enormous creature with a ring of tentacles. All very cartoony, very *Powerpuff Girls*, but the drawing reminded him of what he'd seen below.

In Carmen's drawing, the scale was way off. The little girl was barely a dot, the monster took up most of the page.

The real thing's much bigger.

Nothing a door would hold back, though he couldn't leave her in a room whose door did not even lock. The hinges were bent out of place. He wedged the bent bits with a knife. He found the loose screws in the dirty carpet and angled the door back into place. It wasn't hard. You could close it now. You could lock it and the lock would hold, and his sister would be safe. She'd be fine.

"I'll be back soon," he said.

"Don't go," she said. "Please. *Please.*"

It was still daytime. He'd be back by nightfall. Before dark, for sure.

She told him that she loved him. She hadn't said that since before they'd arrived in Las Vegas, but he did not realize that's what she had said until he was already walking away, he had just nodded and said again that he'd be back soon, he just had to get the check, he just had to talk to Ellie, and he hoped the dog would protect her, that the big brown Lab would prove useful and it didn't occur to him until he was nearly inside the hotel that his sister had dreamed it all, down to the sick pink color of the moldy walls. In the dream, she had called and called for him and he had not answered.

The dream of the Alicia.

His sister had known, somehow.

She had warned him, and he had ignored her. But he was doing the right thing. That much he'd tell you. *Even now*, he'd say, fingers splayed. He wondered—then and now—if the Alvaro who stepped into the Alicia was the same Alvaro who had taken his sister out of the country, who had fled on the telephone, the one who let their family die. *How do I know it's you?* He had wanted to say that it was him. But didn't Carmen have a point? Even if she didn't know what happened. Even if he kept the worst of what happened to their family from her, even if he'd kept as much as he could about the hotel from her—and even so, she *knew*, more than she should. And so maybe she was right, maybe he wasn't really him. He was some other Alvaro. And maybe here's another Alvaro still, telling you what he knows, hoping you'll remember, hoping you'll remember why he's telling you. Here sits another Alvaro. Someone else entirely. Because the real Alvaro wouldn't lie, wouldn't keep things from his sister, even if that's what he had been doing all along.

━ ⅰⅰⅰⅰ

He had already inside in the Alicia when he realized that he had missed a crucial warning. His sister tried to stop him. Why wouldn't he listen?

You couldn't.

Not here. Not with the voice in the corridors insisting on its own truth, its own appetite, its own dreams. You dreamed what the voice dreamed, what the Face Beneath the Face dreamed. His sister had dreamed it also. As had he, as had you. Even if none of us remember, even if you yourself do not remember the telling, even as you tell yourself, *I'm not really hearing this.*

I'm getting this wrong. This isn't happening.

You're not. It is.

Listen.

None of it felt real. He could be dreaming now and not know it. When he awoke, all would be well. The hotel would be just a hotel. Marisol would be alive. His sister would back to her old self. He would too.

When he woke up, he'd finally be himself.

PART FOUR

No Plans for Our Return

CHAPTER 22

THE LIGHT IN THE PIT blurred the crowd, every face a smear of lurid yellow. Alvaro hoped to find his friends in the heat and press of these strangers. No luck.

The red strings hung everywhere. The strings had multiplied and snaked their way from below and crept into the upper floors. They festooned slot machines and snaked around the craps table.

It wasn't until Alvaro saw Steven—and Steven saw him—that he realized how much he'd have to explain.

He had not found B., and he had lost Dan, and Steven's own man was missing, dead and abandoned, and Alvaro could tell that was all on Steven's mind when they saw each other across the roil of tourists with no faces, but Steven's attendants pulled him away, their hands and cheeks inflamed, Steven's swollen index finger jabbing in rage and indignation at Alvaro.

Steven's wet, red face glowed in the yellow light.

The group edged to the Ogden exit, their phones pulsing white with alarms. They'd stayed too long. Yellow plastic covered the windows to keep out the worst of the sun. Nothing could keep out the stink of unwashed bodies. The pale men stalked outside the automated doors. He could make out their faces, their anger, and he forced himself to remember what they'd done to Dan, what they could do to him. He tried to remember that they were dangerous people, stupid sandals and all. They'd be back in the Alicia, they'd be in here, looking for retribution, Steven with his tears and his fanny pack. Steven, who thought nothing of beating a man on crutches. Steven, to whom all was due. Steven, who served the Alicia and profited from her in a way Alvaro could not understand. Who needed B. Who needed Alvaro to find B.

Alvaro saw no one else he recognized. Surely they were here, even if he couldn't find them. Too many people stood between him and the café. He couldn't walk. He couldn't make his way through the press of the crowd. Winifred said she'd be here. He'd find her, all he had to do was look for the hair, the cigarette, the plum blazer. Again: no luck. The cocktail waitress and the pit bosses were all unfamiliar, as alien to him as the tourists. Two strangers wore the plum uniforms of the hotel and darted from desk to hallway, panicked. Bodies pressed and pushed and elbowed and jostled. He didn't want to go into the elevator, but the Alicia waited.

For you.

Your sister and the mother and the daughter, we are waiting.

He didn't want to go anywhere, he knew he should stay in place, but the crowd moved him along, away from the café, where Ellie needed to be told about her dog, needed to be told that her dog was fine. He needed to tell her to leave.

He would.

First he'd get his paycheck, he'd talk to Winifred and see about getting paid, and he'd tell her to leave, he'd tell her *everything*—what he had seen and heard, what he could not believe—and then he'd find his friends and tell them the same thing, and *then* he would leave. Whatever lurked beneath, whatever waited in the malformed corridor—the insects with their unearthly pincers, and Charleen, and Charleen's little girl, and whatever Marisol had become—whatever waited below (*for you*) could wait some more, and it would stay below, it would keep to its rightful place until it wouldn't. Alvaro had time. *They're waiting for me*, he thought. He had just enough time to do what he needed to do, he told himself, in the voice he recognized as his at his steadiest and most pragmatic. The voice sounded very much like his father's.

The crowd moved him through.

The crowd ate him up and pulsed and throbbed his body to where he needed to go. The crowd pushed him from itself, elbows and fat thighs pressed tight in a fog of bad breath, all of them packed in the yellow of the pit.

The crowd pushed him into the welcoming doors of the elevator.

The door did not quite close.

He couldn't make out the faces of the people he had just left, he couldn't make out eyes, even as the crowd settled in the distance, and even as they turned, in concert, every blurred face turned his way, teeth bared, the hungry tourists of the crowd hungry for *him*, for something he held close, something he did not know he held close. What did he have? He had nothing, held nothing. He longed for the index card that read "INVISIBLE." The crowd turned, twitched, refused to come into focus.

The door closed. The roil of the crowd swallowed the groan of the elevator, the buttons as greasy and forlorn as when he last pressed them.

I'll have to see them again, he thought. *I'll have to go through them again, because I have to warn Ellie.*

He couldn't shake the crowd, the thought of the crowd, how the crowd was as much a barrier as the warped corridors below were a labyrinth— the hotel bent on swallowing him whole. Go in, he'd tell you, *and you wouldn't go out.* Go in, listen to the voice long enough, you'd forget all other voices. All other stories. You'd just sit there, you wouldn't know why. That was the problem with listening, and he'd open his hands and smile and you'd see if it was true. If his tooth was really cracked. If it was him, really and truly, down to every broken part.

The elevator lurched to the penthouse. The floors ticked, one by one, the ascent halting and slow.

He hoped to find Winifred or B. in the penthouse, both or either, anyone in charge. Hoped all the harder because humans felt unnecessary, superfluous.

The Alicia steered herself, even as the thing that slumbered beneath her stirred. He could feel it in his bones, the thrum of an immense force on the verge of waking. What Steven called the Face Beneath the Face. The thing he could not name but whose dreams infected his sister, and him, and everyone here.

The doors opened and he was greeted by no one.

Everything was where B. had left it: the painted plywood, the rotting marble, the pale flamingos. But now strings coursed along the ceiling, thick and mostly green. The enormous desk sat unmanned, and the telephone rang as it always did, and there was just enough light to let him know that the walls had grown softer since he'd last been here, the marble whorled with the pale-pink jelly from beneath. *Give it more time and you'd see right through it*, he thought. *You'll see insects coursing through.* Parasites, all. Steven and his people too. Us too, for that matter.

The insects burrowed below, and so they must burrow here as well. Just because you didn't see it didn't mean it wasn't happening.

There was so much he did not see, so much he did not know.

He texted Winifred and B. The texts faded into the void of the hotel. When he tried calling, his phone didn't even bother to pretend. The numbers wouldn't register. They sank into the display and blurred.

He tried calling his sister. The hotel relented. The call squeaked through. He told Carmen that he was having a hard time finding someone to write them a check.

"What?" said Carmen. "What? I can't hear you. What?"

He asked her to hold on, he said he'd call again, that he'd try calling from the landline, which hadn't stopped ringing, and which he didn't want to touch. He was afraid of the receiver, afraid of the voice that could reach him here, the voice that had chased him from the forest and through the phone lines and landed in every nightmare: *We're coming.*

We're coming for you.

Answer the phone and it could be Ernesto, or even your own dead father or whoever chased you out of your own safe corner—the voice of the hotel, the voice of a stranger, the voice of a loved one. The voice of his dead family.

He banged the receiver and hung up on whoever insisted on talking. He dialed his sister.

He said he'd be home soon. He'd have the check in no time.

"What?" said Carmen. "Who is this? Who's calling? Who keeps calling?"

He told his sister that he would be back soon.

Carmen said, "Who is this?"

Maybe it was bad reception on her end, maybe that's why she couldn't hear him, or why he didn't sound like himself. He didn't think so. He blamed the hotel. It closed in, it cut off outside conduits.

He hung up and the phone rang again and he resisted the urge to pick up. Because it wouldn't be his sister calling him back. It wouldn't be anyone he'd recognize. It could be Steven. Or it could be the hotel herself. Worse—what if it was Dan calling from deep inside the hotel, lost still? Lost and wandering and asking why Alvaro had left him there? How could he leave a man on crutches?

But I didn't, he thought. *Dan hobbled away. I couldn't see him, we lost track.*

The phone wailed, and Alvaro grew convinced that whoever was on the other end had been waiting for him, knew that he would make his way here, that the crowd would guide him to this empty green tomb festooned in rot and shadows. He didn't want to talk to whoever wanted to talk to him. The first and last time he answered that phone, it had been B.

You're not my son, B. had said.

Today he'd ask, *What did you do with my son?*

Only then did he notice the couch. It had been pushed to the very back of the cavernous room, into the shadows, into a pool of darkness where the greasy corduroy shone. Two people sat on the couch, in the murk, their forms bulky, hands on their laps. Waiting. He walked closer, hands in his pockets, toward the immense forms. A gift from the hotel. He kept the hotel's other gift: the tooth that had been lodged in the bag of mushrooms. How he would have loved to stab Dan in the stomach with the tooth. How easy it was to imagine. How he could do it to these two, whoever they were. How the urge to hurt never vanished, not in this place, how it refused to go away.

The tooth refused to go away. He'd kept it in his chef's pants all this time. Waiting too. He gripped it and was about to pull it out.

A muzzle wet with blood.

A wet face.

Neither form belonged to Dan.

What he saw, what he faced, were the enormous weeping figures of Lost and Found, the twins in their identical overalls worn under their plum blazers. Marisol had been so afraid of them, and he was too, even now. They called ICE. They watched over everything the staff did. He had meant to talk to them, to ask about Marisol's photograph, but now the photograph was so unimportant, as was the crying. He let go of the tooth and felt its weight against his leg. It'd be easy to pull it out, stab them in their fat fucking bellies. Spill out their secrets, cover every secret thing with blood. The twins had not raised their heads, though he was close enough to put his hands on their shoulders. Close enough to kill them. The phone had not stopped ringing.

Alvaro said, "That's not B. calling."

Lost and Found shook their heads. They wore bright, canary-yellow rubber gloves. Lost wiped his nose. Found patted his brother on the back.

Alvaro was going to introduce himself, but they already knew him— they acted like they knew him. They'd seen him. They'd seen more of him than he wanted them to see. And they'd seen him on camera. In the pit. They saw everything, and they had a sinister reputation in the kitchen, but on the dark-green couch, they looked forlorn. Two fat abandoned children.

"Winifred's not here," Lost said.

Found pointed at the gash on the wall. "They're not in the passage either. Not and B. not Winifred and not Dan. We looked."

"We looked as far down as we dared to look," Lost said.

"It's deeper now," Found said. "Deeper than before. Winifred's not down there. So don't go."

Alvaro said, "Who's on the phone? Who's calling?"

"Why don't you answer?" Found said.

The phone rang. The twins sat.

Alvaro hovered, his hands and arms locked in place, all of him desperate—he needed such a simple thing.

"Cut me a check," he said. "My sister and I need to go."

"What did you do?" Lost said.

"I did nothing." He lied. "Cut me a check. Pay me. I'm owed."

The twins wept.

"What did you *do*?" Lost said again. "It's so much deeper now, and there's so many of them now. We can't see. We can't keep up."

"We tried," Found said.

"We didn't mean to," Lost said, and pointed.

Alvaro was glad that it was dark, because he had missed seeing what Lost pointed to until now. He had not slept, he reminded himself. He missed things, time skipped, voices intruded. It was just as well—that he couldn't make out the faces in the crowd when they turned in concert, or that he could no longer hear the landline, or that the rot on the wall no longer bothered him.

It was *good* that he missed things, that he had not seen the body of the child sprawled over the arm of the couch—that Lost and Found sat and wept and he stood and talked and they all ignored the body of a little girl.

She must have been Alba's age. She must have been young, younger than the girl in the Nightmare Room, though she wore the same pinafore dress and had her hair in the same pigtails. Her neck bent at an impossible angle. She faced the plywood and the occluded view of Fremont.

Lost said, "Don't touch her."

Alvaro ignored him.

The girl's skin felt rubbery and cold, and it stung his hands. When he turned her torso over, the head stayed in place. Her neck had been snapped. Lost or Found must have done it, and now they grieved in the penthouse, their sorrow as deep and as genuine as what one would feel for a family member. Alvaro knew that kind of reaction to loss. He recognized the weeping, the uncontrollable shaking, the incapacity to move or explain or make sense. The reluctance to leave the body, or to move it. Poor Lost. Poor Found. Alvaro had not looked at the dead girl's face. He did not dare. Not yet. She still faced the wrong way. An index card peeked from her dress pocket. "Hymnal," it read. Poor thing. He remembered how Alba had pitied the dead, shortly before she died herself, how she had said, *Poor thing*, and he shared the sorrow for the dead creature he now held with both arms even as the heavy head of the dead girl looked away from them all.

Not a girl.

Not human. The skin didn't feel like skin. The body weighed too much and the weight suggested an odd density—no bones, too many bones, too many things wriggling in there, some wriggling still.

He turned the head so he could see the face.

The eyes were open, the color of the pupil too pale to register in the bad light. The lips parted. The teeth were long and sharp, like needles— smaller versions of the thing he kept in his pocket.

He braced himself for the mouth to snap to life, for the thing that looked like a little girl to speak again, but the figure remained limp and pitiable. He shared in the sorrow of Lost and Found, and as he stood and left the body on the couch, he wiped a tear and realized that he was also mourning Alba. He had left Alba's body in the jungle. He left all the bodies behind.

"Are you going to bury her?" he asked.

Lost shook his head.

"It's against the rules," Found said. "The Face won't let you. Anyway, they're coming."

Alvaro didn't need to ask.

The insects with the long pincers rustled close. His skin itched. The parasites were so close, and he didn't want them near, didn't want them crawling over his kitchen shoes to make their way to the body. He backed away and stepped on one, felt its squelch and crunch, and resisted the urge to apologize. Who did he want to say sorry to? The bugs performed a service. They belonged to the hotel's ecosystem. Alvaro was the interloper. So were Lost and Found. They didn't belong here, or they belonged here as fuel. As food.

"B. has the keys," Found said. "He *promised* us he'd keep them in. But he let them all out, all of the girls. All of the rooms are open. Most of the little girls wait in the walls. Nearly all of them are in the walls still. They're good."

"Good little girls," Lost said.

"So there's time," Found said.

"There's no time," Lost said.

"There *is* time," Found said. "For the girls to be put back to sleep. For them to feed on the stories and not on the guests. We've been working. We're trying. We're trying to get everything back to where it was, but it's B. who has the keys, B. who knows how to close it all up."

"There's no time," Lost said.

Alvaro said, "What did he do?"

Found laughed. "Don't pretend you don't know. Don't pretend. Don't you think we *know*? How you've played us?"

"Why did you think B. brought you here?" Lost said.

"She told him to," Found said. "The hotel told him to and he *obeyed*. You and your sister. You were sacrifices. The hotel wanted you. B. delivered."

B.'s office door was only half-closed.

"You're not supposed to go in there," Lost said.

"That's his private office," Found said. "He's not in here. No one is."

"Don't," Lost said.

Neither twin moved to stop him. Alvaro pushed against whatever had jammed the door. The twins didn't say anything when he gasped.

They had piled dozens of bodies against the corner. The same little girl, the same pinafore dress, the same expression on each of the still faces. The same teeth. The girls looked like they were about to move in the daylit shadows, but they stayed still. The twins had crammed a dozen more in B.'s once-empty bookshelf. There was something unfinished about the girls' features, something uncooked. Again he felt a sorrow he could not explain, because the bodies were not quite human, and because the hunger in the sharp teeth assured him that the girls were dangerous. They wouldn't mourn him. They'd eat him up.

He mourned them all the same. They had been alive, and now they weren't.

"It gets easier when they just come out," Lost said.

"Otherwise they're too strong," Found said. "They come out of the walls, they come out of their rooms. They won't listen. All they do is what they did before."

Alvaro said, "What do they want? Who are they?"

"We don't know," Lost said.

"B. doesn't know," Found said. "We don't know what they are. We don't know who *you* are, why the Alicia picked you. Why she wants you so."

Will you give her to me? Will you give them all to me?

"They like to be sung to," Lost said. "They like stories. They like their little things, so we just write them down on the cards. Mostly they stare at the cards. They zone out. When they don't zone out, they mostly like to eat, and to lead guests astray, and to eat the guests they lead astray, so we try to keep them in check."

"We prune," Found said.

"We try to prune," Lost said.

The twins stared at the office wall. A pinkie finger protruded from the marble, as did a knuckle of a ring finger. The knuckle and the pinkie flexed, aquatic and languid, and through the translucent flesh, he could see some other, smaller life wriggling inside the fingers on the wall. Alvaro thought of jellyfish, of coral reefs—of organisms composed of other organisms. He resisted the urge to touch them with his own fingers.

"They're also coming in from the new doors," Lost said. "Those we just prune. Those we don't even try to sing to."

Three doors had grown on the marble, the edges as irregular and malformed as the corridors below. You could barely see the doors in the bad light. The phone in B.'s office rang. The calls followed them. No one answered. The phone clicked to voice mail. A breath of silence. The phone rang again.

Alvaro asked, "Where do the doors go?"

"Two go below," Found said. "Deep, deep below. Rooms full of red strings. The other we couldn't open."

"We think it's been waiting," Lost said.

Alvaro didn't need to ask who the door waited for.

"I wouldn't," Lost said.

"Oh, I wouldn't either," Found said. "Not even if B. waited to save my brother's life. I wouldn't go. Why would you? Why would anyone?"

Alvaro asked, "Why were you watching? You spied on me and Winifred. In the corridor." He blushed. "Why?"

"B. told us to," Lost said. "It was what the hotel wanted."

"Don't," Found said.

The knob burned, fever-hot and moist as flesh. The tissue of the knob contracted—the same tense, plasticky, wormy sinew animating the walls and the girls. The same life that was like no life he'd ever known.

"Oh no," he heard, and the voice could have come out of Lost or Found or both.

He ignored them and stepped inside and the door snapped shut behind him.

■IIIII

Light burst and fractured. He could smell the acrid sweat of bodies too long in the heat, and he could smell the heat itself—asphalt and scrub and garbage and beer—and he was trapped, pressed on all sides by strangers, and he had no idea where he was, where the hotel had led him.

He heard chants.

He saw the backs of placards that rose high above the backs of heads. The enormous television screen that covered the sky above the street showed a woman in jean shorts, but daylight blared and streaked across her stomach and legs, and he thought of Marisol's flayed body.

And then he saw her—actually saw her—in the press of the crowd: the limbs still red and raw, the face still intact and smiling.

He shuddered in the heat, realized that the light had played a trick. Marisol wasn't there. It was a woman wearing a one-piece bodysuit. Red spandex.

A guitar pealed. A singer urged him to take it easy.

He recognized the song. He'd heard it often enough on his walk to work.

The hotel had spat him out.

He could leave. Walk back to the extended stay, find Carmen. What he realized, what he'd tell you later, was how easily the hotel wound you around itself—promised you a freedom you did not really want. How it spun you round. Like right now. One finger in the air. No wounds on the finger. No blood, no sign of trauma. Not even so much as a tremble. Right now, we are being spun again, you and me. And how we sway. How we say yes. How we lean in to hear what happened next, to read the warnings, missing the real warning.

That we should stop. That we, too, should walk away.

Men held signs and screamed, but their screams blended with the ordinary drunk sounds of the tourists, everyone angry and sweaty and *loud*, even if some held pamphlets and others beer in plastic containers shaped like footballs.

It took him longer than it should have to realize that he had been dropped into the protest, that the protest had already started, and the vertigo arrived late: he had been high in the dark of the penthouse and now he was at ground level and the sun blared, and he was pressed on all sides by people composed of equal parts body odor and bile. It was daylight now. Was it supposed to be daylight?

He could spy the red, blotchy face and the black turtleneck of Steven. Steven had put his hand on the shoulder of a man who held up a poster of a bloodied fetus. They conferred.

The man nodded, pounded his fist, raged at the video of the woman who hovered over him, and moved to where Steven pointed—to the Alicia. The man nodded and the poster turned and the enormous red eye of the fetus nodded along.

There was so much anger here.

An elbow dug into his side and another dead baby floated into view. A brochure. A woman urged him to take it, to think of the unborn, to pray for them. He took the brochure and stuffed it in his pocket—he felt dizzy and sick—and the woman told him to pray, to leave this place, and Alvaro told her that he had every intention of leaving, all the while praying that Steven wouldn't turn around.

Don't let him see me, he thought. *Don't let him see me here.*

"Don't go there," the woman said. "The devil's there."

"I won't," Alvaro said.

The woman shook her head. "I dream of it all the time. The devil waits in that hotel and it's not like the pictures. Not like anything you can—"

"I won't," Alvaro said again, staring at the woman's wrists. How she rubbed them when she talked. How she grimaced.

Steven's neck grew pale in the sunlight, less red. The men from Seattle would soon go into the hotel again. They'd be looking for him there. For B. too. They wouldn't find anyone.

"You will," said the woman, who could have been Ellie's twin. Same pained wrists. Same solid body. The same face. "You say you won't, but you will. Just look at them. They say they're against the devil, but they go into the hotel where the devil waits." That much was true. The Alicia opened her doors and took them in, placards and all. Dark beads dotted the yellow sheeting on the hotel windows. Spilled drinks. The woman handed him a comic strip and opened a panel and pointed at a cartoon of a horned man going "HAW HAW HAW." "The devil's nothing like that," she said.

Steven turned. Alvaro ducked.

It was only because he was trying to keep out of view—only because he crouched—that he spotted the crutches in the welter of feet. Dan had put on a trucker hat, a pair of mirrored aviators, a T-shirt that read "FBI: FEMALE Body Inspector," but Alvaro recognized him anyway, though the recognition took the full length of a Don't Walk signal to coalesce, to turn into certainty.

He followed Dan's slow, halting gait across Fremont. *He's running away*, Alvaro thought. A coward, not like you or me. We stay. We stay and listen. Dan did not. He had run away before, and it was a miracle he had survived Marisol and Charleen, a miracle he was here, free and unharmed. It was an even greater miracle that Alvaro had chanced upon him. Even now, with no sleep and stuffed with voices that were not his own, he feared that it was no coincidence, no miracle: the hotel had set him up, and if not the hotel, then someone else, some other force. Alvaro had been led. Tricked.

Dan walked south, away from the protest, away from the Alicia, Alvaro following as close as he dared in the great sea of demonstrators who walked in the opposite direction. The woman had been right. Everyone else trudged toward the hotel. The protestors held their placards high and chanted until they neared the Alicia. They dropped the signs. They slipped through the yellow doors. More fluid misted the windows. Fine and dark. Not drinks, not cocktails.

Blood.

The Alicia celebrated her great feast. The mountain of placards grew higher.

The woman who looked just like Ellie had not heeded her own warning. The Alicia pulled her in. Alvaro saw her go into the gore of the casino, a fistful of brochures in each hand.

Dan and Alvaro were among the few slipping away from the great conflagration, swimming against the slow current that led to the Alicia, and it was only when the crowd thinned two blocks down, and when Alvaro could see that the men from Seattle had gone back in (they were so pale, so easy to spot, even from this distance), that the younger Melmot hobbled faster. Other people wore the same stupid FBI shirt, and Alvaro feared that he'd lose Dan, but you couldn't lose track of a man on crutches. Other fears sank in, other worries. Dan seemed to be heading toward the extended stay. Alvaro wanted the Melmots as far from his sister as possible.

Another fear arose. If Dan didn't know he was being followed, couldn't the same be said for Alvaro? That he was being followed as well? Some unseen observer (not us, he joked—we're invited) followed him even as he followed Dan, and so he turned, but he couldn't tell, couldn't really know, even if Steven and his group had gone back. But he could feel it. He could feel eyes on him. He didn't know who could possibly know where he had gone.

Even Lost and Found didn't know, and they knew everything.

I'm invisible, he thought.

He turned and lost track of Dan. A quick, frantic scan. The younger Melmot had tossed away his crutches—no, it was someone else in the same stupid shirt. Alvaro yawned, rubbed his eyes, panicked until he saw Dan hobble and stop before the Big Eastern's mustard-and-ochre façade.

That wasn't the Big Eastern's only holdover. The doors had no motion sensors. If you wanted in, you either used your hands or you pushed the handicap button, which Dan missed even though it was right in front of him.

Dan had managed to half-prop the door with an elbow and the tip of a crutch, but he couldn't do more than that. No one helped, not until Alvaro pulled the door open.

Dan yelped and nearly fell.

Alvaro said, "Write me a check."

"I'm not going back there," Dan said.

"I'm not going back either," Alvaro said, wanting it to be true. He had to help Ellie and Winifred and Umberto. "I don't *want* to go back. I just want you to write me a check."

"Dad writes the checks," Dan said. "Dad or Winifred. The checkbook's over there, in Dad's office. Or in his safe room. That's where I'm going." He looked up. "Come with."

"What happened to your eyes?"

"Nothing," Dan said, "I'm fine."

He wasn't. The T-shirt was smeared and wet. Below, a dark stain spread over the injured leg. Dan had aged. He looked puffy. Doughy. More like his dad than ever. And his cheeks burned, as red and inflamed as the Seattle men's, and there was something wrong with his eyes, even if Alvaro couldn't be quite sure what it was. Dan wouldn't take off his polarized sunglasses, even now that they had made their way into the crowded pit.

Alvaro said, "Where's the safe room?"

"We're almost there. Second floor."

Dan moved stiffly, a bad actor who forgot where he was supposed to stand. Every gesture unnatural. It wasn't just his injuries. Dan clenched his mouth and kept his secrets. *I saved your life,* Alvaro thought. *You owe me. Tell me. Tell me everything you know.* Alvaro had so many questions, but he kept those to himself. All he needed was the check, and so all he needed was B. *Just tell me where your dad is.* Did Alvaro care about the rest? He did. How had he survived Charleen? How had he found his way from below? He had slipped past Steven. Past the hotel herself. Her terrible appetites. *Why did she let me go?* he thought. *Why did the Alicia spare me?* He was about to ask, unsure of his phrasing, shy about his English, but he stopped himself, because he could see that Dan was no longer paying attention to him, and because he could see what Dan saw.

He could see it reflected in Dan's mirrored lenses.

Standing behind Alvaro was Jacob in his plum blazer and Charleen in her bright-blue tracksuit. They were close enough to touch. A hand gripped Alvaro's shoulder. The tip of Charleen's X-Acto knife flicked. Dan slipped away once again. Alvaro realized that he'd gotten an answer to all the questions he had not asked: The Alicia had not erred, Dan had not been spared, had not slipped away. A bargain had been made. If Dan had compunctions, they hadn't stopped him. Alvaro was an inconvenience—a small sacrifice, something to discard or trade off.

CHAPTER 23

"**W**E WON'T HURT YOU," JACOB said.

The knife tip grazed Alvaro's neck, and he knew he had to walk, walk or get gutted, but he wasn't afraid—not *truly* afraid—until he saw Carmen's backpack on the bar, the whorls and the pre-Columbian figure bright, fully drawn and finally finished, the eyes startled and startling.

His sister had mourned the family too, of course.

He knew that, but he had somehow missed that what she had drawn was what the family had seen on their last trip together. The family would never camp in San Agustín again, and Alvaro and Carmen could never return.

There was no Alba to return to. No Mom, no Dad. No family.

"Where's my sister?" he said. He kept his voice low and calm. He did not scream. Screaming did not help. Crying didn't help. "What did you do to her?"

"Sit," Jacob said. He pointed to an empty stool.

Alvaro stood, arms locked.

"Sit," the bartender said. The bar counter was pocked with rings. It looked sticky, even as the bartender wiped it down. "We've been waiting for you."

"I'm not sitting," Alvaro said. "Not with you or Jacob or—"

"Don't say her name," Jacob said. "Not here."

Charleen hissed. The bartender turned on the television directly in front of her and switched channels until Charleen stopped hissing and sat down. The other screens showed sports—mostly horse races, though football blared here and there, as did basketball—but Charleen's special screen (*SPECIAL things, her SPECIAL things*) had a faded quality, the lighting and the set the same mustard-and-ochre tones as the casino façade. On the screen, a man fell and screamed and was trailed by a smear of laughter. The man on-screen looked almost familiar, as did the bartender. Both the bartender and Jacob wore the plum blazer usually assigned to Alicia employees, but the color had faded to pale dust, the shoulders had gathered actual dust, and the embroidered flamingo on the back of the jacket had not been in use for years. Below the flamingo were letters once woven in gold thread, but these, too, had faded or fallen off, so Alvaro could barely make out the words, the ghost of the words: "The Hotel Splendor / Serves All." Alvaro felt dizzy.

"Sit," Jacob repeated. "I'll tell you how you can save your sister."

Alvaro sat, flanked by the woman who was not a woman on his left, the old man with the cloudy eyes on his right.

Jacob said, "We talked, your sister and I, we've been talking. Your sister *gave* me her backpack. Listen, the hotel needs something from the both of you. The Alicia has a proposition."

Alvaro shook his head and nearly grazed Charleen's shoulder. She was so much taller than he was.

Charleen turned, her smile fixed, the knife nowhere in sight, an unlit cigarette pincered and expectant. Alvaro had no lighter.

"Don't say her name," Jacob said again, looking at Charleen's dead eyes and fixed smile. "Not here. Not in this company. And don't say your sister's name either." He lit a cigarette, reached across Alvaro so that Charleen could lean in, cigarette already in her mouth. She used the coal of Jacob's cigarette to light her own. "Names carry weight around here."

The smoke crept into Alvaro's own lungs, it crept inside him, even as he realized that there was nothing he could do, nothing but breathe

Charleen's bad air, the hotel's bad air, the bad air of a bar where everyone smoked, even the bartender. They all smoked the same brand, the same thin blue band on the recessed filter. The pack read, "Parliament."

They'd known each other for years, these three. Charleen had not stopped smiling. The old man looked at her with his milk eyes, an elderly couple on their night out. The bartender wiped a cloudy glass with a damp towel. Charleen stared at the television all the while, enraptured and enchanted.

The bartender served Jacob a shot of whiskey and a glass of beer. Jacob sipped the shot in small, unnatural sips. Everything else was off as well: the glasses smeared, the beer flat, the whiskey the wrong shade of yellow. Jacob's eyes also the wrong color, the eyes of a fish left too long on the pier. He sipped again and grimaced until Charleen's show burst to life on the bar's flat, dingy screen, the video grainy and brown, a relic of the late seventies. Charleen leaned into the screen, absorbed still.

The old man nodded to no one.

"Why did you talk to my sister?" Alvaro said. "Why did she give you her backpack? Where is she?"

The laugh track interrupted, insistent and loud, though Alvaro missed out on the joke itself. *I keep missing things*, he thought. If he could say the right thing, he could fix it all. He could get up, find B., get the check, leave. Live. His sister could be kept safe.

Because Jacob wasn't saying anything. The old man looked like he had all the time in the world. He could have waited for hours. Days.

Alvaro said, "I could buy you a new drink." Did it work like this? It worked like this in fairy tales, and it worked like this in Vegas. You comped, you treated, you provided a favor in anticipation of a favor. He said, "A beer? Another shot?"

The old man shook his head. Alvaro tried to stand. Charleen's knife hand twitched, a hand as gleaming and smooth as the knife—the hand of a doll, of a figure human enough to fool you. Don't look too closely and you could trick yourself once more. Nothing wrong here. Alvaro forced to keep himself still, his own hands trembling on the counter.

Liver spots covered Jacob's hands, fat purple veins under the skin, a wine-colored stain streaked around his neck. It was not dark enough in the Big Eastern, always bad news for a bar.

The place smelled too sweet. Part of the problem was the frozen-drink machines with their unnatural half-frozen tankards colored aqua and tangerine. The mixture overflowed and spilled over the bottles on the bottom shelf, the spillage left to dry and go bad. But the other part was the people here, who smelled like they'd been sweating fruit. Alvaro and his sisters had once crossed a mango grove in the middle of the coast. The layer of mangoes on the ground reached halfway up his knees, the smell of decay heavy and cloying, a fog, and that's what the old man smelled like, what the whole bar smelled like.

Everyone here smelled like a wound.

"You worked at the Alicia," Alvaro said.

"I worked at the Splendor," Jacob said. "I still work at the Splendor. I have never not worked at the Splendor." He tugged at the edge of his shirtsleeve, where a flamingo cuff link held together a frayed French cuff. "So the proposition." He tapped on the counter. "We know you, what know what you did, what you're capable of doing. The Face Beneath the Face wants for you to do it. The Alicia too. Do it again."

"I did nothing," Alvaro said, dizzy once more. He was lying, he was telling the truth.

"Your sister did nothing," Jacob said. "Your mother? Nothing. Your father did nothing. They were innocent." He held up a splayed hand. "You? The hotel knows. The Face hungered for you and called you unto her. Back. Back unto her. It does that. It called unto you and had B. draw you in."

"What do you want?" Alvaro said, thinking all the while of B. in his safe room, and Dan too. Dan slipping away. The anger rose, the urge to use the tooth—to stab, to hurt, to tear into the Melmots, who were responsible, had been all along. The urge to jab the tooth into the open, screaming mouth of his own sister. Carmen. A bloody muzzle. A dead dog. Shut them all up. The Melmots, most of all. They had brought them in. Never mind that Carmen had said no. Never mind that Alvaro himself had insisted.

"If you want to save your sister, if you want to save yourself, you better listen." Jacob lit another Parliament. "You can't fight the Alicia," he said. "You can only feed her. And you only win when you feed her yourself." He exhaled and smoke covered his whole body, as though he were exhaling through his sleeves and shirt collar, his whole body up in fumes. "What the Face Beneath the Face wants is a sacrifice. We need one too."

"You want the Melmots gone?" he said. What scared him was how easy it was to see himself doing it. For him to live? For he and Carmen to escape? He could kill, he would do it, he already found himself relieved.

"No," Jacob said. "The Alicia wants you."

The bartender served Alvaro a half-frozen and evil-looking bright-blue drink. On the glass, balanced on the cloudy rim, a molded plastic orange sword speared a chunk of pineapple. The bartender said, "Courtesy of Charleen."

"I wouldn't drink that," the old man said.

"No," Alvaro said.

"We want you," Jacob said. "The Alicia has wanted you a good long while. And we need for you to give yourself to her. You made a promise. In the forest, you promised us."

"No," Alvaro said.

"You promised us," Jacob said. "One or the other."

"No," Alvaro said, and checked his phone. No message from Carmen.

"Charleen tells me things," the old man said. "She's been telling me things for years." His lips hung slack. More smoke. Another sip from the stale glass. "She's telling me things right now. She wants you too."

From the bartender's cigarette rose a thin, straight line of smoke, delicate as a strand of spider silk. Smoke also trailed the other sad cases at the bar: a man with an eyepatch riding a motorized stroller, two men in bowling shirts, another with a goatee and a Hawaiian shirt and sweatpants. Smokers, all. Not unusual. They sat and drank in the Big Eastern, they drank and smoked, but you smoked in Fremont, you smoked in Vegas, just about everyone did.

"You don't believe me," the old man said. "That's the thing. Talk to the Alicia long enough, you get used to being believed. Anything you tell her she'll believe. She'll think it true."

It was time to find the Melmots or Winifred, then time to go. They'd leave right away. He'd find his sister, drag her from this place. He checked his cell phone again. Nothing.

"You can't fight her," the old man said. "You can't fight the hotel. You can't fight something that's in you."

"No," he said.

"You say that and you believe it, but it's not true," the old man said. "Your sister warned you. She told you not to drag her here."

Alvaro forced himself to stay put, to not react, to say nothing that would give him away.

"I fought her," the old man said. "I fought her in the desert. I fought her after I lost my child, I sacrificed the child who followed us. I fought the hotel before the hotel dreamed itself into being. All fighting did was keep me here, draw me closer. I fought her again, fought her for years. Listen. I would know. And I know *you*. Better than you know yourself. You're young, and you're not listening. All she wants is a sacrifice and if you give it to her, she grows, she sleeps, she leaves you alone. If you fight, she feeds on you, on your anger, on your love. She keeps you, she grows fat. She grows fat on Alvaro." The old man tapped Alvaro's wrist. "She grows fat on Jacob," he said, tapping his own wrist. "She grows fat on all the Alvaros, all the Jacobs."

"I'm leaving," Alvaro said.

"You can't leave," Jacob said, and grabbed Alvaro's wrist. "The Alicia's waking up and no one's putting her to sleep. Not your boss. Not the people from Seattle. You leave, you let her go, she'll keep eating. She won't stop." He tapped his temple. "Don't think she doesn't know what happened in Colombia, what happened on that road." He sipped the flat beer. "Why she can't touch you, why she *wants* you. *You.* You slipped. You've been touched elsewhere." He tightened his grip around Alvaro's wrist and smiled, teeth broken, absent, some teeth leaning in, some out. "Don't think we don't know. Don't think I have not sacrificed myself. We all have. We'll take your sister if you won't give us yourself—we need someone you love. That's all we want. We want your love. We want everything you love. Give us something you love and we'll get what we need. Don't think we don't know. Don't think we don't know who you are. Who you really are. Give us you or give us your sister. A sacrifice. That's how it works because that is how the Face Beneath the Face came into being. From the red rock and the red sand, the blood of an innocent. A sacrifice. She was born from a sacrifice and a story and now she demands more. She hungers for offerings but will only go to sleep with a sacrifice. A *true* sacrifice. That's how it works. It took us ages—*ages*—to discover how she grew, how she slept, how she dreamed herself into being. What the Alicia did the first time she does every time. That's what I told your kin: *She'll want a sacrifice.* Listen: we need you to leave your sister here, with us. You slipped out. That's fine. You can slip back in. You or her. Inside the Alicia. A sacrifice. Your sister understands. We all do around here."

No.

"She said yes," Jacob said. "She said she would walk into the Nightmare Room. The Room moves. It shifts. We can't get to it without a sacrifice. The Alicia will trade an innocent for an innocent, an Esther for a Carmen. An Esther for an Alvaro. We need to get Esther out. For her to slip like you slipped. The first Esther. My daughter. My daughter can put the Alicia to sleep."

The old man lied, of course. He had lied to Carmen and he was lying now.

The bar crowd leaned in, waiting for Alvaro to talk, drawing their smoke in the awful half-syncopated rhythms of people engaged in the same activity. Jacob slackened his grip.

"We fought her in the desert," Jacob said. "She was just dust. Dust on the dust of the desert. She stuck to everything. Bright red. Pink. She infected our dreams like she infected yours. Stole our children. *Infected our children,* and so we had to sacrifice them. Free them. It was an awful thing to behold and it did not stop." He ran his spotted hand over his sallow face. "It did not stop even after their deaths. Their first deaths."

Only then did Alvaro put it together. What Esther had said, what Jacob now told him. They had it wrong. They'd been telling each other the wrong version of their own story. Easier to believe. It was *because* they killed the child that the Alicia awoke. That the Face Beneath the Face stirred.

Esther had been innocent, and the men had hallucinated.

And now they played it all out, they kept playing out the same awful play.

Bring me your children, your family.

Bring me all your loved ones.

All of us, all of you. Them. You.

Anyone you care about, anyone who cared enough to listen.

The hotel wanted loved ones. It was awful to think of Carmen here, in this company. Awful to think of Carmen in the same breath as this man, and all because of Alvaro. He brought her here. "I have no intention of fighting the Alicia," he said. "Not me, not my sister." He coughed. "We're not who you want." His voice was small and muffled. Weak. "Let us go. Please."

Jacob was crying.

Charleen twitched, her knife hand ready.

Alvaro said, "You killed your own child because the Alicia infected her?"

"Your sister can free my child." Jacob's tears were cloudy and thick, and they stuck to his face. "You or your sister. A Carmen or an Alvaro for an Esther. And the first Esther can put her mother to sleep." Jacob smeared the tears and they left a milky trail on his cheeks. "What I'm saying is she wants a sacrifice," he said, fiddling with his cuff link. "I fought her too, we all did, all of us. We didn't know. What mattered was the sacrifice. We woke her up. Give her what she wants."

"What does she want?"

The old man wiped his face. "She wants *you*. All of you and all of Carmen. She wants you to keep feeding her. She wants you to do for her what we did for her. Because she cannot stop. Because once we offered a sacrifice, she wanted others."

"You're with her," Alvaro said. He coughed, aware that everyone here was smoking, wanting a cigarette for the first time in his life. "Why should I believe you?"

"Don't," Jacob said. "Don't believe me." He pulled back his sleeve.

His arm had been gutted from the wrist up. The tissue around the cavity glowed a dark red, the color of beef jerky, and it had dried and grown taut, ridged with discarded capillaries and tied-off tendons, as though the hollow had been carefully excavated. Jacob put the filter end of his Parliament by the cavity. A small hand—a hand the color of ordinary flesh, whose fingers were smaller than the pommel of Alvaro's cocktail sword—reached for the cigarette, and soon the head of an infant followed. Its eyes were closed. It sucked at the Parliament with greed.

The crowd leaned in, expectant, the whole bar shrouded in smoke. They smoked as though their whole bodies participated in the act, and he realized why. They were also riddled with cavities.

"They build," Jacob said. "They build their little rooms like the Alicia builds our little rooms. They don't stop building."

Other things grew inside them, and Alvaro imagined that they all looked like the creature nestled in Jacob's arm. He imagined soft rustling. Nothing moved inside the other people in the bar, not that he could see, no telltale disturbance wrinkling their clothing. The man with the eyepatch twiddled with the joystick of the motorized wheelchair.

Alvaro stared at the child. Jacob's child, who looked very much like Jacob. It yawned, its teeth long and sharp.

"You lost your tooth," Jacob said.

Alvaro felt the pocket of his pants. "Still there."

"That's where it starts," Jacob said. "In the mouth. That's where you first feel it."

Alvaro's broken tooth no longer throbbed. His tongue flicked, tried to feel for it. Nothing. An empty space. He probed with his finger. A sharp jolt of pain. A jab.

On his finger: a dot of blood.

Another tooth grew where the broken tooth had fallen, sharp and needle thin.

The TV played a car commercial. When the car roared at the camera, Charleen ducked.

Jacob said, "I'm one of the first Jacobs. Sometimes I dream I'm the only Jacob, and then I remember. We can no longer tell, though—what we dream, what we remember, what's true, what's imagined."

Alvaro remembered the painted flamingos, the index cards, the Strip's love of scale replicas of monuments, the ways in which the city floated on copies and fevered hope. He said nothing, drew his tongue to the sharp sting of the new tooth.

"What I'm telling you, what I've been trying to tell you," Jacob said, feeding the cigarette to his child, "is you fight this thing, it takes you in. It feeds off it. It needs people to fight it to keep it going." His infant clung to the edge of the cavity, not letting go, the scarred flesh of the forearm puckering where the thing's fingers clutched the edges.

"So what do I do?" Alvaro pocketed the little orange spear from his drink. The pineapple chunk settled on the bottom of the glass. Pale yellow through bright blue.

"Feed her. Feed her yourself and save your sister," Jacob said. "Free my daughter. Put the Face to sleep before she wakes up fully. Before the Face eats the world."

Alvaro said, "How come you can talk to me?"

The crowd watched them talk. Charleen stared at the TV. Jacob sipped, said nothing.

"How come she's not stopping this conversation?" Alvaro said. "Why is the Alicia fine with us coming and going?"

The infant rested its fingers on the lip of the wound.

"This is no person, no villain, no creature from the movies," Jacob said. "We don't know what it is, who we are, but it's not a thing you can fight, no more than you can fight the weather. It was dust in the desert and then it grew itself a little world and the little world grew. And now we are in it. It was *nothing*, it was mold, but it grew because we fed her. And then it kept growing. Think of it as a force of nature. As a . . ." His cigarette trembled. "Think of it as a *corrective*. The Alicia bandaged herself around the Face. She protects us from the Face. Keeps the Face slumbering its unspeakable dreams. She's bigger than us. Bigger than anything we know. Bigger and older than anything in the world."

"And the Face?" Alvaro said. "The Face Beneath the Face?"

Jacob shuddered. "It is a *nothing*. A nothing of hunger. It coils around the universe and devours what it can—what the Alicia gives it. We serve the Alicia because she keeps the Face at bay. I've seen the Face. I saw it once. You too. The slime, the coils, the wet black ropes festooned with teeth. If the Alicia wakes, the Face wakes with her."

Jacob slid the backpack toward him and Alvaro picked it up.

Jacob said, "Open it."

Inside, Alvaro found a sheaf of Carmen's drawings. He saw drawings of himself, his face long and worried, and he realized something so obvious and heartrending that he lost his breath: his sister loved him, she loved him deeply. She drew him because she didn't want to lose him. Carmen had drawn herself in their shabby room at the extended stay. She had drawn Clarabelle too.

"She's where you left her," Jacob said. "Her and the dog. They are safe. But you need to give yourself up. Give up all of you, open the Nightmare Room, and then truly give yourself up. We need you to put the Face to sleep."

"Yes," Alvaro said, thinking, *No*.

Jacob lied. Of course he lied. Jacob was part of the thing he claimed he wanted to stop.

What Alvaro and Carmen needed to do was simple: leave. That was all. They had lived through so much, he and Carmen, and they would live through this as well, they had good reason to think they would. They had reason to hope.

There was no hope in Jacob's eyes. The old man's eyes must have died years ago. He must live here, in the Big Eastern, trapped and cared for by the same entity, whatever manipulated Esther and Charleen and even B. and Seattle. Maybe even Alvaro and Winifred. You never knew, how could you? Once inside, once you slipped, it was nearly impossible to tell—whose voice you followed, who guided you to a place of safety. Who told your story. Impossible to tell now, inside. And so he knew, he'd tell you—he knew they had to leave, money or no money. And you wanted to ask, if you had a mouth to ask with, *Why now?* Why now and not before? But you said nothing, could say nothing, and you yourself stayed put. You kept listening.

"We'll come for you," Jacob said. "After you've said your goodbyes. When you're ready. Soon. We'll come for you." He offered his hand. "Just be careful."

Alvaro thought the warning referred to Jacob's hand and to the infant lurking in the sleeve. He shook the hand regardless. Jacob was talking about their predicament—the Alicia waking up, B. and the men from Seattle not reining her in, the Face Beneath the Face stirred to hunger.

"I'll be careful," Alvaro said, thinking, *Leaving this city is about as careful as you can get.* His finger had darkened. It throbbed, not unpleasantly, where it had come into contact with his new tooth.

"Everything here gets amplified," Jacob said. "The Alicia is a giant megaphone of desire. All kinds of desire. Just be careful." He pressed his thumb against Alvaro's forehead. "So you'll find me," he said. "When it's time to find me, you'll know how, you'll know where. I am the conduit. The conduit and the oracle."

Jacob unbuttoned his blazer. His shirt hung loose and open, two other infants sitting in the hollowed-out cavity of his stomach. "Ignorance and want," he said, and the creatures smiled with long, sharp teeth. They clung to the outside flesh, but there were closed flaps into which they could retreat. They could burrow deeper into Jacob if they so wished, and one did, tunneling in headfirst. A small and nimble and highly articulated foot wiggled out of sight. The flap closed.

Alvaro left the bar and hoped against hope he'd find Dan waiting by the elevators. No luck. He told himself not to worry, that Dan could not have gone far—that he could follow Dan and find B., and he'd get what he was owed, and all would be well. They would leave Jacob and his lies and the things that lived inside him. They would leave the Alicia and its soft walls that quivered with the life of insects. They would leave everyone and start anew, he and his sister. He clutched her backpack, but he hadn't zipped it close. A half-crumpled drawing nearly flew out: pale geese, a park bench, an old man. Their day with Ellie. The old man looked almost exactly like Jacob. Same long nose, the long, dolorous limbs. He thought of his father. Alvaro had missed the resemblance until now, until his sister's drawing bore the brunt of the proof, and the fear crept into him again—that there was no escaping, that every decision he made to keep them safe only made things worse. That it was hopeless.

He called his sister. She answered.

"You're OK?" she said. "You're safe?"

"Are you?"

"Yes," she said. "We're just here. One of us is drooling."

"I have your backpack," he said. "Jacob gave it to me. He said you talked."

His sister said nothing.

"I'm fixing this," he said. "We're going to be fine. I'll be there soon. So soon. As soon as I can. Everything's going to be fine. Pack what you need."

The elevator chimed and its door lurched open. Blood dotted the interior, blood dried on the floor, a bloody handprint near the edge of the metal grooves, as perfect a print as you'd find in an art school classroom. Blood covered the broken crutch in the corner.

Alvaro knew that he should not go in but he went in anyway.

Did he tell his sister he loved her before he hung up? He didn't know. They so rarely told each other anything of consequence. He had no business pressing the one button on the elevator that had been colored by Dan's blood, but that was the button he pressed, his own index finger stained now. Stained and throbbing still. He hoped Dan was alive, he hoped he would find B., that the Melmots could make everything all right—that money waited for them, that the safe room was as safe as Dan had assumed, that the Melmots had cut no corners, that they were there, still living and willing to pay their dues. Alvaro hoped to keep his rage inside, but already he trembled, already he looked forward to seeing Dan's bloody face, to maybe bloodying it some more. Alvaro hoped he'd see them soon, that he'd get what was owed to him, that it wasn't too late. The elevator quaked and boomed and promised nothing.

CHAPTER 24

B. **HAD CHOSEN A NONDESCRIPT** room, but Dan trailed blood. All Alvaro had to do was follow the dark stains on the floral carpet—the darker flowers, the darker thorns.

He tried to step lightly but the corridor groaned with age, the carpet worn to almost nothing, the pattern barely visible, the length of it dirty and whorled with cigarette burns, every door but B.'s stained and warped. The steel door had been painted to match the others, but the paint job did not convince. It did not look like wood. It did not look old. It did not have a room number. Every other door had a regular lock, but the safe room did not bother its combination panel, the 5 at the center punctuated with a red dot, the door half-open.

Dan's body was sprawled on the carpet, face up, polarized glasses still on. It was a relief to find him still breathing. Dan's chest rose and fell. His arm twitched.

You owe me, Alvaro thought. Dan would talk. He'd be perfectly willing to pay. Maybe Dan would apologize. *Just show me where the checkbook is. Just move your hand enough to sign. That's all I need.* Alvaro would call an ambulance, of course he would. He wouldn't let poor Dan bleed to death. You didn't do that. You didn't abandon an injured person, not even if the person had betrayed you, had put your own life in danger, had likely left you to die and was now likely dying himself, *by* himself. Dan must have thought he would die alone. Alone and looking for a father who was nowhere in sight.

"B.?" Alvaro said. "Dan?"

B. wasn't here. Dan wasn't saying anything.

Alvaro leaned in. Dan's face bulged, the eye socket puffing, a weak balloon. The silver lens covering the eye ticked and gave way. A stream of bugs poured from the socket. Another burst pipe. Alvaro's steady heart surprised him. His lack of surprise surprised him. Where was Dan's missing eyeball? It must have rolled away, or the bugs had eaten it as they made their way out.

The insects skittered in concert—like flocks of birds, like animals in migration seen from a great height. Alba and Carmen both were giant National Geographic documentary nerds when they were younger, and so he watched them too, and even in Las Vegas, he had caught Carmen putting on Discovery or Animal Planet in their room, whatever was on, it didn't matter, as long as it had animals. The scale of things in documentaries troubled him, made him dizzy. It troubled him now. The bugs could have been much bigger. He could have been looking at them from much farther away. That's what it felt like. He was looking at them from a helicopter, getting an aerial view, and the densely packed creatures moved like a continent-long herd of wet buffaloes.

The bugs shrank from him when he leaned in.

They hollowed the body. The chubby creatures with their long pincers and their peanuty smell poured out of the stomach cavity and from Dan's sweatpants and shirtsleeves, all in panic, and joined their brethren on the walls and on the windows, blocking the light of Vegas and filling the room with their own dark iridescence.

They were all nervous, afraid of him, the poor things. He meant them no harm.

His tongue played with the space where his tooth had fallen out and found the sharp growth in his gum. *Another tooth. A needle.* He told himself to stop. His tongue jabbed itself again. What else grew inside him? What else waited, what nestled?

Ignorance.

Ignorance and want.

Don't—

Don't touch the body.

Dan's pocket buzzed. Alvaro sank his hand into the fold of Dan's sweatpants and felt a bug twitch and flee in a panic. He found the dead man's cell phone. Winifred was calling. The Alicia was allowing it.

Don't answer.

He answered. "Dan's dead," he said.

She didn't say anything, and he tried to imagine how she would feel. Sad, surely. Scared. Maybe she hadn't heard him.

He said, "Dan is dead. I'm next to his body."

"What about B.?"

"I'm in the safe room, I followed Dan to B.'s hiding place, but B.'s not here." Even as he said it, he doubted himself. No way to be sure. The room could hide another room, you never knew. He told Winifred where he was. The smell of death broke through the smell of the bugs, each smell sweet and cloying in its own way.

"I'm coming over," she said, and hung up before he could tell her not to. Before he could say—

"Bad idea."

First he thought he'd said it, then he thought Dan's body had said it. *Anything's possible here.* But Dan lay mute and still, emptied of the creatures that had burrowed inside him.

The voice had come from the wall that was now completely coated in insects. Their shell gave off a green, oily sheen that bounced off the flat desert light. The wall rustled and shimmered. The bugs feared him, and whatever repulsion he had felt had now faded and turned into an inexplicable sadness, a bone-deep regret. They could do whatever they needed to do. He would not impede. They had a job to do. So did he.

"They don't understand, son," the voice said.

The accent had thrown him off. Dan shared that Texas lilt with his dad. Alvaro had forgotten what B. sounded like, it had been so long since people who worked for the Alicia had talked to its putative owner.

"Your son is dead. This is Alvaro."

"I know." B. sounded wet, tired, not quite himself. "I know, son."

A bug fell and cracked open. What was inside was wet and defiantly alive, strands of pale-pink jelly, quivering and licking at the air and redolent with the same sweet peanuty stuff he'd smelled before. *You could eat that*, he thought. *If you needed to, you could live on that.*

"Oh, you could," B. said. "That was the plan for us, for me and Dan. They don't taste half-bad. We had it all worked out. And now—"

"I need you to write me a check," Alvaro said. "I need to leave."

"I need something from you. We have a proposition."

"No."

"It's not what you think."

"I've heard what you want." Alvaro was close enough to the wall to count legs and pincers, for a pincer to reach out, for a bug to jump and crawl on him. He did not move back. He said, "You're not getting us. Not me. Not my sister. We're leaving. I need you cut me a check. You owe me."

"We're just trying to get you home, son," B. said. "Honest."

"We're going. Write me a check."

"It's not the hotel. It's not the hotel's proposition," B. said. "It's me. Us. Hear me out. We're all trying here. We're trying to put her to sleep. We didn't know. Hear me out and I'll cut you a check."

"Where are you?"

"Hard to say."

Alvaro slammed the wall. Most of the bugs moved out of the way, but he clipped one and it stuck, half-smashed, against the floral wallpaper. The bugs crawled back into place. He thought of Egyptians and their love of scarabs. He thought of tombs and pyramids. He thought of the Melmots and how they floated through the world—how money kept them above the mess they made.

Alvaro said, "You *brought* me here. Me and my sister. You wanted to give us up. Why me? Why my sister? Who are we to you?"

"Hard to say," B.'s voice said. "I didn't know. I didn't know what I was doing even as I was doing it, son. Didn't know who you were. Not then.

Not when I asked. What do you want me to do, apologize? I didn't know. I'm sorry I didn't know."

The bugs rustled their wings.

B. said, "But it's not like you do either, son." Water troubled a pipe. "Do you? Do you know who you are?"

"Does it matter?" Alvaro said. "You wanted us dead. You gave us up to die."

"I lost a son," B. said. "I gave up a son. We all lost so much."

"You don't know what we lost," Alvaro said. "Cut me a check."

"Come here and I'll do it."

"Where are you?"

What B. tried to say was swallowed in a low, wet cough—no words, nothing like words. More water caught in an old pipe.

The bugs pulled away, and what they left in their wake was a door-sized portion of the wall. Flowers and thorns. No door. No hint of a door. Alvaro looked for a telltale edge. No luck. The blank space was roughly the same size as the doors the Alicia had built elsewhere, and what he had missed, what he had not seen until his nose grazed the floral pattern, was the fuzz that grew out of the print. At first, he mistook it for mold, but it was darker, more solid. He grasped the fuzz with the tip of his fingers and expected it to wiggle, and when it didn't, he pulled and a clump of fine red thread looped out. He pulled out a clump of yarn that grew thicker as it came out, until it had the heft and weight of a human leg. More threads poked out of the wall, and he remembered Alba's birthday magician in Barranquilla, who pulled a loop of handkerchiefs out of Alba's tiny pocket.

"Leave it, son," B. said.

Alvaro pulled out another clump of red yarn. It came out wet, slick with mold, looking very much like an arm. The air grew cold and sweet with rot.

"That's not how you come in," B. said. "You're doing it wrong. Listen. Listen to me and I'll cut you a check. I promise."

The AC unit clunked to life. The bugs skittered. The yarn was nothing more than yarn. Nothing magical about it. Nothing special. *What if I let the Alicia know? What if I told her? What if I said,* You can cross the yarn, you can ignore it, you can eat it, it's just yarn, it won't harm you? *Because Seattle lied, and B. lied, and the Alicia didn't know, the Face Beneath the Face didn't know.* He pulled another clump from the flowers on the wall and B. gasped, B. nearly screamed, and it was all Alvaro could do to keep from smiling, from taking a great deal of pleasure in knowing that B. was scared, and that what B. feared was *him,* not the hotel. What Alvaro could do. What damage he could cause.

He said, "You'll write a check?"

"Promise, son." A cough. A rush of water. A rustle of pincers and feelers. "Scout's honor."

Alvaro didn't say yes. He didn't move any closer. He was close enough to feel the wall breathe, to know that the tissue belonged to the Big Eastern, and that the hotel was a living thing. It made sense, almost, that B. made a safe room out of unsafe elements, that whatever animated the tunnels and soft apertures could be used against it. If you knew how. And B. had learned, and so had Steven, and they all thought themselves safe.

"You've got that wrong, son." The voice was nothing human, but the Texas accent lingered, and Alvaro imagined B., his red hair and his Yosemite Sam tie, imagined a body cocooned in yarn and surrounded on all sides by walls that were not walls.

B. could hear Alvaro's thoughts, had access to the parts of himself he had kept hidden. Had done his best to keep from everyone. What Alvaro had to do was to walk away, before every horrible secret thing spilled out, before they knew all the things no one could know.

"You got that wrong too, son," B. said. "We don't know everything. We can't hear what you don't want us to hear. We're not mind readers here. We're not magicians. We need you is all. We need you to talk to us is all. Come inside the safe room. Or just lean close and whisper your life to us. Tell us the things you don't want to tell us. That's all we need. Just talk to us for a spell and we let you go. That's a better deal than that old man's giving you. We cut you a check, we let you go. Scout's honor. Why don't you lean in? You pulled out the yarn. Why not finish what you started? Why not pull out the rest?" The voice grew soft. "Why not pull at that *thing* inside you, that thing that's twisting you up inside? Twisting and growing? Why not get it out?" The voice rose and fell and rose again. The B. that was not quite B. now waned. The voice trickled down to almost nothing. A silvery stream. A distant brook. Alvaro leaned in and the voice that belonged to the man who brought him to the Alicia persisted. "What we need for you to do is talk is all. Just tell us what the Face thinks you got that's so special. What did you do? Why did it want you here? Why did it call for you and your sister? *What did you do?* It's hard to keep secrets, son. It's no good. It's why Dan is dead, because I kept so much from him. He didn't know, he didn't know until it was too late. He didn't know that it was time to run, to seek shelter. I had no time to warn him. I thought I had time to fix what needed fixing and now look at us, son." A cough, an errant pipe. "Just look."

There was nothing to look at. The wall was just a wall. The wallpaper was just wallpaper. The insects were just insects.

"Just look, son," the voice said again. "All we need is information, son. That's all we need. You'll be fine. You and your sister will be fine. Because it won't be *you* feeding the Face, see? It'll be *me*. It'll be me telling the Face what it wants to hear. What secret it wants from you. Lean in and tell me yours and I'll cut you a check and you can go. I'll give you a full two weeks. Promise. Scout's honor." The bugs skittered, the sound a chorus, an affirmation, a promise: *Do what B. wants and you'll be fine.* "A full two weeks, son. That's what I gave the other boy in the kitchen. That's what he asked for and that's what I gave him. So he could go. He whispered his secrets and he was fine, wasn't he? All he wanted was enough so his girl could get back to her grandmother. He asked and I made good, son. I always do."

Alvaro said, "Umberto made a deal?"

"He asked and I made good, son. For him and his girl."

Now his girl's dead, Alvaro thought.

"Not *dead*. Come on. I mean, come on. I see her, son. I *hear* her. I feel her in the walls. She's fine, she's happy. She's in the hotel and she's fine as a June rain. We make good is all I'm saying. We're about as fair as fair can be. You give up one thing, you get another."

Alvaro had to go. There was no check, nothing he could get from B. or anyone that wouldn't come with a price too awful to pay. He thought of Marisol's flayed body, of the eyes that were no longer human—what was awful was hearing B. and knowing that the boss of the Alicia truly did not know, had no real awareness of the damage done, did not care about the cost inflicted on others. He and Carmen, they'd make it out of the city somehow. The Alicia had delayed him long enough, had confused him long enough, but at least he had learned what she wanted—knew its true cost.

It had all become clear: Bargain with the hotel and you'd lose. Fight the hotel and you'd lose. You could give in or you could slip away. *Listen* to the hotel and you'd stay, you'd stay forever, you'd forget why you listened in the first place, what force kept you where you least wanted to be.

They had to go. Whatever excuses floated in his mind—their lack of money or a place to go or their uncertain future (go *where*? what waited for them? what job, what prospects?) or the foolish hope that the hotel would spare them, that they were safe and exempt, that Alvaro had it all under control, that he could outsmart the force that slumbered beneath the Alicia and was waking up—all of that was an illusion. All of it a ploy to fix him in place.

The laughter came from the wall and from the door and from all around. Even the insects joined.

Even the insects laughed.

Because his phone rang, and he could not get to it, because his hand had sunk into the wall.

The wallpaper flowers and thorns and brambles leeched into his wrist— the wallpaper was no longer wallpaper, the wall sucked at his hand when he tried pulling. He had been listening to B. for so long, he had not realized he had been lured. He screamed and the voice that was B. and not B. mimicked his scream and laughed and when Alvaro tried to pull his hand again, something ripped. The tip of his pinkie burned and he felt pincers yanking and then the nail ripped off, he heard the rip through the wall even as he felt the sharp, awful burn and realized, briefly, that this would be the last thing he would feel before feeling the awful pain Marisol had gone through, that his own flesh would be flayed, that he, too, would become food. He pulled at the hand and screamed and tried to keep from screaming. The room laughed and the bugs that had kept their distance now crawled back toward him.

Don't pull, he thought.

"Don't, son," B. said. "Don't, or it'll be worse. You'll make it so much worse."

Alvaro pulled and screamed.

"It's awful," B. said. "It was an awful thing, watching my own child go through it. Couldn't do a thing about it. They keep you alive, you know. They need you alive through it all. Because that's when you talk. That's when we *all* talk. It's when we hurt the most that we're most willing to share, son. You've been away a long time. Now you're home."

Alvaro screamed and thought of Charleen and her X-Acto knife. She'd be coming soon.

Coming with a song.

A song and a knife.

We're coming. Waiting. We've been waiting.

He'd be trapped.

Laughter. Not coming from B., no longer B.

"No," it said. "No, son. It's still me. It's still me. And it's not Charleen who's coming. It's your friend. It's the woman who got you in trouble in the first place, and you don't know. You don't even know. She's got her knife too. She's got her little knife and she'll get you like she got my son."

Alvaro's hand was on fire. Pincers ground into the quick of his injured finger and he screamed, and it didn't matter now, he didn't care who killed

Dan, but the voice trickled through the wall and so he put it together, he made sense of what the B. who was no longer B. was telling him. *Marisol*, the thought. *Marisol's coming with a song and a knife and she's no—*

The wall shook with laughter, and there was something again of Texas in the laughter, an almost-human warmth, and then the B. was not B. screamed and the insects fell to the floor, their dense bodies cracked at their backs and spilled out the worms of their insides, and Alvaro did his best to make sense of what had just happened. The wall was letting go. It spat him out, the tip of his finger slick and red and pink and whorled with yarn.

That's when he saw her, her face a blur.

She held what looked like a knife until he blinked. She held the phone that once belonged to the dead asthmatic from Seattle, and she stuck it in the gummy wall and the B. who was no longer B. screamed again, and the wall vomited wet yarn. The face was a blur still, the hair a puff of red.

"Winifred," he said.

She hushed him. She told him to—

He couldn't hear.

The words hardly came across, or they came across and he couldn't make them out, and he kept waiting for the world to resolve itself. Maybe the wall would give up the body of B. Maybe he'd see what his former boss had become, what the safety he bought at the expense of others had turned him into. But no body materialized, and the wall grew more solid, and Winifred stood triumphant, her cigarette lit, her plum blazer neatly buttoned.

The gobs of yarn twitched on the floor. Live limbs, dying now. *That's B.,* Alvaro realized. *That's why he screamed. I was pulling out parts of B.*

"Fuck this," Winifred said.

He nodded. He was on the floor, he could not get up—he had not known that he had fallen until now. "My sister and I are leaving," he said. He could not get up.

Winifred crouched. Her eyes met his. He wanted to kiss her. He wanted to thank her. He wanted to tell her that she needed to go too, that they could all go together.

He had no words. He had run out of words.

She said, "They're all—" She tapped ash on the sodden yarn and the still-wriggling bodies of the dying insects. She shook her head. "You're leaving," she said. "You're up and going, yes?"

He nodded again. "We need money," he said. "I'm owed for last week."

She unbuttoned her blazer and searched a pocket.

In the carnage of the impossible room, by the hollowed body of Dan, surrounded by mounds of yarn that was flesh and not flesh, B. and not B., Winifred cut him a check.

"You could have done that before," he said.

She smiled.

He said, "Why didn't you do it before?"

He knew nothing about this woman, they'd hardly talked since their time in the corridor, and he wanted to tell her everything. Every secret thing. She would understand. Whatever she had done, whatever she had seen, she managed to glide through the worst. She lived. She did what she needed to do in order to live.

She could have written him a check before.

She could have, but she needed him here. She needed him to find B.

Don't trust her.

"Come with," he said.

"I got business here," she said. "I got some fucking questions that need answers." She pulled at a string on the wall and the thing that had been B. screamed. "Go," she said. "Get your sister. I'll see you around, maybe."

She helped him up, and he hoped she didn't feel him shaking. He felt unsteady, unsure, the finger still pulsing and raw and bleeding. *It'd be gone,* he'd tell you. The finger would fall off, he wouldn't even notice. Wouldn't mind. Another finger would grow. He'd feel it grow, he'd feel its pulse in the raw nub. *Not yet, though,* he'd tell you, and laugh. Where we're at, I'm still at ten fingers and all but one of my teeth. He wrapped the injured finger with red yarn. The room still smelled of death, but he could smell her perfume now that he was so close, he could smell limes and cinnamon and money, and it was bittersweet—being so close to this woman and knowing they had no time, that she had her own story, her own secrets.

What awful thing did you do? he wanted to ask.

Surely she too. All of us had. To be called here, into the Alicia. All of us had to have done a terrible thing—him, Umberto. Marisol too.

And Carmen?

All of us. All of us here.

"You don't need that," she said, and pointed at what he'd been clutching the whole time.

He was shaking still, his vision blurred.

He handed it to her—the remains of his sister's backpack, a mess of canvas and zippers and drawings, he'd been holding on to it this whole time—and he staggered out the door and left his friend in the safe room that had been safe for no one, he left Winifred and her wiry, red hair and her lit cigarette. *I'll see you around,* she had said, but he could hardly make her out now in the blare of the room, he could hardly make anything out at all, and it dawned on him that he could die, that people had died already, that he could hardly walk. He walked, hands splayed and raw, the finger a beacon of pain, and what struck him most about his walk down the corridor was how lonely it felt, how much he missed the noise and chatter of Las Vegas.

The Big Eastern had been emptied.

Even the bar was desolate, the barkeep gone, the tankards of frozen drinks whirring and waiting. The motorized wheelchair had been overturned, and its wheels spun, but its owner was also absent. Everyone was gone. There were still drinks on the counter and cigarettes burning in the ashtrays. Orphans, all. Foundlings. Smoke rose into the massive ceiling fans that purified the air for no one.

The slot machines had fallen silent and gone dark.

There was no one to bear witness to his limp, to his halting walk, to the hand that stung and sought refuge in his stained chef's pants. No one to help him should he, in his shaking and blurred transit, happen to fall, and so he did his best not to fall as he made his way through the dead pit of the Big Eastern, even as he pushed the glass door into the blast of heat and light—even as he remembered how he had helped Dan as he staggered in, how he could no longer recognize Dan, his mirrored glasses reflecting Alvaro's own face, Alvaro's own worries and hopes. Those, too, he could not recognize. What worries? What hopes?

There was no one here, and there was nothing left.

CHAPTER 25

FREMONT WAITED, AS EMPTY OF the living as the Big Eastern.
Alvaro could not run. The shaking had subsided, however. His
vision was finally clearing up. The casino lights had been turned off. The
vendors had left their T-shirt booths and spray-paint stations. The enormous television screen that hung over the street was dead. Blood dried on
the asphalt. Blood clotted on the marquees. No bodies, though.

Normally you'd see cops, you'd see a homeless person, but even those
mainstays were absent. Alvaro looked for errant members of the protest—
there had been so many protestors. None now. He could spy a placard on
a bench, the placard half-bent so the photograph of something bloody
and recognizably human peered at the vacant street. A number of plastic
football-shaped beer cups, most of them still full, littered the ground.
Still cold, I'm betting. There was no indication of where anyone could have
gone, what had happened to them, but he knew.

He passed the dead lights of El Cortez and didn't bother to register the
silence or the cold air that leaked out of the half-open door. What caught
his eye was the pattern on the carpet, because it matched the Alicia's.

Flowers and thorns.

Someone had parked a rusted Accord on the sidewalk and left the
driver's door open. Empty food wrappers fluttered out of the car and spun
into the slate of the cloudless, birdless, empty sky.

He could not run, but he did his best to hurry, and he nearly fell, righting himself with his wounded hand. *Don't scream*, he thought. *Don't make a sound. She can*

Hear you.

We hear you.

Hi.

We're waiting.

He could hear nothing in the wake of her voice.

The voice of the Alicia thrummed in his bones and pulsed in every cut, every open wound. He staggered past the empty bars and the deserted streets and heard the great thrum. The hot wind coursed and cut through the part of the city he thought he knew best.

He didn't know the city at all, though. He had not even known that the Alicia and El Cortez used the exact same carpet pattern and that the carpet was just as faded and worn in both. He had never stepped into El Cortez. He had not even registered the bar right by El Cortez that had been done up to look like an enormous Guinness bottle, or that the bowling rink across the street had been shuttered for some time.

All of Fremont was shuttered now.

How long had he been inside the Big Eastern?

He thought he caught a glimpse of a face, a flicker of life. He was wrong. A cheap comic strip floated in the air and stuck to a pole, opened to a cartoon devil who said "HAW HAW HAW." The heat was awful and dry and the sun nowhere in sight. His kitchen sneakers grew soft on the asphalt. He was used to feeling like you were stuck to the ground, it was nothing new in the Vegas heat, even if the ground itself now felt soft and gummy and sticky. He was close to home, close to Carmen, and so he did not want to stop, did not want to think about the streets, because Fremont looked *off*—it wasn't just that it was empty, scooped of life, and it wasn't just that it was silent.

Fremont *wavered*. The street refused to keep itself on a straight angle. It wasn't his blurred vision. The pavement rolled and quivered, the surface fleshy. He thought of an enormous tongue. He thought of an enormous child pulling apart the real street and replacing it with a bad copy made of living tissue. *Where am I? What is this?*

"You're in the dream of the Alicia."

The recognized the voice—low, rough, wet,. The little girl in the Nightmare Room. He said, "Esther?"

"You're in the dream that keeps the Face Beneath the Face from waking up. You're here with all of us. We waited for you."

"I can't see you," he said.

"I'm right here," she said. "I'm right next to you."

She wasn't. No one was. He had slipped into the dream alone, and the real Fremont had faded.

"It hasn't. It's here. I'm here. I'm right next to you."

He staggered and did his best to wake himself up, to remind himself that he walked in a real place, that real people waited for him, needed him. That his sister waited in the extended stay, and so did Clarabelle, Ellie's dog, and that Ellie herself needed to be told—Ellie needed to leave. Everyone had to leave. All the people who were not here, he had to tell them that they should not be here.

"I could touch you." Esther laughed. "I could *bite* you. Wait."

A small hand squeezed his own. He screamed. His swollen, injured finger burst—a spray of pale-pink jelly.

"Wait," Esther said again.

"What do you want?"

"*You.*" The invisible hand caressed his palm. "Come with, and your sister lives. Ellie too. That stupid dog. All the bitches get to live."

He took out his phone and remembered he had missed a call and it was no surprise that it came from one of the people he was thinking about. Of course it did. That's what happened in nightmares.

Ellie had called. She had left a voice mail.

"You forget," Esther said. "You made a promise in the forest and you forgot. You forgot who you were."

"You're not here."

"I'm always here. Always waiting. The first Esther always waits. Will you come? We're waiting. Set me free."

No, he thought.

Esther laughed and let go of his hand.

He walked on. He called Ellie without checking his voice mail first. He'd tell you, *Why bother checking?* He never bothered to. He'd ask you for the last time you checked your own, and told you of a dream he had—a real dream, an ordinary nightmare—where every voice mail was the ghost of a loved one trapped in limbo, and in the dream you could set your loved one free if you listened to their voice, but you never did, even though you knew you were supposed to. The call sank once again into the void. He had no idea who to blame. The Alicia? All of Fremont? This Fremont had dreamed itself into being, soft and empty and just as hot as the Fremont that was as incontrovertibly real, the Fremont where his sister waited and where cars weren't abandoned and where the entirety of the street wasn't now littered with those weird comics. The comics were narrow and small and cheap looking. The pages flew and revealed cartoon devils, cartoon angels, remnants of the protests, everyone in the drawings going to hell, falling into pits, pitchforks drawn as crudely as the devil himself, the devil who went "HAW HAW HAW" on every frame.

Carmen could do better, he thought. She was a better artist. He called Ellie again and nearly dropped his phone, because his finger hurt so badly, and because it was hard to talk and to stagger on the soft sidewalk. It was like walking on sand. He remembered walking on a beach, it must have been at Tayrona, he remembered how Alba had complained of the long slog, and how Carmen had teased her. *Big baby. Big, whiny baby.* He imagined walking the desert that rimmed Fremont. Walk far enough out of the city and you'd get to it. You'd reach sand and scrub and the blank, sullen glare of a world not built for people.

Remember?

He checked his voice mail. No words.

Ellie cried. Ellie whimpered.

And now Alvaro cried too. He ran on unsteady feet down the middle of bloody Fremont, telling himself something he wasn't sure he believed—that he'd see his sister soon, that as soon as he turned the corner, all would be fine, everyone would be restored, and that Ellie would be fine, wherever she was. That the void in which he moved had swallowed only him, and only temporarily, and everything would be fine, everything would be all right as long as he made it home, and as long as he and Carmen left the city, it didn't matter how.

They had the money at least. Finally.

The extended stay was where he'd left it, but the building looked nothing like its old self. The walls had grown soft, pale pink. The windows and doors had been eaten away, so he could stare past the moldy security bars and into the void of the interiors. Normally he'd hear fights, crying babies, daytime TV, but there was nothing, nobody, no movement other than the blurred lumps that burrowed in the translucent walls, a shadow play: the pincers and the legs of the insects' cardboard cutouts.

Don't go, Carmen had said.

The Room moves, Jacob had said.

The wind died. A dog keened.

Clarabelle. It had to be Clarabelle.

He followed the keening of the dog and ran into the pliant courtyard and had enough time to register the silence, how every door leaned in, open and gaping, no children, no one there at all, the whole place sullen and dead. Every barred gate bent open. His sister nowhere to be found. Not here. He had failed her, and she had been taken, and he had obliged. He had walked away and thought she was safe and of course she wasn't, how could she be? (*Don't go. Please.*) Could anyone be safe in his care? The Alicia claimed his sister and he had allowed it to happen, because he should have stayed with her. They should have run away.

Their door had fallen off completely—it looked like a passed-out drunk, a pulled tooth.

Inside he spied the wreckage. He called for his sister and Clarabelle barked. The only living thing. The only innocent.

She sat and howled just outside the room. She had a nasty gash on her muzzle (*cut her up, give her to us*), and she limped when she padded to greet him, and she kept on keening by the door.

"There, girl," he said. "Easy."

She keened and howled and he wished he had something for her, that he could help her, that he did not hunger to give her to the Alicia. He could bash her stupid head with the broken lamp. He could cut her open.

That she was the only living thing was a miracle.

That she had survived whatever took Carmen, that the dog had been spared when no one else had.

No.

No no no no no.

That the hotel *feared* a dog. *Well*, he'd tell you. *That was something.*

Clarabelle flanked the broken door and howled, she barked when he went in. She wouldn't go inside, she wouldn't follow him.

The crumpled blue and red vinyl of Carmen's deflated bed had been ripped in half.

No.

Please, no.

There was nothing. No papers. None of her drawings.

All swallowed by the Room.

By the Alicia.

All of Carmen swallowed whole.

Blood dotted the walls. Blood dotted the passages that opened and pulsed and stretched into the blackness in the room.

Not enough, he told himself. *That is not enough blood. That's just a streak. You'd cut your finger and that's what you see there, nothing much. That could be dog blood.*

He wondered what the strange wailing sound was until he realized that it was *him*—that he'd been crying, that he'd been making a sound he had not heard since the road to Ibagué. A terrible keening. Worse than the dog's. He put his hand over his mouth but the sound came out anyway and there wasn't anything he could do to stop it. To keep himself from pacing the small room that was now just a room, the hotel taking him down to where he could see what they'd done, what the Alicia had arranged. *A sacrifice.* He had given Carmen up. He had left Carmen by herself and had entered the hotel, he had—

But she lived, he thought. *She's supposed to live.*

That was the story, he'd explain. *That she lives.* That's why you'd sit here, listening. That was the whole point of you listening.

The point was that she had lived through the worst. She had been lucky, had always been lucky, even when the rest of the family hadn't. She had missed the road trip. She was too smart, too sweet, too talented.

No.

Anything could happen to you. To us. Anything at all. Anything could happen to anyone, and it didn't matter how nice you were. How good. It didn't matter that the worst had already happened to you. The Alicia didn't care. The world didn't care.

She's not dead, he thought. *She's not.*

He opened the blinds and hoped that the sun would help. That it would give him a clue as to his sister's whereabouts.

You could see the back of the Alicia from where they used to live. He imagined the cages insisting on their emptiness, the courtyard a glare of sunshine even as the day waned, the pool itself finally full of water, full of children playing in the water. Staff had put cones around it, but the cones were ignored. He imagined that the Alicia teemed with life, that the hotel had drawn everyone in and emptied the surrounding streets. The hotel hummed, even if he could not hear her distinctly. The Face Beneath the Face spoke even if he could not make out what it said, and now it spoke to everyone, not just him. But what did it say to him? What did it say to the hotel? *Thank you.* Maybe. *For Carmen. For bringing these people here. These children. For doing what B. asked. For being such a good employee.*

You will be rewarded.

He put his hand over his mouth again and kept the noise from rising. The heat was awful. He wanted to throw up, but he had not eaten anything, he couldn't remember the last time he ate, the last time he slept.

He could walk into the Alicia. He could go find Jacob, he could go to the penthouse, he could reach out to Ellie for help—he could try finding Carmen.

Or he could leave.

He could *live*.

I gave them what they wanted. My whole family. I gave them up.

The little girl asked, in the forest she had asked, and he had lied, he had said yes but spared Carmen until now.

Go in there and you'll die, just like her. Even if she wasn't dead, she would die soon. There was no winning. The Alicia swallowed the world whole.

And it was all his fault. He had kept his worst secrets from Carmen. He had lied. He had taken her from the world she knew and brought her here, because he thought it would be better. Because she would do better here. They both would. But he had done the wrong thing, said the wrong things. He had kept the worst from her and it had all backfired. The worst had come back.

Last time, he had walked away. He had walked away because he thought he had no choice, but he couldn't walk away again. He had no one left. *Calm down*, he thought. *Find Carmen and stop the Alicia and then get out of here.* He had to find someone who could help him, someone who *knew*, and it couldn't be Jacob. Jacob couldn't be found. Couldn't be trusted *if* found.

What did the hotel say to you?

He pulled out his phone and called Winifred. "My sister's missing," he said. He had to repeat the last word so she could hear it over the rush of hot air pouring out of the holes in the room, and then he said it again.

"I know," Winifred said.

"Help me," he said. "Please help me."

What came out of the other end could have been a laugh or a cough or static. Or the hiss of the Alicia. It sounded like no one he knew.

Winifred's voice returned, a low, hoarse whisper. She said, "I can help. You can get your sister back. You need to—"

"What?" he said. "What?"

She had hung up.

He tried to call back. She wouldn't answer.

Carmen had warned him. She had also told him to stay with her. *Don't go,* she had said. *Please.* Still: it wasn't him, right? He waited for you to answer but you couldn't. You could only listen. You have no tongue, no mouth, not at the present moment. You forget this sometimes. He tried telling himself that he had done what he should, but he couldn't fool himself. What did his sister know? Why did he listen to her? He should not have left her alone. They heard the voice of the Alicia, even at the extended stay they heard her, and so they should have known that they were still in it. Still in the dream. Still in the wake of the Face Beneath the Face. *But she said to go, hadn't she?* She hadn't. Never mind. She had *let him go* anyway. They needed money so they could get out. He should have been the one to say no. To say that the others could take care of themselves. That it wasn't his job to help. That all he and Carmen had to do was to live. Had he said anything, had she listened, they could have left—they could have made their way somehow. Or not. This was the story he told himself then. The story he wanted to believe even if he knew better. The story of having no money, and therefore no other choice but for him to go back. They had been down to ten dollars. They needed the check—needed B. and Winifred and the generosity of the hotel. They had nothing. He could have asked Ellie. She would have loaned him the money, he would have paid her back. Sent it once they found their way to California. Ellie. Poor Ellie. It was humiliating to have nothing, and now Carmen was gone, and it dawned on him that maybe the horror of it all was simply having no money.

If they had had money, they could have left.

They didn't have enough for a bus ticket. *But we could have left*, he thought. *We had every opportunity to leave.*

He faced the wreck of their bed that was no longer their bed. Even the television had taken on the same gummy, organic, soft edges of the Alicia. Turn it on and you'd see nothing real. Nothing of their world.

The walls of the room poured open. A waft of rotten meat. Three holes bristled out of the enormous living thing into which they had all wandered, and he knew, he didn't need anyone to tell him, didn't need Esther at all, that one of the passages led directly back to the Alicia. The other two? He could end up anywhere, because that was the awful thing about the Face that dreamed itself into being. He remembered the three bad imitations of doors that had opened in B.'s office. He remembered Lost and Found's warning. *I wouldn't go. Why would you?* He had ignored those warnings and he had ignored his sister too.

Don't go.

He had gone anyway and lied to himself. That was always the great comfort, the easiest lie to believe—that they'd be fine. That things wouldn't get worse. That Carmen, at least, would be fine, she'd be safe even if he wasn't. That the only person he was putting at risk was himself. That he could leave her and she'd be fine. That they needed to wait anyway, that he needed to convince her to wait. Because payday was only a few days away. That was the awful thing. They missed the moment where they could have slipped away and now his sister was trapped. Him too. He'd be trapped if he tried to go after her.

He could walk away. He could leave her behind. He had done so before, he had left the bloody wreckage of his family, and it was an awful thing—it was the most awful thing—but you could live with yourself. You could keep going.

Carmen would understand.

The holes stretched wide enough for him to walk through, and the faint familiar noises of the hotel returned: the birdsong loops of the slot machines, the rustle of a crowd, the air and water that coursed through the pipes and passages of the Alicia. He didn't know which of the three openings was the one he was supposed to go through. He had wandered into a fairy tale. Only one choice was the correct choice, but the sounds and even the sour smells of the Alicia wafted in from all three passages. But, of course, any choice was a bad choice. He had run out of good options.

He stood long enough for his whole arm to hurt. The mangled finger throbbed through the sodden yarn. The pain was real. However much you slipped into the dream of the Alicia, what remained constant and true was the prospect of death and injury.

Carmen was in the hotel, in the dream of the hotel, but so was he. So were you. And me. So were all of us.

What Alvaro had failed to realize until just now, what he had not time to process until he stood in the room that was no longer their room, was that the Alicia was much bigger than he had first imagined. The hotel may have been the outer shell of the thing that dreamed itself into being, but the Face Beneath the Face stretched far and wide. The Face had swallowed Fremont. It had replaced it with something that looked like Fremont but breathed and pulsed, a living organism. It had also swallowed their home and had replaced it with something other.

"No," said Esther. "Not replaced."

Alvaro said, "We've been living in the creature all along, haven't we?"

"All along," said Esther. "You mistake the dream beneath the world for the real world. You don't see."

"Where's everyone else? Why can't I see them? Why can't I see you?"

"They're here," Esther said. "Waiting. Waiting or dead. The Alicia had to eat. She had to feed the Face Beneath the Face."

Now he saw. Now he understood the true nature of what he and his sister moved through. This soft, slumbering, sentient thing. This enormous, live, writhing animal.

I'm not going back to the Alicia, he thought. *I'm going to find my sister.*

Esther laughed.

He hoped that Carmen was alive. But even if she wasn't, he wouldn't leave her—leave her and he'd leave what little remained of him. That was the unuttered, the unvoiced thought he had not been able to disclose, the secret lodged in the back of what he kept silent: he had lost most of himself when he lost his family.

He hoped and realized that as long as he hoped, Carmen lived in him—the part of her that was also him, the best part of him, the most selfless part. Even if he could not find her, even if she was irretrievably lost, what mattered was that he walked back, that he did not run away, that he would never run away again. He would find her. Even if he lost himself, even if he gave himself up to the Alicia, he would find a way to rescue his sister.

He put a foot through one of the holes and was stopped short by a loud bark.

Clarabelle had come into the room.

She bit the cuff of his chef's pants and dragged him back.

"OK," he said. "Not that one?"

She let go and pointed—she pointed poorly, she was a Lab after all. But she held herself steady and pointed with her injured muzzle at the smallest opening. She whined. The poor thing didn't want to be there, she didn't want to guide him, and yet here she was, and he remembered that she'd been through enough—she had lost an owner, she had been horribly injured, she had no reason to be kind. No reason to help him. And here she was, helping.

They went in together, the two of them close and less afraid now, and he was struck by how paltry and sad his newfound optimism was, how fragile its foundation: a dog, and not a particularly brave one at that. But Clarabelle gave him comfort nonetheless. He thought, *It's going to be fine, Carmen. I've got reinforcement. We're on our way.*

CHAPTER 26

THEY EMERGED FROM DARKNESS INTO the garish yellow of the pit. Clarabelle kept herself quiet. Alvaro followed suit, though the pit seemed as empty as the rest of Fremont. The machines were on but unattended, row after row sulking in the shadows. Stacks of chips sat on the game tables. So did ashtrays and drinks and a bereft pink teddy bear. Someone's lucky charm, he supposed.

They walked toward the café. Alvaro crouched and kept low to the ground.

The backs of the machines were smeared with blood. So were the walls and the floral wallpaper. He could make out handprints in the streaks. He could make out what he assumed was viscera. There were globs of something dark and rich on the walls, and the globs reflected the heavy glow of the overhead light. The odd insect worked at cleaning, at eating the soft pink and red bits, but a great number more coursed through the translucent flesh of the structure. He blinked and lost track of the bugs. The walls were walls and he blinked and the walls turned to something else. Solid, then not.

The Alicia can see us, he thought. *She knows we're here. She's—*
waiting
—waiting.
He shook off the voice. *Don't talk back*, he told himself. *Keep still.*

The red handprint of a child on a Kenny Rogers machine stared back. A slip of paper had nearly come loose from the lip of the machine, and whoever had played had won, and won big. Four thousand dollars. A single bloody thumbprint marred the edge. He wondered if the gambler had tried to get at the slip even as the world crumbled around her. He imagined she was a woman, one of the many who turned up at the Alicia, lanyard choking with loyalty cards. She must have tried to snap her winnings off before she ran. He had his own much smaller check safe and secure in his pocket, but where would he go to cash it? Somewhere beyond the Alicia, you'd find banks, surely, and people working counters, going about their lives. Somewhere there were streets that had people in it.

The hotel felt as though it were full and bustling even as it stood empty and still. The hotel digested the dead inside her walls, and he knew that something else was coming, that an additional convulsion awaited, that the Face Beneath the Face would emerge, would continue eating. Once the Face completely woke up. Once the Alicia stopped feeding it. There was no end to the appetite, no stopping it.

"Just stop," said a voice, high and whining. "Tell the oracle. Tell the tributes."

It was Steven. Alvaro recognized the cadence, the sense of entitlement.

The men from Seattle nodded, and their bodies threw long shadows on the pit. They huddled by something red and wet that had been propped and tied to a long craps table: a pile that moved and prodded lazily at the golden eye of the pit. Steven and his men wore robes and hoods, but Alvaro was sure that beneath the costumes they kept on their fleece and hiking gear. Beneath their ceremonial garb you'd find their true ceremonial garb.

The men chanted. They swiped at the light of their phones.

The wet, red pile bubbled in concert: limbs, severed but writhing still and held together with the same red yarn that Seattle and the Melmots had relied on.

Alvaro and Clarabelle slipped by. They ran into the café, unseen and unnoticed, and they ignored the overturned tables and the brown and red on the walls and found their way into the kitchen, where the smell of bloody handprints grew dense enough to overtake the green tiles. *Esther*, he thought. *All the Esthers were here*. He followed the dog as she padded to the very end of the kitchen, to the dented door of the walk-in.

Clarabelle sat and whined and Alvaro hoped that Seattle wouldn't hear them—that whatever awful thing Steven was doing would distract from the noises of the kitchen.

Clarabelle did not stop her keening. Alvaro tried to open the freezer door, but it had been locked from within, and he didn't know if it'd be a good idea to say anything. He hit the lock with his good hand.

Someone gasped, the sound muffled by the door. What he heard next was uncontrollable sobs, and he was sure it was a woman, he was absolutely sure it was a woman. Maybe Carmen.

"Please," said the voice. "Please *please* please—"

"Ellie?" he said. "I've got Clarabelle. She's hurt but she's fine."

"Please let us out, hon," Ellie said. She cried while she fumbled with whatever she'd used to jam the door on her end.

She said "us," he thought, and hoped to find Carmen next to Ellie.

The door yielded. Ellie sat alone in the shadows. Clarabelle barked and shivered, happy to see her owner but refusing to go to her—afraid of the dark place where Ellie had found safety. He couldn't blame the dog.

The cold of the freezer was not enough to hide the smell of rot: everything had gone rancid, every bag dank and moldy. He remembered the smell of the rotten mushrooms from a lifetime ago, and realized that it had only been days since he'd been confronted by Dan and drawn into the Alicia by B.

It all happened so quickly.

He had blinked and the Face Beneath the Face had stirred.

"They're gone?" Ellie said.

He nodded. "I think so," he said, thinking also, *Who? The Esthers? The Melmots? My sister? Everyone? Everyone's gone.*

Everyone's here.

Everyone's waiting.

Inside the Alicia. Deep inside we all wait.

Other sounds troubled the dark of the freezer. Deep where he could not see, where he had no intention of going, something else moved.

"They're gone," Ellie said again. She stood up and walked out.

Clarabelle licked her owner's face. The smell of rot thickened. They needed to leave. Ellie and her dog would live even if Alvaro couldn't make it out alive—even if the hotel swallowed him as he tried to find his sister. Even so, even then, his friend would live. His debt would be repaid.

"Come out, hon," Ellie said, speaking to the shadow in the freezer. "They're not here. The little girls can't get you. Marisol can't get you."

The voice whispered its answer and the sound resonated and echoed. The voice spoke in Spanish. You could hear its bone-deep regret, its wet and tired and almost-familiar sound.

Umberto sounded only a little like Umberto.

"What's he saying, hon?" Ellie said. "What's Umberto saying? He won't speak proper. I haven't been able to make out a thing he's saying. Why won't he talk? What's he saying?"

Alvaro said, "He's saying he's fine and that you don't need to worry. He'll be out in a moment. He says for you to go. He'll be fine."

Ellie still had on her carpal tunnel braces. She pulled at the Velcro and retightened it while she stared at the darkness from where Umberto spoke. You couldn't see so much as a human feature. Umberto had not moved closer to the door. Alvaro imagined him nestled in the rotting bags, a hand over his face, choking on his own regret.

"He says he's fine," Alvaro said. "We should go."

Ellie and Clarabelle looked ready to leave. "Really?" she said. "He's fine?"

Alvaro nodded and told Umberto that he should get up, that he was not to blame, not really, though that was a lie too. Umberto kept talking.

I gave her up, he whispered. *Now they're coming for me. They knew about the terrible thing I did. What I did to my own father. They knew about Marisol too. What she did to her grandmother. They knew about all our terrible pasts. And now they're coming for all of us. Someone gave me up and they're coming for me. Lock the door and let me be. I'll be fine here. I'll be safe. They're coming for me. Marisol's coming for me. Marisol and her knife and her little girls.*

Alvaro wanted to ask him why. Why give up the person you love? What would it give you? What could it possibly give you?

Maybe Umberto heard his thoughts. They did share the same dream, after all—the terrible dream of the Alicia. The answer poured out.

I didn't know, Umberto said. *I didn't know I'd given her up. I didn't know. B. didn't explain. I didn't know. They don't explain. When they ask for things and you give in—I didn't know I was giving in. She's coming for me. She's coming to claim me. Someone gave me up.*

"Who?" Alvaro said.

The scream flared in the darkness. For one burning second, Alvaro saw Umberto's bared teeth, the white of his eyes, and Umberto wouldn't listen, wouldn't quiet down, didn't care about the men from Seattle. Didn't care about anything. Didn't answer.

Alvaro and Ellie abandoned their friend in the depths of the freezer.

They heard the freezer door lock, but they did not turn around, not even the dog. Alvaro wondered how they knew that it was a bad idea to look behind them, that the Alicia found ways to keep you in place. Ellie held on to his arm. She must have been beautiful once. She was beautiful still, despite her weight and her age. She talked low. He wasn't sure if she was talking to him or to herself, but it was heartbreaking nonetheless.

She told herself the same lie—that Umberto was fine, that he just needed a moment, that he would be fine. She didn't believe Alvaro, but she repeated his words as they emerged from the blood of the kitchen and into the blood of the café. "We have to be quiet," Alvaro whispered, and she nodded and kept on talking. She had worked so many shifts here. Every day the same day. Borne endless complaints with good humor. Endless pains. She had worked and worked and worked. Now they were leaving. She'd be fine. He would sneak her to Ogden, he'd help her find her car, and then he'd lie to her again. *I'll see you soon*, he'd say. He would find his sister deep in the bowels of the hotel. All would be fine. He'd never see Ellie again.

She squeezed his arm.

He wanted to tell her that it wasn't the end. That they had a future—they all did—that they were almost out. He was done lying. He wanted to tell her that she was beautiful, but he was done telling the truth as well.

They needed to get out of the café. They needed to get past the men from Seattle and their ceremonies. They needed to be unseen and it struck him that for the most part they were, had always been. If you worked tables, if you cooked, you were practically invisible. Few people thought of you.

Almost out, he thought.

"Caballero," said Steven. He opened his robe to reveal a fanny pack. "You. Muchacho."

Alvaro had no idea that Steven spoke Spanish. He did. He did so through the tears and through the awful sores and swells of his face. He spoke Spanish with an infuriating, irritating over-enunciation of every syllable.

That's not how we talk, Alvaro wanted to say.

Steven pulled a gun from his fanny pack and pointed it at Alvaro. Clarabelle barked. Steven pointed at the dog.

"You *lied*," Steven said. "How is that even possible? Come here. *Aquí.*"

The men from Seattle chanted and tied another limb to the pile. Their own limbs were swollen and red, barely mobile. The men had wrapped themselves in red yarn but whatever protection the yarn afforded had waned. The men could barely stand. They staggered and sweated. One of them continued to consult his smartphone and directed the others, but their movements were halting and troubled, their eyelids so swollen it was a miracle they could see at all. Steven too. It was a miracle he could point a gun.

Steven shot at Clarabelle but missed and the dog jumped behind a *Wheel of Fortune* machine. No hero, that dog. Neither was Alvaro. He wanted to run. Only Ellie kept him in place—Ellie and the hope of finding Carmen. Steven shot and missed again and staggered toward them. The hood slipped and revealed the damage that the Alicia had done to the man's face—Steven was a walking wound, the skin so swollen and inflamed that it resembled Marisol's flayed body, the eyes shut, the neck tattoo engorged and beaded with pus, red strings of yarn looped ineffectually around the worst of the injuries. *Save none*, thought Alvaro. Ellie hung tight to his arm. Alvaro whispered that they had nothing to fear from them, not anymore. Steven tried to point his gun again. Tried to fire.

Alvaro said, "Where's my sister?"

"Who?" Steven said, shaking. "She's not here." He pointed at the pile. "We know everyone who's here. We don't know her."

The men chanted.

"You lied," Steven said. "You said you'd help."

"You serve the Alicia," Alvaro said. "You don't care who gets hurt."

"We're trying to stop her," Steven said. "She won't stop." He pointed the gun and smiled, bloody gums inflamed. Most of his teeth were gone. "Won't you help?" He pointed at the pile, where a bloody finger extended and pointed back. "Won't you?" The pile writhed. "Won't you feed her? She's still hungry. She's always hungry. Now that your boss let her do whatever she wanted, she won't stop."

"B.'s dead."

Steven choked on his own tears. "Don't *lie*. Why do you lie so much? He's not." He pointed below. "She's waking up. She's still eating. No one's put her to sleep, and if she doesn't go to sleep, the thing beneath her will eat us all. We gave her *everyone* and she wants more, and someone's guiding her. Your boss is guiding her. Someone else is feeding her. Someone's telling her all our secrets."

"There's no one left," Alvaro said.

Steven screamed and staggered close, his breath ragged and rank.

If they ran, Steven would kill them. He could shoot, he wouldn't miss now that he was close enough to touch, and Alvaro wanted to wrestle the gun from the bloody hand, he wanted to push Ellie to safety, he wanted to do all the things you saw people do, in stories, in movies. But the awful fact of the gun kept him in place. It kept Ellie in place too.

Not Clarabelle. Poor, brave, stupid Clarabelle.

She had emerged from behind the machine and growled at Steven. She put herself between her owner and the gun. Steven sneered.

"We take all kinds," Steven said. He pointed the gun, the barrel an inch from Clarabelle's dumb, sweet head, and Ellie cried, Ellie said to stop, and Alvaro didn't know if he was saying anything himself, if he pleaded, he couldn't hear anything, he didn't know why he loved the dog so much, why this particular bit of cruelty would get to him when so much hadn't.

Alvaro held his hands and thought, *Just—*

(*Will you? Will you? Will you give him to me? Will you give them all to me?*)

—*take him*, knowing and not knowing who he spoke to, knowing and not knowing the answer, the dark, oily abyss that thrummed in his bones and troubled his own teeth, the pain jagged and bright in his new, sharp needle tooth. The voice that was the answer and that was all hunger burned in every wound. The voice seeped and burned and slipped inside him. A black, cold nothing. Immense. The voice was his own and not his own and it was powerful and *jubilant.*

The Face said, *Yes.*

The Face Beneath the Face opened up beneath them and swallowed Steven.

The moist, translucent flesh of the Alicia bristled open—the petals wet and licking at the air, and he thought again of underwater creatures:

anemone, jellyfish, coral. The Alicia opened a gash and revealed what she kept in slumber.

The Face had no easy analogue. Immense and writhing, a mass of appendages from which other tentacles unspooled, beyond which Alvaro spotted stars and nebulae kept in place by wet, black coils. *Bigger than us. Bigger than anything. Bigger than our world. Bigger and indifferent.* You could fall, you could be swallowed, you could so easily slip in, and the system that kept the coils slithering over each other would barely register your presence, your sacrifice.

Steven was swallowed into the void of the Face: the man was nothing, and the tentacle that squeezed his body until it popped red was as big as a skyscraper.

The floor looped around itself and the Alicia healed herself, the pattern on the carpet returned to its faded flowers, its blunt thorns.

She keeps the Face in check, Alvaro realized. *The Alicia feeds, we feed her, and she feeds the Face, and if we don't—*

The Seattle men cowered in their robes, mute. No chanting now.

Did you see? he wanted to ask. *Did you see what I did to your boss?*

Do you see what I can do?

The limbs in the pile had stopped moving, the smell awful and familiar. Fruit left too long in the sun. The insects crept out of the walls and crawled toward the dead and useless offering.

Ellie had let go. "Hon, what did you do?" she asked, the look on her face filling him with shame.

The men too. Afraid. Their hands shot up.

They reminded him of the crowd by the side of the road to Ibagué. *Cattle,* he thought.

Have them too, he thought. *They're yours anyway. They were always yours. Save none.*

The men screamed, but their screams were cut short.

They were there, and then they were elsewhere, and it was better not to think of their transit. *You could go mad,* he explained. He tried to explain.

Stare at the Face for too long and you'd go mad. Better to let the men go. Better to acknowledge they were dead regardless. They didn't have long to live. No one did, if they chose to stay here.

Ellie and Clarabelle stepped back. Just as well.

It was time for Ellie to go, time for them to part ways.

"What did you do?" Ellie asked again.

"I did nothing," he said, thinking, *I killed my family. I gave them up so I could live. No one knows.*

This is nothing.

I did nothing.

Ellie would live at least. She'd drive out of Vegas. She'd have her dog, she'd be fine. And Alvaro would find Carmen. Maybe he'd see Ellie again. Maybe they would all get together. After it was all said and done, they'd find each other again. He would tell the heavy Irish waitress that she was beautiful, that he had always found her beautiful.

Her face was pale and beaded with sweat, blotchy with fear.

He wanted to tell her that he meant well. She had no reason to be afraid. She and her dog were going to be fine. He had come back for her and for his sister. He was here to save them all.

Ellie's mouth contorted and gaped, and he had a moment to note that her molars were filled with metal, that her tongue was a healthy pink, that her teeth were in far better shape than his own. Ellie's neck bent and cracked, her arms popped out of their sockets, and he screamed as Ellie flailed and made no sound.

Ellie tried to scream and her mouth cracked open.

He stood and did nothing, could do nothing. He thought of her mouth, of her dental work, of the time she must have spent at the dentist.

He had a moment to register her body, to fully witness the beauty and upkeep and fragility of his friend, before the unspeakable thing beneath them swallowed Ellie whole.

Clarabelle whimpered and drew near him.

No, no, he thought. *I can't protect you.* Alvaro was sure that it was him. He had somehow given Ellie up.

He had killed her, surely.

He had killed the others, after all. It had taken so little effort.

But the dog thought him innocent, and he believed the dog. He had nothing to apologize for. He had tried to save Ellie. Someone else was responsible. Not him. Not him.

His breath was ragged. The Alicia waited. The walls opened onto the service corridors and the ballroom, but he didn't know where to go, what to say, until he heard a faint, watery rush. *It could be bugs,* he thought. *It could be anything.*

He thought of fairy tales again, and moved through the yellow light of the pit and into the dark and mold of the ballroom, and then thought of forests.

He followed what sounded like a river. Las Vegas was so dry and the Alicia collected so much water inside herself.

The walls were so wet, the pipes so full.

He didn't know why his forehead throbbed or why he found himself in the center of the ballroom, why the broken generator hummed and sputtered, or why the holes that opened like enormous wounds in the carpet brimmed with black water that smelled like vinegar and rot, or why he sank into the water—why he dipped a naked part of himself into the lifeblood of the Alicia.

He didn't know even if he did know.

He communed with the thing. He felt its wriggling mind inside his own. It was like nothing he had felt—how cold her thoughts were, how hunger coated every impulse, how the Alicia's appetite was pure life, a thriving slime, and how it polluted everything and everyone it came into contact with.

His hand sank deeper into the cold and the black.

When something pulled at his hand—when something grasped and nearly dragged him under—he pulled back until the Alicia yielded one of her own: the hotel's gift to Alvaro and Carmen, the conduit and the oracle, her faithful servant, the person who warned and the one who cajoled.

Jacob.

CHAPTER 27

OUT OF JACOB'S MOUTH POURED the same black liquid that coursed beneath the Alicia's bristling, pink flesh. Alvaro pulled the old man out of the muck. The liquid dribbled out of Jacob's mouth and out of his hollows and spilled onto the broken concrete and torn carpet of the ballroom.

Jacob weighed little, even in his sodden state. *The things living inside him are no longer there,* Alvaro realized. They had torn loose. They had rejoined the Alicia. It was just Jacob now, and there wasn't much to him—he was a husk, his wet flesh folded open and roped around the shreds of his blazer and shirt. A lone insect made its melancholy circuit out of the hole in the man's thigh.

You are the oracle, Alvaro thought, *and the conduit.*

Speak.

Jacob's mouth opened. A hiss. No words. His teeth had all been pulled out, his tongue had been eaten away. Alvaro settled the husk of Jacob against a stack of chairs. Jacob's hand flapped into his pocket and emerged with a wet pack of cigarettes and a blackened book of matches. The old man tried to strike a wet match. He dangled what remained of a cigarette on his lip. He struck match after match and nothing happened.

"OK," Alvaro said. "OK."

Alvaro clambered to the broken stage and found a lighter on the podium, remembered when B. had gathered all his workers. Winifred had been there. She had clicked her high heels to the generator. *That's Winifred's lighter,* he thought. *Please let this work.*

The lighter did its job, but the cigarette looked too damp and soiled to be rescued. The coal came to life against all odds. Jacob sucked with greed. Smoke poured out of him, and that's when Alvaro heard him—the oracle, the conduit of the Alicia, back to life, and what he heard first was a bitter laugh, and he smelled the old man's breath, vinegary and sour and sweet with death, the breath of the Alicia.

Jacob spoke and smoked, though he lacked the anatomy to do either.

Jacob said, "You're too late. The Alicia cannot contain the Face, none of us can. None of us can access the Room. Your sister was supposed to come. She said she'd come, she said she'd give herself up, she was supposed to be here, with us, swimming with us in the dream of the Alicia, but she's gone."

"No," Alvaro said.

"She's not here. She's not in the Nightmare Room. We can't find her. She was our tribute, our willing tribute. You or her. The Alicia hungered for you, for your return. All you had to do was say yes."

"No," Alvaro said again, sure of himself.

"Someone's feeding us. Someone keeps feeding us." Jacob took a long drag and his cloudy eyes filled with smoke. "What she'll do when she awakes we don't know. All the Esthers stir, they move through the hotel, they come for anything with flesh. Can't you hear them?"

Alvaro could. The hotel had been quiet and now the sound was the sound of rain. Even Clarabelle registered the presence of the Esthers: she flattened herself against Alvaro and whined, her ears pressed back.

"They're coming," Jacob said. "There's no stopping them. No stopping because there's no stop to the feeding, no end to the dream. Once they come, they'll only listen to the first Esther—they'll only listen to my daughter. She cannot be reached. You cannot walk out of the Nightmare Room. You cannot walk in. We have no one to let her out, no means to do so. No sacrifice. You give up a loved one. We asked you to give yourself up

and now it's too late, there's nothing. There's no one. There's no one left."
Smoke rose out of his eyelids. "Don't you see? Do you see why we serve?"
His face was the face of a true believer, the face of a man who had killed
his own daughter. "Why we keep the Alicia in her state of slumber? Why
we can't kill the thing that eats?"

"Because the Face is worse," Alvaro said. "Because the Alicia keeps the
Face in check." He saw the Face once more—how it slithered and pulsed,
how it hungered, how enormous was its hunger.

Jacob took another drag of his cigarette. "We're done, at any rate. All
the Jacobs. The first and the last and all of us, called under by the Alicia.
Dispatched. She calls her servants unto her but the Esthers run wild.
They will not listen to their father." He smiled his black toothless smile.
"They will not listen to their mother. They listen to no one because they
still hunger. Because they are still being fed. Still they are fed. Still they
make their transit out of the walls and into the void of your life, and they
run out. The Melmots had their men go after the girls, and now the men
are gone. No more. The ones who profited from the Alicia, the ones who
thought they could channel her energy. You." Again the black smile, the
white smoke. "You have failed, and there's no one. Put me back. Drag me
back to the dark water, lest my children find me. Lest my children tear me
apart. We tried to do good. The Alicia did her best, she wanted you, and
you turned your back, and so you lost your kin, but don't say we didn't try.
You refused to hear. You refused to spill your secrets. To whisper your life
unto her. You said no when you should have said yes."

"No," Alvaro said.

"Put me back."

Alvaro tried to imagine the ballroom restored to its former glory. B.
had been so optimistic, so sure that he could renew the hotel—to turn it
into something magnificent. Something other than itself.

Jacob said, "Please put me back. We're done. The Alicia will awaken,
she will fully awaken, and when she does, the Face will slip out of her
dream and into the thing that the Alicia dreamed into being. *This*." He

waved at the faded carpet and the dead chandelier. "Will you do this? Will you let me rejoin my brethren?"

Alvaro had no reason to be kind, no reason to take pity on Jacob, who belonged to the Alicia, who could be blamed—at least in part—for what Alvaro had lost. It was easy to be cruel, he realized. You could walk away from the pain of others. You could enjoy their suffering, tell yourself that you had little time, that if you wanted to live you had to find a way out, you had to do your best to leave the orbit of the hotel—and how far away could you go, really? How long could you run down the abandoned dream of Fremont before you ran into other people? Before life returned? Alvaro did not know. Did you? You'd have to run far. You'd have to find a car and drive—you could leave Jacob to his little girls and their teeth. You had no time, not if you wanted to live.

If.

If, then.

He dragged Jacob back to the black pool, the old man's cigarette nearly gone, his stained fingers tight against the recessed tip of the filter. Everyone smoked the same brand here. Even Winifred.

A sacrifice.

I didn't know, Umberto had said. *I didn't know I'd given her up. I didn't know. They don't explain. When they ask for things and you give in—I didn't know I was giving in.*

Alvaro had kept Winifred's lighter in his pocket, not knowing why, and it was only as the black waters crept over the face of Jacob that he realized that Winifred had taken something of his even as he had taken something that belonged to her.

You don't need that, she'd said.

Carmen's backpack.

I didn't know I'd given her up.

He ran and Clarabelle ran beside him, the hiss of the Esthers closing in. He knew where he'd find Winifred, and he hoped that he'd find her before the little girls did. A part of him hoped. A part of him wondered if it'd be better if he guessed wrong—if Winifred had already slipped away or had been otherwise dealt with by the hotel.

Alvaro would be absolved. He had tried and he had failed.

I've been wrong about so many things, he thought.

This hiss of the little girls grew louder in the elevators. *They had gotten to her already*, he told himself. They came at her with their teeth, with the knives of their mother, with their hunger. Most of the living had been taken care of. Soon the little girls would take care of him too.

CHAPTER 28

IN WINIFRED'S PENTHOUSE OFFICE, UNDER the startled eyes of the crumbling flamingos, Alvaro pulled a battered U-Haul box up off the floor. Inside were the keepsakes reported missing by the Alicia staff. He found drawings, notes, family photos, too many found things thought lost. More than there should be.

"There's more up here."

Winifred emerged out of the slit in the wall, the one B. had once used to lead Alvaro underground.

"I thought you were gone," he said. "Swallowed up."

She said, "More over there too." She held personnel files in a manila folder and pointed at the space beneath her desk, where she had crammed six more boxes stuffed with what people kept to remember their lives.

He spotted the photo of Ellie and Clarabelle right away. He picked up a sheaf of Crayola drawings next to Ellie's photo. A child had drawn himself next to his mom, the child drawn unreasonably small, the mom unreasonably large. The child wore green pants and a red shirt and the mom had bright-yellow spiky hair and wore bright-blue pants and a bright-blue shirt.

"You took these," Alvaro said. "You stole them."

"I can't tell you everything," Winifred said.

Alvaro said, "You don't have to tell me anything. You just have to stop feeding her."

Winifred nodded but kept going, her pale, freckled face aglow, her hair wiry and red. She dropped a W-2 form. Froth rose on the carpet, bright and pink, and a soft, hungry opening swallowed the form in one gulp. Then the floor turned to floor again.

"Stop," he said.

"I've made mistakes," she said. "You've made mistakes too, but the big ones are all in the past." She looked at the floor, where the puckered opening reemerged. "We all make mistakes. We mean well." She pointed at the box of stolen keepsakes. "Look deeper inside."

Alvaro pocketed Ellie's photo and stuck his arms deep into the box. His arms sank into the rich, peculiar variety of paper stock, some glossy, some crinkly, some pulpy. He pulled out a handful, thinking of the first padlocked corridor, the one he helped Winifred open. The painted beach. The smell of her skin: limes and cinnamon and money. The lost copy of his forged passport.

He said, "Seattle and B. didn't know, did they? That you've been feeding her? What you've been feeding her with?"

Winifred didn't bother answering. "Look at what you're holding," she said. "B. said to get rid of all this. First he asked me to gather them, feed the hotel—expand, expand, expand, you know? Then it was all, *stop.*" She scratched her neck with a corner of the folder. "I mean, grow some fucking balls."

"Now she's helping you find them."

She nodded. "The boxes just appear. Box after box after box. I think it's Lost and Found who's been bringing them in, but who can tell? Who's to know? It's got to be her workers, and there's so many. This one was waiting in room 33."

"You have to stop," he said.

"Look at what you're holding," she said. "Really look. Try to understand."

The photos came from another decade, another century. He held Koda-chrome and Polaroid images. The children in the photograph wore jeans whose waists rode too high, or they wore coats from stores long out of business. All of Vegas vanished over time. He did not leave Fremont but he'd heard the news. Winifred herself had told him. The dead Sears on Tropicana, the gutted Dillard's at the Boulevard Mall, the Burger King on Tropicana and Decatur that burned down and was left in ruins for a year. Malls and strip malls stood with nothing on them, no one in them.

The photos all belonged to Vegas, every photo marked by a Vegas backdrop. He recognized parts of the city he'd never been to, mostly because he couldn't *not* recognize them. He knew the Strip from photos and movies. He even knew the sad vein of motels and forlorn wedding chapels linking the Strip to Fremont, though he had not even ventured that far. He picked up another photograph. An eight-year-old posed in front of the Stratosphere, leaning forward and holding his arms apart, the foreshortened angle making the kid look as though he held the building in his hands. He wore a T-shirt too big for him, the shirt bearing intense faces and terrible hair. "New Kids on the Block," it read. Alvaro picked up another photo, black and white, gone green with age. Another child standing on an empty expanse of road, his hand resting on a monster of a car, the backdrop the camel outline and block letters of the Sahara sign. They were closing that one down too, or they already had but could not find a buyer. He picked up another stack of photographs. A group of brides stood in front of the Sands, the New Frontier, a rundown cafeteria called the White Cross, a small blue shop called Luv-It Frozen Custard, whose typography and general state of decay suggested that it'd close at any moment. The place must be gone now, a remnant of a more innocent past. The brides held their arms in various angles suggesting semaphore flags, ships at sea. Behind the brides in their variegated gowns of taffeta and tulle stood the half-built Stratosphere, the beams and blocks reminding Alvaro of the Death Star in *Return of the Jedi*, the dazzling intersection of massive empty space and massive interlocking matter. Of something massive not quite built.

He said, "These are all from miles and miles away."

"Couple dozen blocks," Winifred said. "Vegas Boulevard and Sahara and beyond." She stood in her black dress, her red hair barely contained by two glossy, oversized combs. That woman was electric. She walked toward him, her heels clicking in the echo chamber of the penthouse, her face and body perfectly composed.

"But that's not all," he said.

She smiled. The eyes of the flamingos troubled him.

"Alvaro, look at me," she said. "Look at the photos."

"The Alicia's not *here*," he said. "She's in the past and in the future. She pulls from everywhere. We're outside of time."

"Look at the fucking *faces* in the photos."

No.

The eyes of the flamingos. Wild and startled and innocent.

They were all dreaming, and they could not wake up.

They dreamed and the Alicia feasted.

Winifred said, "Look at the faces."

He did. He saw. Finally, he saw. There was Winifred in a bridal gown. There was Carmen, his sister—a bridesmaid. There he was too, Alvaro himself, in photo after photo. Ellie too. They reappeared, they showed up in impossible configurations. Umberto too. Everyone here a child of the Alicia.

"How long have we been here?" he said.

"Who knows?" she said. "Who knows what we are?"

My children.

You are my children.

"Why?"

"I think the hotel sends us out," Winifred said. "She sends us out and then she calls us back, after we've done our terrible work. She sends us out to suffer and then she gathers us up. Maybe. Fuck if I know." She laughed.

The children of the Alicia suffered and the Alicia feasted on their suffering.

"Alvaro," she said, "the Alicia wants a sacrifice. She wants a *tribute*. That's why she made us. You give it to her, things work out for you."

"They don't," he said.

She fed the mold on the floor a fistful of drawings.

278 | JUAN MARTINEZ

Carmen's drawings.

"Give me back my sister," he said. "Stop."

"If you don't . . ." She shrugged.

"You're hurting people," he said. "You're hurting my sister. You're hurting Ellie."

She said, "We're not *people*."

He held up the photo. Ellie and her Lab grinned.

He said, "You've got to stop." He didn't care what she'd done. He didn't think, did not know he was not thinking, did not know he had been holding her until she screamed and one of her feet sank into the floor.

The mold pooled around her legs, hungry. It grew fast, thick and pink, hot and vinegary. She threw receipts and an ID card at the puckered surface and yanked her foot from the floor, her foot bloody and raw, the skin scraped. "I can't," she said. "You can't stop. Once you start, you can't stop."

He tried to hold her. She shivered, but her skin felt damp and too warm. Feverish.

She pulled away and dropped photos in her wake. "Your sister is fine. These people are fine," she said. "I'm not hurting anyone." She didn't believe it. "I'm not," she said, arguing with the part of herself that knew better. "It's not like we're people anyway. And these are just memories. Your sister isn't really here. Not here, not beneath. She's fine. She's just elsewhere."

The floor opened, hundreds of soft, puckered orifices pooling about. She fed the openings. The mold bubbled and split into itself, its interior lined with jagged thorns, thorns like teeth, long and black, the flesh on the thorns the same pink as the mold on the wall. He thought of coral reefs, of a squid hiding in a reef, of the beaks you see in squids, remembered that his parents caught squid when they were young and lived in Curaçao, a full year before they had him. He did not keep their Curaçao album. It was likely lost now. It was likely a lie anyway, this past. All of his memories. He was the only one who remembered what his parents did before they had him and his sisters, and he wasn't sure about the memories—if they were real beyond the dream of the Alicia.

Winifred's ankles bled as she moved, but the floor swallowed the red trail.

He followed, Winifred backing away, photos still in hand, the Alicia fully awake now, the Face Beneath the Face rising from its own slumber.

"They're just memories," she said. "And all they do is go away. Wouldn't you want that?"

She threw a journal into the rot and boil of the waiting surface. She threw an iPad and a cell phone.

"Wouldn't you?" she said. "Your parents? Your dead sister? Wouldn't you want to wipe that clean?"

She dropped a flurry of birthday cards and Mother's Day cards.

She said, "She sends us out to kill our loved ones. Did you know that? All of us killed someone we loved. You more than others. She loves you the most."

She fed the holes in the floor and walked around them, always facing Alvaro, never looking at the craters. He thought, *She trusts the Alicia more than she trusts me.* He couldn't blame her.

She said, "Don't you want it all gone? Your guilt? What you did to your sister, your family?"

That much was true, almost. He didn't want his memories, but he didn't want them gone either. He didn't want them swallowed.

"Here," she said, holding a copy of his forged Social Security card. "Wouldn't you want it all gone? All of it? Your whole sorry life?"

She crumpled the paper. He took one step. She threw it at the floor and the floor swallowed it.

He did not bother telling her that the document was not his. He had no idea who it belonged to. She must know. He had told her. She must not be thinking clearly.

He said, "You're running out."

She held a fistful of photographs, but they thinned as she edged the slit in the wall, where another box of photographs waited. More memories. More pain. She bled into the hotel, and when she held on to a photo for too long, the mold licked at her bloody heels. He thought of *The Red Shoes*. The ballerina who could not stop dancing. Winifred's own feet were now mostly red, her face wet with tears, pinched with pain. Her foot sank into the rot again. She said, "Ow," and lifted her mangled foot. "It doesn't stop. It just doesn't stop."

"It does if we leave," he said.

"Leave where? We're home." She threw a photo at the rug. Laughed. "You haven't looked outside in a while, have you?"

The penthouse windows offered no help. No one had moved the plywood.

She held her last photo aloft and he was close enough to make it out in detail: Marisol standing next to her grandmother. Marisol smiled, and so did Winifred.

He did not know that you could love someone who did monstrous things. He was so young, he realized. What did he know about love?

Take her, Alvaro thought. *Take this person that I love. I give her to you.*

When the mold opened again, it was for Winifred herself. She screamed. The Alicia ate her up in three quick bits, the scream cut short, her bones cracking, all of her turning into a wet bag.

The last he saw of her was a shock of red hair, and then the floor insisted that nothing had happened.

The Alicia worked so quickly.

He thought, *Poor Winifred*, but nearly forgot what she looked like. What she smelled like. Who she was.

He tried to remember, but he understood that once she was gone, she was no longer here, no longer anywhere. The hotel claimed her and once it did, there were echoes. The hotel could make more Winifreds, each with the same identical face, but he wouldn't know them. Wouldn't remember them. Echoes, all of them, all of us. She had asked him if he had looked outside. He still had the photographs that belonged to Ellie and to Marisol, and so he kept them safe. The floor hummed. The Face Beneath the Face waited for its tribute. That was all you had to do. It was such a little thing, and you gained so much. You gained the world. You served all, saved none. You forgot everyone.

The photos stayed in his pocket. There were other forms of tribute, other ways of quieting the Face. He knew that now.

He moved the plywood.

Instead of Fremont, what he saw, what he almost touched, was a solid wall of pink, wet mold.

"Come."

He turned around. Not surprised. He had given up someone he loved, had been given in return what Jacob promised.

Esther waited for him by the elevator in her pigtails, her dress. Ellie's dog sat by the girl's side. Clarabelle. The dog practically as tall as the little girl. Such a tiny thing, and not a little girl at all. The dog keened and howled.

Poor Clarabelle.

"Her owner was sacrificed," Esther said, petting the dog, "but Clarabelle lived. She survived."

"Why does she help us? Why a dog?"

"Because the world has good," Esther said. "Because she's good." The girl pushed a button and they stood in silence until the doors groaned. "Come," she said. "We haven't much time. We can still stop the Face."

He did not believe it, but he hoped it was true, that what Jacob had told him was true—here was the first Esther, the one Jacob had killed, the one that Alvaro's sacrifice of Winifred released, and because she had been the first, she was innocent, she could lead him to Carmen. He could trust her. He hoped he could trust her. He followed her, and so did the dog.

They had nowhere else to go.

CHAPTER 29

ESTHER SAID, "WE NEED TO get to the Nightmare Room." The elevator rattled and the little girl pressed the only clean button on the panel. Mold and blood covered everything else.

"Was that button there before?" he said.

"Have you dreamed of the Room?" she said. "The wet pile of bodies? The wet sounds in the dark? The flashlight in the corner?"

He nodded. He'd dreamed it, he remembered it, he wasn't sure. The elevator lurched.

They descended.

"You've been there," she said.

The wet pile waited for sacrifice and grew fat with it. Grew all the more unsteady, all the more immobile. The thing that ate and ate and ate. The thing that would not stop eating.

He said, "What are we?"

"We're people," she said, her teeth inhuman. "We're as much people as anyone. Even if the Alicia made us, trapped us, sent us out into the world. You ran. You and your family made it out so far and she called you out eventually. My sister came for you."

"The little girl in the forest."

She tapped her nose. "We're people," she said. "We're instruments of pain."

"My sister isn't," he said.

The elevator lurched to a halt. The doors refused to open.

"I dream of your sister. We all do. I dream of the Room all the time," she said. "I dreamed of it when I was there and I dream it now that I am not there. All of us there and not there." Her eyes shone red in the wet, and it was not entirely possible to tell whether or not she cried. "All of us lost ourselves here. We grew out of the walls, our dreams the dreams of the Esthers before us, the Jacobs, the Alvaros. Nobody leaves." She squeezed his hand. "Even when we think we've left, we haven't. She comes for us. Gathers us in. Her instruments of pain."

The doors lurched open. She pointed. Through the casino pit, up the service corridor, down the back of the third floor.

Alvaro petted Clarabelle and said, "Let's go."

They walked the pit of the casino. The dream of the Alicia differed in no regard from waking life, because you dreamed yourself into thinking you were awake, alive, real. So did the Face. They may be dreaming of it even now, even as you listen to him, as he himself dreamed of it. He kept a hand on Clarabelle and tried to keep steady.

The dreams of the Alicia intruded.

The hotel gleamed, all of its lights on, the room a gaudy yellow, its floors dark with slaughter.

Handprints on the wall.

He imagined flamingos and for a moment saw them, a jagged band of pink directly overhead.

They walked on.

Rain fell hard on the roof, their steps swallowed by the sound. The rain grew louder and drowned out the sulk of the Alicia, and only when Esther spoke did he realize he was wrong. The rain was not really rain.

"They're coming," she said.

Voices flooded the cavern of the pit.

The girls streamed from every entrance. They filled the room, too many of them, hundreds, arms outstretched, arms open.

They wore calico dresses, the patterns delicate, floral, each of their gummy hair done up in a ponytail. They had faces like the faces he'd seen in the dream of the Alicia. No eyes. No nose. Their skin shone like rubber, slick and wet, skin like no skin he'd seen on anyone: puckered, scarred with pinprick holes that sucked in the air and hissed it out.

That's my face too, he realized. *My true face.* They were all alike, all made of the same wriggling, spongy material—the children of the Alicia.

Their mouths gaped and their needle teeth gleamed in the yellow light. The insides of their mouths too pink. They screamed and ran, teeth snapping, their awful sound the only sound in the world. A rain to end all rains. A hiss.

Clarabelle barked, but he could not hear her.

Esther tugged on his shirt, smiled, a rotting needle held tight in one hand.

She ran at the froth of teeth.

He ran after her, screaming something he himself could not hear, thinking all the while, *I guess we're charging.*

Thinking, too, *I guess the Alicia doesn't want us here. She's blocking our way.* There was some relief in that, in knowing they were doing the right thing, going against the wishes of their mother.

He picked up a café chair. *We can do this*, he thought.

The teeth snapped and his relief vanished.

Alvaro and Esther and Clarabelle cut their way through a river of girls.

There were too many of the things (*not things: family*), too many to count, but the corridor narrowed, so the numbers mattered less, the girls all charging at once, their teeth chattering, their anger too pure. They trampled each other. They jammed shoulder to shoulder in their pinafore dresses and could not move. The pinpricks coursing through their skin hissed.

A girl snapped a chunk of Esther's shoulder, red and black, a mess of blood and flesh and fabric.

He swung the chair hard on a jaw, the jaw attached to what looked for all the world like a little girl. His own sister. He swung it again, swung it hard, until the jaw stopped moving.

Her teeth were clotted, and then they were broken, and then she was off.

Alvaro said, "You're fine," but Esther could not hear. Alvaro himself could not hear.

Keep going, he told himself. *Keep moving.*

He ran, teeth snapping behind him. Esther running, keeping up.

They cleared the stairs and turned a corner and ran headlong into nothing and no one.

No girls.

The corridor glared, the carpet alive with flowers and thorns. The pattern throbbed in the stillness and emptiness and did the best to fill the void.

That was part of the problem of the Nightmare Room. It split off. It fractured. They dreamed the same dream, but now they dreamed it apart, dreamed it close and far away.

Esther smiled and leaned against a wall and then was elsewhere.

Not here.

Not somewhere else.

Stay still, don't move, Alvaro told himself. It was difficult. He was so used to moving. That was how he and Carmen had ended up here. How the family had escaped the orbit of their mother in the first place. They could not stay still, could not wait to be elsewhere, couldn't be anywhere for long. Stay rooted and your own worst self caught up with you. Your worst fears caught up with you. All of your regret, your anger, your shame. The shame was worst of all. He thought, *My family knows. I let them go. I shot Alba. They know I've lost Carmen. They know everything. My mother knows. My sister knows.* Never mind that the Alicia herself had sent them forth, had set them up to replicate the sacrifice that brought her to life. (*Will you give them to me?*) He thought of how ashamed Alba must be, how sad he would have made her. Had she lived.

"I was never ashamed," Alba said. "Never. Not of you."

She stood in the corridor of the hotel, his little sister, her arms propped on her stomach.

She wasn't there, it wasn't her. Her face and arms as long as yours. As ours. The whole family too long. Spindly.

She said, "Let's go. It's time."

The wrong sister, he thought. The one who died.

She stood by the open door of the Nightmare Room, her arms waiting to embrace him. "Carmen's here," she said. "We all are. All of us."

"No," he said.

She smiled, she agreed. *Yes*, she seemed to say. *Alvaro is not going. Fine.* Her eyes focused elsewhere.

That smile, that nod, they weren't for him.

They were for whoever stood behind him.

The X-Acto knife gleamed in Charleen's hand. He froze. She sliced his cheek. She wore the same blue tracksuit. Three white stripes. Adidas. The light of the room was the yellow light of the Vegas streets. His cheek burned, it had not hurt and now half his face screamed, his cheek wet.

Blood fell onto the carpet.

"I was never ashamed," his sister said again, but he could no longer see her.

Charleen held the knife high above her, her smile frozen.

I tried to help, he thought.

Carmen would have to manage without him.

Even Esther would—the Esther who had broken free for a while.

Because we let you.

The Alicia sets you free on the world. So you can suffer.

Then she brings you back.

He ducked. The knife missed and cut at the air by his neck. The woman held the knife up again, but moved slowly, in hesitant jerks. The Alicia struggled, and with her all of her helpers. In growing large, the hotel also grew slow. Sluggish. He felt sluggish himself, his blood still dripping onto the carpet, the flowers and thorns stained and wet, too much of him puddled in there.

He threw himself at the woman, hoping he'd be of some help, hoping he was doing good, not really knowing, sure only that this was it. He was dying.

Charleen would finish him off. He hoped he could slow her down, thinking, *I should have done that in Colombia. I let them die. I helped. I was complicit. I could have helped.* He could have said no.

Shoot me before they make me shoot you.

Will you give them all to me?

No.

He hoped there was something beyond the Alicia, something good, something other than the voice of the Face Beneath the Face, but the darkness yawned and took him in. It did not speak, because it did not need to. Nothing waited for him. That was the sound of the universe, the sound in his head, the buzz of hornets and hunger, all of his life adding up to nothing. You end up at the heart of what you ran from. The fear. The dead sister he tried to leave behind. The edge of the Nightmare Room. The edge of a knife closing in on his eye.

Surely he was done. He had been lucky and now he was done with luck. Done with everything.

He was out of the little time he had been given.

He had too much time now that the knife crept close. Too much time to think and doubt and regret before he died.

The world grew dark.

He assumed he was dead.

A weight pressed heavy on his chest, and he recognized the good fur smell of a Labrador. Clarabelle stood on top of him and blocked his field of vision.

She also blocked the thrust of the knife.

Clarabelle growled and tugged at a mass, but he could not make it out, not from the floor. He thought, *No, girl. Charleen has a knife. She could hurt you.*

Something tore, the sound like Velcro coming apart.

The air hissed, the rug hot beneath him. Wet. Wetter. The Lab yowled in the darkness and lunged and he was finally able to see, he was finally able to get on his knees.

The dumb, enormous dog bled from her haunch, the cut awful and bleeding still, but she wasn't letting go of what she had in her bloody muzzle, what she held on to, which licked at the air still, nubs hissing and reaching out like worms, like the insides of a pomegranate, like an aquatic creature, pale and gelatinous. The writhing nubs reached for Clarabelle even as Clarabelle growled and held on to it, the thing as big as Clarabelle's head.

He finally recognized it, only because the tracksuit twitched, the X-Acto knife still jerking about ineffectually in a blind hand, the torso of the woman who now had no head.

Because that is what Clarabelle had in her mouth, what the dog shook and tore at.

Charleen's head.

"Let go," Alvaro said. "Let it be." He grabbed at the twitching mess, the nubs groping blindly at his own fingers, and played tug-of-war with Clarabelle until she finally let go. "Thank you," he said.

The dog limped closer and licked his face. She whimpered.

Please be OK, he thought. Maybe the cut wasn't so bad. Maybe she could make it. Maybe the big, stupid dog who saved his stupid life would make it.

"Thank you," he said again.

Alvaro and Clarabelle stood by the closed door of the Nightmare Room, his chef's pants torn to shreds, a single bloody handprint on his T-shirt, the print too small. A kid's. A little girl's.

Something fell out of his own shredded pocket. A tooth, long and rotting.

He had pulled it out of the mushroom bag a lifetime ago.

A gift.

A gift from Jacob, torn from the Alicia herself, lodged deep in the freezer, where it waited for him.

And he had kept it all this time, this tooth that cut into his hand and felt good and light and as capable of inflicting pain as Charleen's knife.

He'd mistaken what the little girl held for a knitting needle. He'd seen her holding it in front of her. She had been given a gift too.

Alvaro didn't want to ask, figured it'd be better if he kept his mouth shut, but as the corridor settled into itself, their path to the Nightmare Room finally clear, he knew what the problem was, what had nagged his relief since Alba had spoken to him.

What he had lost track of.

Who.

"Esther?" he said.

"Here." The voice came from inside the closed door of the Nightmare Room.

The door opened, the entryway too dark to see in, but the little girl who had gathered him and the dog and led them here now waited in the shadows, she was lost, and he didn't know what to say or what to do. He thought, *I should pray*. He didn't. Clarabelle whimpered, the only sound troubling the silence of the Alicia.

The hotel gloated.

Alvaro staggered, tried to move, tried to get back to the little girl, who had allowed him to open a door that should not open. He was afraid, but he walked in anyway, they both did, the wounded man and the wounded dog.

CHAPTER 30

CLARABELLE WHIMPERED. THE POOR DOG. Her back leg shook when she stood still. She'd been hurt too, she'd been hurt badly, but she stayed close to Alvaro and kept going.

Any other animal would have fled, he thought.

All of Vegas had fled, anyone originally here gone already, his friends and coworkers included. Gone or swallowed. It was just him and a dog, Ellie and Winifred and B. and Dan and all the rest of them swallowed by the darkness of the Alicia. He remembered Marisol and her lost photograph, her flayed body, her soulless eyes. He didn't want to worry about her or about Umberto. *The Alicia sent us elsewhere, had us deliver a sacrifice—a loved one—and she called us back.* Better not to know right now. Better not to think of what he had lost, what he had been made to lose, because they had lost so much, all of them, and now they were going to lose more.

He walked toward the pile of flayed bodies, where Esther waited.

The two of them each held a long, thin tooth, each knew that what they were doing was ancient. Jacob had done this to Esther. People in the Bible had done this.

He knew, he must have known, why they were here, why they needed to get beyond the Room.

They needed to feed the Alicia the wrong things.

Esther and Alvaro walked closer to the pile, each already knowing that *they* were the wrong things, the things that would put the hotel to sleep (*The Alicia sets you free on the world. So you can suffer. Then she brings you back*)—hopefully to sleep for good. Or for a while at least.

"It's OK," Esther said. "I've done this before. You won't remember it hurting."

The pile extended its flayed arms, its hunger wet and ready, waiting.

Esther said, "The girls are coming, they're coming still. When we are swallowed, when we are gone, they'll keep coming. I don't think it just stops. It takes a while."

"You don't know," Alvaro said.

"We know we can stop it," Esther said.

"You don't know if we're helping her or hurting her," Alvaro said.

"We don't know," Esther said.

"But we know we dreamed it," Alvaro said. "We dreamed of this place and we dreamed of each other and we dreamed we were here. We're dreaming it right now even as it is happening."

Esther said nothing. She didn't need to.

Alvaro looked at the little girl by his side and desperately wanted to apologize, but they were out of words, they were out of time, they could feel the Alicia fumble into wakefulness.

Esther squeezed his free hand with hers.

They ran before they could say anything else, before they had time to really think, their teeth in hand.

It was only when he was about to jump into the wet pile that he saw the blur by his side, which he at first mistook for another Esther. He thought that the hotel was trying to stop them.

It wasn't.

Clarabelle ran alongside them. The dog jumped when they jumped.

The flayed hands took the three of them in.

––

The ballroom was aglow, the light from the chandeliers soft and constant and gauzy. Alvaro, Esther, and Clarabelle walked close together. The room was nothing like his first memory of the place, when B. gathered his staff and asked them to call him Loco, and nothing like the rest of the Alicia, with its moldering fixtures and green walls. The hotel repainted itself, presented itself anew. The partitions separating the rooms had been removed, so the banquet table stretched unbroken and out of sight. The linen stretched unbroken too. The silverware glittered. It was a kind of heaven, he supposed, since everyone seated at the table must have died— must have been swallowed, like they had been.

Waiters in plum blazers arrived with loaded silver trays of rare roast beef and boiled potatoes and glasses of water and red wine.

The dead sat in their chairs and ate and talked and laughed. It was entirely possible that Alvaro and Esther were expected to join them, that two chairs waited for them here. No one approached.

B. sat next to his son, who sat next to Winifred.

Winifred popped a sliver of beef into her mouth, caught Alvaro's eyes, and looked away, her red hair turning too.

"We keep walking," Esther said.

Alvaro nodded, his grip tight around the ancient tooth. He thought, *I found it in a bag of rotten mushrooms. I found it a whole lifetime ago, before I knew I had nothing like a life, long after I lost my parents, before I thought I could lose or find anything else.* They walked. They had not been invited to the feast. They were interlopers.

"This isn't what it looks like," he said.

"It isn't," Esther said.

Meat glistened on the rows of plates. The men and women huddled close over the food, the conversation low but pleasant, their faces convincing. They looked like the people they'd been.

"And we're not dead," he said. "Not yet."

He didn't say, *And this isn't the ballroom of the Alicia.*

This isn't a place—this border between the Alicia and the thing that the Alicia keeps in check.

The Face Beneath the Face was nothing they had the right words for. They neared the enormous wet, black tentacles, the coils that coiled around whatever approached, whatever the Face could eat.

The hungry thing as big as their universe. Bigger still.

They had constructed a language for it, they had made up an enormous room to stand in for a place they could not understand. The place barely held together. The beef smelled right but looked as though it came out of an animal they wouldn't recognize. The conversation of the dead sounded pleasant enough, but when he forced himself to listen, it buzzed like radio static.

The long table turned into an enormous organ—something aquatic and immense and *alive*, all pores and nubs, pink and spiked with thorns, and the Face Beneath the Face throbbed, the whole room filling itself with its own hunger.

We came here, he thought. *Or we were led here.*

The organ turned once again into a banquet table, and they walked along its edge until Esther stopped short and said, "Oh!"

Jacob, her father, sat and ate. He wore a dinner jacket. He had shaven, his face clean, his hair neat. He drank water, his wine glass turned upside down on the table.

"Come," Jacob said. "Sit. It'd be much better if you sat."

Clarabelle whined. Ellie waited for them two seats from Jacob, her wrists free from their braces, her face broad and tanned and at rest. She sat directly across another freshly shaven man in a green shirt.

"Here, girl," the man said.

But Clarabelle wouldn't go near him, wouldn't go near Ellie. The poor dog whined and keened.

"She doesn't remember me," the man said.

Alvaro remembered, though: the homeless man by the Alicia, the one who had lost his dog, who had paid honest money for Clarabelle's leash.

"Sit," Jacob said.

Esther shook her head.

"She doesn't love me anymore," the homeless man said.

"She does, hon," Ellie said, "but she won't go near you." She ate a bit of meat and her fork glimmered in the ballroom light. "She loves you, but she won't go near you because you are dead, and because you smell like a dead thing."

"We need to go," Alvaro said.

Ellie nodded. Her eyes watered.

Two chairs waited for them here, next to the poor man and Jacob and Ellie.

Alvaro said, "We can't sit. We can't stay."

Esther wiped her face with her bloody arm, her tears cutting through the grime. They walked, knowing others waited for them beyond the partition, in the next room. They walked to meet them.

CHAPTER 31

ALVARO'S DEAD FATHER SAT AT the end of the table next to Alvaro's mother and Alba. They waved. His mother cried. He had been ready for all of that. He supposed there was no helping it. He had not been ready to see Carmen close to them, her back to the table, drawing.

He supposed he cried, he didn't know, he could hardly think, he could hardly brush Esther off him, he could hardly walk with her holding on to him, and Clarabelle barking—alarmed about what he did not know. His dad huddled in his chair, as sweet and irritating as ever.

For years, he had wanted to look like his dad. And when he turned seventeen, it happened, it felt like it happened overnight, because everyone who knew the both of them had told him. They'd said, *You look just like your dad.* They'd said, *Alvaro and you, you look just the same.* And that's when it started bothering him. Because his father held his arms tight around himself, and because he laughed and looked at the ground when he was nervous or shy, and because he tilted his head in the exact same way that the son did, in photographs. People would say, *Your dad is a very handsome man*, but all he could see was his dad's shyness, his insecurity, his deep sense of unease around people.

Because we were never people.

We were fodder.

Sent out. Called back. Sent out again.

He walked to his dad and stopped, uneasy and insecure himself. Again. After all this time on his own, with no mirror to point out these flaws, these fissures in his deepest self. The father he'd last seen in Colombia now returned, ready to make another corny joke. Ready to embarrass him again. Ready to remind him, through no fault of anyone, of his deepest fears, the small things he disliked most about himself, magnified and glaring. His father. Who was innocent. Who could not help but be who he was, even now, long after he had been left behind in a field in Colombia.

In Colombia.

He imagined a tunnel running through the continent, the tunnel filled with the pink jelly of the Alicia.

The Face Beneath the Face, beneath all of the Americas, the whole of it huge, so much larger than their little corner of the world.

Of course.

The Alicia began as a spore. As dust. And dust covered the world, dust traveled, dust traveled impossible distances—galaxies, distant planets, the edge of the known universe.

You flew over land and water, you flew over islands, everything below vast and cloud covered, and small only from a great height. Beneath the skin of the land waited the coiled black hunger they thought they could stop, a young man and a little girl and an injured dog, orphans all.

His mom said that she was so happy to see him, that he looked so well. So healthy.

Alvaro was covered in blood and grime. He still wore the same unlaundered chef's pants, the fabric torn and soiled. He wiped his dirty hands on the dirty pants and smiled, and the smile hurt, it hurt because he'd been hit and cut.

His mother said that he could stay. That he should stay. That he should eat something at least. "Before," she said, nodding at the pores on the wall that opened and closed and waited.

It was his dad who saved them. Who saved them all. "You don't even have to cook," he said. "They bring it all to you. No *self-service*." He said the last bit in English, his accent heavy, everything about the words what Alvaro most feared about the way he himself sounded.

Funny, he thought.

We sound funny. We sound wrong.

Esther tugged at his sleeve and Clarabelle growled at the wall openings that licked the air and sucked in the light from the room. The Alicia waited for them to give in, give up.

Alvaro said nothing to his father. He flinched at how his father sounded and what he said, though he knew his poor father was blameless, at least here. At least now. As for what happened in Colombia, he was blameless enough. They all were, all but him. He remembered what he'd said at the roadblock, how he'd told the boy on the Kawasaki that they had nothing, that the family had no money, which was when the guerillas decided to take all of them in. Now his family sat at the table and blamed him for nothing and all they wanted him to do was to join them for a nice meal. How hard was that?

Carmen glared.

"I'm so sorry," he said.

Carmen shrugged. She said, "You don't want to know what we are. We're not who you think we are."

"I found out," he said. "Come with me."

Carmen shook her head. "Esther will tell you. We're not who you think we are." She pointed at the drawing in her pad: an old man borne aloft on a goose.

She had drawn it a lifetime ago, in a park. In sunlight.

"Please," he said.

"Look at the old man's face," she said, but pointed at the goose.

The old man was Jacob, who had led them here. Who had drawn them in. Who had hoped against hope they could stop the Alicia.

"He told me it'd be my choice," Carmen said. "He said I could say no, and I said no, but I think I meant yes. I wanted you to live. We're special, you and me." She pointed at the albino goose again. "The hotel makes copies. Some of those copies go awry, Jacob explained, and that was us, the two of us. Copies gone wrong. Set free. Like that goose. But for you to live I had to stay. The wrong sacrifice. That was the compromise. Jacob had found a way to trade with the Alicia. When the Face Beneath the Face came for me, when my sisters came for me, I said, *Yes*. I said, *Please*. I said, *Let him live. Let my brother live.*"

She folded her drawing, rested her hands on her lap.

"So live," she said.

I am leaving you here, he thought.

I can't believe I'm leaving you.

I am leaving you here because that is what the Alicia wants. It wants me to see you and it wants me to give you to her.

Or: *I am leaving you here because if I don't, I will lose myself. I will stay here. I will sit here forever with all of you and there will be no returning, no Esther to ask, Will you give them all to me?*

Carmen shook her head. "You're not leaving me." She pointed at Esther. "She carries me. We all carry each other. She's got my dreams. My memories." She held up a pen. "One day you'll remember. One day you'll sit with her in a park and you'll see her draw, and you'll remember."

A gift. A gift or a sacrifice or both.

You stayed or you left, but the Alicia grew fat regardless.

He did not say goodbye. His father held himself, as shy as always, his mother smiled and her eyes closed when she smiled, and his sisters did the same. His mother and his sisters smiled the same way. All three were beautiful. He knew this already, had always known it, had been told so often, as often as he'd been told that he looked like his father. He thought, *Carmen would have grown up to be a beautiful woman.* What an odd burden that must be, to be beautiful, to know you are beautiful.

"Alvaro?" Esther said.

"Yes," he said, meaning *No*.

That's not my name, not really.

That's my dad's name.

The pores closed and opened and closed again and revealed immense coiled tentacles, the cold breath of the Face Beneath the Face sweet with rot and decay and dirt.

They fed it a journal that once belonged to the Hotel Splendor, and they fed it a notebook he'd been carrying all this time, the handwriting feminine and vaguely familiar. They fed her all the scraps of paper they carried. Receipts, a brochure, what looked like a dollar bill but was actually a coupon for a free dinner. The pores opened and closed again, waiting for more.

Esther leaned into the openings, her cheek almost brushing the nubs and bristles, and she whispered her life into the puckered wall.

He did the same, he told the Face everything about himself, every secret, every secret shame, everything he'd ever done he could remember, everything he'd heard. They fed her their lives. They made up stories about themselves when they could not remember the truth, or they embellished, or they borrowed the stories of others.

"I had a dad once," Esther said. "He was a reverend. He was a good man. He was learned. He was a shoemaker."

"My sisters flew to Cuba once," Alvaro said. "They were on the swim team."

Unsure if that was true or not.

Unsure if it was his life he was sharing—his life and yours—or someone else's.

They told every story they could think of, about everyone they could think of.

The Alicia swallowed it all.

Esther told her every Bible story she remembered, and then she made some up. Alvaro pieced together every movie that unspooled from his late nights at the extended stay, and he shared them, he mixed them up, thinking all the while, *We'll run out of stories before she falls asleep, we'll just exhaust ourselves and fall silent and it'll wake up and keep eating.*

We're not Scheherazade, he thought, remembering his grandmother's set of *The Thousand and One Nights*, and then realizing that it wasn't his memory, it belonged to someone else—*a night manager from the Alicia's time as the Splendor*—and that the man's dreams and memories tumbled into him. (*We carry each other*.) He told the Face every story he remembered from the set. Every djinn. Every secret wish. Every concubine. Every shocking reversal. Every twist.

We'll be done telling stories in no time, he thought. *We'll stop soon. Soon we'll stop.*

━━▪▪▪▪▪

They talked for days.

━━▪▪▪▪▪

He told the Face of the road trips the family took to the coast, all of them singing along to *Don Giovanni*, and then he told her the plot of *Don Giovanni*, and then he remembered an episode of *Three's Company* that sounded an awful lot like the end of *Don Giovanni*, with Jack Tripper convincing a woman to go out with him despite her being engaged to someone else, and despite it being Halloween, rumors of a ghost roaming the Regal Beagle, the ghost dragging Jack from the Beagle for his philandering ways. But that was all a dream, Jack woke up, whereas Don Giovanni was truly dragged to hell. No dream there. Not like yours. No chance to wake up, or go back. And Alvaro not sure if he conjured an actual episode or if it was just him doing the conjuring, making it up. He kept going. He thought, *We have to do this, we can't stop.* Like Jimmy Stewart in *Mr. Smith Goes to Washington*, like Mohammed in the cave, like Joseph Smith unspooling stories from whatever he saw in his hat, the stories changing, evolving, flowing through the pores of the Alicia and into the waiting black coils of the Face.

The wall grew dark, engorged, the pores swollen and red, the nubs and bristles incandescent pink.

They could not stop, thinking always, *We'll run out of story, we'll run out of things to tell her*, and somehow they kept going, feeding her the wrong things, and the Face Beneath the Face drank it all in, even when the stories lacked sense or coherence or when they were peopled with no one they knew, no one they remembered, no one that could possibly exist.

Alvaro said, "The saints saw nothing but rock and scrub," and he saw desert and wind and a raw sky and a single tree with two broken branches. A fallen man. A fallen prophet. He told the story of Jacob, unsure of how much of it was true, how much of it was distorted by his own telling and by the haze of the dream they all shared, the dream of the Alicia. And in the dream, he could see the Alicia herself, and he could see the Face Beneath the Face, the coils unspooling to reveal row after row of black, glistening teeth, opening still to reveal the moment it gave birth to itself— the red spores on the red earth, the black, hungry truth beneath. He saw the first Esther, her head severed from her body. She sang "Abide with Me" and Jacob sang with her. Alvaro thought, *Jacob must be here, in this room*, but did not turn around to find him, the enormous coils and teeth lulled with story.

Esther said that her father had been a gambler, a poker player, that he'd circled the Alicia when it sat abandoned next to all the other abandoned hotels in Fremont. "It was so dark," she said. "The hotel gathered its darkness into the cage, the pool, the lot, the newly built and pointless parking lot. Too little, too late. You could not see the hotel unless you brought a flashlight." They thought of the flashlight abandoned in the Nightmare Room, unnecessary now, the ballroom aglow, all the chandeliers finally working. She told the Face the story of the poker player who could not let the hotel go, and who left everything behind and walked into the history of the hotel, all while Alvaro talked too, all while he told another story, of when the hotel was called the Splendor and was circled by a river of dogs. He talked, thinking, *Surely the night manager is here, in this room.*

Surely the night manager was called back, as Alvaro himself had been. But Alvaro did not turn, he had to keep talking, they both did.

So they did not see that they had emptied the room.

That as they told the stories, they used up the people behind them. The people were eating and talking and then they were gone. Out, perhaps. Elsewhere. Or thrown out of the Alicia, the Splendor, and into the void of the Face Beneath the Face. There was no way of telling. They had no way of knowing. They just talked, they did not stop talking.

They said, "This city gets its water from the Colorado River," not sure if that was true or not. They made up a story of Las Vegas, how it had come to be, how it had flourished.

"A bird landed here," they said, "a flamingo, and here the city grew."

No, it was Latter-day Saints, or gamblers in search of a way station.

Someone dreamed the city up. Someone dammed the water in Lake Mead. Someone made this impossible thing happen, a place with a mayor perpetually flanked by showgirls, where people gathered to watch the bloom of a nuclear test explosion from their hotel balcony, and where residents later drove to the desert and gathered the green glass at the test site, and where nothing stopped, no one slept, no one dreamed, no one was ever alone and everyone was always alone, and where you could lose yourself and you could become anyone, you could turn into anyone, where the best and worst of you would be amplified, the city buzzing you into being whatever you felt like being that day. Yourself. Someone else. Someone else entirely.

They told the story, and in so doing, they gave the city up, though they had no way of knowing, they knew nothing but their own telling, which they kept expanding, they kept making up, well past the point of coherence, until the puckered wall of the Alicia grew taut with her own blood, taut with her own engorged appetite, so full of what they fed her that the tissue strained, it looked like a water balloon filled past its breaking point. *It should burst*, they thought. *It should just pop.*

Which is when they drove the teeth into the wall and the Alicia convulsed, all of Vegas convulsing with her, but they of course did not know that, not at the time, not ever.

━║║

They did not even known their own names, since they'd given those up.

━║║

They did not know who they were, or why the drove the needle teeth through the tissue of the Alicia and deep into the Face Beneath the Face, or why the Face screamed.

━║║

They did not remember those they'd left behind, they did not even know they'd left anyone behind.

━║║

All they knew was the living wall of the Alicia bursting and the world bursting with her, the ballroom turning into something other, something squirming with a form of life they could neither understand nor even really see. It looked very much like a jellyfish. It looked very much like something you would see deep underwater, but not here, not where they were, wherever that was, the place for which they had no name, of which they had no memory.

They thought, *We could be anywhere.*

She wants you. All of you, Jacob had said.

Him.

But not Carmen.

Not the sister who sat at the table but whose plate was empty.

Who could draw.

Who could still do things the Alicia did not understand.

She had offered herself in exchange for Esther, but so could he. He could still free his sister (*We all carry each other*, you had said), there was hope, there was something like hope.

He could not fight the Alicia, but he could give her all of him—the wrong sacrifice, the aberrant copy, the wrong thing. The Alicia had lost him, had not touched him.

You've been touched elsewhere, Jacob had said.

———

Feed her.

———

He jabbed the tooth into his own neck, the pain so sharp it must belong to someone else, surely it couldn't be his, couldn't be this bad, surely it'd get better. He gasped and the blood spilled on the pink wall, the black, shuddering coil, the blood burst everywhere—the blood spilled onto the first Esther and onto Clarabelle.

That, too, was part of the ritual. That, too, was expected.

Esther screamed and Clarabelle whimpered, but he could not explain, he had no time to explain, he could not talk, and what burst forth from him was blood and hope in equal measures.

He thought he could do it again, he had not done it hard enough, but he flinched.

Spare her, he thought.

Spare her and take me.

Spare her and take me, please.

It was easy if you didn't think, if you remembered that the tooth had waited for this exact moment, this exact sacrifice. This simple exchange. The Alicia took in the wrong blood and he hoped it worked, he knew it would, because everyone balked—even Jacob balked, in the end. Even Jacob let his daughter die, and it wasn't until Carmen stepped in and freed her, the first Esther, that the Alicia truly convulsed, as she was convulsing now.

He gripped the bloody tooth and jabbed at his neck one more time, all of him saying, *No,* his throat white-hot, the tooth long and hot and lodged deep inside him, and no thoughts now. Nothing he could say or think. He thought he'd been safe, he thought he was untouched, had kept himself apart, but he had never been safe, he could keep no one safe, and he could no longer hold himself—he was no longer himself. He gasped, inhaled a thick, hot liquid, his own sour blood, and he panicked and tried to calm himself, and then he grew calm, he had nothing to do, nowhere to go, no name to hold on to—

He did not know that he was dying, he did not know anything at all, he did not know why he could not say what he wanted to say, why one word stuck wet and red to his throat.

Please.

The young man fell, and his last thoughts had nearly nothing to do with his sister, whom he loved dearly but whose name slipped out of his grasp, and his thoughts had nothing to do with the hotel, whose name also vanished, and what came back, what persisted, was a wide and bright and inexplicably joyous image: a stone face, birds in flight, black water.

You'll remember, a young woman had told him. *You'll remember.*
We all carry each other.

The child in the calico dress jabbed at the sputtering coils, and this place that was no place at all screamed and convulsed and she kept at it—the first Esther, the last form standing—until the world was as still and sullen as a desert sky.

EPILOGUE

THE LITTLE GIRL AND THE young woman and the dog did not know each other, but they huddled close. The young woman asked the girl if she was all right, the young woman's face a mess, her nails torn and bloody, each nail sporting the drawing of a face.

The little girl asked her the same question. Was she all right?

They'd lost their names. They didn't know what else they'd lost.

The three stepped out of the silent building and into a silent parking lot stuffed with abandoned cars.

"We should go," said the young woman. She touched her shoulder and flinched. "We should find a hospital." Her face was ashen, her shirt dark with blood and bloody handprints. Tattered.

The little girl said, "We have to leave. We can't stay here."

"We need to find the people we left behind," the young woman said.

Maybe the only people missing were here, in Fremont, and the city beyond bustled, the Strip a hive of activity, Summerlin and North Vegas and the rest still alive with motion and commerce and loved ones. The little girl doubted it. So did her companion, and so did the dog, whose injury was not so bad anymore. Who seemed to be recovering.

The little girl said, "I hope we find them."

You won't find them, but you don't know that yet. So you hope.

A box of keys sat by the abandoned valet station. No one would be coming for any of those cars. The young woman—you—imagined the cars in a hundred years, the parking lot swallowed by sand, the cars still waiting for drivers long gone, long forgotten.

"We'll be fine," you said.

You will, but you don't know that yet. You're just hoping.

▬▮▮▮▮

The three drove out of the city, you behind the wheel, the little girl keeping an eye on the atlas she found in the back pocket of the car, the dog poking her nose out of a half-open window.

You drove through empty streets and saw no one.

The little girl whose name had once been Esther thought, *Soon this whole city will give way to the desert. The lake will burn dry. The river too. Soon all of this is going away.*

They drove past a desolate park. You remembered black water, a stone face, an old man, a bird in flight, but the image flickered and vanished.

The city persisted as you drove away from it, all the buildings empty but stately, sure that they'd be stocked with inhabitants. Sure that they'd be made anew. The buildings waited. The Alicia waited. The Face Beneath the Face waited also. The little girl did not remember what she'd done, did not remember what she and I had done, but even so the thought lingered in the back of her head. She did not know if she had helped or stopped the hotel. Neither do I.

You drove through the streets in the wake of no human voice and kept your eyes on the road and hoped to see some sign of life, to see someone else along the way, but you carved your way through nothing, the sky blue and cloudless and as mute and absent as the abandoned city.

"There," the little girl said, pointing at an exit, the car gliding into the bright, gleaming ribbon of a desert interstate. *Off we go*, she thought, petting the dog. *She needs a name*, she thought. *We all do. We can call ourselves anything we want. We can go anywhere.*

That was when she remembered her mother.

It happened briefly. Her name popped into her head and she tried to hold on to it, she tried to hold on to the voice of her mother singing her to sleep by a campground fire, her mom by her side singing "Abide with Me."

You drove away from nothing.

The little girl did her best to hold on to the memory of her mother but it vanished before she registered its loss, and so she kept her eye on the highway signs and the billboards and hoped to see traffic, to see a sign that they weren't the only people left, the only people driving, leaving, heading elsewhere, heading anywhere, heading toward something new.

You remembered another road trip in another country. The whole car sang, badly and off key. Happy. We sang in a language not our own, the car full of the good smell of the coast—salt and fish and roasting meat. The boy who sat next to you sulked, you'd just had an argument, something about the window, about hogging the back seat, but now we all sang, and it was so good when you caught my eye, when you told me I looked like a deer, with my long face, my long nose, my long lashes. He was so sweet to you, this stranger, this ghost of a memory talking to you right now, telling you your own story. Your family's story. Listen.

You'll forget.

You'll forget, but I'll come back one night. I'll come back in a dream. I'll tell you everything. You'll dream that the voice you're hearing is just a voice and not your brother, you'll wonder if I'm lying, you'll count my fingers.

You'll remember us. Mom, Dad, Alba, me.

We carry each other.

But that is years from now.

As you're driving, all you remembered was your own name—Carmen—and you said it, and it sounded right, but you thought, *No. That's the wrong name. That's not my name anymore.*

You turned to your new friend, your hands on the wheel.

You passed loops of concrete, sky, sagebrush, a vast expanse of broken airplanes, ghost towns, gas stations. You drove. You wondered if you'd see any people, if there were any people besides the two of you left.

I wish I could tell you.

The girl in the calico dress kept her eye on the atlas, proud of her role as a navigator.

"That's our next exit," she told you, guiding your way.

ACKNOWLEDGMENTS

A HUGE THANK-YOU TO MARK BAUMGARTNER, Robin Becht, Benjamin Healy, Mary Kinzie, Kelly Link, and Robin Rozanski for their generous feedback on multiple drafts of the novel.

Thank you, also, everyone at the University of Arizona Press and Camino del Sol, with special thanks to Elizabeth Wilder and Scott C. De Herrera for welcoming this weird beast of a book into their editorial home, to Leigh McDonald for the stunning cover, to Marie Landau for the careful and rigorous copyedits, and to Rigoberto González for the beautiful foreword and for bringing the novel in and for his invaluable work as a mentor and a champion.

Another huge thank-you to my friends and colleagues and students at Whitman College, Lebanon Valley College, and Northwestern University for their companionship and support. Thank you, especially, Christopher Leise and Johanna Stoberock and Katrina Roberts and Jim Hodge and John Alba Cutler and Harris Feinsod and Reginald Gibbons and Kasey Evans and Kelly Wisecup and Brian Bouldrey and Michelle Huang and everyone else, and big thanks to Laurie Shannon, Susan Manning, and Katherine Breen for steering the ship. Big hugs and love to the Chicago writing community and its bounty of reading series, bookstores, and institutions.

This novel owes a lot to writers and filmmakers who have worked in this same bloody vein. So thank you, Nathan Ballingrud, Ramsey Campbell, Dan Chaon, David Cronenberg, Brian Evenson, Shirley Jackson,

Stephen Graham Jones, Stephen King, Terry Lamsley, Victor LaValle, Thomas Ligotti, David Lynch, Robert McCammon, Michael McDowell, Benjamin Percy, George Romero, Peter Straub, and Lisa Tuttle. Thank you, Mario Mendoza, for being such a patient teacher when I was young and lost, and also for teaching me the value of transgression in literature. Thank you, Susan Hubbard, for being such a terrific model and mentor. And thank you, Philip K. Dick, for showing up at exactly the right time in my early life as a reader and exposing the fragility of our time, the unreliability of our experience on this earth. This novel is a love letter to all of you, and to the city of Las Vegas.

Thank you, my Vegas friends, without whom living there would have been unimaginable, and thank you, too, to coeditors Geoff Schumacher and Andrew Kiraly, anthologist extraordinaire Jarret Keene, and professor Mehmet Erdem, whose assignments (a walk across the entire city, a Lovecraft-inspired story for an anthology, a set of interviews with kitchen workers) provided the initial spark for the novel.

I thank my family, my parents for their love and support and for shuttling us back and forth between Colombia and the United States, and my sister, Maria, and Brad and Lucas and Nico.

I give thanks most of all to Sarah and to our children, Saúl and Rosa. I love you all so much, and I don't know where I would be without you.

ABOUT THE AUTHOR

Juan Martinez is the author of the story collection *Best Worst American* (Small Beer Press), which won the Neukom Institute Literary Arts Award for Debut Speculative Fiction. He lives near Chicago and is an associate professor at Northwestern University. His work has appeared in many literary journals and anthologies, including *McSweeney's*, *Huizache*, *Ecotone*, *Glimmer Train*, *NIGHTMARE*, *The Sunday Morning Transport*, *Shenandoah*, NPR's *Selected Shorts*, *Mississippi Review*, and elsewhere. Visit and say hi at fulmerford.com.